CW00665740

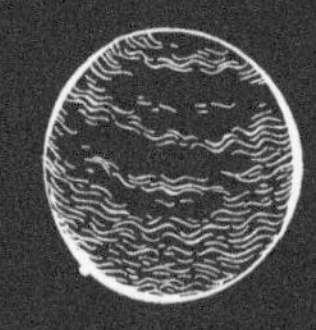
Fae

Avalon

Gaia

Tuonela

Erebus

Styx
Hades
Purgatory
Annwn
Tartarus

Somewhere Out There

Somewhere Out There

Book One in the Shadows and Regrets Series

6/11/23

To Amy,

Thanks for entering the read along giveaway!

Happy reading!

Caroline Astiago x

Caroline Astiago

This is a work of fiction. Names, characters, places, and incidents either are the product of the author's imagination or are used fictitiously. Any resemblance to actual persons, living, dead or immortal, events, or locales is entirely coincidental.

Copyright © 2023 by Caroline Astiago

All rights reserved. No part of this book may be reproduced or used in any manner without written permission of the copyright owner except for the use of quotations in a book review. For more information, contact: hello@carolineastiago.com

First paperback edition 2023

Book design by Publishing Push
Cover design and illustrations by Scott Eckersley

ISBNs
Paperback: 978-1-80541-089-8
eBook: 978-1-80541-090-4

www.carolineastiago.co.uk
Instagram: caroline_astiago

My thanks to my day job.

Much of this book (and all of the second) was written whilst at work. Your choice in double-sided printers is second to none.

*And thank you to those who never gave up asking "when are you going to finish the f***ing book?!" I owe you and I hope it was worth the wait.*

I would be remiss to not include Jess. Sorry for the lack of unicorns.

Character List

Benjamin/Ben – (he/him) A shtriga and Guardian of Gaia. Former court physician to King Arthur and assistant to Merlin. He was a warlock in his human life and his magic is called Ambrosius.

Jack – (he/him) A vampire and Benjamin's partner.

April – (she/her) A hunter.

Fate – (she/her) The God of time and creator of the universe. She writes history and builds worlds.

Dirmynd – (he/him) A supernatural artefacts collector

Mórrígan – (she/her) The God of War. Ex-wife to Merlin. As War she is responsible for creating and resolving conflict.

Barqan – (she/her) A Djinn queen and Guardian to Avalon.

Chaos – (they/them) Creator of the Gods and the first universe.

King Arthur – (he/him) Deceased. Former king of Gaia.

Merlin – (he/him) Deceased. Advisor to King Arthur. Fate's husband and Benjamin's mentor and best friend. Merlin was responsible for creating the Guardianship. His magic was called Emrys.

Magic – (shares its owner's pronouns). Magic manifests itself in characters with natural magical abilities (Benjamin, Merlin, for example). Their magic has its own identity and personality.

Realms and Guardians

Avalon – The uppermost realm, inhabited by the Gods. Guardian: Barqan. God: Fate.

Gaia – An upper realm populated by mortals. Guardian: Benjamin. God: Freyja.

Fae – An upper realm populated by witches, wizards, warlocks and mages. Guardian: Hecate. God: Nyx.

Erebus – An under realm populated by vampires. Guardian: Keres. God: Lamia.

Tuonela – An under realm populated by werewolves. Guardian: Kalma. God: Tuoni & Tuonetar.

Annwn – An under realm populated by shtrigas. Guardian: Cerridwen. God: Arawn.

Styx – The first level of hell where souls come to cross over. Populated by ghosts and ghouls. Guardian: Charon, The Ferryman. God: Mórrígan.

Hades – The second level of hell populated by demons and the damned souls. Guardian: Artemis. God: Hades.

Tartarus – The third level of hell where the evillest souls and disgraced Gods who have broken the law are imprisoned.

Populated by nightshades, shapeshifters and tricksters. Guardian: Menoetius. God: Chaos.

Purgatory – A featureless plane inhabited by deceased supernatural beings. It takes its shape around the individual's insecurities, fears and worst memories.

Travel between the realms is only possible if characters can find the static portals or are magic users powerful enough to create their own portals. Guardians are the only group allowed to travel freely.

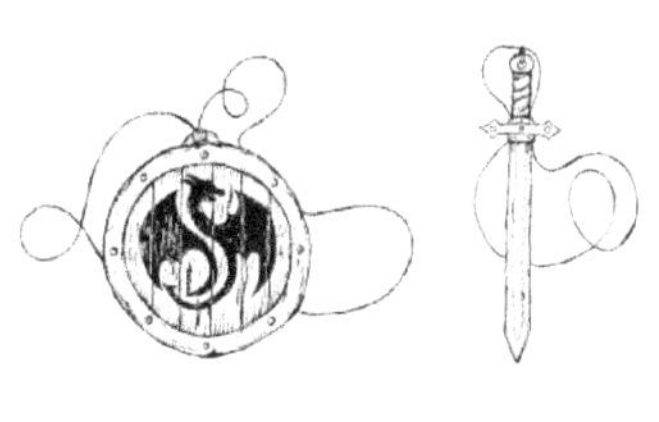

1

Drag My Body

31st October, 537AD, Camlann, Cornwall

Benjamin's legs skidded out from under him, his torn tunic and trousers heavy with a putrid mix of blood, mud and silt from the fast-flowing, red water of the river, which sent him crashing into the sludge. He'd only realised it was blood when he'd gone under briefly.

Swords clanged against one another, setting an erratic beat to the cries of men dying. Behind him, Percival grunted in pain. The knight turned unusually slowly, his hands clamped to his neck. His eyes found Benjamin's and he dropped his hands. Bile burned Benjamin's throat. A gaping red hole sat where Percival's neck should have been. Percival sank to his knees, slumping into Benjamin's lap. Dead eyes stared into his. Benjamin kicked the body off him and crawled away. The chill of late October clung onto his bones, stiffening his movements.

The mud was up to his elbows, trying to swallow Benjamin and everything else that dared stay still long enough.

They were losing Gaia to the Gods and supernatural clans from the other realms.

From deep within the woods lining the ordinary field in Cornwall, the lone howl of a werewolf was answered by its pack in bloodcurdling unison. No doubt they'd taken the village on the other side of the woods. And then they came, shaking the orange and red leaves from the trees like confetti as they pounced on the mass of soldiers. The earth shook violently, aiding his uncooperative limbs in preventing him from standing. Benjamin planted his hands in the squelching mud to push himself up, and impaled his right hand on a discarded sword without a flinch. The ground split open in front of him. A tumultuous, murky-green cloud of demonic entities tore their way free from the under realms. A dark figure sighted Benjamin and charged. Benjamin fired a shot of burnt-orange magic over his shoulder at the twisting mass of evil. The demon fled with a sharp hiss of pain. Benjamin drove his legs backwards, accidentally tripping somebody. A pained whimper came from behind. Benjamin turned back. Regardless of what was happening to him, he was still the court physician. He had to help. His exhausted heart broke for the hundredth time that day.

A soldier of about sixteen lay beside him, his body peppered with arrows, a horrible mixture of hope and desperation on his face. The boy's eyes widened in silent horror as he clocked Benjamin's eyes. His monstrous, kaleidoscope eyes.

'You're one of *them*.'

Ambrosius, Benjamin's magic, screamed inside his head, louder than the battle itself, as it rallied against the new darkness within. The curse was five days old, but it felt like centuries had passed. The young soldier rolled onto his back, all hope lost, and breathed his last. The weak autumn sun, deciding it had seen enough, slipped behind its clouds. But the pangs of his newly acquired hunger were stealing his concentration … Wobbling with exhaustion, Benjamin sat up, fumbling with the greasy strands of black hair plastered to his dirt-encrusted face. He choked on a sob, his shoulders dropping, pulling him forward to meet the silvery-white soul as it poured out of the newly dead body's mouth. It offered no resistance. Done, he collapsed next to the lifeless body, feeling some of his weariness subside. Benjamin would lie there in the accumulating mud, piss and blood forever. It was where he belonged.

Above him the soldiers danced on. The dead kept dropping. Humanity couldn't swim against such a tide of evil. Ambrosius sent a sharp pain shooting across Benjamin's chest. His magic was dying, along with the king's army.

The air was full with souls fleeing bodies, Benjamin confused them with the fog at first. Silver phantoms that awakened his deepest, darkest desire. Two soldiers teetered above him, about to fall. Benjamin dragged himself to his feet, out of their way.

They'd all be dead by supper.

A corkscrewing green cloud of a demon tore past, close enough for Benjamin to see the dissolute smiles on its many grotesque faces, the different strands of its unique sense of evil. As it approached its target, hundreds of wispy arms reached out, pulled back the soldier's mouth and forced their way past the scream. No sooner had the man's mouth shut, than his eyes flared green, his mouth twisted into a distorted, depraved smile. Without looking, his hand shot out and caught another soldier running past at the wrong time. The possessed soldier's head turned towards its captive so violently that Benjamin heard bones break.

Disorientated, he stumbled through the middle of a sword fight; around him, steel clashed and blood flew. A blade whipped towards Benjamin's chest. Lancelot shoved him out of harm's way with a harsh word, and there was Arthur, parrying attacks in a flurry of ash.

The air here was thick with smoke from a raging fire, setting the king's armour aglow. Arthur was surrounded by enemies. The fire – overturned wagons – blocked his only retreat. Arthur's knights fought in a tight circle around him, a tangle of swords, shields and limbs. Benjamin's trembling hands freed his knife from its sheath, marvelling at how the flames seemed to snag in the blade's teeth. The possessed solider rushed Arthur. Benjamin tensed. The king's knights turned as one to swarm around the attacker, isolating the threat. Lancelot's sword slashed across the demon's neck. It howled like nothing Benjamin had heard before, and tore free of the ruined body, fleeing into the cold air.

Arthur staggered on, his knights falling, one by one, caught on spears or torn apart by claws, swords and axes. Only Lancelot remained, back-to-back with Arthur. With one strong swing of his sword, his king decapitated another attacker. As the headless body slumped to the ground, Arthur's gaze found Benjamin's face in the melee. Arthur pushed his visor up, eyes widening with recognition, a smile on his face.

That smile stole Benjamin's breath.

His eyes flickered over his king, taking in every little detail: the silver armour dashed with blood; the ruffled, sweat-drenched blond hair exposed beneath his helmet. The hooded figure, approaching from behind …

Instinct tried to move Benjamin but his legs had grown roots. He tried to call out a warning, but his words wedged together in his throat. Benjamin reached for Ambrosius, but, for the first time in his thirty-two years, his magic didn't answer. Benjamin had never felt so helpless. 'Arthur!'

Distracted, Lancelot turned towards Benjamin's voice, leaving himself off balance. The hooded figure rushed in, shoving Lancelot to the ground. Arthur wheeled for the newcomer, sword raised, but the attacker's blade glinted as it flashed across his king's neck.

Arthur's muffled cry emptied the world of war, colour and sound, leaving behind Arthur, Benjamin and the stranger who had taken everything away.

No matter how big a breath he took, air wasn't finding its way in. Benjamin was going to drown on dry land. The king fell backwards into the waiting arms of his assailant. With his head bent over Arthur's, the man lowered the king to the ground with a gentleness completely out of place amidst the scene of destruction. Benjamin managed a staggered step forward and tripped over his own feet. A cloaked head snapped up before he fled, engulfed by the fog and the battle. Benjamin's mind understood nothing besides reaching Arthur. Arthur, whose armour was now stained red. Arthur, who wasn't moving. Benjamin fell to his knees beside his king, his hands automatically tearing strips from his tunic, all the while knowing there was nothing to be done.

'Arthur?'

The king's eyes fluttered, but there was no response. Benjamin backed away, buffeted by soldiers rushing past in a blur of red and silver, and panicked cries of 'The king! Save the king!' Benjamin could only move backwards, as if doing so would rewind time. He wanted to be back in Caerleon, with Arthur. Or even Tintagel's draught-filled halls. Wherever Arthur was safe and well.

'Benjamin!' He couldn't remember who the voice belonged to. He couldn't think of anything. Benjamin was stuck, held in place by Arthur's tortured, wet, gasping, final breaths.

'Merlin?' Benjamin screamed for his best friend. The warlock could fix anything. He couldn't be far away. 'Somebody needs to find Merlin.' Benjamin's lungs gasped for air, trying to breathe for Arthur. The soldiers picked their king up as gently as men taught to fight could, and carried him from the field, still calling to Benjamin, their cries fraught with desperation and despair, looking to him to command. Looking at him with confusion and fear.

Benjamin turned and fled the scene as Arthur drew his last breath. He couldn't watch that soul drift free of its body. Benjamin knew it would be the brightest of them all.

31st October 2023, Oxford

Dearest Arthur,

There's a bitterly cold wind tonight. Do you remember how the wind screamed over the castle rooftops, the last night we were together? Perhaps that's why the wind always reminds me of you. I hope it's not cold where you are. Me? I've been trying to outrun memories that time should have allowed me to forget.

Lately, Gaia has been feeling less like home and more like a prison. You'd have a few words for me, I'm sure, if you could see me. Something along the lines of: 'this is no way for a Guardian to act', a train wreck of a life notwithstanding. The trouble is, I've not learnt much from the peaks and troughs of existence. I have come to better understand certain things – as you said I would. Everything I was and everything I've become stretches away further than I can see.

It's Samhain Eve, again. Mayhap this will be the year I see you once more. There's much I should have said. I'm still waiting for your prophesied return. You're running late, I suppose. Is Merlin with you? He always had a loose relationship with time. I never did learn the manner of his death. Merlin should have seen it coming, being a prophet. It was good of him to force me into replacing you as Guardian. Merlin called it 'a temporary solution'. After 1,486 years, one thing is clear: Merlin didn't know the meaning of the word. After what happened on the battlefield, it's the least I deserve. Hindsight is a detestable gift and hope is hard to find on dark days and even darker nights.

Speaking of which, it's after midnight! Much too late (or too early) for such fatalism. It's not as if I'll finally find the answers hidden on this page. If I constructed a house out of my unanswered questions in my letters to you, used my doubts and fears as mortar, the roof would scrape against Heaven's door.

It's been a long time, love, many lifetimes in fact. Perhaps time is telling me, with its juggernaut subtlety, that it's time to be done with a past which has slipped through my fingers.

Always Yours,
Benjamin

2

City of Devils

The night crashed down around Benjamin as he rushed through another calamitous Samhain Eve, hoping to outrun his responsibilities on the rain-soaked slate rooftops surrounding Oxford Castle. The remaining tower silently kept its watch over the spires, domes and peaks piercing the sky.

Above High Street, the pitched roofs of sleeping shops and raucous bars huddled together, tucked into the sandstone and black-and-white Tudor facades darkened by time. Pumpkins adorned the cobbled streets below as people, dressed in their Halloween best, tumbled into the road, causing the buses to swerve around them. The edge of the church-like Ivy restaurant flashed into view. Ben didn't slow, jumping the gap with ease, his breath trailing behind him like steam in the cold air.

'Ohhh,' Ben's magic cooed, *'that one looks like Merlin!'* Ambrosius usually presented himself as a tiny human-shaped figure. Most of the time he stayed out of sight, choosing to crash about inside Ben's head. This was one of those times. A screech from below interrupted Ben's stride. A woman dressed as the devil was laughing in the arms of somebody

wearing a wizard costume as they fell out of a taxi, outside a pub.

'It's a costume, Ambrosius.' Although Ben stole another glance. *'Merlin wouldn't wear that parody of an outfit.'* His eyes easily picked out constellations and planets muted in the tones of a winter's night, shining above the light pollution. *'How did Gaia's traditions slip into this tacky display? Nobody remembers.'*

'We'll go to Mexico next year – you liked how colourful it was. And we've not left Oxford in ten years.'

'There won't be a next year. You know that.'

Fearing a deep period of introspection, Ambrosius pleaded, *'Don't get hung up on the past. You spend most of the year doing that.'*

'Sometimes I think I would be grateful for the peace your absence would bring.'

'They're not coming back.' Offended, Ambrosius stormed off.

'For crying … Samhain puts me in a foul mood.'

Loose bricks scattered over the edge as Ben landed on the roof of St Mary's Church. *'And I know.'* Ben snuck a quick glance at the revellers, looking for familiar faces. *'I know.'* Pins and needles broke out on both arms.

'Demons,' Ambrosius snapped. *'University Park.'*

With a huff that failed to blow hair from his eyes, Ben jumped into a deserted alleyway nestled between the quiet university buildings and overlooked by his beloved dreaming spires. The landing should have broken his legs – a long time ago it would have. Skidding round a corner, Ben tripped over a black cat that tore across his path. *'Is it too much to ask for a quiet Samhain?'* Ambrosius gave him the magical equivalent of a shrug. This night belonged to ghosts. Every year, with the fading light, they came, free to cause chaos in their home realm. '*We've dealt with two poltergeists, one vengeful spirit, a possessed jack-in-a-box, and a bunch of other nonsense.*' Five minutes. That's all Ben wanted. Five minutes alone on the quiet Bodleian rooftop. But the chance of that happening was as far off as dawn.

'*Stop whining.*' Ambrosius was right. The past was never going to be present.

The Natural History Museum looked wickedly distorted, draped in the night's cloak. Ben fixed his gaze on the floor. He had enough to do.

Ben shot through the park gates, his shadow a devil at his tail as he passed the cricket pavilion and the pitches tucked in for the winter. The sounds of screaming directed him to some teenagers who were trapped between the river and the demonic shadows cavorting around them. Adrenaline emptied Ben's mind, readying him to fight. Time slowed to a crawl under the scrutiny of his soldier's vision, every movement gracefully drawn out, allowing him to read the pattern of an unlearnt dance. His breathing slowed, his shoulders dropped a little, and his hands curled into fists. Ambrosius pulled back, giving him space to assess the situation. The four teens were drunk; the demons – of which there were also four – had taken an adult human form. Demons had to possess a body of some sort if they wanted to do real damage. Otherwise, they were mixed-up remains of a soul winging its way around the realms. He could see them for what they were – snakes who'd developed legs. They wore their true nature over the body, like an ill-fitting jacket. Layers upon layers of all their past wrongs. The numbers were fair, but the odds were stacked. The teenagers screamed and ran, but the demons were quicker. One pulled the nearest boy into its steel-like grip, whilst demon number two lunged for the other boy. Ambrosius sparked into life, his energy surrounding Ben. Swords clanging against armour and dying breaths stormed Ben's mind, propelling him into a demon, shoulder first, shunting it to the ground. Rough hands pulled Ben back to his feet before he could hit the deck. He caught a raised fist with one hand, the other grabbed a fistful of fabric. With a grunt, Ben swept the demon's legs out from under him, and pirouetted to his right, like a dancer in a grotesque ballet, revealing another snarling demon. Its twisted, featureless soul wiped away the facial features of the body it possessed. Ben jumped to the left, narrowly avoiding a punch. His reply cracked upwards into his opponent's jaw. The strike shattered the mandible of the human's body, but did nothing to the demon.

Whatever humanity demons had owned in life was squeezed out of them in death. A few years in Hades or Styx would do that to a soul. Ben ducked a sharp left hook, his fist colliding with a demon's head, sending teeth flying in opposite directions. His knee connected with a stomach, knocking the air out of its lungs. An involuntary snarl tore free of his throat. There were some things about his nature he couldn't change. No matter how much he tried. And Ben was tired of feeling uncomfortable in his own skin. A cold streak slithered down his cheek, his hand came away red. Ben's fist collided with another demon, freeing two of the teens who fled to the other side of the field and stopped.

Orange magic flared in the palm of Ben's hands, he thrust it forward, flinging two demons onto their backs, far from hurt. *'Oh Ambrosius, you can do better.'* The remaining two were looking on with a mixture of shock and fear, holding tight to the struggling prey.

'You've not fed in years. Give me a break.'

The taller of the two spectating demons dropped its hostage, and finding its mediocre courage, snarled. Ben sighed and stood his ground, his hand hovering over the hilt of a knife on his belt. He had overused Ambrosius. At the last possible moment, Ben whipped the knife up, sinking it into the demon's shoulder, scraping bone. It blinked in shock at the blood welling around the blade. Pulling the knife free, Ben slashed up and across the demon's neck, drenching himself in blood.

'That shirt is definitely ruined.' In the palm of his hand, Ambrosius was a furious ball of magic waiting for the demon to flee the body. The green mist flooded out of its mouth in a hurry. Ben muttered a quick exorcism spell and threw Ambrosius at the demon-soul, before it drilled into the ground. Ambrosius's burnt-orange glow engulfed the green mist, destroying it. Devoid of life, the body crumpled to the ground. Ben couldn't look at it.

'Come on then!' Ben squared up to them, 'if you're feeling brave.' The demons exchanged a look. And charged. Ben calmly raised the knife, moonlight reflecting in the blade. Tonight had gone badly enough. He might as well make a complete mess of it. They slammed into him with the force of a speeding train. His blade found its mark twice more whilst Ambrosius took care of the last one.

Blood roared in Ben's ears, as he fought to expel the adrenaline with deep breaths, the real world slowly returning to him. A few more breaths and ...

'*Ben!*' Ambrosius's concern for the terrified teens broke through the white noise. Ben allowed himself one more breath before letting Ambrosius go to work, carefully removing their memories of the fight.

'Go straight home, do you hear?' Four confused faces nodded at Ben before they took off. His skin erupted in pinpricks heralding the appearance of a tiny Ambrosius in his hand. 'No! No way.' Ben jabbed the person-shaped bundle of burnt-orange embers with a finger. 'I'm going home.' He had some letters to write.

'Whilst I enjoy listening to your greatest hits, there's one last thing to take care of.' Ambrosius nodded to the low hedges off to their right. 'Then you can return to perching on roofs like an overgrown raven.' Ben catapulted Ambrosius into the air with the slightest flick of his wrist. The figure broke apart into thousands of tiny glowing embers in the sky.

****

April quietly observed the hellish scene unfolding in front of her from the cover of the hedges stretching the length of the field like leafy walls. She clutched the saltshaker and her homemade wooden sword close to her chest. It was getting harder to keep her heart rate down. And the only thing she could do about her body temperature was pray to a higher power that nothing supernatural looked her way. It was at times like these, April wished she had more than shrubbery and a couple of party tricks to help her stay hidden. As if materialising from the air itself, a tall, scrawny-looking vampire burst onto the scene, blurring in and out of focus, his progress marked by airborne demons. April was dreaming. It looked like the vampire was trying to save the teens. A bad feeling crawled into her gut, right on cue.

This was no ordinary Dracula.

The air rushed from her lungs, replaced by an overwhelming and absolute sense of impending doom. Hers or his, April couldn't say. Every nerve in her body was screaming for her to run, to put as much distance between them as possible. April adjusted her grip on her sword, the weight of the smooth wood reassuring in her hands, and ducked behind the hedge. Dirmynd had told her to take salt. Dirmynd knew about ghosts. April had only figured out vampires. He'd asked her to help out. April took a deep breath and peered over the hedge. 'Where'd he go?' The leaves rustled a reply.

'Did we enjoy the show?'

April's heart lurched into her mouth. Leaves don't talk. April spun around, sword aimed at his heart. She lunged forward but he casually halted her with a raised hand.

'I wouldn't bother if I were you. You'd never make contact.' He effortlessly grabbed the sword from her grasp, holding it up to the moonlight for inspection. His eyes never left the would-be weapon and yet April knew he was watching her. 'Be careful. You could hurt someone with this.'

In between the fear and morbid curiosity, April took his warning as a rare compliment. By the light of the full moon, she tried not to stare at his intriguing silver eyes, drowning in sadness. It was probably rude to ask a vampire when he last ate, but his skin had that greyish tint to it. Something about the way in which he carried himself, his long black hair, waistcoat and jacket, black jeans and scuffed biker boots gave the impression that he was constantly out of place in time. His gaze jumped from the sword, alighting on the saltshaker clutched to April's chest. 'What in the hells is that for?'

With all traces of smugness now gone, April jutted out her chin and said with confidence, 'Demons don't like salt.' His rusty chuckle took her aback slightly.

'You have the right idea but your methods are severely lacking.' Ben didn't usually find such naivety amusing, but on her, it was endearing. No doubt she'd watched far too many horror films. There wasn't much of her to see. She was all bundled up, head to toe, in black. Tall boots, jeans and a faded black leather jacket which had more miles on it than she'd ever travelled. Her green eyes stood out against the dark material of a scarf that covered the bottom half of her tawny beige face, despite it being a mild night.

'Is she supernatural?' Ambrosius pointed to the intriguing jade aura outlining her. It matched her eyes. *'Find an excuse to touch her. I can't connect with her energy.'*

'I am not touching her without permission! What's the matter with you?'

'You're the one noticing how her aura and eyes match!'

An overexaggerated cough from the girl caused Ben to jump a little. He flashed her a quick smile, cheeks turning red.

'*You've been caught staring!*' Ambrosius's laughter filled his mind. Ben felt himself turn a deeper shade of red.

'Who are you talking to?' she asked.

Ambrosius choked on his laughter. *'Can she hear me?! She shouldn't be able to!'*

'What's your name?' It was a pathetic subject change, but she took mercy.

'April. What's yours?'

'Benjamin.' He executed a small yet exquisitely sarcastic bow. 'A word of advice, April, wooden swords and saltshakers are no use against demons. They're for vampires and ghosts. Trust me.' Her eyes grew wide, much to Ben's amusement. A slight tremor ran up her arms, her attention fixed on her wooden sword that he still held captive. 'I don't know why you're here, but you won't remember this part of it.' April surprised both of them by lunging forward and batting his outstretched hand away in disdain. Benjamin took a respectful step back.

'No, you don't. I saw what you did to those kids.' A sharp poke of an accusing finger sent his eyebrows up. April stood, defiant, silently daring him to try it.

She was different enough to hold his interest hostage, but he'd best release her back into the wild. There were no accidents, only Fate. 'I'll escort you home.'

April's fingers twitched around the saltshaker. 'Don't you dare erase my memory when we get there.'

Ben held his hands up in mock surrender, smiled, and lied through his teeth. 'I wouldn't dream of such a thing.' He stepped aside. 'After you.' But April hesitated, chewing her bottom lip. Out of politeness, Ben tuned out the thoughts tumbling back and forth in her perplexed mind.

'Do you know a lot about supernatural stuff?' April enquired sharply.

'Yes, I suppose I do,' Ben paused, 'and you don't. By chance, are you a mage?' The words left his mouth before he had a chance to curse himself.

'What's a mage?'

'Never mind.' Ambrosius's laughter exploded in his mind. Ben closed his eyes. *'One, two, three …'*

'Isn't killing,' April vaguely gestured at him, 'your lot, frowned upon?'

'It's complicated.' Ben wasn't sure what he'd said, but April shrank back into the hedge, a look of apprehension in her eyes.

'Can I have my sword back, please?' Polite, even when face-to-face with danger. Ben flipped the bokken over, offering it to her hilt first. April nodded her thanks with saucer eyes. 'You're not worried by the sword?'

'At best, it'll give me a splinter. Perhaps a headache, if you hit me hard enough.' Her confusion was amusing and irritating in equal measures. *'She thinks I'm a vampire …'*

A branch snapped in the distance. Ben silenced her with a raised hand. Mixed in amongst the rustling leaves was the faintest sound of heavy wool snagging against branches. He quickly scanned the deserted park, his sharp senses straining to find the cause.

'Were you trying to ask me for help earlier on?'

There it was again. Another twig breaking underfoot. Ben edged towards April, who took a few distrustful steps backwards, planting her hands on her hips.

'I don't need you to save me, *thanks*.'

'Forgive me, sweetheart, but you brought a saltshaker to a demon fight so, yes, you look like you need some help.'

'Hey, the 1940s called. They want their condescending term of endearment back.' Ben frowned into the awkward silence; light footsteps ahead of them stole his attention. The faintest whiff of burnt air prickled his nose, and there was something else … static was building around them.

'*Something magical this way comes.*'

'*Aye. Djinn. A whole pack.*' Ambrosius paused, straining to recognise the energies coming towards them.

'*Because what I need right now is more argumentative beings in my general vicinity. See what you can find out.*' The air around Ben crackled, signalling Ambrosius's release into the atmosphere. His head felt heavy from the night's antics, the pain in his stomach felt ready to tear him apart. He should have fed before Samhain Eve.

'*Barqan is with them, Ben.*'

The Guardian of Avalon could only mean trouble. 'You might not want saving, April, but I'm going to have to insist upon it.' Urgent conviction lent gravity to Ben's words and still her distrustful eyes bore into his.

'I don't hang out with people who feed on humans.'

'Nor should you. However, something far worse than I is coming.' Silhouettes with blue flames for eyes, appeared like dots and dashes amongst the trees at the other end of the field. 'I won't hurt you – but I can't promise that they won't.'

A djinn let out a high-pitched shriek, and April flinched in pain, her hands flying to her ears. Before she had a chance to protest, Ben snatched her up, threw her over his shoulder and ran. He could ask for forgiveness later.

'What the hell are those *things*?'

'Djinn. Kind of like a genie, but they ain't granting wishes.'

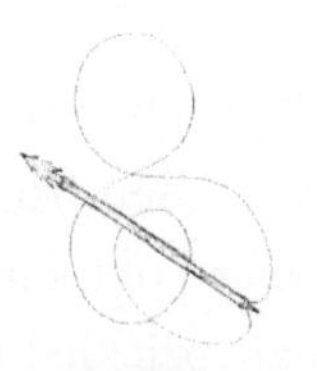

3

Too Much Whiskey, Not Enough Blankets

In his haste, Ben tripped over a "please keep off the grass" sign, stumbling into a controlled skid and took a sharp left out of the park.

The pursuing footsteps halted at the gates. Eight pairs of flaming blue eyes burning in the dark watched his retreat.

'Fate must have assigned them an urgent task for Barqan to leave Avalon.'

A chill of realisation embraced Ben as he shot across the crossroads onto Cattle Street. *'If it was an attack, there would have been no snapping twigs.'*

Djinn were Fate's creatures. Ben associated them with death, not necessarily his, just death, which was to say he thought of them as the premonition to a bad omen he wanted no part in.

They could shape their appearance at will, allowing them to be anything to anyone. A helpful skill when luring prey. The near-perfect glimmers didn't fool Benjamin. He could always spot those shimmering blue eyes.

Ben saw them in the streets, in the coffee shops, in the parks.

They were everywhere, looking at you like they knew what shape your future would take. Ben's spare hand clutched at his sword-shaped talisman. He rounded a corner sharply, his grip on April momentarily slipping.

'Ugh.' April's voice sounded strained, battling to be heard over the wind rushing past. 'This is how I die.'

'It most certainly isn't. I'm very surefooted.'

'Where are we going?' It wasn't easy hitching a ride on his back. April seemed to be handling it reasonably well. And by well, Ben meant that she hadn't thrown up all over him. Yet.

'Bodleian.' Here, where the spires stretched up above them and the university buildings closed in, his pace slowed a little. It was his personal purgatory where time stilled and he could exist.

'Safe?' April lifted her head slightly.

'Nowhere is safe from djinn. But I doubt they'll check the library roof first.' He made a beeline for the Divinity school, which was quietly waiting for him across the courtyard, and leapt high into the air. From his back, April let out a startled yelp but before she could finish it, they had landed.

Ben returned April to her unsteady feet. She promptly stumbled back against the crenelations and vomited over the side.

'That's no way to treat a Grade One listed building.' Benjamin peered over the edge. April stared at him, disorientated and unimpressed. Ben ducked into a quick bow, to hide his smile. 'Apologies.' April leant back a little too far, her arms windmilling over the steep drop. 'I've got you …'

Eight silhouettes with slits of blue flames for eyes strode into the courtyard, two by two, their footsteps bouncing off stone. Ben pulled April to the centre of the tower with a put-upon sigh.

'Hey …' Ben's hand flew to her mouth, his nerves jumping with her every breath. April's furious green eyes found his pleading orbs. He inclined his head to the right. April hesitated before trying to follow his gaze, bobbing onto tiptoes, still swaying a little. Ambrosius rose to the surface in a wash of pins and needles, ready to be used. Ordinarily, Ben would have confronted Barqan by now. Ordinarily, he didn't have an April in tow. Below them, wood groaned in protest as doors were rattled.

'Just a thought, Ben. Perhaps it's not you they're following …'

'No.' April was so … *'She has a saltshaker and a wooden sword! April is not the reason why Barqan …'* Silence. Ben edged to the side, cursing the full moon and lack of clouds. Footsteps carried the djinn out of the courtyard. One turned back for a moment, seeming to stare right at him.

'Barqan.' Ambrosius sparked at Ben's fingertips. The blue eyes turned away and rejoined the pack waiting on the street.

'Are they gone?' April mumbled behind his hand.

'Careful, Ben. She might bite!' Ben let go of Ambrosius.

'April, I'm going to take my hand away. Please, for the love of the Gods, don't yell. Ok?' April, who apparently wasn't quite ready to forgive, shrugged him off and promptly lost her balance. He left her to stagger about this time. 'You're looking a little pale.' Ben cringed. At least he hadn't pointed out the dried sick on her top. April wobbled up to him, a pointy finger jabbing his chest.

'You're in for it now, Ben.' His mouth twitched, as he tried his hardest not to laugh.

'Remind me to enter you ...' Benjamin's eyes widened in horror. 'Oh. Oh, God. That wasn't what I meant!' April pulled her scarf further up her face and promptly sat down. 'Was trying to say, enter you in the Grand National. Oh, God.'

'Your brain believes you have been poisoned.' Ben spoke quickly, blushing. 'Humans aren't built to travel so fast. Take some deep breaths and think no more of it.' Ben took a few deep breaths too, as if it would help April. 'Ok?' She nodded.

'I have a question.'

'Of course, ask away.' Ben leant back against the cold stonework, keeping one eye on the courtyard.

'What, exactly, are djinn? Were they chasing us? Or was it a convenient excuse to kidnap me? Why are we on a rooftop?'

'Finished?' Benjamin had the novel idea that she'd explode if she didn't ask all her questions. 'Splendid. Djinn are divine creatures that can trap you in a dream state. Avoid them. Their intentions were unclear. I *assisted* us in escaping – there's a difference. I happen to like it up here. As for being safe,' Ben shrugged, 'if it's meant to be, the djinn will find us. In my company, you're as safe as ...' he couldn't think of a reassuring verb, 'can be. If you were referring to the structural integrity of the building, it hasn't collapsed yet.'

'You're a vampire that hangs out on rooftops. It's not creepy at all.' Her words tripped over themselves on their way out.

'It's a world away from the hustle and bustle below.'

'Still creepy.' April's heartbeat was settling, although her bokken had found its way back into her hands. But Ben's casual honesty was working its way around them whilst his cool demeanour forced her to calm down. 'Did you say hustle and bustle? Nobody says that anymore.' April wished the world would stop spinning. It was making it difficult to maintain a suitable level of sassiness towards the vampire. Benjamin folded his arms and raised his eyebrows, drawing her attention to eyes that had definitely been silver in the park. Now shifting from silver to pale green, lilac and yellow. Beautiful, unique and unnerving, they revealed nothing of what crossed Ben's mind. The ever-changing spectrum of colours weren't as bright as could be, she thought.

'Is something the matter?'

'I was cursing you for having healthier hair than mine.' April's face flushed with heat. Benjamin looked eternally weary, like he'd carried years of responsibility on his broad shoulders. The true cause was probably something far less romantic. The dark circles under his eyes stood out in stark contrast to his pale skin. Ben didn't look like a vampire, born or turned. More like somewhere along the way he'd taken a wrong turn and this was the end result.

'Right. So, what, exactly, is it you think I can assist you with?'

April inadvertently grunted at him in response, her attention partly devoted to not throwing up again. She zipped her jacket up against the cold, plucking up the courage to ask another question. 'Why did you kill the demons?'

'You must know the answer! You are a hunter, yes?' Ben unfolded his arms, freeing his fingers to lightly drum against the stone.

'Not exactly ...' April noticed him glance into the courtyard. She hoped the genies hadn't come back. She didn't want to hitch a ride on the giant's shoulders again. 'What are you? 6'5, 6'7?'

'What?' Ben's brows furrowed.

'I'm … looking for some demons, to, you know, kill. When I saw you …' April held up the bokken. 'I may be out of my depth.'

'Are you looking for a specific demon, or will any old one do?' Ben's speech and mannerisms were a patchwork quilt of old and new, hinting at his age.

'What?'

'Allow me to surmise: either you were possessed or – and I think this is more the case, for I do not see any marks on your soul – somebody you loved was.'

April's mouth twitched. 'They were possessed.' Although she didn't remember upsetting a witch, April thought she might be cursed. People had a horrible habit of dying. And Danny … she was not enduring that kind of loss, ever again. Benjamin's sigh told her that it was a tale as old as time. No doubt he was trying to find the quickest way to get rid of her.

'Is revenge worth it?' Benjamin asked gently. 'I've yet to see it bring happiness to those who seek it.'

'Happiness is alright; I'm looking for closure. I didn't want to be a hunter, but I have to finish what I started. But I never progressed past staking vampires.'

'Indeed?' Ben wanted to laugh at the ridiculousness of April trying to exorcise a demon, but his chest tightened with concern. Despite being brave, her lack of knowledge would be the death of her.

'*You've got enough problems of your own,*' Ambrosius warned.

'It's most regrettable. There is a certain rhythm to life. You won't truly understand it until you look back on it from death.' Buses trundled past on Broad Street, heading home for the night.

'Ugh, don't tell me everything happens for a reason. You're worse than a self-help book.'

'Everything *does* happen for a reason and that *reason* ...' it hit Ben, stealing his breath for a second, 'is called Fate.'

'Fate sent Barqan to ensure I left with April. Or to prevent it.'

'So, it's not so farfetched after all!' Ambrosius huffed. *'Do we want to find out which it is?'*

Ben's fingers tapped staccato beats on the rough stone. 'Look, April, you don't want to hang around me.'

'Why not?'

Baffled, Ben stared. 'Because you'll wind up dead, that's why not.'

'How do you know I won't kill you?' April quickly met his gaze before looking away.

'You don't even know what I am!' The traffic, the people, and the twinkling city lights dimmed on their own accord. 'I miss the days when street lamps didn't bleed into the night sky, banishing the stars from sight.' Ben stared into the blinking lights of a city that never settled. Carefree laughter pulled him from the skyline, and his entire being ached to be something else. Mortals grew old, suffered the trials of their lives and died whilst he remained.

'Alright, I'll bite. What are you?'

'How to explain it in terms you'll understand?' Soldiers rushed past him, pushing him aside, running to Arthur's aid. 'I was a physician. Now I'm a Guardian missing its other half.'

'Ok ...'

'It was a busy week!'

'What are you guarding against?'

'Whatever threatens the realm.' The Gods had been mercifully quiet for the longest time, leaving only the occasional supernatural nuisance. He was a glorified hunter these days.

'Like genies and demons?' April leant forward a little, fixed on his eyes, trying to read him.

'Djinn. And yes, among other things.' Ben's fingers continued to drum against the stonework, not enjoying being the sole object of her intense curiosity.

'That explains you killing demons.' Doubt was still present in April's voice.

'I didn't do it for fun, did I? They are a small part of a much bigger picture. A picture that looks a lot like war.' The bokken in April's hands trembled slightly. 'You shouldn't be getting yourself mixed up in something larger than you.' Ben absentmindedly plucked the wooden sword from her tenuous grip.

'Hey! Well now you have to tell me.'

'You know,' Ben continued, sitting next to her, bokken balanced on his knees, 'I'd meant to see you safely from the park. I hadn't intended on this.' He gestured at the tower.

'And what is this?' April mimicked his hand gesture.

'You, still being here and asking questions.'

'Questions that you don't like to answer?' Mischief glinted in April's eyes.

'Questions that *you* wouldn't like the answers to.' April's face knotted itself into thoughtful lines. She understood what he hadn't said. 'A sensible person would leave,' Ben warned her, unsure as to whether or not he wanted her to leave. He so rarely felt comfortable with people.

April's curiosity overpowered her rationality. 'Help me with my problem, I'll help you with yours?'

Benjamin snorted in disbelief. 'Don't be so quick to make my trouble yours. Mine will be my end.'

'What's so bad that you risk putting yourself in harm's way?' April asked.

'The End of Days.' It sounded so simple and so huge when said aloud.

April's laughter startled Ben. 'You're serious, huh?'

'Deadly serious.'

'Oh. Sorry. You're aware of how this sounds, right?' April paused expectantly. Ben gave her a nonchalant shrug, hoping it would discourage her. It did not. 'Like some crappy vampire novel? We have a conflict, demons and a tortured vampire trying to save the world. All we're missing is a love interest.'

April gave him a little grin and the Gods be damned, Ben surprised himself, and he let the worry lines stretch themselves back out into a smile. 'I've read a couple – oh, don't look so surprised!' He wasn't going to tell her about Arthur. Not yet anyway.

'Is it like reading a biography?' April teased, leaning in a little.

'They're inaccurate and whiny.' Ben scrunched his face up in disgust. 'However, I do appreciate the irony.' He let his attention settle on the bokken. It felt so flimsy! 'I can't believe you hunt vampires with this. Do you have the strength to break through the rib cage?' April shot Ben a sideways glance. Her narrowed eyes screaming at how insulted she was. 'I could carve a spell into the blade, douse it with holy water if you like? Give it a little more oomph.'

'If you think it will help?' April asked uncertainly. Ben nodded to himself. He'd do that before they parted company, see if he could keep her alive a bit longer. Especially with sunrise fast approaching. Those still yet to return to their dismal abodes would be desperately seeking a way to stay in Gaia. 'Why is Halloween always so busy?' April cocked her head, listing to the shouts of revellers going home.

'With the stroke of midnight, dresses turn into rags, carriages into pumpkins and the boundaries between the realms are compromised until sunrise.'

'Who decided that was a good idea?'

'As with most questionable ideas, it was a compromise.' Arthur had been struggling to keep the supernatural clans at bay. So, Merlin intervened. 'They're sealed in their separate realms. Except for one night a year.'

April shook her head, clearly judging. Of course she didn't understand. She'd not known a war-torn realm.

'It wasn't my decision!' Over a thousand years later and Ben was still defending Arthur and Merlin's legacy.

Every so often, an inexplicable feeling enveloped April. It wasn't intuition.

It was something infallible, something not to be ignored.

There was trouble ahead and it was unavoidably April's. And whatever it was, it was bad enough to worry a vampire-guardian. It had been unusually busy on the demon front and quiet on the vampire front recently, like the calm before the storm. Perhaps Benjamin could shed some light into the dark corners. His voice rose with concern as he continued on, unaware that April wasn't listening. It was a bad habit, a by-product of her inquisitiveness. Plus, a compulsive tendency to overthink everything allowed April's questions to out-noise the world.

'It's a disturbing sign.'

Case in point. April straightened up, opening her eyes wide in an attempt to force focus. But holding onto her questions was a distracting type of torture. For example, she was dying to know why Benjamin was bothering. What was it to him whether or not she survived?

'The End of Days have been a long time coming. And now, well,' Benjamin frowned at her bokken in his lap. 'If it's allowed to succeed, the disaster wrought will reach all nine realms. They'll leave no stone unturned in their quest to regain control. Freyja's not going to come to your rescue this time.'

'Nine realms?!' Freyja?' She should have listened.

'Yes.' Ben laughed, shaking his head in wonder. It wasn't April's fault – she seldom left the county, let alone the realm. 'Look.' Fire the colour of autumn leaves engulfed Ben's hands. April couldn't scoot away fast enough. Ben chuckled and launched the flames into the air. April watched in awe as nine orbs of burnt embers lined themselves up, hovering like jewels in the night. 'Avalon, where Fate and the djinn live, is at the top. We're here – Gaia. Below lurks the seven under-realms. Each more odious and unfathomable than the last.'

'Sounds great …' Ben swiped his hand and the embers vanished. Magic. It was beautiful. He wielded it with ease born of practice. Vampires didn't have magic.

'If you and your fellow mortals could see the underrealms, you'd realise how lucky you are.' April slipped her phone from her pocket but resisted the urge to look it up. She didn't know what she'd search anyway.

'The vast majority of mortals are blissfully unaware that magic and monsters exist.' As if Benjamin had ordered it, a thick mist rolled in, eager to devour them all. April couldn't fathom how nine realms could disappear.

'Humans are not the be-all and end-all. You jostle about on the carousel of mortality, waiting to be delivered to the realm in which you will spend your afterlife.'

'Who's they?' The fog brought a new, crisp cold to nip at her fingers and settle into her bones. April dug through the bunched-up tissues, odd glove and loose change in her pocket, looking for a hot hand pocket. 'You know, the ones who want to *leave no stone unturned*?'

'The Gods, Fate, Chaos.' Benjamin's eyes widened. 'I assumed you'd know some of it.'

'I kill vampires. I assumed there was a God at some point but …' April shrugged.

'I'm going to have to start from the beginning, aren't I?'

'Yup.' April burrowed further into her scarf; she couldn't feel her nose. 'What will the End of Days entail, exactly?' Benjamin looked skyward, uttering something that sounded like a plea for strength. 'Some sort of apocalypse?' April caught Benjamin rolling his eyes.

'Close enough.' Ben tilted his head to the side, considering her. 'You'll have to trust me, if you want my help.'

'If somebody says you can trust them, that usually means you can't.' It came out harsher than intended, but April was exhausted.

'A hunter doesn't trust me! I am shocked!' Benjamin frowned in thought. 'I think you need to see it, to believe me.'

That unnamed feeling crept back up April's spine, urging her to pay attention and making her squirm. Her head was swimming. Benjamin might not need sleep, but she did. Apocalypses, evil not-granting-wishes genies, helpful vampires – nine realms! It was too much. 'Say again?' April turned to see the orange glow engulfing his hands again. Ben's deathly cold fingers brushed against April's temple. Oxford melted away.

4

Life in the Embers

April's chest burned as if she'd run thousands of miles in the dead of a frozen night.

Terror clawed at her throat. Above her, the sky shone with an entire galaxy of stars. The full moon's light struggled to cut through the thick tar of night.

The shadows filtering through the trees had to be branches swaying in the ...

'Shadows don't carry pitchforks, April, nor torches.' A hundred burning torches were approaching her with purpose.

'Benjamin?!' Pure blind terror ripped apart her composure. The smoke-filled air burned her throat, angering her lungs. April doubled over, trying to catch a breath between coughs. Soldiers, their armour glowing orange, transforming them into spirits made of fire, hemmed her in. The faces of townsfolk swam in and out of hazy vision in the heat. There wasn't a sound to be heard, like the world had been paused. April's arms ached inexplicably. Puzzled, she glanced down. She'd lost a glove. In her right hand, a steel sword. In her left, a well-used wooden shield. Realisation crept over her like the cold dawn she'd left behind in Oxford. 'This is your memory.'

'Yes.' The shouting of soldiers and townsfolk shoved aside Benjamin's disembodied voice. She'd let them down. She'd let someone important die.

'Monster!' the townsfolk yelled. 'Demon!' They spat, some making the cross gesture of the new God.

'What do I do, Benjamin?' April spun in frantic circles, her heart in her mouth as she realised the assortment of weapons were meant for her. The mob bled into the clearing, surrounding April.

'Kill it!' A thunderous conflict raged inside her. It was true – April was a monster now. Perhaps she should stop running. Let them end it for her. She didn't know, wasn't sure, couldn't concentrate over the roar of the crowd. 'Please go away, please ...' she whispered, pressing balled-up fists to her eyes. She didn't know why her friends, people who she'd attended to as a physician, the soldiers, didn't recognise her. Hunger crippled her. April was going to be sick. In the centre of their chests sat a swirling ball of warm light – home to her pain, the salvation from the hunger. Their souls sang such a sweet song. If she could bask in the majesty of the symphony, it would all be over. 'I am your physician.' She wasn't the curse twisting her soul into a balloon-animal parody of itself. Seeing no understanding there, April turned sharply and fled.

Weak and still unused to her own body, she tripped and stumbled through the woods, seeking distance. The mob chanted as it marched. They had no hope of catching up, given the miles she'd put between them. April's legs nearly buckled as the world blurred by. 'I'm going to crash into the trees!' April flinched with every knotted gigantic tree trunk she passed, tense with the anticipation of a collision.

'You won't. My reaction time is beyond your comprehension,' Benjamin replied, unseen.

'Why am I covered in blood?' The odd patch of brown floated in the middle of rusty red. 'Is it yours?' She'd never seen so much mud either; his trousers were caked in it.

'No.'

April crested a hill and spotted a clump of prickly bushes that looked like a hiding place. Under the bushes, it felt like even the earth was trying to crawl away from her.

Peering through the slits of leaves, April spied a familiar, foreboding landmark – rather, Benjamin recognised the jigsaw of bricks and mortar of a curtain wall of a castle.

'Where am I?' April knew she'd run hundreds of miles in fifteen minutes.

'Caerleon, Wales. Why I didn't return to Tintagel, I don't know. It was nearer.'

April's soul reached for her adoptive home; she'd forever be a stranger now. A tall knight in armour stepped out onto the edge of the moat. His visor obscured his face. Home was wherever *he* was, and *he* wasn't anywhere. Not anymore.

'Who is he, Benjamin?' This man was her albatross.

'Everything.' Benjamin quickly buried the memory where April couldn't reach it.

'You couldn't save him.' April curled into a ball, trying not to get caught on the rough edges of the trauma lurking close by. 'But you didn't kill him. You were trying to survive because you'd been changed.' April hadn't considered whether or not a changed vampire was less evil than a born vampire. 'How did it happen?'

Benjamin didn't respond, she could feel the weight of it bearing down on him. April lay, staring at the alien sky, smelling the wet soil and moss, trying to keep her head above the water.

'Benjamin?'

Big cracks shot across the sky, shattering it into sections. The ground shook so violently, jolting April from her hiding place. The world was rupturing, her head with it. April shut her eyes, hoping that whatever was happening would overlook her. She couldn't tell if it was part of the memory or if Benjamin had terrible luck. The light on the other side of her eyelids softened from a faraway frosty night to the soft hues of sunrise. The sounds of the mob switched places with the more familiar soundscape of traffic and pigeons.

Everything sounded so muffled in comparison to Benjamin's hearing. April didn't dare believe she was back within herself, and in the correct time period, so she stayed as still as she could for a minute, listening to the whirr of the milk float passing by on its route, oblivious to what was taking place above his head.

Hearing no angry mobs, April slowly opened one eye.

The Bodleian's rooftop greeted her, its stonework beginning to reveal some of its distinctive sandy colour in the early morning light. April opened her other eye. Benjamin had retreated to the far wall, considering her through haunted eyes and looking as shaken as she felt.

'A little warning would have been nice.' April was furious. Rather, she was going to be. Just as soon as the tremors of relief mingled with utter horror subsided. 'Did you run out of words?'

Benjamin said nothing, his eyes riveted to the ground. As his terror echoed in her mind, April wrapped her arms around her legs. No amount of rubbing her eyes would expunge the scene. Somewhere, in the jumble of feelings, both April's and Ben's, she realised the point of it all.

April had seen it in his eyes in the park but hadn't been able to name it. She'd felt it in every second of the flashback. 'You were human.'

'And then I wasn't. It took me a long time to make peace with the curse. I'd survived all of those battles and … I didn't understand it, so I tried to fight it.' Ben snorted at his own ignorance. 'The devil that did this to me said, "A life you didn't live is still lost. You haven't fallen, you have risen anew." As if that made it any better.'

'What a douche.' April pulled her scarf over her face to hide the cringe. 'If your story doesn't get better soon, I'm going to start feeling sorry for you.' Her back cracked as she stretched into the quiet. 'There was a lesson here, right? Life is a delicate balance so easily upset by the thousands of imbalances lying in wait; it's all too easy to find yourself on the wrong side of the sword.'

'Close enough.' Ben nodded, his unfocused eyes staring into the blinking lights as a moth would.

'Why didn't you show me your turning?' The mob yelled in her mind, causing her to shiver.

'Ah, well,' Benjamin's fingers tapped out an agitated rhythm on April's wooden sword, 'that would be too much for you, I fear.'

'Or too much for you.' The memory she'd lived through was as sharp as glass, as it had been on the day, hundreds of years ago. And Benjamin tortured himself with it. 'You keep calling it a curse.' April's brows pulled down, fear edging her voice. 'That's a funny way of a describing a vampire.'

'I am a shtriga. You are forgiven for confusing me with a vampire; we are, in a way, related. Shtrigas are vampiric witches. We are created from magic.'

'Staking you wouldn't have worked, would it?' April's wide eyes travelled down to her bokken, sitting loosely in his hands. She should get that back.

'No,' Ben laughed darkly. 'Only consecrated iron will do. And I'd have to be feeding, so you won't have many opportunities, I'm afraid.' April's eyes widened further in surprise. 'Ah, you're fresh out of consecrated iron rods? No matter, I'm not hungry.' He was joking, April knew that, but this was the line. It had to be.

'Do you feed?'

'I was wondering when you'd ask.' Benjamin's sigh carried hundreds of years' worth of being judged. 'Would it change your opinion of me?'

'Well …' April hesitated, 'you saved me, so … you're not all bad. How often?' she asked because he was leaning away from the question.

'Once a year, usually. I can't abstain forever.' Ben shrugged. 'The pain is debilitating.'

'Yeah. I get hangry if I skip a meal.'

'I don't understand … I gave up trying to follow the language of youth.'

'The language of youth?' April's laughter startled Benjamin and a nearby pigeon. 'You don't talk to many people, do you?'

'I try to avoid it.' Something else they had in common.

'So, who are these poor people? Is that a cat?' There was no way a black cat could be up this high, but there one was, slinking across the tower behind them. She grabbed Benjamin's sleeve. The cat vanished by the time he turned his head. Typical.

'What? I feed on those I catch committing particularly despicable crimes.'

'Right.' April could imagine this usually reserved cliché chasing thieves up the high street. 'Sounds like self-inflicted unorthodox community service.'

'More like a public service. In some small way, I'm atoning for my many sins.' April thought he might be trying to nullify some guilt too. 'I'd barely call it surviving, existing at the most basic level. It's exhausting, April.'

April's hands were shaking. Whether they were itching to hold the bokken once more, or whether Benjamin had articulated some shared sentiment, he didn't know.

'So,' April purposefully stepped over the moment, 'what's the rest of your story? You've left out a few hundred years.' She met his gaze straight on. 'Feels like I've walked into a film halfway through.'

'Is that so?' Benjamin half-smiled. For years he'd waited for the world to move on, willed it to do so. And the winds of fate had answered by pushing April into his path. Forgetting himself and how traumatic the previous link had been for April, Benjamin raised his hand.

'No!' She violently batted him away. 'We're not doing that again. Use your words.'

Benjamin nodded. Twice in one day was too much. He didn't enjoy raking up the past – and with a live audience. His resolve shook and caved-in under the scrutiny of April's steady, inquisitive gaze. 'You're nosey and mildly annoying.' Ben said playfully, knowing she wouldn't be deterred.

'It's been said before.' Somewhere in the distance, birds began their song, welcoming another uncertain day. Benjamin often thought they were singing to the sun – persuading it to rise and shine. 'And this business with the End of Days?' April asked.

'It will start with the Gods, I think. It's bad news for *everyone*. Vampires, demons,' Ben paused, 'and humans. A war that has been a long time coming.'

'*A long time coming*, sounds like it has an epic backstory and it's bloody freezing out here.'

Benjamin blinked in amazement. 'You wish to accompany me onwards?' People tried to avoid conversations with him, not prolong them.

'You might have forgotten this, but mortals are susceptible to temperature. It's a little below freezing. So, to the bat cave?' April gave him a cheeky grin.

Benjamin snorted, pushing himself up and offered her the bokken. She grabbed it and allowed him to pull her to her feet. She quickly made it vanish into the sheath whilst peering over the edge at the long drop to the flagstones. Having already guessed her next question, Benjamin tried to look remorseful. His face had a habit of fixing itself into a grimace regardless of how he felt.

'There are these things called stairs. You should try them. They're great.'

'As lovely as stairs are, there are none here. The shtriga elevator is the only way down.'

'Fine,' April groaned. 'But I want to walk once we're down.'

'As you wish.' Ben bowed. 'Close your eyes and try to ignore the way your stomach drops as we fall.'

'If I throw up on you, it's deserved.' April hopped up onto Ben's back, her hands knotted tightly around his neck.

As far as Samhain Eves went, this one had been on track to be the worst. Until he'd come across April. Now it was top twenty. 'Are you ready?'

'No.'

Ben smiled to himself, scanning the courtyard for djinn. 'Here we go.'

Despite his warning, April shrieked as they plummeted towards the unforgiving ground.

Dearest Arthur,

If I close my eyes, I am home.

Caerleon's halls, bustling with servants. The chatter of court. The sea of people pushing through the markets. I hated it then! You thrived in and amongst the noise and dirt (progress, you called it). I stayed for you. I wonder, from time to time, if we were too different. Separated by twelve years and social standing. You were cocky; I was quiet. You loved to hunt; I preferred to read. If we'd have met even a year later, well, timing is everything and it has a wicked humour.

Caerleon was gripped by fear, depleted by preparations for yet another raid from the supernatural clans. The squabbling over land and, who should rule what, was just that – squabbling. The Gods' bid to take over Gaia didn't seem worth their trouble. Yes, their freedom from their oppressive creator, Chaos, had been hard won, but they had the clans to appease them. They had free travel. I wish I could have seen Merlin sealing them away in their adopted realms. Merlin saw straight to the depths of a soul, so why didn't he recognise the curse on our last parting? Did he have a premonition? Did he try to stop it? Did Merlin tell you? Of course, Merlin left me with more questions than answers. The impossible-to-please and cantankerous man spoke in riddles. Having the Guardianship to occupy me has been a blessing. It gave me a reason to keep moving. Although it was a rubbish parting gift on Merlin's part. Would you have accepted me? I hope so.

The night we met, you were glowing – from the roaring fire! You were captivating, dressed in gold-studded red velvet. I knocked my goblet over. I tried to forget, but I'll always know you, the ever-present undercurrent in my mind. I have your talisman. The tiny sword. It threw splinters of light onto the walls as we lay in bed. I asked you why you never took it off. You laughed and said, 'If I am not wearing it, the worst has happened. The Gods help whoever succeeds me!' Of all your alternative endings, did you ever imagine it would be me? Nor did I. The history books speak of you and battles won. They tell of Merlin's unparalleled skill with magic and his knowledge. There's no word of the court physician who remains, trapped in time, trying to remember who we all were.

With love,
Benjamin

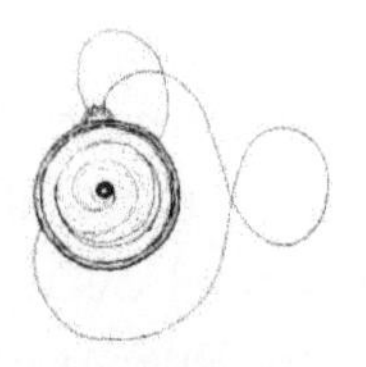

5

Feel the Void

Something darted past April.

She'd only taken one step out of the courtyard.

It tugged her sleeve.

April froze, peering through the fog-choked air. A cold breeze trailed icy fingers across her shoulder. She was alone on the cobbled streets that snaked away in all directions. A sizeable stone skittered towards her, propelled from the shadows. April's heart leapt in her chest. She squared her shoulders and hurried after Benjamin, whose long stride had given him a daunting lead. If she was aware of the thing skulking along beside her, Ben would be too. And he didn't seem concerned. But he felt too far away. Worry pushed her legs to match her racing heartbeat. April rummaged in her pockets, but her headphones were gone. Humming wasn't as world-muting but needs must. As she'd cleared the intro to *Enter Sandman*, the shadows shifted. Any sense of calmness that the chords had brought, vanished. Benjamin slipped from view around the side of the drum-shaped Radcliff Camera with its domed top. April's pride chased Benjamin's name from her lips. Nerves propelled her into the second verse, and around the corner, expecting to see Benjamin. How did he make no sound? The gravel crunched under April's feet as if it were in cahoots with Satan. Cold, bony fingers locked around her forearm, spinning her around. April stared back at the way she'd come. No drunks. No Benjamins. No genies. Only the feeling of being watched from the parapet guarding the upper gallery of the Radcliff Camera.

'Lurking in the shadows is a dick move!' With a glare into the dark, April set off along Cattle Street. A stone hit her square in the back. April was going to have to run – a scarier prospect than any vampire. 'Please don't be a genie.' She took a deep breath and glanced behind her. Nothing. She turned and came nose-to-nose with a gaunt, pale, glitching face leering down.

'Oh, ghost!' The phantom smiled and it was all jagged, razor-sharp teeth, thin lips and sunken eyes. 'Ben …' The phantom's hands wrapped tightly around April's throat, delighting in the dwindling air in her lungs, its distorted face sneering down at her. April's fear-muddled brain spluttered back into action. She managed to curl her hand around the saltshaker, freeing it from its pocket prison. She shook it furiously in the general direction of the ghost, despairing at the thin stream of salt trickling free. The fingers with no form squeezed tighter still. In desperation, she fought to unscrew the lid. With a strength that no ghost had any business possessing, it lifted April into the air, the tips of her boots scraping the ground. The saltshaker's lid clicked free, the contents spilling onto the ghost's hip. The ghost let out a surprised hiss of pain, and its knowing gaze found April's for a split second. It turned to wisps of smoke and drifted away. April crashed to the ground, saltshaker and all. She'd been aiming for its head, but beggars couldn't be choosers.

Despite her burning lungs, April forced herself to take big gulps of air. Her hands explored her throat, certain that huge red welts were forming there. The furious ghost flickered back into view on the other side of the street.

'Translucent piece of crap.'

Exhausted and aching, April reached for the saltshaker, dismayed to find it empty. The ghost saw it too, its head leaning to one side as it considered its options. Something solid stepped in front of her, obscuring the ghost. Fear propelled April backwards. She scrabbled to stand up, chased by a strange wheezing sound. She reached for her bokken and '*You*!' April croaked, her throat burning. 'Where the hell were you?'

'I'm …' Ben tried to speak around bursts of laughter, hands on knees. 'I thought it would scare you, nothing more.' Keeping one furious eye on Benjamin, April peered around him in time to catch the ghost melt into the air.

'What?'

Benjamin was trying and failing to regain control of his face. 'Saltshaker.' He lost control again, his whole body shaking.

'You were welcome to step in at any point. It could have killed me!' April bypassed "angry" and went straight to "woman scorned". She ripped her sword case from her back, not bothering to take the bokken out, and began her assault on Ben. The attack only added fuel to his laughter.

'I wouldn't have let it come to that,' Ben protested, putting little effort into blocking her blows. 'There was no danger of it attacking again, not after the amount of salt you threw at it. It's probably having a stroke.' Ben ran out of air himself as he continued silently laughing, tears streaming down his face.

'Prat,' April muttered darkly and Ben's laughter returned, bouncing off the stone walls, filling the space. April hated to admit it, but the music of Ben's laughter was annoyingly infectious.

'It's not funny!' Ben held his thumb and forefinger up to indicate that he thought it was, at least, a little funny.

'It strangled me!' Ben's laughter stopped. Within a single breath, he smoothed his face and tone out.

'I appear to have forgotten myself. Well, I'll be ...'

'The ghost?' April stepped closer to Ben, her hands brushing his arm.

'No. It's ... I saw the same black cat in the park.' Ben's eyes followed its progress.

'I saw a cat on the roof. Don't ever let a ghost get the drop on me again, is that clear?' April poked him in the chest with the sword case.

'Crystal.' Ben glanced at his watch, his thumb smoothing over the cracks. 'We should be on our way.' He turned and carried on, his pace a little slower.

With a last hateful glare at the shadows, April hurried to catch up. This time, she wasn't letting her pride keep her from dogging Ben's heels. 'What's the time, Mr Shtriga?'

'It's four a.m.' Ben laced his fingers behind his back.

'Really?' Hours had slipped by, unannounced and unmarked by the early morning's events, and all the while time had stopped. April drifted back into the mess that was Ben's story. Shtrigas and apocalyptic wars had never featured on her bucket list. 'It's funny how things work out; you went to Caerleon for herbs and found your forever home instead. Fate works in mysterious ways.' April grinned at him, but Ben was staring into the distance.

'She does.'

'I'm still trying to wrap my head around shtrigas and realms, never mind Gods …' Shtrigas – the differences were subtle, bordering on being technicalities. Or identity issues. 'I understand vampires. I know what makes them tick. More importantly, I can stop the ticking.'

Ben kept his attention fixed on the passing vehicles as shops and offices thinned out, giving way to houses. 'Indeed.'

'Your world sounds brutal.'

'The living think death isn't fair, and the dead think life isn't fair. It is what it is.' Ben shrugged. 'The world reinvents itself. It's not necessarily a bad thing. Magic use declined steeply after Merlin's death. People remembered the battle. They were scared of anything that wasn't human. There was a purge.'

'Just when I thought it couldn't get any worse …'

'There wasn't a place for me in the new world.'

April heard the shutters drop. Her questions would keep for a while, she supposed. Besides, climbing up Headington Road at a half-run left no room for talking *and* breathing. April wasn't flagging so much as dying. Behind them, the sleeping city unfolded in the valley, stretching its arms upwards and yawning.

The distance between them had lengthened and the silence had grown to fit the gap.

'Why don't I go to the gym? I have a membership. Ridiculous.' April lengthened her stride. Even at this time, cars shot past the hushed houses lining both sides of the street. April couldn't stop herself from peering into windows unguarded by closed curtains. Houses that would be right at home in *Good Housekeeping* magazine soon gave way to homes that wouldn't even grace the back cover. 'So where exactly do shtrigas *live*? Bird boxes? Under rocks?' She ticked each ridiculous suggestion off on her fingers, trying to gauge when Ben's patience would snap. 'In a tree?' Ben dipped his head in exasperation. 'You know,' she panted, 'just because you're *technically* dead, doesn't mean you have to kill me by walking at breakneck speed.'

'I am not *technically* dead.' Ben slowed a little, frowning over his shoulder at her breathlessness. 'Do you want me to carry you?'

April furiously shook her head. Once was plenty. 'So how dead are you?'

'I'm alive and dead. It's …'

'A curse, I *know*.' April turned this new-found fact over in her mind. 'So … you're like Schrödinger's cat?'

'Not quite. As with vampires, there are two types of shtriga – those who are born and those who are made …'

'Sooooo, you are dead?'

'You're asking me to condense thousands of years' worth of history and magic into a few sentences?'

'A short paragraph would be fine.'

'You are pribbling!' April mimed zipping her lips. Ben was a strange one, but she didn't mind strange, she understood it. 'To change a human into a shtriga, your target must have natural magic. The curse turns it against them. The end result is a creature who's not alive by human standards, but isn't dead either.'

'Right,' April replied sceptically. It was a tricky dichotomy to wrap her head around at four a.m.

'My heart still beats. Check my pulse if you like.' Ben rolled up his sleeve, spinning around and walking backwards, his arm outstretched for her inspection.

'Um, maybe later?' April stopped, hands on her hips. At least she wasn't cold now. 'Leave me here. I'm not going to make it.' The sight of Benjamin walking backwards up the hill with one sleeve rolled up, had her smiling. He appeared in a pool of one streetlamp light and vanished into the blackness of the night, a solitary blip on a radar. Perhaps being carried wouldn't be so bad. 'If shtrigas use chat-up lines, you should definitely use the "check my pulse" line.'

His answering amused laugh drifted to her on the breeze. 'Thank you for the advice.' Benjamin stopped under a lamppost, leaning against it.

With a groan, April jogged to catch up. 'Human speed from now on, or I'll start singing.'

'Can you sing?'

'Obviously not. Wouldn't be much of a threat otherwise.' The lamplight never lasted long enough for April to steal a decent look. Being in Ben's head had been a claustrophobic experience. She'd seen loneliness creep towards him when he'd been chased from town. She'd felt it wrap itself around him when Arthur and Merlin died. Ben clung too tightly to his failures. He'd stuffed so much into cupboards and drawers, it was a miracle he hadn't imploded. April sympathised; her own head was a self-made torture chamber of what-ifs and if-onlys.

April's fingers kept worrying at the strap of the sword case. She generally wasn't keen on people (supernatural or otherwise). At some point, she was going to say the wrong thing. He'd covered so much ground in his lifetime, across fields littered with emotional landmines that could be easily triggered by the questions gathering speed in her mind. It was only a matter of time before one broke free and … 'Arthur and Merlin?' Unfortunately, the ground didn't swallow her whole.

'What of them?' Benjamin voice sounded strained.

Oh well, she'd already breathed life into the tired ghosts, so, 'As in *The Sword in The Stone?*'

'That film couldn't have been further from the truth.' Ben's disdain was noted.

'It wasn't meant to be a biography, I think.'

'Beside the point.'

'Hey,' April held her hands up. 'Just because it's your history, doesn't mean it's somebody else's fiction.' She folded her arms in case he had any doubt about her not backing down. 'What were they like?'

'Merlin wasn't a kind, eccentric old man with a beard down to his knees.'

'I sense that you're about to ruin my childhood.' April narrowed her eyes.

'They were people, April. They bore a lot of responsibility. Responsibility doesn't leave much room for nice personalities. Merlin was chaotic by nature; cold and calculating. He broke more than he fixed. And Arthur ...' Benjamin had to pause as the ever-present sense of loss squeezed his vocal cords. 'You've heard the stories.'

'Why were you friends with somebody who was cold and calculating? Low self-esteem? Oh, and this is important, did he have a talking owl?'

'Did he have ... No, he ... ugh!'

'Did he turn people into squirrels?'

'No. Actually, there was one such instance. It involved an unfortunate squire who'd disturbed Merlin whilst he'd been brewing a potion. It took me a full day to persuade him to reverse the spell.'

'Incredible!'

'Have I ruined your childhood?' Ben asked in a mock dramatic voice.

'I'm not surprised, I'm disappointed. I didn't think anybody could be so ...' She searched around for the word that would describe somebody who seemed to be the embodiment of hope and salvation for so many people.

'Distinguished?'

'Yeah.' A gate creaked as she passed it. April froze. 'There's somebody leaning on that gate.' The dog let out a low growl. Ben's surefooted step faltered for a split second. Maybe he'd seen it too, or maybe ... 'You still miss him.' The four words had barged past her better judgement.

'No.' April wasn't interested in the lie.

'Doesn't it get easier?'

Benjamin's laugh was the sad laugh of someone who had learnt the hard way that time had no healing properties. 'No. You get better at disguising the wounds from yourself.'

April huffed. He exhausted her, both mentally and physically. Although it probably had more to do with their half-an-hour trek. And she had too many layers on. 'I never dress for the weather.'

'What do you dress for?'

'The worst-case scenario.' The combined irritants of heat and tired legs had April tugging at her scarf. In her struggle to free herself from the mass of knotted fabric, her long jet-black hair was falling loose from its ponytail. April collided with a stationary Benjamin, bouncing off him. 'Hey!' She rubbed indignantly at her aching shoulder.

'You are a walking, talking omnishambles. What are you doing?'

'What does it look like? I'm taking my scarf off.' April bundled the thick black bedsheet of a scarf into Ben's confused hands.

'Could you not have waited? We're here now.'

April slipped past him. Her confidence failed her at his front gate. She tentatively nudged it open, triggering the security light. '*This* is your house?'

It was everything that April had expected and nothing like she had imagined.

A rundown house with a view of the city below. The paint looked to be white beneath the grime, whilst the tired, red bricks framing the bay window and arched porch door had surrendered to the sun after years of fighting to keep their colour. Judging by the untidy flower beds inhabited solely by the skeletal remains of plants, April guessed he wasn't going to be entering the Chelsea Flower Show. The only living plant was a single intruding branch from his neighbour's cherry blossom tree. In spring it would make for a stark contrast to the overgrown grass and overturned wheelie bins. It suited Benjamin perfectly.

Keys in hand, Ben pushed through his gate, praying that he'd remembered to put his laundry away. He had a sinking feeling he'd left it stranded on the clothes horse. He turned to apologise for the state of his house, and saw her leaning slightly on the gate, admiring his collection of dead flowers. Her apprehension hung in the air as she squinted against the harsh glare of the security light.

The clothes horse was going to be the least of his worries.

'*Why do you care?*' Ambrosius asked, genuinely perplexed by Ben's uncharacteristic house proudness.

'*I don't,*' Ben shot back. '*It's too soon for her to see my washing, don't you think?*' The scarf had hidden the dark pink flush painted across April's tawny skin and had softened her strong cheekbones. There was a crook in her nose that spoke of past fights. Something inside Ben twinged. '*She can't be more than 20...*'

'*At some point she's going to see more of your metaphorical dirty laundry.*'

'*Ambrosius, please.*' Benjamin sighed internally, leaning against the doorframe.

'*Try and look reassuring,*' Ambrosius advised in a know-it-all tone he'd learnt from Merlin. Benjamin locked gazes with April, fixing his mouth into what he hoped was a wide, reassuring grin.

'*You've overshot it. Less teeth. That's better. Less serial killer-esque.*'

A young lady indecisively loitering on his doorstep simply wouldn't do. '*I hope she doesn't become a bother.*'

'*You decided to entertain her, Ben,*' Ambrosius chuckled.

'*What was I supposed to do? Leave her for Barqan?*'

'Hi!' April waved at him. Ben blinked rapidly, letting his eyes refocus on her.

'*Ask her if she hears something because ...*'

'Seriously, I swear you're talking to someone when you do that.' April raised her eyebrows.

'*Witch!*'

'*Ambrosius! Don't be rude!*'

'*No, I meant: is she a witch? Fairy? 'Cause she's something!*'

Ben counted to three, a not-so-subtle warning to Ambrosius to settle down. 'Sometimes my mind wanders.'

The sound of a key turning in a lock reminded April that Ben was expecting her to actually go inside. She tentatively swung the rickety gate open. It was a big house. Lots of rooms to clean. More space than one person needed.

'If you're waiting for me to carry you over the threshold, you're gonna be there a long time, *Princess*.' April drew the saltshaker back, despite knowing she'd never reach him with her crappy pitch. 'Do you know how many ghosts are currently stood next to you? No ghosts in here though.'

'No. Nope. No.' April rushed up the path and into the gloomy hallway. Smiling to himself, Benjamin leant past her and flicked on the hallway light. The dim glow of an energy-saving bulb blinked awake. April couldn't make out much past the chair that sat next to a neatly organised shoe rack and side table. The house was mostly trapped in darkness, the curtained windows standing ready to refuse entry to the dawn. She glanced back to the street, and spotted a pool of light in the darkness. 'How judgy are your neighbours? You're out all night and return in the small hours with a woman,' she said in a mock scandalised tone. 'Tongues will wag.'

'Come on in, for goodness' sake,' Benjamin laughed.

'Shoes on or off?' A line of white powder ran across the threshold. April arched her eyebrows by way of enquiry and shut the door without a second thought.

'It's salt. Rock salt to be precise. I'm not lavishly decorating my home with cocaine,' Ben snorted, kicking off his boots.

'Shouldn't it trap you at the door?' Ben rolled his eyes at her reasonable question. 'Have you tested the theory with a human in the house?'

'You're thinking of ghosts. I'm not yet a ghost.' Ben reached into a cupboard under the stairs; April peered over his shoulder, mouthing a silent "wow" at the cupboard entirely dedicated to salt. 'It prevents those who wish you harm from crossing the line.' Ben carefully rebuilt the lines disturbed by the door's draught.

'Makes sense. You don't wish yourself harm.'

'Usually.' Ben tossed in a dark laugh. 'I'm a Guardian. Therefore, I'm not popular. So don't break the lines of salt.' Ben leant forward like an expectant teacher. 'Say it with me.' April hiked her eyebrows further up her forehead. Ben dismissed her with a wave of his hand and disappeared through a doorway to his left.

'You're scared of ghosts?!' April called out in disbelief and took her first tentative boots-on step into the inner bowels of the house.

The layout was consigned to memory without much conscious thought. Every possible escape route and hiding place was duly noted, anything that would make a good weapon catalogued. 'It's a bit of a fixer-upper, isn't it?' April asked as she took in the worn-out carpets and shabby curtains. Benjamin didn't have much furniture, but what he did have was kept clean and tidy, very at odds with its surroundings.

'I like a project. One day I'll finish it.'

April followed his voice to the living room, where Ben was perched on the bay window's bench. 'You have eternity and you've got as far as … nothing. It looks like you've done nothing.' She picked at a hole in the plastering, chunks drifting to the ground.

'I changed the handles on the kitchen cabinets last month.' Ben's smug tone suggested that he was open to compliments.

'When did you buy this place?' April picked up an old snow globe from a bookshelf. The little flurry settled to reveal a miniature library with ghosts swirling about inside.

'Let's see …' Ben looked at the ground as if the answer was etched into the floorboards.

'Before the war so …'

'Which war?'

'Two? Two. Late 1920s/early 1930s. I forget.' Benjamin shrugged as if it was inconsequential.

'That explains the wallpaper in the hallway ...' Turning away from Ben, she scanned the bookcases groaning under the weight of the numerous tomes and novels stacked haphazardly on the shelves. Everything was so *normal* – wood floors, sofas and a TV in the living room. She had been expecting a dark, dingy cellar with ...

'A coffin, bats and candles dripping wax.' Benjamin finished April's thought aloud.

'What the hell?' She whirled around to find him casually leaning against a door frame that he definitely hadn't been leaning against five seconds ago, arms crossed against his chest. 'You best not make a habit of that. It's mildly terrifying.' April's furious glare was ignored.

'And *you* best learn the difference between a vampire and a shtriga,' Benjamin huffed. 'And perhaps give the horror films a rest. Humans never get 'em right.'

'Yeah, you're a regular Edward.' April rolled her eyes.

'Edward?' April toyed with putting Benjamin out of his misery before he hurt himself. 'Oh. Was that a reference?'

'Yes ...' April's stomach chose that moment to interrupt. Embarrassed, she crossed her arms over it as if she could hold the sounds in.

'The kitchen ...' Ben tilted his head towards the hallway. 'Help yourself.'

April inspected the small rectangular room that lay beyond the hallway. The table held court with four chairs, the pile of plates and utensils cluttering the draining rack suggested that he had cooked for friends the night before. An engraved brass antique kettle gurgled away on the Aga oven, and the potted plants adorning the windowsill lent a peaceful feel to the room. The only sinister fact was that it was owned by Schrödinger's shtriga. April opened the knackered fridge slowly, convinced she was going to find loads of takeout Tupperware filled with trapped souls. Benjamin let out a snort of laughter as he entered. April grabbed the cheese and set about making a sandwich in furious embarrassment. 'What happens when the sun comes up?' April licked the knife clean and turned in time to see Ben's shoulders slump. 'Right. *Not* a vampire.'

'Right.' Ben settled himself into a chair across from her with an involuntary groan that seemed to attach itself to people over the age of 30.

'You eat normal food?' For some reason, this surprised her more than anything else.

'When I'm nostalgic for flavours and textures. It's more about blending in. No good if the neighbours pop round and find souls in the spice rack.'

Choking with laugher and a mouthful, April put her sandwich down. 'Your neighbours are human?'

Benjamin watched April with a quiet amusement, unable to remember the last time he'd entertained a human. His old mind tended to forget smaller details. 'Yes. Apart from two witches and a wizard, who live directly opposite.' They'd arrived on Samhain and he hadn't moved them on. Ben hadn't realised how much he'd missed the hum of another's magic until they'd moved in. Vampires made ghosts of their victims. Shtrigas ended existences altogether.

April's eyes widened with worry. 'So, any supernatural d-bags in your realm steer clear of you because it's your job to send them back to theirs?' April looked at him thoughtfully.

'Something like that.' He flashed her a quick smile, watching her sword case swing from the back of her chair. Benjamin pulled back his sleeve to check the time, his thumb running over the glass of his antique, as if he could wipe the scratches from the clock face.

'You need a new watch.'

'It was a present.' His reflection looked back at him with eyes the black of mourning clothes.

'Who from?'

'A ... friend.' Ben tugged his sleeve down.

'Merlin?' Ben looked back in exasperation, waiting for her to do the maths.

'Right.' April couldn't let a silence breathe, so he steeled himself. In the battle of whether or not to ask questions, April would always lose. 'How much longer are you meant to be holding the fort? Given that they're ... dead.'

Ben leant forward. 'Merlin acted as if death would never touch him.'

'And here you are, a few thousand years later, with nothing more than a necklace to show for your troubles.'

'A few thousand? Try halving that. And it's a talisman. All the Guardians have their own equivalent.' This was why Ben hardly spoke of Merlin. They were different times; kind people didn't last very long.

'My mistake. Why didn't Merlin tell you how the world ends, if he saw it?' April propped herself up on her elbows, her triumphant smile declaring that she'd figured out a thousand-year-old riddle.

'Kids.' Ambrosius shook his head. *'Although it must have come as a shock to Merlin, when the world didn't end with him.'*

'Merlin was an enigma, even to me. If there had been a way, he would have found it.' The minute hand raced around the clock behind April, whilst the seconds lasted forever. Ben drifted off into the distance with his thoughts, grief hanging heavily from his shoulders. 'I'm not completely on my own. There are the other Guardians ...' Nine realms to choose from and he was the epitome of an awkward round peg in a square hole. 'And Ambrosius is always there to save me from my own company.'

'Who the hell is Ambrosius?'

'*I thought she might have worked it out! Sometimes it's like she's looking at me.*'

'My magic,' Ben smiled. 'I might introduce you to him later.'

April's eyes widened in amused curiosity. Ambrosius cackled in pure delight.

'If,' April mercifully moved on, 'the humans are gone, you no longer have a realm to guard. So, why not let the Gods destroy it?'

'My responsibility ends when the realm dies. If the Gods win, I have failed.'

6

Three Angels

31st October, Oxford, Dirmynd's house

Dirmynd's eyes hopped from word-to-word, rereading the sentence for the sixth time. The hum of a portal opening had ruined his concentration.

Not wanting to find a small gaggle of djinn when he turned, Dirmynd continued reading, content in his tatty wingback chair.

'Ahem.' Dirmynd turned the page with a passive-aggressive flick, enjoying their impatience. 'Ahem!'

'Barqan.' Dirmynd looked for cracks in the ceiling of his cramped living room for inspiration and, finding none, heaved himself up with the most exasperated sigh ever witnessed. 'You look well.' He swept the floor with his exaggerated, sarcastic bow to the djinn queen. 'Considering it's been five hundred years since last we met.' The cold blue flames flared in annoyance at the blatant disrespect. The inky, bold black lines shivered and reached for her hands. An unmissable warning written across the deep red-brown of her ochre forearms. Dirmynd couldn't remember why they didn't like one another.

'Oh, stop it. I'm embarrassed for the both of us.' Barqan's goons gathered around their queen in a semi-circle, magic engulfing their arms. 'The royal guard. Very intimidating.'

'You're a slow learner,' Barqan tutted. 'You can't hide from Fate.'

'But my cover was perfect this time.' He'd taken a job at a bookshop, although that was growing tiresome. Dirmynd wasn't cut out for the workplace. Magic and technology did not mix well. This, combined with an extremely short fuse and rusty people skills, was a customer service disaster waiting to happen.

'How many times have I had to fetch you home? Too many to count.'

'Do you remember when you found me at court? King-what-was-his-name? The one with all the wives?' If he kept talking, Barqan couldn't deliver her message. 'Now he was an interesting soul! He graciously invited me into his court …'

'And you repaid him by conducting yourself poorly with one of those wives? You're recycling your stories.' Barqan crossed her arms, her round face pinched into a stern look. 'I'm not interested in your ramblings, Dirmynd. Fate has summoned you to Avalon, as you well know.' It would be Barqan who suffered for his tardiness. Fate had a great capacity for cruelness; Dirmynd had caught the sharper side of Fate more often than he hadn't. Perhaps being shunned by the other Gods had eroded her personal skills.

'If she sent a text message or called, I have not received them. Smartphones are not so smart, in my opinion. I despise the current generation, with their endless whining, skinny lattes and swiping.'

'Fate did not text you ...' Barqan's voice was crisp, but it brooked no argument.

'Hateful things. Had mine for ten minutes. I threw it in the general direction of the Atlantic Ocean.'

'You never cease to try my patience.' Barqan let out a slow, controlled breath. 'You must return home.'

'Home?' Dirmynd laughed darkly, exhaustion scraping at his eyelids. Had he been an average warlock, Fate would have left him to linger with time. She was drawn to those with magic. 'What does Fate want from me now?' Dirmynd's temper blew its first fuse. Ignoring Barqan's huffing, his bare feet slapped the well-worn floorboards, his fingers trailing over the spines of books in their cases. 'Le—' A book, its cover rough with age, stopped him. 'I told Fate that my service to her had ended.' The book's spine cracked open, freeing a photograph that drifted down to his feet. 'My exact words were *"find somebody else to lie at your feet."* Her response? She tried to stab me!'

'You fool.' Barqan laughed softly. 'It's a lifetime of service or nothing at all. She's left you to play amongst the mortals for long enough. Do not keep her waiting. For both our sakes.'

'Look at this photograph – Elvis!' Barqan kept her gaze locked on him. 'And this book – *The Tempest* – signed by the author. Freedom. It's a beautiful idea.' Disheartened, Dirmynd flopped down into his armchair. He'd known this day would come. It was probably why he never gave anything too much attention. It was all temporary. The next big thing was always peeking round the corner of the present.

'Have you heard Chaos rumbling away in Tartarus?' Barqan nodded curtly, not wanting to say anything out of place. 'They've been growing restless for some time now.' Dirmynd reluctantly closed the book. 'It was inevitable – I warned Fate, you will recall. She listened not.' Dirmynd stood, his creaking bones reminding him how many years had passed by. Too old for this, he thought to himself. 'Fate didn't respond well to authority.'

'Chaos wants the Gods to return to Tartarus.' Barqan took a menacing step forward, tattoos crawling over her skin. 'The Gods have had their rest, according to Chaos. They say the Guardians can take care of the realms. Fate will not return to living under their rule. Have you spoken to Chaos? You're their friend.'

'Chaos will not listen to me. Not on this.' Dirmynd had bent back and forth for Fate, travelled a million empty miles alone across infinite universes. He wasn't the one to stop her. 'I can only but wonder what it is Fate expects me to do about it.' With a click of his bony fingers, he extinguished all the candles in the room, plunging it into darkness and earning him a disapproving sigh.

'This city,' Barqan sneered in the darkness, 'is barely breathing. Buildings, people – they all go missing with time.'

'I know this place and it knows me.' Dirmynd's sapphire cloak obediently materialized in his outstretched hand.

'What's left for you here?'

'The streets will never take me anywhere else.' With a well-practised flick of the wrist, Dirmynd positioned the cloak, fastening the clasp. 'I *detest* Avalon's perpetual spring and winter.'

'I do not know how you put up with so many humans about the place.'

'Make no mistake, if I am forced to choose between these transitory meat-bags and you, I will choose them. I followed my ghosts here, Barqan. I have business to conclude before I pay my respects.' Seemingly satisfied with his sincerity, the gaggle of djinn opened their portal and left.

Finally alone, Dirmynd stood in the empty, darkened room and cleared a mental workspace. With shaking hands, he tore a rip in the divide between realms, before he lost his nerve.

****

Tuonela

Having concluded her business with Dirmynd, Barqan slipped effortlessly into the vastness of the universe. Only the impatient called the space empty. It took her eyes a few seconds to adjust to the light of the field of stars that burned above, below and all around her, embracing the realms in a cape of priceless jewels. She turned herself towards the under realms.

Tuonela was a world painted in varying shades of grey, the towering mountains' darker pastel smudges brooding over the light shades of barren fields below. It never quite managed full darkness, nor did it ever fully accept the pallid sun's light. The lakes and open landscape provided few places to hide and so Barqan thought it wouldn't be too hard to find Kalma. The werewolves she passed had the good sense to shrink away from her, lest they found themselves to be her quarry. Not that their fear would stop their murmurings. Barqan trod carefully through the central square, the sound of claws scratching on cobbles setting her nerves on edge. News would reach Kalma before she did. Tuonela was busier than expected for Samhain Eve, not that there would be any survivors. Unlike the vampires. But she would see to Jack shortly.

Distancing herself from the realm's inhabitants was effortless. Barqan had not made it this far in life by concerning herself with the atrocities of war. So long as Avalon was safe, she was content. And yet, as a Guardian herself, dispatching her colleagues was uncomfortable. The truth was a hard obstacle, almost impossible to ignore.

A werewolf in his human form stumbled across Barqan's path. He turned to growl a warning, saw her glaring, flaming blue eyes and dropped his own straight to the ground, terrified.

'S … s … sorry.'

'Get out of my way!' Barqan shoved him roughly without breaking her stride, bursting through a pack of grown wolves cowering with their tails between their legs. She slowed to a walk, her head turning from side to side, sniffing. The quickest way to find Kalma was to follow her nose to where the stench of rotting corpses was strongest.

There was a great Gothic church on the edge of town. Its brown stone arches and towering stained-glass windows overlooked a graveyard swamped with shadows. Barqan wandered amongst the headstones, listening to the panting of Surka, Kalma's hellhound-like dog, trying to pick out Kalma's scent over the rest of the dead.

'Barqan?' She'd expected the voice but still it froze her to the spot, unable to turn around. Surka's wet nose nudged the back of Barqan's legs in greeting. The dog let out a short low whine that set the djinn's heart racing. Dogs were so much more perceptive to guilt than people. Barqan forced herself to turn and face Tuonela's Guardian.

Kalma's dull black eyes sparkled with curiosity, or so Barqan thought. It was difficult to gauge emotion in a death-ravaged face so pale, it looked to be painted on. Thick black shadows ringed Kalma's eyes whilst once-red lipstick, smeared like rust, provided a nod to colour. Kalma's dishevelled, lank hair had grown past the small of her back. It could have been brown or black but centuries of neglect had obscured the colour with grime. What had once been a delicate silver sweetheart dress proudly sported many rips and tears. There had been sleeves the last time Barqan saw her. In Gaia, this was fashionable. Whatever it was called, Kalma would be the envy of them all.

'Barqan, what are you doing here?' Kalma was circling around her, bringing herself in for a hug in which Barqan remained rigid.

'Is everything alright? You are quiet and a little off colour.'

'Fate sent me,' was all Barqan's contralto voice managed. She'd wanted to take Kalma by surprise, as cowardly as it was. Barqan was finding it harder and harder to look her friend in the eye.

'Nobody has left this realm in over ten years, aside from Samhain, of course.' Kalma pulled back out of the hug, a look of genuine concern and confusion animating her corpse-face. 'Whatever does Fate want?'

'That, my dear, is the tricky part.' Kalma's face folded into a deep frown as she reached down to pat Surka absent-mindedly.

'I don't suppose there's any way I can convince you to give me your talisman and leave Tuonela?' Barqan ventured.

'What? Why would I flee?' Kalma laughed at the preposterous suggestion.

'At the very least, I need your talisman.' Barqan held out her hand, her voice devoid of emotion. 'Do not make me fight you.' Kalma's hand curled around the Surka-shaped pendant, understanding and disgust lighting up her eyes.

'I am not leaving my realm. Not without good reason.'

'Fate wants you dead. Is that reason enough?'

Kalma thought about this, one foot sliding backwards. 'If Fate wants me dead, I am as good as gone. She won't know where, or for how long, but she will know me to be alive. There is no wisdom in running.'

'I do not want to kill you.' Barqan drew her magic all the same. Feelings were irrelevant. She had orders. Guardians can't refuse their Gods.

'Why are you doing this? You've always been your own master.' Kalma stood firm, one hand on Surka's growling head.

'Fate feels Chaos creeping closer. Chaos wants control of the Gods again. And if the Gods won't come home, Chaos will force them.' Barqan's attention was split between Kalma, Surka, and a lone werewolf, creeping closer, claws extended, a silent growl vibrating through its substantial form.

'Fate is trying to starve Chaos of attention, thus killing them? She is willing to destroy all of that life to preserve hers. And you are helping her.' The venom in Kalma's voice cut Barqan a little and sent her magic flaring up her arms.

'I am choosing survival, Kalma! You should do the same. You'll be safe in Hades.' Without looking, Barqan fired a whirling ball of blue magic into the lone werewolf, flinging him backwards. He didn't get back up.

'Whilst my realm burns, I would be no better than you.' Barqan deserved that, she supposed. 'We have reached an impasse. It has already been written – the look on your face tells me so. I am the God of Death and Decay.' Kalma drew herself to her full height, which wasn't particularly tall. 'I will meet my destiny but not without a fight.' Barqan's chest tightened with a mixture of admiration and deep sadness for Kalma.

'Then I shall have to close your eyes.'

As if she'd been cued, Surka growled and charged. Another ball of blue magic came instantly to the space between Barqan's hands. It flew true, catapulting the dog into a marble monument of a werewolf. White shards rained down. Kalma cried out in shared pain, her talisman glowing silver in her hands. Barqan channelled her magic to her own talisman, a miniature spinning wheel carved from wood, that she wore on her left wrist. Inky black lines shot down both arms, flooding her veins with poison. A relatively painless death was the least Barqan could do. Kalma drew her hands back and sent a wall of silver magic hurtling towards Barqan. Her spinning wheel erupted, engulfing her a second before Kalma's attack arrived. Sparks flew as Kalma's spells ricocheted off the rippling energy. Barqan's own talisman surged forward, eager to deal with the threat. With a push, both physical and mental, Barqan shouldered her misgivings aside and shouted the incantation with conviction. The death spell tore itself free of her hands and hurtled towards Kalma. It caught her square. Kalma's eyes registered surprise and she crumpled to the ground, her head cracking on the side of a headstone. Breathing heavily, Barqan stepped close enough to watch the magic flicker and fade from Kalma's onyx talisman, taking her adrenaline with it. Barqan allowed her magic to die down. She didn't need it for what came next.

Barqan bent over Kalma's unconscious form, taking care not to kneel in the blood leaking from the back of her head. She caressed Kalma's face, letting her poison seep from her fingertips. Barqan's were the kind of dreams in which the occupant perished, regardless of whether or not they hit the ground. Usually, they kept falling straight into Purgatory. Kalma's body convulsed one final time, she uttered a single moan and succumbed to the poison. She had fought well, better than most, but when a djinn struck, few escaped. Barqan found herself pushing hair off Kalma's face, and straightening her dress without knowing why but aware that this moment would haunt her later.

'Flimsy things, Guardians.' Mórrígan's thick, melodic accent appeared behind Barqan along with the pop and fizzle of a portal tearing a rip in reality. 'I never understood Merlin's thinking. They can't defend realms. At least this one was a fair fight, so it was.'

'It wasn't. Avalon would never be as easily disarmed as Tuonela and Erebus.' She felt Mórrígan roll her eyes. Barqan couldn't lift hers from Kalma's face. 'Did Fate tell you why the Guardians must die?' the djinn queen enquired pointlessly, trying to find the motivation to stand. 'Some of us are Gods.' Lesser Gods, but Gods nonetheless.

'Soldiers do not ask questions. In this case, ignorance serves you best.' It almost sounded like advice.

'It does not feel right. That is my sole observation.' Barqan frowned at the splashes of blood on her knuckles. She scraped her hand on a nearby patch of wet grass. Mórrígan was right, her place was not to question Fate. Hers was to protect Avalon, and if Fate had identified the other Guardians as a threat, she had no choice. 'Killing my colleagues is a somewhat unusual assignment, do you not agree?' Carefully, she extracted the onyx miniature of Surka from around Kalma's neck, acutely aware of Mórrígan's foot tapping an impatient beat. Nobody questioned War.

'Wipe the blood off before you give it to me!' Barqan complied silently, rubbing the pendant in brown grass.

'What do you stand to gain from this, Mórrígan?' Barqan asked carefully.

'Whatever is left and the survival of Styx. Fate had best not expect me to take in the Gods without a realm. Avalon is plenty big enough for that.'

Barqan had expected more. Ensuring the survival of Styx didn't seem enough to persuade Mórrígan into working with Fate. Perhaps even War worried about survival from time to time. Either way, Barqan would be left to suffer the fallout. 'Caerridwen next?'

'Change of plan.' Barqan closed her eyes in relief. 'Benjamin is next.' That would be easier. Barqan had little to no relationship with the shtriga. 'There is a girl travelling with him.'

'Mortal?' Barqan had her suspicions.

'What does it matter? They're all going to die.' Barqan took one last look around, feeling the vengeful glares of an entire realm's worth of werewolves. They wouldn't be glaring for much longer. 'Why are you still here? I have work to do that is not for your eyes.'

So, Barqan, Guardian of Avalon, Third Queen of the Djinn, stood and opened a portal of her own. The realms were toppling like dominoes, heading towards Gaia.

With Barqan gone, Mórrígan inhaled a lungful of damp air. She held her arms out wide, allowing her magic to stretch out into the space. This was the part that she delighted in. The utter destruction of an entire world and no requirement to show mercy. Opportunities to destroy whole planets had been so scarce of late, she couldn't possibly resist assisting Fate. It was a surprisingly short spell, considering that it had to rip through the fabric of the entire realm, destroying the world from its core outwards.

There was nothing more beautiful than this moment. The realm see-sawed over the edge, waiting, knowing its fate but unable to change it. The boiling lakes, the storm that bore down on them and the deep rumbles from the bowels of the planet, all sounded like a symphony to Mórrígan. The first rumble of an earthquake shook the realm, gouging cracks into the ground which raced off into the distance.

The screaming, the terror, the yelling, set underneath the rolling thunder, was her favourite sound in the entire universe.

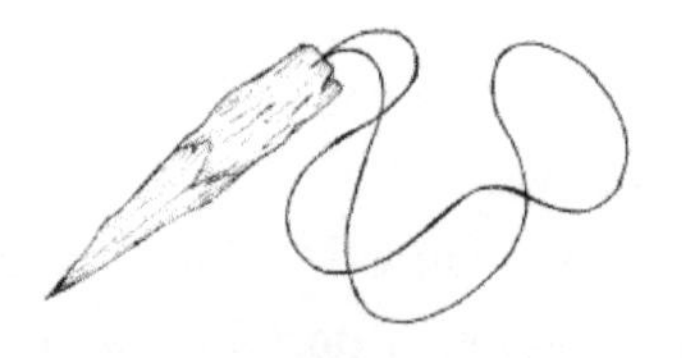

7

Silence

Oxford, Ben's house

Benjamin was drowning.

For all of April's questions ricocheting off him, she hadn't asked the right ones.

The Gods help him, he sounded like Merlin.

When Benjamin grew up, he'd wanted to be a warlock but not *that* warlock.

'*Ben.*' Ambrosius shifted restlessly on the edge of his mind.

'*I don't know when she'll run out of questions, ok?*' Ambrosius's burnt-orange glow peeked out from underneath Ben's hands.

'*No!*' Ambrosius's little voice was shrill with concern. '*There is a huge amount of residual magic approaching.*' Ambrosius was twisting about so much that Benjamin worried his magic would tie itself in knots.

'Time to go!' Benjamin pushed back from the table, toppling his chair in his haste to make ready.

'We've just got here!' April cried out in protest, no doubt fearing more walking. 'What about the salt lines?'

Ben ducked into the cupboard under the stairs, emerging with backpacks, he stepped backwards without looking and collided with April.

'What's wrong?'

Ben darted into his living room, April at his heels. 'At a guess … djinn.' Ben dislodged a stack of papers and books on his coffee table, scanning over the mess, not finding the book.

'You're not sure what you're running away from, are you?'

'I'm certain it's something that we don't want to meet.' Especially now he'd accidentally acquired a sidekick, of sorts. 'Best keep your saltshaker close.' And to Ambrosius he asked *'Where did I last have the book?'*

'Um, the office.'

Benjamin pushed past April, taking the stairs two at a time. To his ears, April was shouting at him from the riverbank as he slipped underwater. In his head, Ambrosius's urge to leave was an overwhelming siren, muffling everything else.

'What have you lost?' April followed, dancing out of Ben's way as he searched the drawers of his oak desk and rummaged through the bookcase and shelves.

'A book. Spells, mostly.' He paused in the flurry of paper, mentally retracing his steps.

'Perhaps the fairies spirited it away.'

'No, I put an end to that.'

Fairies? 'I was being sarcastic …' April paused on the landing, straining to hear the sound prowling about downstairs. 'Can you hear … accordions?' As soon as the words had left April's mouth, the disjointed notes faded away.

'Hmm?' Benjamin knocked a box over, spilling hundreds of sealed white and brown envelopes.

'Didn't you hear the music?' Benjamin surfaced from his frantic search to blink at her. 'It sounded like the theme tune to …' The show's title was on the tip of her tongue and then it was gone. April's thumbs circled above her phone, not sure what to search. 'Seriously, you have bat-like hear—' The same lazy tune floated up the stairs.

'That's my doorbell.' He frowned, carefully setting aside a box and joined April.

'Why does your doorbell play the …' April stealthily glanced at her phone. '*'Allo 'Allo!* theme?'

'What?' Benjamin peered down the stairs, trying to see through the frosted glass.

'Never mind. Are you expecting visitors?' April reached for her sword.

'No. Are you?' Ben looked at her expectantly.

'It's *your* house! Why would *I* be expecting visitors?'

'Good point.' The wail of the French accordion rang out for the third time.

'You'd better answer it.'

'In a minute! I'm trying to work out who it is.'

'If only there was an easy way to do that.' Ben dismissed her with a wave.

The door masked most of the magic gathering on Benjamin's doorstep. All Ambrosius could say for sure was that it didn't belong with whoever was wearing his doorbell out.

Ben took off down the stairs with April in pursuit. *'It's like she wants to die!'* As their feet hit the floor, Ben grabbed her arm and dragged her down the hallway. He eased the door of the cupboard open. Ben threw the bags in first and then shoved April in. Furious and indignant, she managed to bite back the protest that formed on impact. Ben would get an earful later on, but for now he trusted her to keep quiet.

April had the horrible idea the ghost had followed them home. Ghosts wouldn't ring the doorbell. But ghost couldn't pass the salt lines, so … Dust rained down on her as Ben stomped down the stairs. April hadn't heard him go up. Was he making noise in an attempt to hide the sound of her breathing? She gulped down a breath as the front door cracked open. She could breathe when this was all over.

'Jack.' Benjamin's cold voice sliced the silence in two.

'Benjamin.' This deep voice was grave with a hint of suspicion.

'What are you doing here?'

'*Not the time for a catch up*!' April clamped her hands over her mouth as if that gesture would dampen the thoughts in her head from ringing out like church bells. The front door shut with an ominous thud. Two pairs of footsteps tapped staccato beats on the floor, stopping outside her cupboard. '*Go away*,' April thought, making mental shooing gestures. She didn't need bat-like hearing to hear Benjamin snort back laughter. The latch scraped back slowly. Bokken in hand, April shifted into a crouch, eyeing up the boxes of salt. The door creaked open, allowing the morning light to blaze into the cramped space. Through the slats of her fingers, two faces peered in. One was amused, the other sheepish.

'Well,' the unfamiliar face lit up with mischief, 'what have we here?'

Perfect pale skin and a grin that was all teeth, Jack *was* definitely a vampire. Sure, his amusement might be innocent, but forced into a corner and on display, April felt like a quick snack.

Her attention turned to Benjamin, who had stepped back from the scene. So, he had a friend after all. April forced a smile onto her face, preferring to be the first to navigate the awkward pause.

'Hi!' She waved her sword coyly at Jack. Not waiting for Benjamin's approval, and feeling uncomfortable in last night's outfit, April scurried out of her hiding place, keen to stretch.

'When did you begin keeping pretty girls in your closet, Ben?' Jack sprawled against the cupboard door. 'She has a sword as well! That's adorable.' Jack tried to pull said sword from April's hand, laughing at her swatting him away.

'I like to give people a fighting chance.' Ben shrugged, content to let Jack and April figure each other out. 'You do realise it's a wooden sword?'

Unlike his sullen friend, Jack's smile was effortless and lit up his piercing blue eyes. Like Ben, Jack had high cheekbones and a razor-straight nose. At a guess, Jack had been turned somewhere in his early twenties, remaining as a snapshot of youth. He straightened up and promptly slumped to the other side, his unruly weave of golden curls spilling onto Ben's shoulder and dark top. Arms folded, he observed April considering him. They were polar opposites in personality.

Benjamin was reserved and prudent whereas Jack seemed coltish and effervescent.

'Going somewhere?' Jack noticed the discarded backpacks and raised enquiring eyebrows at Ben. 'Oh no! Are you eloping?' April blushed, failing to hide her embarrassment.

'April's a hunter. Vampires specifically. If I were you, I would refrain from antagonising her … too much. April, this is Jack. He *is* a vampire. Don't worry, he doesn't bite. He's …' Ben hesitated, glancing uncertainly at Jack, who met his gaze expectantly. '… a good friend of mine.' Neither April nor Benjamin missed Jack's scowl. Ben had the good grace to drop his eyes to the floor.

'*Friend*?' Jack asked in exasperation. 'It's been eight hundred and sixty-eight years!' April heard the undertone of an ancient argument rear up and wondered if she should go back into the cupboard.

'Would you pass me my bags, April?'

'Allow me.' Jack sprung forwards. Benjamin had to duck to avoid being assaulted by airborne rucksacks. 'You should probably tell me what's going on.' Unimpressed, Jack launched the last bag at Ben. 'What possessed you to bring a hunter home? No offence, kid.'

Benjamin tried to smile reassuringly at April who was a little bit offended.

****

'Huh,' was Jack's assessment, as he fidgeted on the wooden chair at the kitchen table. 'You should have gone trick or treating. Or to buy some cushions.'

'And to top the night off, Ambrosius mistook you for a threat. We couldn't recognise you for all the magic. Where have you been?'

Jack took a moment. There was worry in his partner's eyes, but sometimes Ben's concern bumped into his self-doubt and sharpened his words unintentionally. 'With Dirmynd.'

'Why do you waste your time with that charlatan? And why didn't you let yourself in?'

'I forgot my key!' Jack stood up to show off his empty pockets.

'Well,' Ben's chair creaked as he sat back, 'I don't appreciate you coming back covered in somebody else's magic. It upsets Ambrosius.'

'It won't happen again. Besides, it's Halloween! It's foggy and there's so much magic about.' Jack flashed a cheeky grin at April. The kid was sliding under the table to avoid the brewing argument. He'd like to see her spend close to a millennium with the same person and not have the occasional spat.

'And how goes Dirmynd's search for Gaia's second Guardian?' Ben wasn't going to let this one go, but neither was Jack.

'Barqan was in Gaia last night.' Jack tried to fish a just-out-of-reach apple from the fruit bowl.

'I saw her.' Benjamin caught the oranges dislodged by Jack's unwillingness to stand. He huffed a put-upon sigh and tossed Jack an apple. 'I feel guilty for failing to follow them. Do you know what they were up to?'

'They ...' Jack found himself choking on the reality of the situation. 'Ben, they were hunting down any vampires and werewolves they could find. And Tuonela is gone. Kalma's dead.'

'Dirmynd told you this?' Shock dampened Ben's voice. 'So, it's begun.'

'I thought there would be more of a build-up than this. Ben, you need to be careful.' The threat was beginning to seem all too real and it was too close to home. 'Being a widower wouldn't suit me.' Black clothing washed him out. And crying was tiresome. Besides, Jack vaguely recalled spending most of his human life alone – he wasn't letting his eternal life go the same way.

'I'll check in with the other Guardians.' As predicted, Ben didn't sound thrilled about the prospect of reaching out to his colleagues. 'I've not heard from them in a while. It's hard to tell whether or not this bout of silence is due to disinterest or a legitimate cause for concern.'

'They can't ignore you forever.' Ben shifted in his seat in anticipation. 'Fate has left Avalon.' Jack ran a hand through his hair, his grim smile filled nobody with confidence. 'She found a way around the warding.'

'It was only a matter of time.' Ben slumped back, his eyes dull with exhaustion. 'Did Dirmynd say where she'd gone?' Jack shook his head apologetically, sharing Ben's sense of foreboding.

'Why is it a bad thing?' April asked.

'If Fate is away, the other Gods can play. There's nobody spinning the wheel,' Ben said grimily. 'I'm more concerned with what she's after.'

'And if Fate has figured out how to escape, the other Gods can't be far behind.' Jack worried at the apple core, unintentionally crushing pips into the table. 'The magic is failing.'

'Or …' Jack looked up sharply; Ben was about to make things worse. 'Somebody let Fate out.'

'That's so much worse. That somebody would have to be as powerful as Merlin.'

April raised her hand before a concerned silence could settle. 'About the werewolves, didn't they put salt down?' Resigned to his situation, Ben shrugged and they turned as one to look at her incredulously. 'If Ben's using salt, I don't see why others aren't. Unless they can't hold it in their little paws.'

'Little paws?' Jack stared at the kid in disbelief. 'You say she's a hunter?' Ben nodded. There was nothing to be read in his eyes. 'And she's gonna help us?' Jack's concern was rooted in his belief that they had yet to arrive at the darkest part of this mess. It would leave an impression on even the sturdiest of souls and she looked so young.

'Everybody looks young when you're pushing on for 900 years old,' Ben reached out.

'Can April handle this?'

'Yes.' Ben answered both questions out loud. To Jack, he said, *'She's stood her ground so far. And …'* he hesitated, *'I don't think she has anybody else.'*

'Colour me impressed. Look at you, making friends.'

'Hello!' April waved furiously. 'I'm right here! Quit talking about me like I'm not.' She locked eyes with Jack, unwilling to back down. She had guts but was a little slow on the uptake. Perhaps he was being harsh. When sleep was a pastime long forgotten, Jack tended to forget that humans didn't function so well without it.

Well, Ben could worry about April. Jack had other concerns. Dirmynd's cautionary tales of realms being torn apart had Jack trying to shift a mountain of dread. Ben was going to find himself tied up in the centre of it all. Guardians, Dirmynd had said, were martyrs-in-waiting.

'You can't run salt lines around an entire realm. And they won't defend you from Gods.' Jack hoped that answered her question, because Ben had slipped off into his thoughts.

Tuonela was gone. Samhain was the perfect time. Kalma would have been distracted, keeping an eye on where her clan travelled in their brief window of freedom. For this to happen, Kalma must have fallen first. 'It takes an unimaginable amount of power to erase a realm from existence.' Jack and April's bickering drowned him out, but Ambrosius radiated sympathy. 'How many more realms have fallen without me noticing?' Jack reached across the table, but Ben folded his hands into his lap. Physical contact wasn't going to help. He felt sick to his stomach.

'You weren't to know, Ben. There's nothing you could have done.'

'Merlin's warding was visible tonight,' Ben sighed, as if he could exhale the sadness. 'They shimmer above the clouds in curtains made of green and purple.'

'You mean the Northern Lights?' April asked carefully.

'Exactly that. They're fading rapidly.' There was only so much patching up Ben could do before he ended up being the last line of defence. Across the table, Jack continued to fidget, his unease palpable. Ben had a sense of being stood at the bottom of a mountain, watching an avalanche careering towards them. 'Would you please stop mushing apple into my table?' Jack looked up quickly, conviction flashing in his eyes. Ben squashed down another sigh and waited for the "*I told you so*".

'We should have listened to Dirmynd!' There it was, right on cue. 'But no, a Guardian couldn't possibly be behind it.'

'I don't trust the majority of the Guardians, but they take their duties seriously. And, if you recall, I *knew* something was afoot; I was just terribly wrong in my timing.' Ben had anticipated the first move being made in the new year.

'If the djinn caught your scent ...' Jack's hands clenched into fists. 'You need to get out of town.'

'And go where exactly? If Barqan is killing Guardians, she'll find me.' Images of Kalma suffering, whilst her realm crumbled around her, came unbidden to mind. They had their differences, but Ben hoped her end had been swift.

'Anywhere but here!' Jack was getting himself worked up over nothing. 'I wish you wouldn't put yourself at risk so,' he added quietly.

'Are you talking about me?' April pushed back her chair and rounded on Jack.

'If I didn't help those kids, they'd be dead.' Ben grabbed a handful of April's jacket, pulling her back. Jack opened his mouth but realised he couldn't argue.

April crashed into her chair, and an intense pain engulfed her, boring into her skull, above her left eye. Neither Jack nor Ben noticed her distress. Somehow, she remained upright, fingernails digging into the table. April screwed her eyes shut and was immediately lost in a confusing kaleidoscope of images painted in colours she knew and didn't know. It was nice of the pain not to show up empty-handed.

Through the throbbing red haze, April began to recognise shapes in an alien environment. The kitchen had been replaced by a damp wooded area, different to the one she'd seen earlier. Ben and somebody April didn't know, dominated the landscape. April didn't know where it was, but she was actually there. The meeting sat, suspended in time, waiting to begin.

Ben's serenity seemed out of place. There was nothing here to cause April to worry, but instinct insisted she needed to intervene.

April was repeatedly drawn to the stranger with his bird's nest brown hair. Beneath it sat a long aquiline nose and pitch-black eyes which burned in determination. He had a purpose here. He was a little over five foot tall, but he gave off an energy that seemed to fill the entire realm. Catastrophe followed in his wake. Held loosely in the stranger's right hand was something short and metallic. Sunlight bounced from it, blinding April and obscuring her view. She took a hesitant step forward but the colours drained from the scene, reducing it to a monochrome diorama. Determined to learn something, April pushed through the encroaching darkness to get closer to Ben. She hadn't noticed that he too held something. Hanging from worn leather cords were two glowing pendants. Perplexed, April reached for them. As her fingers brushed the worn leather, the stranger turned sharply to look at her. April tripped over her feet as she hurried backwards. The stranger stared down at her and April understood: wherever he currently was, he knew she was there. And he knew her. Behind her, Jack was screaming for Ben, pain and fear splintering his voice – the sound of it chilled her to the bone. She wasn't sure who was in trouble here. The stranger's mouth twitched into a condescending smile and dropped the curtain on the vision.

As if they'd been sucked up by a hoover, the wall of noise in her head, the pain and the disturbing images all vanished, transporting her back to the kitchen.

The boys were still in their places, debating – with conviction – the merits of staying versus going. Sensing April's stare, Ben glanced over to her, whilst Jack's cries rang in her ears. Tears welled of their own accord – that sound was going to haunt April until her death. The stranger and Ben knew each other. April had felt it. Perhaps that's why Benjamin had looked so calm? She needed answers, but how to describe what she'd seen when she didn't know what it was. A vision? A very vivid dream? Dream being the preferable option.

'Are you alright?' Ben asked, holding up a hand to silence Jack. April didn't trust herself to answer so she nodded and pulled on her jacket. 'Only you're shaking, you're looking a little pale and you've not asked me a question in five minutes.'

And she wasn't going to. April would figure it out on her own. No point in worrying them. 'I'm fine.' Her response was too quick, her smile forced.

'Are you in shock? That's an incredibly delayed reaction.' As Ben leant forward to check her temperature, part of an old, leather cord slipped out from his shirt.

'I'm fine.' April's voice squeaked. A miniature silver sword hung from the cord, a glaring premonition that destroyed the last remaining shreds of April's composure. Too many world-shattering revelations in one day tended to rob a girl of her sanity. April stared as Ben absentmindedly tucked the cord back under his shirt.

'Okkkkk.' Jack rounded up the stray mugs and plates from the table in a not-so-subtle hint. 'You're a crappy liar, kid.'

It was true. Danny used to laugh at how she'd look anywhere but at him. Her tells, he had said, were so blatantly obvious he knew she was lying with his eyes closed.

'Um, you said you were looking for a second Guardian?'

'We've been looking for the second Guardian for a lifetime.' The vampire was washing up – that's how April knew she was going crazy. 'Find the Guardian, find the second talisman. Or so we thought.' Jack carefully set a mug in the drying rack.

Ben pulled the sword out. Dread ran its cold fingers down April's back as Ben buffed the pendant with his sleeve. 'Arthur's was a shield. It was lost, most likely at the bottom of a lake. Wherever it is, it's useless without its Guardian.'

'But you don't want certain people to find it?' Like the man in her vision.

'The sword and the shield are two halves. If we find it, Ben's might do something other than … well, nothing.' Jack knocked a plate into the sink, drenching his top. 'Ugh!'

'I wonder what's happened to Kalma's talisman.' Ben got up to fetch a tea towel and dabbed at the soapy mess.

'What happens if somebody completes the set?'

'We're talking end of the world stuff.' Jack picked up two of the bags and handed the other two to Ben.

'There's still some of Merlin's magic in them. Pool that energy together, introduce somebody else's magic …' The lightest tread of feet at the front door stopped Ben and Jack dead in their tracks. He had enough time to look at Jack before the sound of the front door handle rattling filled the house, followed by his bay window smashing. Ben pulled April behind him as hellish noises crawled in through the broken window.

'I told you we had to leave.'

'And look, we're leaving.' Ben readied Ambrosius, trying to ignore the mounting pressure.

'They're not being subtle about it, are they?' April quipped, trying to push in front of Ben.

'They're either confident or extremely stupid,' Jack summarised. 'Or both.'

'Back door … now!' Ben ushered Jack and April outside. Turning back to make sure they weren't being followed, Ben got one last look at his kitchen. April had described it as shabby; he disagreed. He inexplicably felt like this part of his life was coming to an end. As long as Benjamin was a Guardian, he'd never know peace.

'Play your part,' a disembodied voice whispered to him. The three words conjured up a strange mixture of panic and grief, catapulting him back to Cornwall. He was looking down at the last remnants of the battle. Merlin pushed the talisman into his hand and told him to "*Play my part*". A shadow appeared at the end of the hallway, dragging itself towards him. Ben froze, his mind half-stuck on the past. The sound of armour scraping along the floor and tortured breathing scrambled his common sense. It sounded like … but it couldn't be …

'Arthur?' The smell of smoke seeped into Ben's confusion, choking him back to reality. They'd set his house on fire. 'Explaining this to the insurance company will be a challenge,' Ben grumbled to Ambrosius, but Ambrosius wasn't listening. His magic was focused on the shadow that was solidifying into a featureless figure as it crossed the threshold. Its head tilted from side-to-side, sizing him up. Ben drew Ambrosius close, ready to throw a spell.

'What are you doing?' Jack materialised in front of him, shoving Ben back towards the door. 'Is the house on fire?' The sound of Jack's voice shook the cobwebs from Ben's mind. He grabbed Jack's arm and pulled them both away. 'Wait, you didn't lock the door.'

In the garden, April was turning this way and that, bokken raised, unable to keep track of their movements. Aware of something moving at the edges of his vision, Ben skidded to a halt and offered no apology as he slung an arm around April's waist, flipping her onto his back.

'So much for salt!' April gave a short sarcastic laugh, squirming to look about. 'Where's Jack?'

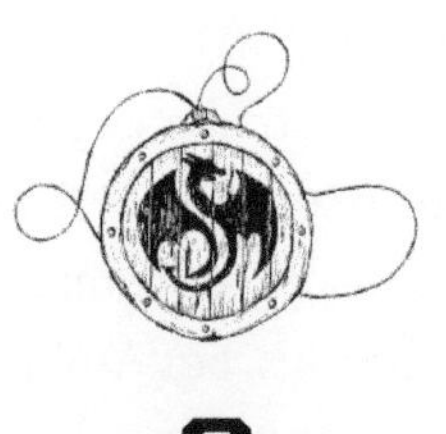

8

New Eyes Open

Oxford, Ben's house

Barqan snatched her burning hand from the door handle with a hiss of pain.

'Salt and iron door handles. How tedious.'

The wooden door splintered under the weight of her frustration. Seeing no more use for stealth, Barqan called her magic to the surface and threw it into the air. It split into segments which manifested into snarling, screeching silver draugrs. The phantoms of illusion whipped around the house, embracing it, rattling windows and doors. Benjamin's warding was thorough. Barqan expected no less of the careful, detail-orientated shtriga. What a sad thing it was. Benjamin was minutes away from death and the only description she could offer was *thorough*. There wasn't a spell to ward off errant rocks, so Barqan smashed the window. A draugr slithered in and dropped out of sight. Barqan held her breath. Bones cracked into place as the draugr dragged its now-skeletal form further into the house. It was a satisfying sight.

The sound of another door opening pulled Barqan round towards the back of the house. Skidding on the frost-covered pathway in her haste, she arrived at the back gate in time to see Benjamin scoop the girl up.

The back door slammed shut at the same time as realisation slapped Ben in the face. Silence. No growling, no rattling door handles, just eerie silence. They were trapped outside. Exposed and without Jack.

'Have they gone?' April asked.

'Unlikely …'

'Fuck!'

'Excuse me! Less of the … ooohh, fuck.' Flaming blue eyes watched them from the bottom of the garden. April pawed at his shoulder, wanting to be let down. Somewhat distracted, Ben dropped her without warning. 'You could have knocked, Barqan!'

'If you hadn't fortified your domain, I could have gained sufficient access to knock.' The djinn stuck her chin out, hands on hips.

'Clearly, I needed to. Why are you in my realm?' Beside him, April muttered what sounded like another curse and upended her empty saltshaker.

'Where are you, Jack?' Nothing. If Jack was trapped in the house …

'I've come to collect something.' Barqan took a threatening step towards them.

'Good luck with that. You've locked me out.'

'What I need isn't inside.' Barqan's smile looked more like a grimace so Ben stepped in front of April.

'I don't have much on me.' The djinn raised an eyebrow at the small mountain of rucksacks beside him. 'Those? They're April's.' Barqan raised her other eyebrow, eternally unamused by his sense of humour. 'Fine, I may have a few essentials. Do you need to borrow some sugar?'

'Your talisman, Benjamin.' She held out her hand. It was hard to read eyes made of fire, but Barqan's were dead and her voice matched. A flicker of an idea sparked in Ben's mind. He motioned for April to grab a bag.

'I heard about Tuonela. Of all the Guardians, I didn't expect you to be involved. How are you destroying entire planets? I must admit, begrudgingly, that is impressive.'

'With magic like yours,' Barqan stalked closer, 'you could go anywhere in this universe and beyond. There's no need for you to die today. The other Guardians will not judge you.'

'Oh, but they will.' Charon had tried to warn Ben, with time-earned wisdom, that the Guardians would never truly accept a simple physician. Elitist bastards. 'How magnanimous of you, allowing me to choose life or death.' He couldn't tell if the guilt trip was working. 'I'm not going to die today, Barqan.' Ben held Ambrosius close to the surface, ready to strike.

'Your path has already been decided,' Barqan replied as if he was stupid to think otherwise.

'Fate wants me dead? Shocking. It's a shame she isn't here. Turning her Guardian into an assassin – it's poor form.'

'It is not my place to question Fate.' The tired party line meant negotiation was pointless.

'Alright.' Benjamin charged towards her. He opened his fists so Ambrosius could manifest as two fiery balls of energy. As he ran, Ben shed his human appearance, and the colour drained from his eyes, leaving behind pitch-black orbs that matched the abyss of his mouth. His already pale skin became almost translucent and mottled, his hair faded to white. Ambrosius washed over him and his jawline contorted and stretched. Behind him, April screamed. The blue flames danced from April to him. Barqan darted forward. She sidestepped Ben, shoving him aside. Ben lunged forward, his fingers clutching at her rough cotton robe. With a grunt and sheer determination, he hooked an arm around Barqan's stomach and hauled her down the bottom of garden. She was on her feet in seconds.

They met like two missiles colliding. Barqan sank her knee into his gut and Ben's confidence faltered as he lost his balance. Barqan kicked him over, raining down punches. Ambrosius's glow inexplicably dimmed. Winded and slightly panicked, Ben reached for Ambrosius again. Barqan landed another blow, her spare hand reaching for his talisman. Familiar pins and needles tingled down his arms and it felt like sweet relief. Ben thrust his palms into Barqan's abdomen, sending her hurtling backwards and scrambled to reverse the scenario. If this became a battle of spellcasting, he wouldn't win. Djinn were spirit-like creatures born of smokeless flame in the God's pantheon. He had …

'April! The containers.'

Barqan clawed at his face, her elbows digging into his sides, trying to grab the talisman. Behind him, April tipped the contents of the bag onto the floor as she frantically searched.

'Got them! Now what?'

'Wait for Barqan to die of old age? What do you think?' His impatient sarcasm cost him a swift boot to his ribs. 'Salt her!' Benjamin caught a flailing wrist and almost dropped it. Barqan's arms were becoming consumed with the smokeless blue flame of her magic. The tribal-like tattoos grew until they covered all of her visible skin. 'Keep your dream state. My life is a waking nightmare. April!'

'Coming!' With a speed that surprised both of them, April upended the container, pouring the salt directly into Barqan's face. The flames flickered twice and extinguished. Barqan's face contorted with pain but she refrained from screaming, trying to roll free of Ben. He didn't let up, but allowed her to snatch her wrists back.

'Rubbing salt into your eyes isn't a good idea.' Barqan's empty eye sockets locked on his, somehow radiating disdain and loathing. The tattoos reached her fingertips. All Barqan had to do was press her hand against Ben's skin for a few seconds, and he'd be trapped in a dream state. 'More salt! I poked the bear one too many times!' Ben pinned both wrists to the ground, contorting himself into what Jack referred to as a cat pose. In her blind panic, Barqan pulled one arm free, but Ben threw himself backwards, narrowly avoiding being touched. A blast of magic hit him square in the chest. He hunched forward, trying to minimise the searing pain.

'Son of a ...'

Barqan found the outline of his talisman. Ben desperately tried to prise Barqan's fingers apart but she clung on for dear life. The ancient knot in the worn-out cord fought to hold on, but the strain was too much and it gave way.

'No!' Barqan's magic flared up into a giant ball of agitated energy, forcing Ben to retreat from whatever was attacking her.

'Move!' April shot past him, dumping another heap of salt onto Barqan. Ben's blood ran cold with her screeching, but it didn't stop him from pushing her magic back with Ambrosius. Ben grabbed at the loose end of the cord, pulling with all his strength, but Barqan wouldn't let go. The smell of burning flesh rose up to greet him. What in the hells?' Ben forced her hand open. The pendant had fused itself to Barqan's skin. Ben let go of her hand, dumbfounded. In the gaps between Barqan's clenched fist, glowed aquamarine magic that Ben hadn't seen in a very long time.

'It can't be ...' Out of the corner of his eye, Ben clocked April charging towards him, another container of salt held above her head. 'Hold on.' April paused, her hands shaking with adrenaline.

'How unusual,' Ben murmured, trying not to inhale too deeply.

'You would,' Barqan gasped, 'do what your God asked.'

'Freyja leaves me be.' He hadn't seen her in over five hundred years. Ben's eyes shifted to a murky green to match the disgust in his voice. 'It would take a very compelling argument for me to attack another Guardian.' Barqan snorted, despite her wounds.

'I was referring to my talisman. It's been dormant since Merlin's death.' The soft tread of retreating feet wrenched Ben's attention from the pulsating glow. 'April!' Her eyes were so wide, Ben thought they'd never shut again. He shook his head and chased the monster from his appearance. 'I should have warned you.' Barqan arched her back, trying to topple him. 'Seems a little simple for Fate. I thought there'd be more fire.' The wet grass was chilling his knees and staining his jeans. 'Which of the Gods are helping her?'

'Fate works alone.' Ben pushed his knee down hard into Barqan's throat, leaning forward to stare into the empty eye sockets.

'Fate can't destroy her own worlds, so who is she working with?' Ben happened to be looking down when Barqan stopped squirming. She didn't let go of his talisman. 'We are meant to be united against injustice and discord.' Ben had grown sick of the Gods a long time ago. This was the final nail in the coffin. 'The Gods can't keep bringing their squabbles to Gaia. There are millions of lives at stake.' Barqan gritted her teeth against the pain of the talisman's burn. 'That must hurt like hell but I promise you, it'll pale in comparison to what I'll do if you try to destroy Gaia.' Ben squeezed his hand over hers, trying not to gag at the sound of sizzling skin.

'One name, Barqan.' Barqan bit her lip. 'You're hesitating? Surely, it's simple?' Ben was a bit of a wuss when it came to pain. 'What'll it be? I can stay here for eternity.'

'Mórrígan.' The name sent an unconscious shudder through Ben.

'I was hoping you wouldn't say that. There aren't many candidates, granted, but the Goddess of War? Although it seems unlikely Fate would forgive Mórrígan.' Whilst on a particularly bad rebound from his breakup with Fate, Merlin, in his infinite wisdom, had sought comfort in Mórrígan's arms. It wasn't long before they wed. Fate was neither pleased nor fair about the situation. It had ended, as most of their interactions did, in a fight. It was a miracle Avalon wasn't destroyed.

'Call it a truce met through mutual goals.'

'Isn't that lovely? Two Gods setting aside their differences to destroy realms.' The repercussions of Merlin's decisions were still rippling through time. Ben shouldn't be surprised. 'All the Gods know Mórrígan cannot be trusted.'

Through the pain, Barqan managed a smirk. 'Because Merlin is the epitome of trust?' Ben wasn't going to justify that with an answer. 'Mórrígan has no intention of delivering the talismans to Fate.'

'Naturally.' If Mórrígan had all the talismans, she would have enough power to overthrow Fate.

'This should be Merlin's fight, Benjamin.'

'Yeah, the universe is laughing at me. And what of you? What will be your reward?' Ben asked coldly, his hands scrunching into fists.

'To relinquish my Guardianship.'

Ben was no stranger to that particular pipe dream. 'I never had you pegged as a fool, Barqan. If Fate doesn't kill you to make an example, Mórrígan will, to keep her secret.'

Barqan's free hand gripped Ben's shirt. 'Make it stop!' she sobbed, violently shaking her head in an attempt to dislodge the combined pain of the salt and the sword's magic.

'Let go of it! I'm not forcing you. I'm certainly not in control of it.' Benjamin tried once more to gain control of the talisman's energy. It slipped from his grasp once more. 'Shouldn't controlling my talisman be second nature? Trust Merlin to make something complicated.'

'Mórrígan will kill me if I don't return with it,' Barqan pleaded.

'Why does she need the talisman?' April asked, still poised to pour more salt.

'Magic has a long memory.' Ben pulled his top free from Barqan's grasp. 'It's not in Mórrígan's nature to create. Merlin could. With the talismans, Mórrígan could manipulate Merlin's residual magic. She'd be able to build and destroy realms. Mórrígan would be untouchable.' Understanding flashed like lightning. 'So you, Barqan, kill the Guardian, Mórrígan destroys the realm and steals the talisman. Fate lands another blow against Chaos ...' Barqan drove her fist into his unsuspecting stomach. 'Let go, Barqan!' Rolling on top of her, Ben pinned her other arm to her side, his spare hand wrapped around her throat. Barqan's thrashing legs stilled.

'Have you killed her?' April's tone was one of pure terror.

'She's playing dead,' Ben said pointedly but Barqan didn't so much as twitch. 'It's an act.'

'She's not breathing.'

'Hmm.' Ben was staring at the cord dangling from her closed fist. If he was quick enough, and careful not to shift his weight ... He wrapped the cord around his hand. Barqan's eyes flew open as the talisman tore free, taking skin with it. Barqan let out an unholy wail and scrambled to her feet, cradling her hand.

'I told you she was fine.' April took one look at the sword-shaped wound and gagged.

'This isn't over.' Barqan cut through the air with her magic. Ben dived forward, his fingers grazing Barqan's ankle as she vanished through a portal.

'Where'd she go?' April whirled about.

'She'll return. Once she's recovered.' Ben picked himself up from the floor with a groan. 'We'd best not be here when she does.' An unusual pain sent him poking at his chest.

'Are you ok? It looked like you fell over.' April sniggered. Apparently, she'd forgotten the earlier trauma of seeing his true form.

'Barqan broke my ribs! A minor inconvenience, I'll heal shortly. At least she didn't poison me. You wouldn't have been able to free me from a dream state.' Ben double knotted the leather cord and slipped it on. The still-warm pendant settled against his chest, dispelling most of his tension.

'I hope you got Barqan's skin off first! Gross.' Ben's thumb rubbed over the watch. There was nobody moving in the neighbouring gardens. 'I emptied two boxes of salt over her.' There was a hint of pride in April's voice.

'You did.' Ben tried to smile but his jaw didn't feel right. 'Works better than a saltshaker, right?' Bottles of holy water and boxes of salt were scattered around the backpack like a debris field, and …

'The book!' Ben wiped the mud from the cover, his fingers tracing the letters of the title: *Prophecies, potions, and spells of Merlin*. The pages were all dog-eared and faded, the cover a little ripped. The frosty grass had embraced it and Ben wasn't sure he could salvage the damp pages. 'I suppose it's time to make another copy. It's older than you.'

'Everything you own is older than me.' April sheepishly retrieved another book and slipped it into the bag. 'I can take photos of each page and show you how to back it up in the cloud.'

'Photos in the cloud?' April might as well have offered to teach the neighbour's cat how to tap dance.

'So you'd always have a copy.'

Ben glanced skywards. Perhaps that's why the puffy grey stratus clouds looked so heavy. 'I suppose nobody would find it up there.'

'Never mind, I'll show you later.'

April couldn't quite cover her smile with her hands. 'Hmm. Talk to Jack about it. When we find him.' Ben clutched the book to his chest, scanning the gardens for signs of his vampire. 'Are you alright?'

'Never better.'

'Good.' Ben absentmindedly patted her on the shoulder, still occupied with Barqan, talismans, Gods and … 'We need to find …' right on cue, a cool breeze disturbed April's hair.

'Oh. My. God,' April shrieked. 'Stop suddenly appearing beside me.' Jack laughed, tussling April's hair. 'Get off!' Ben's heart tightened at the dark red stain on his vampire's top.

'What?' Jack followed Ben's gaze down to the patch and pulled his jacket over it, giving Ben a big, reassuring grin that eased Ben's concern.

'Where in the hells have you been?' Ben winced. Why he had to pick a fight, he didn't know.

'Barqan can raise draugrs. Did you know that?'

'That explains the noise. I was concerned with the skeleton dragging itself up the hall. I had April to worry about.'

'Great.' Jack stared at the ground, seeming to hear the ghost of Arthur. 'The bastards hit me with a sharp stick!'

Ben gently pulled Jack's hands away from the wound. ''Tis but a scratch. You'll live. The only real casualty is your shirt.' And Ben had been trying to get rid of that one for years.

'I knew it! And being stabbed hurt, you know?'

'It's healing. You chose to fight the magically animated skeleton,' Ben teased. He couldn't always be there. He wanted the choice. One of these days, the boisterous vampire was going to run right into something he couldn't handle. As Arthur had.

'Why are you glowing, Ben?' Jack pointed to the greeny-blue glow emanating underneath Ben's shirt.

'Oh, the talisman seems to have activated itself.'

'You finally figured out how to control it?' Jack's face lit up. 'Talk about timing!'

'Not exactly. Barqan attempted to strangle me with the cord. It decided to work.' Jack's excitement vanished in a puff of smoke.

'That can't be good. And you sound exhausted.' Jack prodded Ben in his chest. 'Did you overuse Ambrosius?'

'I'm fine.' Ben wasn't going to admit that he really needed to feed.

'Anybody else hear the sirens?' April asked over her shoulder as she finished repacking the backpacks.

'Yes. We should leave.' In Ben's experience, it was hard convincing somebody that he was of sound mind when his house was filled with salt, demon traps and spell books.

'Agreed. Ben's too old to go to prison.' Jack beamed at him.

Ben decided to let Jack have that one, pleased to have avoided a full-blown argument.

'And go where?' April asked suspiciously.

'Jack's apartment.' Ben needed a minute to think.

'You don't live together? What are you waiting for, your two-thousand-year anniversary?'

'We do,' Jack replied.

'Come on.' Ben held out his hand. 'We're going to have to run again.' April groaned but allowed herself to be hoisted up onto his back.

From around the side of the house, Dirmynd watched the three leave.

1st November 2023

Hello,

I've been thinking a lot of late – how to begin this letter for one.

The words "dearest" and "Merlin" have lost much of their meaning. Whether this is due to the myriad of times I've scrawled it on parchment and paper, or if the passing years have robbed them of their worth, I don't know. There must come a point where all the words have been spoken. That day is not today.

I'm sure you had your reasons for not warning me. I suppose my becoming Guardian was for the "good of the realm". Did you ever consider what was right for me? You made these decisions in isolation, and now look at us. You and Arthur, dead. Me, miserable as sin. I saw your magic today. The tiny residual glow of your spell. I realised something – it didn't matter then; it shouldn't matter now. Only, it does matter, doesn't it? It wasn't your soul that was tarnished – it was mine. How could you let it happen, Merlin? Perhaps you were right. Only fools gather friends close. As Guardian, you couldn't pick friendship over Gaia.

I'm about to tangle with your widow and ex-wife. They want to destroy what you built. Thanks for leaving that mess for me.

Speaking of Fate, the funniest thing happened. I wonder what you'd make of her, this hunter who isn't quite a hunter. I am unable to dissuade April from leaving and I like her company. She was going to attack a demon with a condiment receptacle, if you could believe such a thing! She's got an attitude and a quick wit to match yours. You'd like her. April does not like you, despite death and over a thousand years separating you. She's suspicious, that's to be expected. There's hurt somewhere in her past. I know, I know, I should send her away. I tried. I hope that that won't be her undoing.

April asked me a lot of pointed questions about you. I surprised myself with how few answers I have. She wanted to know if I'd ever seen your spirit. April thought it odd that somebody such as you hadn't found a way to cross over. She has a point. I gave up waiting on your spirit centuries ago. Besides, knowing your timekeeping, you'll show up as I take my last breath. Please don't get any ideas. I've no desire to see your ugly face at the end.

If I had to guess, I'd say that you chose to remain a ghost, walking through a world that you can no longer affect. Perhaps that's for the best.

Benjamin

9

Indelible

31st October, Avalon

'Fantastic.' Dirmynd materialised right in the middle of the palace's rose bed, sitting atop the tallest of the seven hills.

His mind drifted away with the intoxicating perfume on the light summer breeze.

The sunlight always seemed brighter in Avalon. It gave Dirmynd the false illusion that nothing could touch him. Below, the turquoise waters of Lake Albion glistened invitingly in the golden sunlight; beyond that lay the timeless city of stone and marble. If Dirmynd closed his eyes, he could picture the cobbled streets. In the squares, the citizens would be chattering beside extravagant fountains, enjoying the heat of the day. Seasons didn't so much linger in Avalon as hurtle past in the blink of an eye. On a particularly clear day, he could see all the way over to the Hall of Folkvangr – it might have been heaven for most, but heaven wasn't for everybody. With closed eyes, Dirmynd listened to the breeze rustling the leaves of the trees, and enjoyed the warmth of the stone wall beneath him. Avalon was a tranquil spot when the spectacular marble-domed Pantheon sat empty – as it had for some time. When the Gods did gather in their frantic epicentre, the wind was heavy with the discord. But since their liberation from Chaos, the Gods had little to no reason to congregate. And there hadn't been a trial for many years now – trials helped pass the time. The building, which strongly resembled Oxford's circular Radcliffe Camera, had been so long forgotten, the dust had given up forming.

Dirmynd grabbed hold of his common sense before it fled entirely. This wasn't the place to lose his wits. He hadn't recognised the prison bars hiding beneath the fancy trappings of freedom. Dirmynd's captor had convinced him he was safely home and locked the door. Fate's glass palace glinted in the sun – a ridiculous ode to her delusions of grandeur. Beneath Dirmynd's feet, the mud squelched in protest at the mess of trampled rose petals and stems. He winced. He should move before …

'You promised to return, once your business with the Tudors was complete.' Dirmynd reluctantly opened his eyes to see Fate standing in the shade. She appeared to carry the light within her. Long silver hair tumbled down to her waist in a loose plait. It wasn't awful, but it was new.

'I really don't know why I came.' Dirmynd wanted to see her again, despite knowing that he never wanted to see her again.

'You had forgotten about me.' Fate's eyes were the same delicate shade of lavender that Dirmynd saw when he closed his. A person could stare into those pupils for the rest of eternity and consider it time well spent. They could see down into the deepest, darkest reaches of Dirmynd's soul, to the man he could have been. He'd forsaken his moral compass somewhere in the Roman Empire.

'How could I forget you, Fate? You who have destroyed me so.' Fate looked resplendent in a silk gown of turquoise, its blue and green shades bleeding into one another in the same way a sunset's colours faded together. The sloping V-neck gave way to a skirt that trailed off behind her, peacock feathers hanging from the delicate slits that revealed a deep-blue underskirt. The sunlight bounced lazily off the miniature spinning wheels and open-palmed hands strewn across the entire dress. Dirmynd particularly disliked the billowing sleeves – he preferred at least the chance to see the blow that would send him down the rabbit hole.

'Dispense with the dramatics, it does not suit you. You should thank me rather than squabble with me, Dirmynd.'

Presumably, he had enjoyed her company once, but his memory didn't stretch that far back. Passion eventually faded, leaving nowhere to hide; they'd taken their first good look at one another. The truth wasn't pretty. Their last row had crashed against the glass walls of Fate's palace for two days. After they'd finished laying atrocities at each other's feet, Dirmynd had looked at the woman he supposedly loved and realised that he should abhor her, but he could never quite bring himself to that point. It was a terrible conflicting thing, to still care for the person who had been responsible for the death of their child. Whatever he was, whatever they had been, it had ended with their child's life.

'I'm not here voluntarily,' Dirmynd said through gritted teeth. 'I didn't fancy tangling with Barqan. She was … on edge. You wouldn't have been pleased if I'd scratched your favourite toy.' Dirmynd forced himself to check his anger; it did no good to argue.

'Do you recall the first time you watched me spin a life?'

'It was awe-inspiring, watching you spinning your gold threads. Like an omnipotent spider.' Distrust sharpened Dirmynd's tongue. 'I was easily impressed as a young man.' Fate wove with such vision. Her fingers danced along the delicate golden thread, knowing where to drop a patch of sorrow and when to allow happiness to grow. Dirmynd had been captivated by this angel who created life. 'What's it like for you, Fate, writing time and watching it slip by?'

Fate's cold, barren eyes bulged. 'You forget your place, Dirmynd. You are nothing more than a soldier.'

The words tore through his chest like shrapnel. Dirmynd searched Fate's face for any traces of compassion and found a beautiful abyss. He was always one wrong move away from tumbling into the dark void of black magic that waited below the safe harbour of his.

'What do you want from me?' Dirmynd needed to pull himself out of repeat. The past always ensnared him, and she knew that. 'It can't be as simple as you missing me. What plot are you hatching now?' Fate's silence was going to drive him mad. 'Come on, out with it. I don't have time to waste.' She'd already asked the worst of him and yet he braced for the impact of hitting a new low. Fate's gentle but dark laugh had him readying his magic. Order or attack, Dirmynd wasn't going without a fight.

'Dearest, you have nothing but time until I say you can go.' Dirmynd drew his cloak tighter around him, feeling quite cold in the shade of the palace. He should have heeded his predecessor's warning. It was absolute loyalty or nothing.

'How much longer do you intend to continue this waltz?' Dirmynd let exhaustion flood his voice.

'I made it clear to you that you would be with me for the rest of your existence.'

'Aye, I didn't realise just how long a time forever is.' Dirmynd looked around at the lengthening shadows and shivered. The day was drawing to a close. He needed to leave before the weather turned. Here, in this strange realm inhabited by a questionable mix of Gods, demigods, djinn, and the odd warlock, weather held little meaning. The plants grew and flowered during the day only to be destroyed at nightfall by bitterly cold arctic blizzards. By dawn's first light, the snow melted away, only for the unforgiving cycle to renew. If there was any peace to be found in the gardens surrounding the enormous glass palace, Dirmynd could no longer find it. If he didn't leave soon, he'd be forced to take shelter inside Fate's palace. And *that* scenario only had one ending.

'How many times can you change something before it loses its shape and structure?' Dirmynd looked at his calloused hands, struggling to recognise them or the suffering they had caused.

'Why do you ask?'

'You've forced me to be so many different things, I've misplaced something important of myself.'

'What have you lost, Dirmynd? Perhaps we can find it.'

'I'm not sure. But I know it's not coming back.' Dirmynd was a sandcastle on a deserted beach. Fate was the wind, slowly eroding away the walls. 'One day, if I'm lucky, all of this will cease to be. You, me, Gaia, Avalon. All of it.'

'Be careful what you wish for, it might come to pass ...'

Fate continued to talk but her warning tumbled around in his head. His suspicion shifted ever so slightly, stretching its tentacle-like arms.

'Will it end?' he interrupted her.

'You are preparing for the End of Days. It must be a possibility otherwise you would not be so worried,' Fate cooed.

'Regardless of the outcome, the realm will not end.' Dirmynd drew back his cloak so she could see his magic swirling around both hands. 'Civilisations will rise and fall, but the worlds will continue to spin until the stars die. Or you end them.' The slightest twitch of Fate's eyes confirmed more than Dirmynd's measured words had insinuated.

'Don't be so melodramatic. I am forbidden from destroying a world that I have built, as you know.'

'I didn't say that you would. Although it's not an impossibility.' Dirmynd's fingers caught on the knots in his hair. 'You will put me in an impossible position if you try to destroy Gaia. Chaos cannot make you return to Tartarus, so there is no need for all of this world-ending business.' Fate's hands flew to cover her mouth, gasping as if he'd stabbed her. 'Oh, don't pretend to be clueless.'

'It's the principle! You have no idea what it's like to live under the thumb of a lunatic obsessed with themselves.'

'No, I can't possibly imagine. It must be terrible for you.' Fate missed his sarcasm.

'I will not go back.'

'Oh, everybody says that at the end of a holiday. I suppose you could use another three thousand years?'

'Enough of this nonsense, what cause have you had to speak to Jack.'

'A-ha! We've arrived at the point!' Dirmynd's magic prickled away, urging him to do the sensible thing and leave. 'You wanted me to gather information on the Guardian. One can achieve that goal by befriending his partner.'

'And you've never reported back,' Fate snapped as if he was an unruly teenager who had neglected to clean his room. 'I have more than enough to keep my eye on.'

'And yet you have found the time to interfere with my life. How lucky I am, truly.'

Fate took a slow small step towards him. Outwardly, he remained calm and composed, with a slightly bored look on his face. Dirmynd portrayed himself as fearless to the world, but there were three hairline cracks running through that image, Fate being one of them. Dirmynd was her coward here, now. Forever.

'Time will never be on your side; you cannot wait for it, nor it for you.'

'Time is a thief.' Dirmynd opened a portal with a snap of his fingers.

Fate closed the distance between them and grabbed Dirmynd's wrists.

'As are you. Where's the king?' Fate's lavender eyes bore into Dirmynd's, but he held fast.

'For the love of the Gods, he's dead, Fate. You yourself ordered me to kill him and I did. I slit his throat.'

'He never crossed the shores of Hades.'

'Oh, I suppose you wanted me to guide him through the afterlife? Is his thread cut?'

'Yes.'

'And can you sense his existence?'

'No.'

'Then accept that he is dead and you only have one Guardian to worry about. I even killed Merlin for you.' Dirmynd snatched his wrists free of her steel-like grasp. 'Why make this so difficult when the narrative is all yours to do with as you please?'

'You misinterpret my orders. Your stories always sound like obedience, but I hear disobedience in the gaps between words. If the second Guardian exists ...'

Dirmynd turned away from her, barely contained anger radiating out from him, his magic heavy in the air around them as he stepped into the portal back to Gaia.

'You've run out of moves,' Dirmynd said coldly.

'Not quite.' Fate's lips curled into a cruel smile as thunder growled in the distance.

Dirmynd hung his head – he'd been so close! He slid his foot out of the portal and turned reluctantly. From her pocket Fate produced what, at first glance, looked to be a smooth, perfect ball of pitch-black onyx. Dirmynd knew better. He'd seen this show before.

'Look.' Fate beckoned with her free hand.

Dirmynd left the portal shimmering in the air, warily watching the light of dawn chase itself across the globe of the seeing-glass.

'Do you see them?'

From where Dirmynd stood, he could make out two silhouettes in motion. He hesitated, reluctant to move further away from the portal, and not remotely curious to see what form her shapeshifting manipulation would take this time.

'I don't need to. I know who it will be.' Fate rolled her eyes and tossed the seeing-glass to him. Dirmynd should have let the bastard thing hit the deck, but his instinctive reflex caught the ball. He dropped his gaze to the smooth surface, and recognised Benjamin, the girl a shadow at his heels.

'What is following them?' It was keeping a safe distance, but still Dirmynd's grip tightened around the glass.

'The ghost is a delightful coincidence.' Fate sounded giddy with excitement. 'The djinn is mine.' There was that cruel smile again. The one that wanted to know what Dirmynd was planning on doing about it. 'Benjamin is too trusting. He accepted the girl immediately.' Fate's brows knitted together.

'My, my, is that fear I hear in your voice, my love?'

'Of course not!' Fate snapped back, flustered.

'You can't see her future, can you? She's a puzzle you can't solve.'

'I can!' Dirmynd didn't believe Fate. 'You cannot be too careful with strangers.'

'All of my best friends are strangers.' Dirmynd tossed the seeing-glass back with a confidence he hadn't felt in a long time. 'I see them and I am leaving now.' He put one foot over the portal's threshold, and …

'You'll not get there in time.' Fate threw the casual taunt over her shoulder.

Without turning back, Dirmynd asked, 'Why show me that scene at all?'

'To make a point and it is this: destiny cares not for want. Gaia will fall. Just as Tuonela and Erebus did. Even you, with your tricks, cannot alter my endings.' He shuddered at the lack of emotion in her voice.

'Then let me be gone. I have to pack.'

'Do you know what your weakness is?' Fate moved her hand over the ball, killing the image.

'You're about to tell me, I think.'

'You love.' Coming from Fate, the word was twisted and barbed. 'You love me, you love humanity. Your job would be easier if you cared less. Do not disappoint me. Again.'

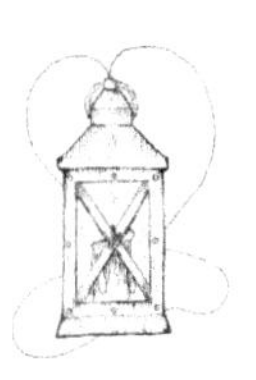

10

Impossible

Avalon

And like that, Dirmynd was gone as quickly and as quietly as he had arrived.

Their constant bickering exhausted Fate.

Love! It was such a delicate and temporary thing. She had no use for delicate and temporary things.

Fate glared at the mess that Dirmynd had made of her flower beds and knelt down to see what could be saved. She could magic them back to health, but it was satisfying to tend to them herself. After all, creating and nurturing life was what Fate did best. The roses' most attractive quality was how they depended on her for survival. The characters in her stories survived by other means. Roses were a rewarding distraction. Usually.

Dirmynd had been a thrilling distraction for a few moments. But Dirmynd was a mage, and like all mages, he got bogged down in the minute details. Things like the death of their daughter. What was she supposed to do? She had a universe to run. The child shouldn't have been so sickly.

Dirmynd never knew when to let things go. And now he had her mind slipping back into the past.

The battle in 537AD had not played out as Fate had expected. She was content in her new home of Avalon, although she could understand the frustrations of those who had been assigned the under realms – they were so dark and damp, filled with the worst of Chaos's creations. They had retreated to Avalon and she'd had enough of their clattering about. And Gaia was a big enough realm. It was funny, nothing permanent lasted. Chaos had been so delighted and distracted with the new realms and the endless possibilities. And the continued disaster of existence sustained Chaos. But lately, they'd grown bored and their attention had returned to their original creations. The Gods. Perhaps it was paranoia, but Fate swore she saw Chaos's face in the clouds most days. So, if the realms were no longer enough for Chaos, Fate would destroy them. Some of the Gods would perish but for them, death was temporary. A few might flee to another universe and the others, they would come to her. She would have to learn to live with them again, but that was preferable to returning to Tartarus.

The air fizzled and popped with the opening of another portal behind Fate. She had collected nearly a dozen roses beside her.

'I think Dirmynd tramples my plants on purpose.' Fate kept her eyes firmly on the delicate stems. 'I thought you weren't coming, Mórrígan.'

'And I thought Dirmynd would never leave,' the Goddess of War replied, exasperation dragging her words out, reinforcing her thick Irish accent.

'He doesn't know when to stop talking. Or when to step out of the flower bed.' Fate scowled at the tortured soil. She shouldn't be surprised. His carelessness had cost her the war.

'Most do not. Even their silence is loud.' Mórrígan carelessly plucked a rose from a nearby rosebush and began pulling its petals off. Fate stiffened. It would not do to chide Mórrígan for such a small thing, so she swallowed her displeasure. Destructive behaviour was to be expected of War.

'Dirmynd will likely interfere in Gaia.'

'Seems like the nerves are at Dirmynd. That's unfortunate.' Mórrígan held Fate's gaze, slowly stripping the tortured rose, its petals dropped to the ground like velvety red drops of blood. 'Did you ask about the king?'

'Dirmynd insists he killed him. You shouldn't have a problem.'

Mórrígan threw her head back and laughed darkly, long black hair brushing the ground. 'I wouldn't have a problem either way.'

'A modicum of caution would serve you well, Mórrígan.' Fate rescued another of Dirmynd's rose casualties from the ground. 'The more I dwell on it, the more I'm convinced that Chaos is working through Dirmynd.' Fate had wanted to ensure that every trace of Arthur was destroyed, but the king's ghost had drifted away on the breeze. It could be nothing or it could be everything and it was a page straight out of Chaos's playbook.

'I'll have no choice but to kill Dirmynd, if he gets in the way. There's no margin for error now. Dirmynd has proved that he can't be trusted.' War stamped her foot. 'Are you listening? Stop fussing over flowers!'

'I can still hear you, even with my back turned.'

'If Benjamin doesn't die, our plan will come to an end and the world will not,' Mórrígan said in a dramatic voice that was dangerously close to sounding like whining. 'I'll not go back to live with Chaos!'

Fate returned to pruning, not wanting to indulge War's impatience. 'Nor I. So, you had best succeed in Gaia.'

Mórrígan mulled this over, twirling the rose stem in between her fingers. 'There's not been a good battle for centuries. I regret creating guns. They make the killing too easy and oh so dull.'

Fate nodded in sympathy. It was best not to get too attached to a particular period in time. She favoured the sixth century herself. 'You have to change with time as we all did, and will have to do again.'

'Well, I have realms to burn, Guardians to kill.'

Fate resisted the urge to roll her eyes; destiny was her forte and she thanked the other deities for not forgetting it.

'Barqan will strike soon.'

'And if she fails, I shall step in.' Mórrígan grinned in anticipation. 'Barqan asked about the girl. Is she one of Chaos's plants, do you think?'

'I am uncertain.' Fate frowned. 'We'll see soon enough.'

11

21st Century Survival Blues

1st November, Oxford

April wondered if the boys ever collided with anything. Which was tempting Fate, to think about it whilst hitching a shtriga ride.

They moved like silk, slipping easily around corners and gliding down roads, dodging sleepy-eyed commuters without so much as brushing their sleeves. One or two shivered in an unexpected cold breeze, otherwise, nobody clocked the one living and two not-quite-alive ghosts, silently retracing their steps into town, heading for Jericho. She thought that they'd passed by the Bodleian but it was gone in a flash. April wasn't sure if she should throw up first or ask Jack how he managed to afford to live here. Maybe he had a part time job working nights at Tesco. Unsure of how sound travelled when running at what felt like the speed of light, April made a mental note to ask him later. Although it was tempting to give somebody a good fright with her disembodied voice.

Safe in the quiet, bohemian suburb of Jericho, the boys slowed their pace a little. At least April thought so. It was hard to tell. The world was spinning and the buildings looked like they were bending around corners. April put this down to motion sickness and clung a little tighter to Ben. He was the only object in her vision retaining its correct orientation.

April still had a lot of questions, but looking at the swanky apartment blocks around them, she thought she had her answer regarding their living arrangement. Jack was waiting for Ben to redecorate.

'For the love of …' The vampire dropped out of hyper-speed and forced Ben to hit the brakes. 'Do that one more time, and I'm gonna throw up.

'Don't do it again, Jack. For the sake of my jacket.' Jack grinned over his shoulder and cut across the street to the new estate overlooking the canal. Nobody could tell April that at least one pair of curtains didn't twitch in the hundreds of windows looming above them. Jack strode across the courtyard as if he owned the red-brick apartment building. April squinted up into the morning sun, wishing she'd remembered her sunglasses, but glad for the warmth of her scarf. If April had to guess, she'd say that Jack lived on the top floor, where the penthouses seemed to be made entirely of glass. Ben carried her into the building and sure enough, they flew up the stairs to the fifth floor where Jack awaited them at his front door.

'Welcome to my humble abode. It's not as big as Ben's place, but it doesn't have a djinn infestation. And the decor doesn't date back to the 1920s.' Jack winked at April but she was too busy feeling dizzy to respond. With the greatest of care, Ben put her down in the widest armchair that April had ever encountered. Feeling like a new-born giraffe, she clumsily folded her legs underneath her and sank back into it, grateful for soft furnishings. If she sat still, the ensuing feelings of nausea, light-headedness and worst of all, pins and needles would eventually subside.

'Um, isn't your home a tiny bit obvious?' Jack locked the front door; the sound of the chamber turning was so pathetic when April thought about the things he needed to keep out.

'We're not going to stay long enough for them to find us,' Ben replied, sprawling on the leather sofa that dominated the centre of the room, his expression unreadable. A solitary shaft of sunlight drifted in through the windows and fell across his chest like a wound, his eyes following Jack back and forth as the vampire darted from room to room.

'What are you looking for?' Ben called out, shrugging at the lack of reply.

April surveyed Jack's kingdom. The open-plan kitchen gave way to a cosy living space. A hallway lay beyond, leading off to the bedrooms. The ridiculous amount of glass made the place feel airy and a little like a greenhouse. Or a fishbowl. Either way, it gave the exposed brickwork a faint glow. 'There's a lot of wood and glass in here …' April didn't think that the wooden beams criss-crossing above her were real but the flooring and bookcases definitely were. Jack briefly appeared in the kitchen before a stack of papers drifted through the air in the living room.

'Is this normal?' April jumped as a pile of books that had been stacked haphazardly on the coffee table next to her, toppled to the floor.

'It's how he is,' Ben said as if she was mad for thinking that he expected anything else from Jack.

'Must be tiring.' April heard a thud come from the hallway. 'Is that why you guys don't live together?' Ben raised his eyebrows.

'No. Fine! It's one of the reasons.' Ben rubbed at his chest as if he was trying to displace pain.

'Are you … Jack!' April swatted at the vampire as he materialised beside her.

'What's the matter?' Jack's eyes narrowed at Ben.

'I'm fine.'

'Are we going to ignore how the talisman miraculously resurrected itself?' Jack bent to scoop up the fallen books.

'The colour of the magic wasn't yours.'

'I don't know what to tell you.' Ben sounded a little stand-offish. 'It was nothing that I did.'

'Did you …?'

'You know full well that I recognised the magic. It was never going to be any other colour.' April caught the slight twitch of Jack's hands before the vampire took off down the hallway.

Safely out of sight, Jack paused midway through pulling the entire contents of a filing cabinet out, resting his head on his arms. He couldn't remember his human life. He felt like he should mourn the person he had been, but the grief wasn't genuine. Grief wasn't the right word either. For starters, his old self might not be worth mourning. Still, Jack hated feeling so adrift within himself, second guessing his own tastes and beliefs. He picked absent-mindedly at the frayed edge of a file divider, trying to hit pause on this endless playlist of self-pity. At least Ben was never too far away when he got into this particular funk. He knew who he was with Ben. And Ben wasn't going to change into something else and leave. They were so similar but on this one point, they were poles apart. Ben's past was ever-present. Ben could even open a book and read about the people he'd outlived. And if Ben figured out how to use the laptop, he'd be able to find pages and pages on Arthur and Merlin. Must be nice, to know yourself. Or to believe that to be the case.

'What did Barqan say to you?' Jack called out, fighting to keep his voice light. 'You looked like she took the stars with her when she left.'

'Mórrígan and Fate are collaborating. Mórrígan is double-crossing Fate; Barqan is working for them both, I think.'

'That's a mess and a half.' Jack gently banged his head on his arms and forced himself to resume his search. 'So, Mórrígan is the one ending worlds. Delayed reaction.'

'How so?'

'She doesn't seem the sort to deal with breakups well.'

'Who's Mórrígan?' Jack heard April returning from the kitchen, having gone in search of water.

'She's the God of War and Merlin's ex-wife.'

Jack poked his head through in time to see April spit water over Ben in surprise. 'Ha!'

'Sorry.' Abashed, April offered Ben the box of tissues from the coffee table.

Ben snatched a few with as much grace as he could muster. 'Where Mórrígan walks, civilisations fall. For example, the bloody defeat of the Aztecs via the Spanish.'

'And the time she wiped out the Minoans via a volcanic eruption, because she could.' Jack wished he'd been around to see half of the things Mórrígan had destroyed.

'Merlin had a type, I suppose you'd say.' Ben's face contorted into a look of intent disapproval.

'Destructive and all powerful?' April asked in disbelief.

'I tried to make Merlin see sense. A warlock had no business courting omnipotent beings.'

According to Ben, Merlin had listened, thanked him for his advice and ignored it. 'His true love was Fate,' Jack added, crossing back through the living room. 'I never understood why he married Mórrígan.'

'I think it was out of spite. Merlin was an emotional train wreck. And that was before he married Fate. He was a genius when it came to most things, but relationships ...'

'...were toxic.' Jack finished for Ben as he retraced his steps. Ben sighed in frustration, side-eyeing him. 'Oh, come on, you can't deny it! Fate, Mórrígan and Merlin were the originators of toxic relationships!' Every supernatural creature knew the story of how that particular love triangle had torn a rift amongst the Gods. It had taken all of Merlin's cunning and magic to get him away from a furious Mórrígan and all of Arthur's diplomacy to persuade her to not destroy the warlock.

'That's one hell of a rebound,' April remarked. 'You're always defending Merlin.'

Jack stifled a cheer as another soul joined him on the not-a-fan-of-Merlin cart. It had been a lonely ride thus far.

'The point,' Ben cut in before April could enquire further, 'is that their collaboration does not bode well for us. Fate can only create; Mórrígan can only destroy.'

'I can see why they teamed up.' April puffed out her cheeks. 'Practically unstoppable.'

'Practically unstoppable? Completely unstoppable, that's something to discuss later.' Jack glanced at the time and realised it had done what it did best, crept past without him noticing.

'We should probably think about leaving,' Ben called out. Back in his room, Jack shook his head, resuming the search with more urgency. They'd been together so long, they didn't need telepathy to read each other's minds.

'I know.' Jack's distracted voice earned him Ben's curiosity which Jack batted away. He'd finally found what he was looking for! In his haste, he forgot to announce himself and appeared behind April who leapt up out of her chair.

'You have got to stop doing that!' Jack let her swat at his shoulder, his attention focused on Ben.

'Our plan jumped out the window when you picked up April. Where do you want to go? The other realms are out of the question.'

'We're in a stronger position now the talisman is working.'

'Yeah, about that.' Jack dragged a chair away from the table tucked in a corner. He purposely set it down in front of Ben, crossed arms resting on the back of the chair, chin on his arms. 'We need to talk about how much of a coincidence it is. Something or someone activated it. And if that wasn't you, who was it?' Jack hadn't been looking forward to *this* conversation.

'It hadn't occurred to me that the magic might still be active. I've never felt so much as a tingle from it.' Sensing an unspoken accusation woven into uncomfortable truths he'd rather not confront, Ben shifted awkwardly on the sofa, avoiding the subject and Jack's gaze.

'How are the talismans powered?' April asked, hugging her knees and looking rather pale again. Perhaps she was allergic to conflict.

'After Merlin's death, the spell looked to the Guardian for its power.' Ben absentmindedly wound the cord round his finger.

'Your magic is orange,' Jack stated flatly.

'It's the same shade as autumn leaves,' April piled on. 'That magic looked kind of greeny-blue. Like the sea.'

'I am by no means an expert on magic, but isn't it strange?' Ben didn't appreciate it when Jack faked ignorance to prove a point. Ben considered arguments to be tedious things; he resolved problems with as little discussion as possible. Preferably none. 'It's enchanted or it's not, there is no in between. Merlin's magic is alive or it's not.' Jack leant back smugly, pleased with his deductions. 'Everybody else's continued to work; they adopted the Guardian's magic.'

'So why,' Ben pulled the pendant over his head, letting it dangle in front of his eyes, 'did mine stop?' Jack threw the talisman a dark look. Until today, it had been little more than a jumped-up keepsake. Now it had morphed into a living extension of Merlin – the ghost that refused to die.

'The talisman changes colour to reflect the Guardian's magic, yes?'

'Ordinarily, yes.' Ben's voice was full of wonder as he watched the sword spin. 'If I hadn't have seen the colour myself, I wouldn't have believed it.'

'Walk me through the likely scenarios.' If Ben came to the conclusion himself, Jack wouldn't have to be the bad guy.

'There aren't any. The talisman works only for its assigned Guardian. I assumed it didn't work because I'm lacking the second Guardian.' Jack found himself scratching at a freckle. He'd had months to cultivate his argument, but the words wouldn't budge. Whenever Ben vanished down a Merlin-and-Arthur-shaped rabbit hole, it didn't end well. This time, Jack was going to have to push Ben into freefall.

'Or … oh.' Ben's hand shot forward, gripping Jack's knee tightly. Jack braced himself and forced an interested, worry-free smile onto his face. 'I thought we needed the other talisman for it to work. Mórrígan!' Ben's face lit up with excitement. 'If she's been collecting the talismans, she's probably got Merlin's. We've been wasting time looking in museums, castle ruins, graves …'

'What?' April asked in horror. Jack wanted to reassure her, but Ben's train of thought wasn't stopping for passengers.

'We should have been looking to the Gods. She's found it, Jack. I know she has!'

'So, you think yours is doing its thing because Mórrígan's using its twin?' Jack had hoped for a different conclusion.

'It's possible. It's logical, I suppose.'

'Oh sure, because we're drowning in logic! Because a Guardian killing another Guardian is logical. Fate wanting to destroy the realms is logical …'

'Alright, you've made your point.' Ben huffed. 'I heard that Mórrígan attended Merlin's funeral. I can picture the God of War, her face streaked by crocodile tears, wailing over the coffin as she slipped the shield from unresisting hands.'

'Merlin shouldn't have given Arthur's to you,' Jack said bitterly.

'He must have seen death's shadow behind him. He ensured that at least one talisman would be protected with a Guardian who would never let it go.' Jack rolled his eyes. 'Merlin once told me that Fate both admired and feared his power. He thought it the only reasonable explanation for her attraction to him. As for Mórrígan, well, she likes power too. She's placed herself perfectly for acquiring all the talismans and what's left of Merlin's magic ...' Ben's own words settled like a chill in his mind. 'Fate needs Merlin's magic. She's looking for it in whatever form it still exists. She's planning to take on Chaos – I must contact the remaining Guardians.' Ben shot to his feet, opened a portal to Annwn, and left a confused Jack and April behind.

****

Annwn

Something was wrong.

Ben became aware of that as soon as the portal closed behind him.

Where there should have been eight points of light, there were only six. Where Erebus and Tuonela should have been, there was nothing but patches devoid of matter. Two dark smudges on the universe's canvas. Dread rose in his stomach. His colleagues ... they'd had no warning, no time to call for help. There wasn't much Ben could have done, but still ... two realms and all the creatures thereof had perished without him lifting a finger. Ben felt a coldness that had nothing to do with space gripping him. If April hadn't been with him, Barqan would have erased Gaia.

A blur of blue flame streaked past him. Ben threw himself forward, desperate to reach Annwn first.

He shot out of the portal beside the River Dulais at a run and tripped over the bulging root of an ancient tree. Annwn was a world of lush green forests, high peaks, crystal-blue lakes, and towering waterfalls. It was hard to get his bearings – the river was in full flood, rushing over Aberdulais Falls and slamming onto the pennant sandstone below. 'Damn it!' He'd landed a little short of Cerridwen's cauldron cave.

'Benjamin?' A curious shtriga whose name Ben couldn't remember, approached.

'Where is she?' Ben shook the shocked shtriga by his lapels.

'Who? What's the matter?'

'No time.' Ben set off at a dead run, weaving in and out of trees, pushing aside low hanging branches and following the sounds of water crashing off the waterfall.

'Benjamin?' Footsteps pounded the ground in pursuit.

'Leave! Now!' Desperate determination pushed Ben on. The ground was littered with twisted roots; Ben had to keep his eyes cast down. He didn't see Cerridwen. The pair tumbled over, landing in a heap.

'Benjamin! Sut wyt ti?' Cerridwen blurted out in her native Welsh tongue, shock quickly turning to delight.

'I'm fine, but we must leave. Now, Cerri.' Ben grabbed her hand but Cerridwen didn't budge. 'Please! Barqan is right behind me.'

'I'm not being funny,' Cerridwen flicked her long black hair over one shoulder of her deep red dress, 'but I've not heard from you in ages. You can't show up …'

'We must leave. Now!' Ben gripped her slender shoulders, as if he could shake all of his concerns and fears into her. 'Barqan is coming to kill you.'

'What?' Cerridwen laughed.

'Kalma and Keres – dead. She tried to kill me …'

'Don't be daft …' Cerridwen paused in her reply, tentatively wiping at the blood trickling down from her mouth.

'Oh.' Cerridwen's eyes grew wide. She stared at the spear protruding from her chest in disbelief. Her hands fluttered around the blood-stained tip, as if she was thinking about pushing it back out. 'Benjamin?' The Guardian of Annwn stumbled forward, collapsing into Ben's arms, revealing a stony-faced Barqan behind her.

'No!' Ben fired a death spell at Barqan with shaking hands. The shot went wide but it made for a convenient distraction. He slipped Cerri's talisman of a bow with three arrows from her wrist, into his pocket, without pausing to feel like a grave-robber.

'You cannot outrun this, Benjamin.' Barqan watched Ben's attempt to stop the bleeding with a bored expression. 'Still, you have to admire the poetry of the situation. You brought yourself a handful of extra hours only to perish in Annwn with your own kind.' Ben was half-listening to Barqan. In his arms, Cerridwen's eyes shut and she ceased to be. He bowed his head, silently apologising to Cerridwen as he laid her on the ground.

'Your vampire is without a home, too. Erebus is gone.'

'Jack's home is with me, in Gaia.'

'Is that so? Are you sure he'll still be there when you return? You left your post, Guardian.'

Ben tore an angry arc in the air, squeezing himself into the portal, long legs first, before it had fully opened. Ambrosius made sure to seal it as soon as they were in.

'Mórrígan arrived as we left.' Ambrosius bristled. *'Did you feel Merlin's magic? Ben?'*

'Yes. It's the talismans she's already stolen.'

'Or she has the shield.' Ambrosius was angry, determined to retrieve what was rightfully theirs.

'We'll get it back.'

Annwn was being consumed by flames and no one was going to stop it. Behind them, a third light blinked out, leaving another black smudge. Ben screamed into the void, hearing nothing in reply.

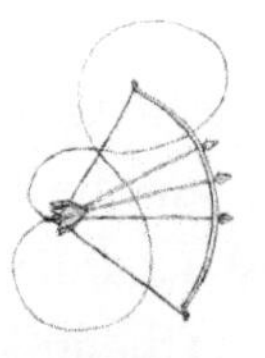

12

Right There With You / It Suits You

Oxford

'Ben!' Jack sounded frantic. 'Let go!'

'What's burning?' Ben's thoughts were scattering left and right.

'You! What are you holding?'

Smoke curled its way past Ben's nose, and he followed it down to see it climbing out of the gaps between his fingers, like a row of chimneys. 'Oh.' Ben let Jack pull his hand this way and that, not too sure what Jack wanted. 'This should be hurting.'

'Ya think?' Jack's fingers wriggled underneath Ben's. 'What is it?'

'Cerridwen's talisman.' Ben said numbly, seeing the spear tear its way through her chest. 'I couldn't help. I couldn't … ah!' Searing pain exploded into his consciousness, dropping him to the floor and jolting him back into the moment.

It overrode his grip on the talisman, letting Jack see the offending object. 'It's consecrated iron. For the love of the Gods, give it to me!' Jack snatched the bracelet before he lost the chance.

Free of the burden, Ben cradled his burnt hand, watching Jack inspect the miniature bow and arrows.

'There was nothing to be done. Barqan killed Cerridwen.' The news stilled Jack's fussing.

'Does that mean …?' April asked, wringing her hands. Ben nodded, slumping under the weight of what had happened. 'Oh. Um, sorry.'

'Are you hurt?' Jack asked.

'Besides a sore hand, I'm fine. Which is more than I can say for Annwn. And Cerri.' Ben scrubbed at his eyes, trying to erase the image of her dying. 'Mórrígan was there. Ambrosius thinks that Mórrígan has the shield.'

'That can't be. Did you actually see it?' Jack turned away, setting Cerridwen's talisman down, breathing quickly.

'No.' Ben could feel Jack's nerves from the floor. 'Merlin's magic connected with Ambrosius.' Jack looked to be on the verge of pacing. 'Why are you questioning this?'

'Because Mórrígan doesn't have it!' Jack blurted out, his voice rising. 'It's where it's always been.'

'What do you mean?' Ben asked carefully. Instead of answering, Jack took a deep breath and closed his eyes. Ben sat up, waiting. When Jack opened his eyes, the usual playful light was dulled by an earnest and strangely apologetic look.

'Whoever has it, has used an impressive masking spell to hide it.'

'What are you suggesting?' Beneath Ben's top, the sword was heating up. Not wanting to be burned by his own talisman, he pulled it off, letting it hang over his knee. The pendant swung back and forth in the air, counting the beats of the pregnant pause.

'The colour of the magic?' Jack hesitated, apparently needing permission to continue. Ben nodded once, tension making his jaw ache.

'Even with fortification from Guardians, Merlin's magic would have burned out a decade after his death.' Jack faltered under Ben's heavy stare but pushed through his reservations. 'The magic shouldn't have been aquamarine. Not if Merlin was …'

'What, Jack?' Ben's voice was low, dangerous.

'The magic in the talisman hasn't faded; if anything, it's as powerful as the day it was created.' Jack's eyes locked onto Ben's. 'It's not responded to you because …'

'Jack.' Ben warned, hoping to scare Jack away from his preposterous theory. April's head swivelled between the two.

'You're going to make me say it?' Jack snapped, his words an invitation to bicker.

'If you don't want to say it then keep it to yourself,' Ben cautioned, his tone a little harsher. 'What do you want me to say, Jack? That Merlin isn't dead? That he committed the medieval equivalent of popping out for cigarettes?'

'Ben.' Jack bent to help him, but Ben pushed himself up and out of Jack's reach. The vampire had started this fight, he could finish it. 'You've thought about it – you said so yourself.'

'Death is the right answer. Ambrosius sensed the moment that Merlin's magic perished.' Ben's stomach lurched, his mouth dryer than a desert. 'I have had multiple lifetimes in which to consider …'

'You didn't see Merlin die!' Jack tried to grab Ben by the shoulders.

'No, get off.' Ben didn't want anybody around him. 'I saw the body!' Ben couldn't think, couldn't hear over the static. 'Let go!' Ben pushed Jack; the vampire crashed into the coffee table, the elderly oak groaned and collapsed into a pile of splinters.

'Jack!' Shocked, April rushed to help him up. 'You're bleeding.' Jack sat up, his hand covering a cut on his arm. 'This. This is why a vampire shouldn't have wooden furniture.'

The anger drained from Ben. He fumbled behind him until he was sure there was enough sofa to catch him.

'I'm sorry, Jack. It's …' Ben couldn't look at Jack. He'd promised himself that he'd never lose his temper with a partner like that, like Arthur had on occasion.

'I'm alright.' Jack didn't look away from Ben.

'It's a lot. To hear it from you.' Ben couldn't accept that his never-ending sadness was the product of lies told – no matter how well intentioned – by the only person with the foresight to prevent the worst from happening. 'Do you know why I know Merlin is dead?' Jack shook his head, afraid to speak. 'Merlin loved to meddle in the affairs of those around him.' Jack opened his mouth but thought better of it. 'Merlin wouldn't have lasted this long without meddling in mine.'

And now they dangled over the edge with a frayed rope made of the past.

Jack watched the paranoia work its way under Ben's skin with a conflicting sense of dread and relief. Doubt was ripping down the smokescreens built from half-truths and outright lies. This anger and torment – it wasn't Ben. It was all the years of carrying Merlin's responsibilities around.

'Why won't you talk about this? It's so glaringly obvious, Ben!' Jack failed to mask the ancient frustration. He'd come close to having this fight so often. He'd even rehearsed it in his head, but he couldn't remember any of his carefully considered lines.

'I have no more answers than you do!' Ben shouted, his eyes wide. Jack noticed April flinching away but he didn't move to reassure her. This felt like progress and if Jack looked away now, he'd bottle it. Bringing all of this up because somebody's world had actually ended – not his best decision.

'Magic is fickle. It's a law unto itself and Merlin disappears – it's what he does. You told me that!'

'Merlin is dead!'

The next sentence that elbowed its way into the conversation didn't care what it broke. 'Perhaps Merlin's magic survived his death. Perhaps Merlin survived his death. Perhaps it was a show for you.'

Ben's face emptied, leaving behind the ghost of his angered expression. With so little effort, Ben's suspicion was finally free to reignite the flames that had taken years to reduce to embers.

'Ben …' Jack's sorrowful voice cautiously crept into the suffocating silence. 'I didn't mean to say it like that.' He wanted desperately to say something to cover up the glaring hole he'd uncovered, but nothing would fit. 'You deserve to know the truth.'

'All spells disappear with the death of the caster.' Ben insisted, but with less certainty than before. Why are you bringing this up now?'

'It's been relentlessly pecking at the back of my mind for ... forever actually.' Jack tried to catch Ben's eye, but the shtriga wouldn't look at him. 'I think it's all connected, somehow. If Merlin's alive. I'll bet anything that he's the solution.' Ben clenched his fists. 'The shield was never lost. It was never parted from its Guardian.'

'Let's say that you're right.' Propelled by his restlessness, Ben paced. 'If Merlin is,' Ben struggled with the next word, 'alive, he would have reached out to me. He wouldn't just leave. Would he?'

The question left a horrible metallic taste in Ben's mouth.

'Maybe,' Jack softened a little, 'he had to leave to keep you safe ...'

'Or Fate trapped him and gave Mórrígan the shield ...'

'Clutching at straws, much?' April's question cut through the fog. 'Merlin could have returned willingly.'

Horror rooted Ben to the floor. 'The ramifications – I can't face Merlin across a battlefield.' Nor could he tolerate the idea that Merlin had left him to this life.

'There are a million scenarios,' Jack cut in. 'Alive or dead, surely it's better to know for certain.' He offered Ben a scroll. 'Let's draw a line under any and all suspicions.'

'How?' Ben's eyes darted from the scroll to Jack's unwavering gaze. 'You would have me perform a summoning spell?'

Jack nodded, nudging Ben's clenched fist with the rough parchment. Sufficiently annoyed, Ben clumsily snatched the battered parchment. 'I've probably already tried the spell.'

He unrolled the scroll and the bottom fell out of his world. Familiar spider-like writing stared up at him.

'What's wrong?' April asked.

'Merlin wrote this. The spell crosses the veils, simultaneously able to summon the living and the dead.' Ben couldn't tear his eyes away from it. Excitement sent him pacing again. 'It could work! This could work!'

'What happens if Ben's right and Merlin's, you know, dead?' April's practical question brought Ben's anxious excitement crashing to the ground.

'We'll either get a ghost or a living, breathing warlock.' Ben studied the earnest look on his vampire's face and knew, without doubt, Jack was convinced that, somewhere out there, Merlin was waiting to be found.

'The bastard,' Ben muttered. 'He knew I'd need this spell. There's no other reason for him writing it down.'

'Correct me if I'm wrong, but that's Merlin's deal.' Jack tensed, knowing that he was swimming in dangerous waters. 'Merlin has all the pieces but drops you blindly into situations. Take the night he gave you the talisman.'

'Merlin knew I'd keep Gaia safe. The intention wasn't for me to become the permanent Guardian.' Even in death, Merlin had managed to make him question his own wisdom. Ben should hate him for that alone.

'Right.' Jack fished a dog-eared book from where it sat, forgotten on the arm of the sofa, and tossed it at Ben. 'Maybe he's had to wait.'

'*The Once and Future King*.' Ben pulled a face. 'Why do you waste your time with such nonsense?'

'Maybe it wasn't Arthur who's meant to be coming back. Maybe it's Merlin!'

'Don't be ridiculous! It's a myth. Nobody is riding to our rescue.' A hollow sadness coloured his voice a dark shade of bitter. 'Don't fall for the propaganda.' But Ben quietly allowed a flicker of hope to spark.

'Souls don't just disappear. Unless you've eaten them.' Ben scowled at Jack. 'My point is, you searched the under realms extensively.'

'Charon, Styx's Guardian, hasn't seen Merlin pass through Hades.'

'So, what about the spell?' Jack asked tentatively. 'Will you try it?' There would be no peace for Ben, not until he'd rid himself of the tiny speck of doubt lodged in his brain.

'I can hardly read it. Merlin's handwriting was awful.' Ben squinted at the page. 'It would take a considerable amount of dark magic to execute. I would have to cross the night plane.'

'That doesn't sound good.' April frowned, reading over Ben's shoulder.

'It's not ideal. Anything and everything in existence would have the opportunity of a lifetime to corrupt a Guardian.' Ben shivered, the potential damage he could cause by opening himself up to dark magic … 'Have you ever known me to use such magic?'

'It's one spell. I hardly think you'll go all dark side on us.'

'Can't you use, like, non-dark magic?' April naively asked.

'White magic draws on nature for its power. Death is natural and thus can't be reversed by white magic.' Ben shook his head. 'It requires a life to replace the one returned. Dark magic bypasses the exchange of life.'

'I'm not gonna lie, the black magic option sounds better.' April pulled a cushion towards her and hugged it tightly. 'What are you worried about?'

'Nobody comes back the same.' Ben set the scroll aside. 'You can't live the same life twice. Death magic twists the negatives in your character.'

'Or,' Jack picked up the parchment, holding it out like it was a prize to be envied, 'we could try this nifty two-in-one spell. All we need is something that was Merlin's – the talisman should work ...'

'Jack ...'

'If Merlin's dead, you can ask what you want of his ghost. Hells, hit me if you like.' Ben raised his eyebrows. 'If Merlin's alive, you can hit him.'

An equally attractive offer. And Ben wanted answers. 'Do you have any idea how grumpy Merlin's going to be?'

'Come again?' April had been watching the volley between them closely.

'Merlin will be apocalyptically furious with us for dragging him back from wherever he went.' It had been an attempt at humour, but judging by Jack's uncertain smile, it fell flat.

'I spent years trying to find the summoning spell. At least give it a go.' Jack batted his eyelashes, so Ben took the parchment back reluctantly. Merlin had always warned him not to use dark magic. But Merlin wasn't here right now.

However Ben looked at the evidence, he couldn't escape the feeling that Merlin had been the architect of a long-running game, leaving a trail of breadcrumbs scattered throughout the centuries for Ben to follow. If Merlin was alive, he would be the true Guardian of the realm, regardless of who held the sword. It would explain why the talisman had never worked for Ben. He traced the letters, trying to place where or when Merlin became the darkness in his world. The words blurred into one as hot, frustrated tears littered his vision. Ben willed them not to fall. He tried to still shaking hands, exhausted from picking up and setting down the past. 'Ah!' he exclaimed, slapping the page and ignoring Jack's wince at the mistreatment of the elderly object.

'It's almost as old as you are, so be gentle with it.' Ben ignored the chiding, rereading the spell.

'We have to return to the place of death to complete the spell.'

Ben looked up to find that Jack had journeyed to the bookcase on the other side of the room. 'Wales.' He addressed the back of Jack's head. 'I am not going back there.'

'What did Wales do to you?' April asked. 'It seems a little drastic to swear off an entire country.' Jack choked back laughter and settled on the arm of the sofa.

'Don't they teach you kids about the Arthurian legends?'

'Maybe. To be fair, I didn't have much time for school.' April shrugged, looking awkwardly away, absent-mindedly touching her bokken, something that didn't go unnoticed by either shtriga or vampire.

'Wales, my uneducated human, is where our Lord Merlin supposedly met his demise.' Jack looked pointedly to Ben.

'It's where I left him. Nobody in their right mind would have taken him to Avalon.'

'Have you been to Avalon to check?' Both Ben and Jack turned to look at April in disbelief.

'Go to Avalon?' Jack laughed like it was the craziest thing he'd ever heard. 'None of us want to meet Fate any time soon. Trust me.'

'Merlin would not have remained there for long. Fate would have banished him within a week.' The smile on Ben's lips died quickly. 'I enquired, April. He was never there.'

'Ok, and you don't want to go to Wales because ...?'

Ben groaned internally. There was nothing wrong with it as such. There were too many metaphorical ghosts. Ben's past was so present there, it was hard to tell the two apart.

'There was an incident.'

'Don't you dare Jack ...'

'Let's just say that it involved a sacred forest, fifty furious fairies, and a fire.'

'I can never return to that forest.'

'Yeah, because it burned to the ground!'

'Back up.' April leant forward. 'Tell me everything.'

Ben's only retort was to roll his eyes in exasperation. 'Can't you two find someone else to annoy?'

Jack threw up his hands in mock surrender, and stood, hinting at his departure. 'I need to meet Dirmynd, so ...'

'Isn't that where you'd been prior to arriving at my house?'

Jack gave up trying to work out what Ben was accusing him of. This always happened when the shtriga slipped off into his dark place. They butted heads and it bothered Jack that he couldn't break through the white noise. He only ever seemed to make things worse, no matter how much patience he showed when picking up the pieces. 'I had a feeling I'd be needing him again, so I text him.'

'I thought you would have sent a raven or something,' April chimed in, seeming to miss the tension that was wrapping itself around the couple.

'Why would we use ravens? We have technology.' Jack yanked his jacket out from behind April, earning him a scowl. 'Seriously, let go of the stereotypes.'

'Hey! Why don't you get me a wooden stake and a hammer and we'll test that stereotype?'

'Bite me, April.'

'What? You're the vampire. So, what do we do next?'

Ben inclined his head towards the parchment. 'How certain are you that this will work?'

Jack paused on his way to the door. He could blag it if he didn't look at Ben. 'Ninety percent.'

'I need more than ninety percent. I don't want to put myself through this again.'

'If you don't want to try summoning Merlin, I understand.' Jack slowly pulled his jacket on. 'Others will have put two and two together. It's only a matter of time before somebody tries to summon him. Better you find him than Mórrígan's hench-monkeys.' Ben's restless thoughts pulled him up from the sofa and deposited him against the mantlepiece. Leaning awkwardly against it, he tried to calm the raging storm inside his head. Jack let go of the door handle with a sigh.

'I can't fail Merlin again. Or for the first time, depending on your perspective.' Jack shrugged out of his jacket. If he could rearrange the past, put Merlin and Ben on opposite paths, he would have done so in a heartbeat to avoid having this conversation.

'You're duty-bound to find the second Guardian. Plus, I can't think of a better defence against Fate and War, can you?' Guardians were often the subject of such gloomy prophecies and messy endings. A prospect worse than any awkward conversation.

'When you put it like that, no.' Ben dragged his gaze from the hearth to look at Jack. There was a hint of worry in his voice that Jack could understand but at the same time, couldn't. If he was Ben, he'd be nothing but angry right now. And he'd have cast the spell already.

'What scares you more? Looking Merlin in the eye and being confronted with your imagined shortcomings, or the small chance that I'm wrong?' Ben had a way of letting himself be plagued by outcomes beyond his control. 'Whichever it is, you don't have to face Merlin alone.' And Jack meant that with all his heart.

Ben tried and failed to reply. He couldn't articulate how badly he wanted to know the truth but the closer he got, the more it terrified him. What if the Gods' honest truth chipped away too much of his history? What if Ben didn't like what was left? He'd outgrown devastation. He could even manage the sadness most days. Hells, Ben had thought that he'd memorised the worst-case scenario, but it kept reinventing itself.

'The only way to solve this is to raise the dead.'

'Are you sure? No, wait. I don't want you to change your mind.' Jack rushed over to plant a kiss on Ben's cheek. 'I have to go.'

'Are you going to be on time for something for once?' Returning to his spot on the sofa, Ben forced himself to sound brighter than he actually felt.

Jack spun to look at him, a hand on his chest and a faked hurt expression on his face. 'What are you suggesting? My timekeeping is exceptional.'

'It never has been and it never will be, love.' Fondness filled Ben's entire being. 'I'll need to get some bits for the spell.'

'Great.'

'I can get what I need whilst you're conducting your meeting.' Ben wanted to stay close to Jack. He'd never met Dirmynd, but he had a sense that the man wasn't to be trusted.

'Alright, but hurry up!' Jack called through the open door, having already made it to the stairwell.

'Are you guys good? It got a bit heated there,' April asked.

'Fine. I got a bit caught up in it all, you know? It's difficult to have your life story torn apart and questioned. It won't happen again.' And Ben meant that with all his heart.

April nodded. 'Are we going to Wales or not? I lost track of who won.'

Ben chuckled and hoisted a backpack onto his shoulder.

'Jack won. He usually does. Come on, we'd best catch him up or he'll leave without us.'

1st November 2023

Merlin,

We need to talk.

I sense you rolling your eyes. I'm not being dramatic. I have questions and it's high time you answered them. We always avoided awkward conversations. But we're having this one.

Your handwriting looks like a drunken spider crawled across the page on its way home. Grabbing onto the bottom of s's and snagging on r's as it trips over its own feet, dragging the letters down with it. Seeing a spell ensnared in your untidy hand ... But here's the rub: Jack – you'll laugh – thinks you faked your death. Arthur's too. And then you vanished somewhere over the rainbow.

Doubt. It's been there all along, underlining everything, criss-crossing my mind, cutting fault lines into fact and carving out foundations for lies. I didn't want to think you capable of something so heinous. So, I filled in the gaps with a story most likely written by you. And I looked for the things I wanted to see.

I find myself reimagining over a thousand years. You are alive, but absent. The world doesn't look at all different. It feels incredibly empty. In this alternate reality, you – my best friend – stood by whilst I was captured and changed. And, to cap it off, you abandoned me! Jack's blatant dislike for you is warranted.

Why Merlin?

You wielded words better than any knight commanded a sword, and you said nothing. Perhaps for one reason or another, you couldn't tell me where you were going. But you could have said goodbye – properly, and with an apology! If you have been out there all these years, I hope for your sake that you are dead.

Should you be alive, there is a storage locker and a house full of letters for you. You will read them all. It's the least you can do. Whilst you read the one, two, sometimes five-page tragedies, I'd like you to think long and hard about your answers to my many questions.

And here's one more: did you ever consider the magnitude of the suffering you caused?

I've changed my mind about the rub.

In my letters, I asked you for forgiveness, for what Jack refers to as my imagined sins. It's you who needs to seek my forgiveness.

I pray you found some trouble that got the better of you. Perhaps somebody with more sense than I banished you to a place not even you know how to return from.

I can forgive those things.

For my own sanity, I must know. So I can put you from my mind, forever.

Ben.

13

Bustin' Makes Me Feel Good

The rain threw itself at the car window, ushering out the golden calm of October.

November arrived, bringing with it the promise of a long, grey month.

Things weren't any brighter inside the car, either. April shivered.

'We have two talismans and a summoning spell.' Ben's words dragged themselves along, his voice hoarse. 'Not exactly a plan, is it?'

'What's that? Thanks for finding a spell that will bring back your best friend? You're welcome, Ben. It only took thirty years, but it's no bother.'

April caught the roll of Jack's eyes in the rear-view mirror. She felt sorry for Ben, and whilst she was inclined to believe his version of events, Jack's point had merit also. It seemed a little far-fetched that Merlin had faked his death, no matter how terrible he was at goodbyes.

'Do you have a backup plan? In case Ben's right.' Because it felt like Jack had thrown all of his eggs into the Merlin-is-alive-basket.

'Find the shield. Get the pair to work properly.'

'Why do you want to find Merlin so much?' Ben's eyes were glued to the parchment. The tick-tock of the car's indicator sprang back and forth, counting the pause between question and answer.

'I've been thinking about Fate and destiny.' Jack's hands shuffled on the wheel, like he was trying to cover something up.

'You can't fight destiny,' Ben shrugged, 'regardless of how determined you are to change it.' Jack's hands tightened their grip and April understood: Merlin was Jack's only solution, his best hope of saving Ben from his fate.

'Surely you've memorised the spell by now?' Jack shot his partner a sceptical look, trying to change the subject without changing the subject.

'There can be no hesitation, no fumbling of words. I must be certain of the spell. I prefer to be off-book.' Ben's hands grew restless at the possibility of casting, his unease an ever-growing pit at the core of his being, threating to consume him.

Ambrosius was pacing in tight circles. '*There's so much that could go wrong, Ben, and that's before we find out if Merlin is, in fact, alive.*' Ambrosius continued to pace, trampling over Ben's concentration, causing the words to jump on the page. Ben rolled the parchment back up, unable to miss Jack's sigh of relief.

'It's not so impossible.'

'What?'

'To imagine Merlin hanging around for centuries like a useless fairy godmother.' Ben's heart swung back and forth from wanting to know the truth, and throwing the talisman out of the window. His replacement would do a better job, he was sure. But that was Jack's point – Ben was coping but he wasn't succeeding. In hindsight, promising Merlin that he'd not forsake his duty had been a monumentally stupid thing to do.

'A large amount of magic, a few sentences, and a great deal of risk and you'll have the truth of it.' Ambrosius retreated to worry in a corner. Out loud, Ben said, 'We don't know what nest of vipers we'd disturb by bringing Merlin back. In my experience, what's dead should stay dead.' For a moment, Ben actually considered going against his sound advice. He was already dabbling in death magic. It wasn't that much further to go.

'Wait, resurrection isn't part of the plan.' Jack pulled the car over in a side street near the park. 'Where did you get that from?' He pulled the handbrake on, reaching for the document with his spare hand.

'The last three paragraphs are dedicated to it. This is what you intended, right?'

'Let me see!' Forgetting his earlier plea of care, Jack snatched the parchment. 'No, I say no to the resurrection.'

'But calling up his ghost is alright? That's the hill you're choosing to die on?'

'I'm not facilitating a resurrection. We want to know if Merlin's alive. I have a couple of things to say to his ghost.'

Ben wasn't sure if it was the unrecognisable harshness in Jack's voice, or the casual snarky remark, that had his back up. 'Everything's so black and white to you, Jack. You're too young to understand the way the world was. Merlin was preserving his realm. If I was a casualty, so be it.' Ben had been telling himself that for years, eventually he'd stop questioning it.

'We're not returning anybody to life.'

'It's not Merlin you're worried about, is it?' Jack stared back with big, hurt eyes. 'I'm not sure I could manage it anyway.' Ben wanted to let his accusation fly, but he plucked the parchment from Jack, thus ending the discussion.

'What good is a ghost to you?' April poked her head through the middle of the seats.

Ben glanced at Jack's hard face. The only good kind of ghost was an exorcised one.

'I wish you'd let me meet Dirmynd.' April had been petitioning Jack for the entire journey.

'Why?' he swivelled to look at her.

'I want to meet the person whose parents hated him enough to call him Dirmynd. It sounds like a noise of disgust.'

'And that's exactly why you're not coming.'

'Only weirdos loiter in the park after dark.' Jack pushed April into her seat. She bounced back and jabbed Ben in his collar bone.

Ben turned to give her his attention. 'Yes, April?'

'Can a talisman kill? It's so tiny.'

'Yes.' Ben gripped the sword. The need to protect his talisman had him opening the car door.

'Easy, Ben.' Jack leant across, shut the door and eyed him with concern. 'April's asking a question, not trying to steal it.'

With a deep breath, Ben forced his hand back down to his lap. April wasn't the first to show interest. Nor was she the first to look at it as if she wanted to throw it into the river. Jack would tackle her for the honour. 'You tie it to a weapon, transforming it into a blade that kills everything.'

'Huh.' April sat back in her seat, puzzling it over, Ben tucked the talisman safely away under his top.

'Hang on, why did you make me attack Barqan with salt if you could have done it with the sword?'

'It stubbornly refused to work. In theory, it should have worked because I was being threatened,' Ben said with a laugh. 'That wasn't the time to test a theory.'

'You could have tried it first, and kept me as the backup plan!' April spluttered, outraged at having almost been sacrificed. Ben shrugged, giving her a coy smile. 'Alright.' April shook her head. 'Riddle me this, why can't Fate see a Guardian's death?'

'It's a good question.' Jack nudged Ben's knee, his fingers toying with the door handle. Ben's reservations invited themselves back to the stage. They weighed heavy on his tongue but he swallowed them whole.

'It was one of Merlin's clauses. Knowledge is power. Merlin preferred to keep Fate in the dark.'

'Is that why he never told you how the world ends?'

'I don't know, April. Merlin claimed it wouldn't be my concern.'

'What does that mean?' Jack asked bluntly.

'Either I can't stop it. Or I die before the end. I never asked.'

'We'll come back to your lack of curiosity later. What did Merlin do?'

'He used a binding spell that prevented Fate from cutting the threads of Guardians. Nor can she write the stories of future Guardians.'

'What happens if a Guardian dies?' April asked, eyes glued to her phone.

'Merlin selected replacements.'

April's fingers paused in their dance across the screen. She felt something dark clinging to Ben's words. 'Like you?'

'Yes, I suppose so,' Ben pre-empted the next question, 'and if the backup Guardian dies, Merlin tasked Freyja with selecting new candidates.'

'Merlin certainly was a busy bee,' Jack said in a measured voice.

'Merlin did what was required to ensure the safety of the realms.' Ben fired back the worn-out line.

'I wonder if he foresaw Barqan's deceit? Was he happy to put you in a position where you might have to kill another Guardian?' Ben tried to slow his anger.

'If that's what is required, that's what I will do. Merlin was a prophet. The prophesies were not his creation!'

'Unbelievable,' Jack said under his breath, his gaze fixed straight ahead. Ben suspected he wasn't meant to hear it.

'Shouldn't you be going? You were in a rush to get here …'

'I suppose so.' Jack glanced at his phone. 'I'll not be long.' Ben's hand darted out and grabbed Jack's wrist, pulling him back into the car. 'What?'

'Can Dirmynd be trusted?' Ben tried not to sound like he worried about the company Jack kept.

'He's not steered me wrong yet.' Jack smiled his biggest, brightest smile. No doubt it was designed to reassure Ben but he preferred to cling to his concern all the same. 'He's a little odd. Like most people in his line of work. A tad eccentric.'

'Fine.' Ben listened to everything Jack said, and everything he didn't, and he found cause for concern in the gaps between words.

'You're the best.' Jack leant over to plant a kiss on Ben's cheek before disappearing into the park, leaving Ben alone with April and his thoughts.

'So?'

Ben braced himself. Of course, April wouldn't leave him be. Since the arrival of the summoning spell, Ben had wanted nothing more than to quietly work through it. 'You have to sleep at some point, right?'

'I'm an insomniac.' Without much grace, and zero elegance, April clambered through the gap in the seats, falling head first into the driver's seat. 'Today's been pretty rubbish. Or are you two *that* couple? It's ok if you are. Everybody has at least one set of *dramatic couple* friends.'

'We're not ...' Jack certainly had his moments. 'It's ...' Ben's distress threatened to slingshot him off into the unknown. Ben couldn't quite explain his feelings to himself, let alone articulate it to April. 'Jack's so quick to disregard my version of events.' Sadness had scooped his heart out, betrayal had hollowed him completely and anger had driven him with no visible horizon. He'd been this way since Arthur's passing. A matryoshka doll of depression. Ben worried at a stubborn hangnail.

'Jack could have handled it better.' April jangled the keyrings dangling from the ignition. Nestled amongst a miniature guitar, a snowboard and a Lego figure from their trip to Legoland, was a Welsh dragon. 'Judging by this little guy, Jack isn't wholly dismissive of your past.'

'Jack would prefer it if I didn't have a past at all,' Ben muttered darkly, scanning the entrance to the park for his vampire.

'I think that's pretty standard. I mean, I was never thrilled to hear about Danny's exes.'

Intrigue pulled Ben from his dark thoughts. April groaned, eyes wide. 'And who is Danny?'

'No one,' April replied quickly. Ben held onto the silence a little longer. 'Fine! He was someone, and now he's gone.'

Ah. Ben knew the sound of lost love when he heard it. Best leave it there; no sense in both of them having their traumas dragged kicking and screaming into the light. Danny could wait.

'My mind won't stop conjuring up "what-if" scenarios. I keep thinking ... perhaps I missed something. Merlin hasn't been a very good friend, has he?'

'Not to take sides, but from what I've heard, no, he hasn't.'

'Yeah. I thought not.'

'Have you thought about what you'll say to him if he appears?'

Ben hadn't thought of anything else. 'If the spell produces a living Merlin ...' Ben's fists would probably speak first. 'Nothing adventurous. Probably ask him where he's been. I imagine you won't be able to hear me over the sound of Merlin judging me.'

'Right, your wayward years as a newbie shtriga.' April rolled her eyes. 'They weren't your responsibilities to run away from. They were Merlin's.' Ben nodded in agreement. 'Let me ask you this – what scares you most?'

'An empty circle. To know, unequivocally, that Merlin's thread has been severed.'

'Yeah, that sounds rather final.' April grimaced.

It was times like these that Ben wished for sleep. To be able to retreat under the covers and hide behind closed eyelids. He'd likely waste the gift by being a quivering wreck in his dreams. On some days the simplest thing, no matter how big or small, threatened to shatter him. Today was one of those days. Beside him, April was rummaging around in her pockets, but Ben didn't bother to ask her what she'd lost. She was stalling whilst she thought of what to say next. 'This is a weird situation, I appreciate that. You can leave if you want. We won't judge you.'

'I thought you needed my help?' April fired back with a confidence she likely didn't feel.

'We do. But I don't need your death on my conscience.'

'I'm a hunter, Ben,' April pointed out reasonably. 'I'll get caught up in this sooner or later. And I hear the end of the world is best enjoyed with friends. Besides, it might even be a laugh.'

Ben groaned softly. 'You're gonna get yourself killed, kid.'

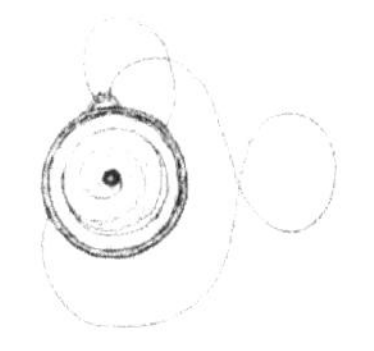

14

Stranger in Town

Twilight stretched and yawned as it prepared to give way to night.

The clumsy clinking of metal on metal came from inside the cricket pavilion.

From the steps, Jack stared hard into the inky blackness of the empty hall.

Nobody sat at the trestle tables that ran the length of the wood-panelled room with its arches. The door slowly creaked open despite it staying firmly shut.

'Glass is transparent.' A resounding silence came back to Jack. He turned back to the park and leant against one of the latticed beams. 'Not like you to be shy.'

'Hmph!' The disgruntled sound, muffled by wood and glass, brought a smile to Jack's face. 'I suppose you want me to leave, do you?' Through the door, the figure of a wizened man materialised. He did not look pleased.

'Aye. Tonight is one of those nights, Tobias.'

Jack smiled and pushed off from the beam. A huge chain of keys dangled from Tobias's belt like a rusted windchime. 'Those keys make it sound like you're being chased by Marley's chains.'

'This is my place, not yours,' the older man wheezed.

'And I apologise for the inconvenience of having to send you away for a few hours.' Jack bowed his head slightly.

'Doubt a ghost would bother this fellow. Seems he's seen much of the world,' Tobias grumbled. 'I won't cause him any trouble.'

'Better safe than sorry.' Jack flashed the ghost a cheeky smile.

'How much more can one person tell you, Jack?'

'I'm not sure, but he's consistently right.' Jack laced his hands behind his back. 'And late.'

With a final huff, the park keeper shuffled past, the rhythmic jangling of keys playing him out.

Not seeing anybody, Jack called out, 'Because I love waiting in the lengthening shadows like a stereotype.'

April had caused the first delay. The "cat-astrophe" as Jack had named it, had taken up more time that it should have. Jack's suggestion that the cat would be fine on its own for an indeterminate amount of time wasn't received well.

A lightning bolt of memory illuminated the fact that human-Jack had been deathly allergic to cats. 'That explains why I don't like 'em.'

Jack wished he could recall more of these little nuggets of his former life. Each new fact was another peg in the ground, but the recollections were so few and far between. He wasn't entirely sure that his name was "Jack"; it had been the only name he could think of. Identity crisis and historical allergy aside, Jack didn't want a cat trapped in his car for hours.

The ease with which April had tied up her loose ends amazed Jack. All too often it felt to him and Ben like they were passing through city after city, never forming any firm ties. Nowhere felt like home, unless the other one was there.

'Whoever robbed you had plenty of time to do it,' Jack had remarked upon entering April's dilapidated flat with its makeshift furniture, scattered piles of books and the occasional photo. There were no clues about the occupant. In fact, the cat had more stuff than April did. 'Is this your cat's flat? Because it looks like you rent a room here during the week.'

'Don't you like cats, Jack?' April had tried not to laugh as the feline made a beeline for him.

'More of a dog person.' Jack had attempted to discreetly move away from said cat as it gleefully rubbed up against his legs, purring unnecessarily loudly. 'Do you have a lint roller?'

A sharp meow had Jack spinning back to reality and back on himself. Less than a foot away from him sat a black cat with piercing eyes.

'Are you meant to be good or bad luck? I forget.' The intensity of the cat's stare was loaded with human intelligence. Against his better judgement, Jack crouched down. 'Hmm, you're either a shapeshifter, a witch's familiar, or a walker.' Each one of the options was worse than an ordinary cat. As clichéd as it was, the fact that it was a black cat with pitch-black eyes had Jack routing for options two and three.

'Whichever you are, you're here to scope me out, aren't you?' The cat cocked its head to one side, studying him with bored disdain. Jack rocked back onto his heels. 'Ben would recognise you. My guess? Walker. Meow once for yes, twice for no.' The cat continued its silent and unnerving judgement. 'Suit yourself.' Jack hadn't met somebody with enough natural magic to transfer their consciousness into another living being before and he didn't want to. If they had that much power to wield, they weren't far off the Gods. Jack had sensed magic on Dirmynd, concealed, but there, so he couldn't rule Dirmynd out. The cat had the same eye colour, after all. With a stern meow, the cat slinked gracefully into the bushes. Jack caught one last glimpse of those cold, pitch-black eyes before they too vanished from sight.

'It could have been a normal cat,' he reasoned with himself. 'One that enjoys staring into the depths of peoples' souls.' A perfectly content stone sat close to Jack's right foot – until he booted it in annoyance. Paranoia was contagious. There were villains lurking at the edges of Jack's vision, all because of Ben. It wasn't helped by the fact that Dirmynd made his skin crawl because the man always felt half-familiar. Like a persistent itch Jack couldn't scratch. Perhaps they'd crossed paths in another life. Ask no questions; hear no lies. That was Jack's motto.

'There's nobody but me present, Dirmynd. You can come out now. Some of us have places to be.' Jack stretched out the last few words so they filled the air around him. 'You're a quarter of an hour late!'

Nobody answered, not even a cat.

Resigned to further waiting, Jack sat on the pavilion steps. With nothing else to occupy his mind, it turned unbidden towards Merlin, an uncertain force lurking in the centre of the confusing collage of unfortunate events. Jack couldn't find an angle from which Merlin's disseverance from the realm made sense. He couldn't work out if time had blinded Ben to the truth, or if the delusion was intentional. Merlin had used Ben and now Jack wanted to use Merlin to free Ben of his responsibilities. It was desperate, but when it came to Ben, he'd do whatever he needed to do. But Jack was getting ahead of himself. First, they had to try the summoning spell, find the other talisman, save the world and try not to die.

A bony finger lightly tapped him on his shoulder. Jack's left hand closed on the wrist attached to the tapping finger, twisting the arm down and round as he spun. Jack uncurled his fingers – he'd grabbed a handful of air and nothing else. He stared into the fading light, trying to make out a shape and felt the familiar weariness settle in. Every encounter with Dirmynd felt like an attack. In fact, fists had been thrown the first time they met.

'Hello, Dirmynd. Are you well? Didn't have you pegged as a cat person.' The space in front of Jack began to shimmer, etching out the outline of a small figure. It filled in to reveal Dirmynd, the man who had dropped himself in a heap on a barstool all those years ago. Jack had looked around at the otherwise empty pub, wondering why the stranger hadn't opted for some personal space. Jack had shrugged and turned back to his pint, only to be set upon thirty seconds later.

'Let's dispense with the small talk. What is it that you need now? Twice in one day is quite excessive.' Time hadn't gifted Dirmynd patience. Jack recalled the man being far more inclined to chat in the pub. Coincidently, it was the same pub where he'd met Ben.

'When we met, Dirmynd, you told me that you were a collector of stories and artefacts. You said, and I quote, "Mayhap I have what you need".'

'I remember you taking a swing at me.' Dirmynd's cackle of a laugh split his face into a rare, toothy grin. 'And I put you on your arse.'

'You need to go to a dentist.' Jack shuddered at the cigarette-stained teeth. 'And *you* started it!' Jack had tried to forget *that* embarrassing incident. The landlord, who had been conveniently absent, assumed Jack was drunk and cut him off. 'The only reason we still speak is because you claimed to know where the second talisman is. Well, we need it now. Alternatively, I will accept the second Guardian.' In the near-darkness, Jack noticed that Dirmynd's hair was more dishevelled than usual, his clothing all askew. Ask no questions, hear no lies.

'Even if I found it, you won't be able to use it – you're not a Guardian.'

'But Ben is.' Jack knocked Dirmynd's wagging finger out of his face, recoiling at the contact. 'If we have both parts, it should work.'

'That's your plan?' Dirmynd snorted. 'Sounds a bit wishy-washy.'

'I didn't say it was a good one. I wish Ben could appoint a second Guardian.'

'Well, Benjamin can't. He's not a God.' Dirmynd stepped closer, making Jack feel cornered, despite being in a park. 'What would you do with a second Guardian if you had one?' Dirmynd peered cautiously over Jack's shoulder.

Worried that Ben had doubled back, Jack glanced behind him and saw nothing but trees swaying gently in a light breeze. 'It's good to have a spare. I hear they're dropping like flies'

'So, you want a decoy Guardian to take the fall. Is that the measure of it?' Jack nodded, cursing Dirmynd for leaving him nowhere to go. Jack knew it was petty and selfish but there would be nothing left to fight for if Ben wasn't around. 'You'd condemn somebody else to save your friend?' Dirmynd scoffed. 'Fate has more power than Benjamin and both parts of the talisman put together. So, you need to be smarter than she is.'

'How? She knows where we're going before we've even decided.'

'She doesn't know the Guardian's path. She's oblivious to the events that deliver them to their final day. Split up if necessary.' Dirmynd's all-seeing eyes bored into Jack's, sending a shiver down his spine. 'What's bothering you, Jack?' The lilt of Dirmynd's voice triggered an overwhelming sense of déja vu that made no sense but scrambled Jack's thoughts all the same. 'Is it the reality that Benjamin's destiny might not align with your desire for a happily-ever-after? Or is it something else?' Electricity flew through Jack; he couldn't breathe and he was much too warm. Fear pried Jack's resolve out of his grip and he crumbled inside.

'Something you mentioned months ago. It's been going round and round in my head until I think that your thoughts are my own.'

'If a notion of mine has got under your skin, it is because there was an opening for it to burrow into.' Dirmynd snuck another look over Jack's shoulder.

'Precisely my point. I've allowed my paranoia to make something out of nothing.' A gust of biting wind blew through the park, leaves trailing in its wake. Jack turned his face into the wind, but the cold didn't soothe his suspicion. Dirmynd knew more than he was letting on.

'What was it I said?' Dirmynd's face folded up in thought.

'It was that prophecy of Merlin's.'

'Your interest in Merlin is bordering on obsession, but continue.'

'Merlin was right when he predicted that one of the Guardian's would go dark side.'

'Did you think he meant Benjamin?' Dirmynd's sharp laughter went straight through Jack, causing him to feel three feet tall. 'I highly doubt that Benjamin would eat himself out of house and home.'

Nervous laughter bubbled in Jack's throat. He was overthinking the Arthur prophecy, but he bottled his question.

'You shouldn't pay too much attention to the ramblings of a warlock. When he wrote those prophecies, Merlin was a madman living in the Caledonian Forest.' Dirmynd rolled his eyes, his head leaning to one side.

'Exactly!' Jack blurted out, distracted by his phone buzzing in his jacket pocket. 'I wouldn't have picked Ben for the job. He's wound tighter than a piano string, has a ton of baggage, powerful magic and an irregular feeding pattern.' Jack wasn't sure why he was trying to convince Dirmynd to demote Ben. It wasn't like he could do anything about it. 'Ben hasn't fed in a long time. You know how it is when we abstain; we're one light tremor away from crashing to the ground.' A small pothole would be enough to do it.

'Benjamin has lived as he is for longer than you have.' Dirmynd shifted from foot to foot. 'Presumably, Merlin saw traits he admired in Benjamin.'

'We're going to try the spell.' Duller eyes would have missed the twitch of Dirmynd's hands. His restlessness evaporated, his face an unreadable slab of marble whilst Dirmynd's pitch-black eyes held Jack in place.

'Might I enquire as to who you are attempting to summon?' Dirmynd kept his voice cool and idle, faking nonchalance, but Jack had the scent now.

'Merlin.' The word stuck to the roof of Jack's mouth like ashes.

'Your second Guardian, I presume? Why not pick somebody who is alive?' Dirmynd's all-knowing smirk pushed Jack a little further than he'd wanted to go.

'You're right, Dirmynd. Ben's magic is no match for Fate's, but Merlin's is.' He stepped over his reservations and advanced on Dirmynd, eager for the truth. 'Merlin knows Fate better than anyone. See, I can be smart and play games like you, Dirmynd.'

'What makes you so sure that Merlin wouldn't return to Fate?' Dirmynd smiled smugly and pushed Jack back. 'Have you thought of that, lad?'

'Aye. I'm banking on the fact that somewhere out there, Merlin is waiting to be called back to serve his realm once more.' Dirmynd's silence told Jack exactly what he thought. 'Like I said, it's not a good plan.'

'Have you considered the consequences?'

Jack's irritation burned hot in the back of his throat. 'Ben will be upset but we can work through that. In the end, he'll be glad to have Merlin back.'

Dirmynd snorted at Jack's ignorance. 'That's a rather naive view for somebody who knows what's hiding in the shadows. If something is dead, it should stay dead. Be careful, lad. You are playing with dark magic, and you are no warlock. You're casting a very wide net when you throw that spell.' Dirmynd's warning – and Ben's reluctance – should have been enough to dissuade Jack. But it wasn't.

'We're summoning Merlin. We'll get Merlin in one form or another.'

Dirmynd's body shook with laughter and disbelief. Jack didn't enjoy the sound. 'I'm not sure how your luck is, lad, but if Merlin appears, you're blessed. Did Benjamin not warn you of what's on the night plane?'

'He mentioned it.' Jack had downgraded the risk to "acceptable".

'If the wrong people happen to be listening when Benjamin casts, they will learn his location. Save yourself some time and send Fate an invitation instead.' Dirmynd cackled again.

Jack should have listened to Ben, that's what he was getting from Dirmynd's mocking. Ben was scared of finally getting what he wanted, that's what Jack had thought. But Ben's concerns had been legitimate. Shame sent Jack's gaze to the treetops. He was so concerned with trying to keep Benjamin out of harm's way that he was pushing his partner into the path of an oncoming train. 'Ben knows what he's doing.'

'I should hope so! Benjamin mustn't let his emotions get tangled up in the spell, or else he'll run into trouble. He feels things a little more sharply than the rest of us.' Dirmynd paused and caught Jack's gaze pointedly. 'I've heard some outrageously stupid ideas in my time, but this is the dumbest of them all.'

'You're always unequivocally right, aren't you, Dirmynd?' Jack raised his hands to prevent an answer. 'I want to know that you're true to our cause.' Jack only had enough hands to hold onto his concern for Ben and his suspicion that Dirmynd was looking for Merlin as well. But Jack felt like he'd missed something.

'Hmph!' Dirmynd spluttered. 'This is an outrage! I have forgotten more than you'll ever know, *lad*. Keep that in mind before you question my allegiance. If I thought this battle would go the other way, I wouldn't be wasting my time with you.' Dirmynd's gaze drifted again over Jack's shoulders.

'There's nobody there, Dirmynd.'

Dirmynd's amused eyes slid back to Jack. 'Cast the spell, lad. But don't come crying to me when you're unhappy with the outcome.'

'Why did you give it to me if … you know what? Never mind. Do you know where the shield is?' The mischievous glint in Dirmynd's eyes backed Jack up a step. Intuition fought to hold him in place. He spun back through the conversation, looking for what he might have missed. Ben was right, Jack watched too many conspiracy-theory and true-crime shows.

'I've not seen the shield for some time. Now,' Dirmynd looked to the sky in thought, distracted by recollection and clouds, 'where did I last see it?' he wondered as if it was a pair of glasses he'd misplaced. 'Oh, yes! Wales, that's where I saw it last.' Dirmynd giggled, struggling to keep a grin from his pointy face.

'Dirmynd.' Jack tried to sound threatening and not like he was freaking out. 'Narrow it down a bit.' Driving around

Wales until Ben's magic told them to stop sounded like it could take an eternity.

'You're leaving for Wales now, aren't you? Benjamin's with you?'

'Of course he is. Why do you ask?'

Dirmynd's demeanour changed to something altogether more sinister. 'His path is long and winding. Mayhap that road takes him home, or perhaps it takes him elsewhere.'

Somewhere in the back of Jack's mind, a dusty lightbulb spluttered and sparked into life. 'Have the two of you met before?'

'He is the Guardian of the Realm.' Dirmynd shrugged. 'Every supernatural creature knows him by name. In another life, another realm, another time, it's possible we met.'

Jack's stomach dropped. 'Where? When? If you and Ben have a past, I need to know. If he gets hurt because of you ...' Jack let the threat hang in the air, unspoken.

'Benjamin didn't deserve the horrors that befell him.' Dirmynd's tone softened which only served to convince Jack that he wasn't mad. 'A lesser mortal would have given in to the pull of his new instincts, left all alone as Benjamin was. But he fought against it with all of his might! He could have killed Arthur that day.' Jack's mouth dropped open, shock muting his voice. Meanwhile, Dirmynd straightened up, his voice shifting to something more nasal. 'Benjamin might need a moment to gather his thoughts on the matter, but I assure you that he will rise in defence of his realm. I'll be seeing you, Jack.'

'Wait ...'

Dirmynd vanished in front of his eyes.

'Warlocks!'

The lightbulb shattered with a flash of intense light, letting the nagging feeling of familiarity in via the front door, seamlessly fusing association with intuition.

Jack's gentle, disbelieving laugh rippled through the silence. He didn't consider himself to be dense, but Dirmynd had deceived him. How wonderfully ironic, that the thing they'd been searching for had been right under Jack's nose the entire time. How frustratingly sad that Jack hadn't seen it sooner.

Credit where credit was due, Merlin had done a terrific job of covering his tracks.

Because the second Guardian was still alive.

15

Captain, Captain

Merlin's house, Oxford

It didn't matter how long Merlin lived, he'd never tire of seeing the shock on people's faces when he "vanished into thin air".

And now, Merlin could drop all pretences.

There was no longer a need to hide behind trees or don disguises. He could see Benjamin without having to be somebody else.

Merlin's anticipation of this day had morphed into dread. It was nerves that had set his heart racing and returned him to his living room, rather than to Wales.

Jack's curses were pathetic but they were welcome. It had been some time since anybody cared enough to hate him. Life had become extremely tedious around the two-thousand-year mark and so he'd been forced to find enjoyment in the small things. Vanishing was one of them.

Nobody else endured the burden of time quite the way that Merlin did, which tended to make him feel rather isolated. He had acquaintances in every corner of every universe of course, but not friends. Even Benjamin would reject him soon enough.

'*You don't know that,*' Emrys, his magic, piped up. Merlin stomped over to his coffee table and snatched up the book he'd been forced to put down.

'*I'd poured a whiskey – the lad always calls at the most inconvenient times.*' Merlin threw himself into his armchair, too exhausted to hold back anger and what he assumed was defeat. His work sent him to the furthest, most remote corners of one world or other, and always a million miles from where he wanted to be – anywhere with decent whiskey.

'*You've enough years on you to know that whiskey isn't the answer.*' Emrys buzzed about in his head. Emrys was always nagging!

'*Says you!*'

Merlin allowed Emrys to flicker into view. The little aquamarine figure leant his back against Merlin's fingers, considering him with a disapproving look.

'You've put Jack in an awful position.'

Irritated, Merlin blew Emrys onto the arm of the chair.

'That's life. Benjamin has to find out one way or the other. Besides, Jack is a vampire. He has no business being so sensitive.' Caring about people was a hard thing to do. It was energy that could be better spent. 'And what of my position? I've been forced to have snatched meetings with Jack in parks. Always with fingers crossed that Fate didn't catch me.' For the most part, Merlin had been able to toe the line and maintain a distance. Until the threats to Benjamin became greater than the distance. 'Hmph.' Merlin idly traced the letters of the play he'd been reading. 'Shakespeare based Prospero on me, you know.'

'I know. His Miranda has a happier ending than yours.' Sadness settled into Merlin's fossil bones. Vivien had deserved better. She was nothing like her parents – a miracle. Merlin held his hand out for Emrys. His magic sat himself on the book's spine, looking up at Merlin with more empathy than he deserved.

'Aye. And to be set free by applause – it's a beautiful idea. Only Death will release me.' Merlin reached for his tumbler but caught Emrys's disapproving stare. 'Fine!' He reluctantly returned the glass to the table. 'I'm Fate's undisputed fool. I could have broken the cycle at any point.'

'Leaving sounded so easy – it was incredibly difficult to action. You loved her.'

'I did. I was killing time for the most part. All I could do was wait for my next cue. And I play my part well.' Life was nothing more than a script. The fool wasn't an ideal role, but it suited him fine. 'Fate thinks I'm not a threat. Best let her think of me as her puppet. We'll end up where we're supposed to.' Merlin considered himself to have two great accomplishments – his daughter and the nine realms. It was a pity that he couldn't save them all. 'A few casualties seem acceptable if I can rid the universe of Fate.' Emrys jumped up and paced back and forth across the dark blue and blacks of the stormy sea on the cover.

'You're risking a lot, Merlin. I still can't see past that scene by the oak tree. If you don't succeed …' Merlin cut Emrys off with a raised hand.

'I won't fail. Fate doesn't suspect me. Do not forget that we are doing this for Vivien. It's high time people were able to decide their own paths.' Revenge was beneath Merlin, but he could stoop if required. Fate's death was the only way to cleanse the bitter taste of Viven's passing from his palate. Let him right some wrongs whilst he had the chance. 'Fate will slip up eventually, Emrys. We have to be ready. There can be no hesitation.' Being immortal only meant that she was harder to kill. Merlin had already sourced his weapon. He rose and crossed to a bookshelf, running his fingers along the spines until he found *Macbeth*. From the cavernous depths of his robe sleeves, Fate's golden dagger slid into his hand. Merlin promptly dropped it onto the cover and held the book out for Emrys, watching as the blade shrunk to fit the bloody dagger on the cover.

'Your plan might make you as bad as she is.' Emrys watched Merlin replace the book, unease filling his tiny frame.

'I can live with that. I can die with that. Everything dies eventually.' The glint of Merlin's wedding band caught his eye. Not content to let time separate them, he slid the ring from his finger.

'What are you going to do with that?' Emrys asked.

Merlin rolled the ring back and forth, wishing that he'd had the courage to throw it at her, in Avalon. The band from his marriage to Mórrígan winked at him from his right index finger. If he'd managed to leave War, Merlin should be able to leave Fate. Merlin told himself that if he absorbed her abuse, others would be spared. But really, he was terrified of leaving Fate.

'We've been tangled up for so long that I can't recognise myself without her. Perhaps a part of me likes that.' With a heavy sigh, Merlin slipped the ring onto his right ring finger.

'I'm not sure that's how divorce works.' Emrys inspected the ring's new placement.

'I wonder what the girl will make of us. What's her name?'

'April, as well you know it is.' Emrys rolled his eyes. 'You'll have to make a good first impression. For once.'

Merlin returned himself to his armchair. 'She doesn't have to like me. None of them do.' He had worked his fingers to the bone to keep the universe safe. Fate had systematically removed everything he cared about until she was the only distraction left.

'Well, nobody can help you if you continue to sulk, Merlin.' He held out his hand for Emrys. 'They'll be trying the spell soon. I suppose we should get ready for our entrance.'

The hairs on the back of Merlin's neck stood on end as he felt the proverbial net closing around him. It felt too much like a noose for his liking. 'Best not to keep them waiting.'

'The Gods know it's taken Jack long enough!' Merlin had been dropping subtle hints for some time, hoping that Jack would call him out and end this sorry charade. 'Do you think Benjamin will hit me?' Oh, to be a fly on that wall when Jack broke the news to Benjamin!

'I think he'll kill you,' Emrys said with sincerity, 'and when he does, you can't say that you're undeserving.' The magic hopped onto the arm of the chair, freeing Merlin's hand to open the book.

'Ha! Benjamin doesn't have it in him. Besides, we know who will be responsible for our death. It isn't Benjamin.' An uncomfortable feeling settled in the pit of his stomach at the thought of the truth finally finding its shameful way into the light. Merlin eyed the abandoned whiskey. 'Sod it!' He downed it in one go.

'Merlin!' Emrys could chide all he wanted, this was one reunion that Merlin couldn't weather sober.

16

Way Out There

University Parks, Oxford

Jack had searched the seventy-acre park until the light had fled.

Having eventually arrived back at the cricket pavilion, he finally admitted defeat.

Merlin had vanished.

He stood for a moment, listening to the wind rustling the leaves of the ancient trees. The End of Days, Ben, Merlin, Barqan and Fate were all worries suspended in the corners of Jack's mind, held there by the steady rhythm of his breathing in and out, in and out. His eyes screwed shut. As soon as the dam broke, Jack would be swept away to tell Ben that he'd found …

'Oh no!'

Jack ran. If Merlin had gone anywhere, he'd have gone to Ben. If Merlin waltzed up to Ben after years of supposed death – that wasn't going to end well. How would Merlin even start that conversation? *'It's good to see you,'* wasn't going to bridge the one-and-a-half thousand-year gap.

Jack narrowly avoided being hit by a car as he exited the park, speeding across to his car, parked alongside the university buildings and bicycle racks. As he neared the vehicle, he became aware of somebody yelling Merlin's name. He spun in circles. Merlin wasn't here, so why was somebody … Strong hands gripped his shoulder. Jack pulled back to throw a punch …

'Jack? Are you alright?'

'I … um … fine.' Merlin wasn't here but still the lump of fear wouldn't shift. A potent mix of nausea and exhaustion washed Jack into Ben's arms. He leant in, letting Ben take his weight, burying his head into his partner's shoulder. Arms folded around him and Jack felt utterly helpless.

'Are you sure?' Ben rubbed Jack's back. 'You were yelling something. I didn't quite catch what. April was talking my ear off.' Ben pulled back, looking him up and down. 'It looked like you were fleeing from hell hounds.' Ben gently squeezed Jack's arm, reminding him to reply.

'Oh.' Jack forced a smile, tightening his grip on Ben. 'I thought something was chasing me. It wasn't, so …' Jack's way-too-high, silly-me laugh did him no favours.

Ben's eyes narrowed slightly. 'Right. Shall we go? April has found us a place to stay. She did it on her phone. Used an app. The one with the bird?'

Jack couldn't help but chuckle at Ben's lack of understanding. 'The one with the bird is for getting into two-hundred-and-eighty-character arguments with random strangers.'

'That's what they use the app for? Ridiculous.'

'Why are you still so bad with technology?'

'Because, when I was human, I used actual birds to send messages.'

'Showing your age, much? Maybe April can teach you how to use a smartphone properly. Bring you into this century.' Jack kept his voice light, although he felt anything but. With a final curious look, Ben returned to the passenger seat. Drawing in a deep breath, Jack attempted to mask the tension that pushed his shoulders up and forward as he slid into the driver's seat.

'Did Dirmynd prove useful?' Ben asked almost as soon as Jack's seatbelt had clicked in. The sound of the engine turning over rushed into the gap where Jack's answer should have been, stalling him.

'It was more what he didn't say.' He paused, still trying to pick out a path that wouldn't send his partner racing around the park. 'Ben?'

'Yes?'

Jack pulled off and watched the man he loved struggling to type on his phone with one finger. He couldn't tell Ben. And the truth didn't change anything. Merlin had retreated to who-knew-where. Their only option was the summoning spell. 'Never mind.' Jack's fingers absentmindedly tapped the steering wheel as an idea repeated in his head. Merlin had been feeding him information and providing counsel for years. Jack had been Merlin's pawn and through him, Merlin had gained a tiny amount of influence over Ben's life. And Jack couldn't let sleeping dogs lie.

'Are you 100% certain, beyond a reasonable doubt, that Merlin's death wasn't one of his tricks?' Jack kept his gaze fixed on the road ahead. He'd confess all his sins if he made eye contact. He wanted Ben to see it for himself, as cowardly as that was.

'We've been over this!' Ben threw his hands up, aggrieved once more.

'I know, I know!' Jack felt sorry for Ben's phone. He was jabbing away at the screen as if he was trying to spear salmon. 'But think about it. Merlin had his own agenda. If leaving served that, he wouldn't have hesitated.' Jack's fingers resumed their irregular beat on the steering wheel. 'Men like Merlin know their friends by the parts they've played in their schemes. If faking his death allowed you to move on with your life ...' He let his words fall away. Jack wasn't defending Merlin, more sugar-coating a jagged truth.

Ben's head snapped up sharply, angry eyes daring Jack to say it. 'So, you've exchanged past tense for present?'

'I thought you hadn't noticed.'

'Oh no, I noticed you trying to unpick history.' Jack watched Ben's fingers curl around the door handle, flexing as if he was trying to let go, but still fighting to commit.

'Merlin was a glorified trickster.' Jack regretted it instantly. His left hand hovered in the gap between them, ready to grab Ben if he threw himself from the car.

'He wasn't a trickster!' Ben's face wrinkled up in disgust.

'Why are you so offended? I didn't call you ... never mind.' Jack navigated a few roundabouts in silence. 'You can't see him for what he is, can you?' Ben sat up straight, staring ahead. 'His constant meddling with the course of history, based on his knowledge of the future, coupled with his job as Fate's errand boy, makes him a trickster.'

'Why must you discredit Merlin so?'

'It's the truth, Ben. Nothing more, nothing less.'

'Sometimes, Jack,' April ventured into the conversation, her voice firm but quiet, 'I think you forget that your truth isn't the same as others.'

'Oh, come on, April. You don't like Merlin either!'

'You make him sound like a jester!' Ben whined.

'Yes, an incredibly unfunny jester, and you, my love, bought a season ticket for the Merlin show.' Jack sighed, checking his blind spot before merging onto the motorway. 'It's like Meatloaf said, "Objects in the rear-view mirror may appear closer than they are".'

'I don't understand.'

'Of course you don't. That spell's going to prove me right, Ben.'

Ben couldn't fathom where Jack's scathing tone was coming from. What Ben did know was that he was sick to his back teeth of this conversation.

'I do not wish to fight with you. Jack?' There was much on Ben's mind that he wanted to talk about – had to talk about – before it strangled him. There were truths that were uncomfortable to sit with, like Merlin's blatant disregard for him. But Ben couldn't seem to dress his concerns up to sound like anything other than denial and disagreement.

'Who said we're fighting? We're not fighting. This isn't a fight.'

Ben felt the familiar exasperation rise up. Jack's stubborn silence only prolonged their disagreements. And it wasn't like Ben couldn't see the cracks and coincidences littering his past. He didn't look too closely, lest he find Merlin hiding in Fate's shadow. There was no such thing as a coincidence, only Fate.

'It's fifty on this stretch of road.' Ben's caution was ignored. 'I said it's fifty. Jack? Slow down a little.'

'Why?' The word squeezed its way past gritted teeth.

'Well, for one thing, there are humans out there. We also have a human inside the car.' Jack eased off the pedal without a word.

'Why won't he tell me?' Ben watched Jack quietly work over some concerns.

'You've tried asking him, Ben.' Ambrosius surfaced from his hiding place at the back of Ben's mind, trying to tune out the brewing conflict. *'He'll tell you when he's ready. He's probably worried about resurrecting ghosts.'*

'And I'm not?' But Ambrosius had a point, so Ben settled into his seat, content to let silence reclaim the space.

'Do you think that Merlin was a false friend?' Ben squinted into the glare of oncoming headlights. It was possible that he'd been blind all along.

'You've always been so quick to see the best in others,' Ambrosius replied carefully.

Ben rested his head against the window as another wave of nerves slammed into him. *'I never did have any patience for waiting, always rushing through life.'*

'And you never did learn your lesson. Merlin was always telling you to slow down. Remember when you mucked up a spell and turned yourself into—'

'I remember! And I take your point.' A rummaging from the back of the car startled Ben.

April bravely poked her head through the gap in the seats, looking from Jack to Ben. Her hands were starting to cramp from attempting to connect all the dots. Diffusing the fight seemed like the best option when she was staring down the barrel of a four-hour car journey with a rowing supernatural couple. And she was going to do it the only way she knew how: questions.

'Let me get this straight: end of the world is nigh, other worlds have literally ended, and instead of taking the fight to Fate, we are going to Wales to find a bit of jewellery and a terrible trickster-warlock?' Ben and Jack nodded in unison. April trusted the boys, but this felt like a long shot at best, and a distraction at worst. 'Say we find the shield, what do we do?'

'Well, that depends,' Ben said.

'On how the Merlin thing plays out?' April asked carefully, not liking the way that Jack tensed at the M word. Ben nodded.

'About that, I have questions.'

'When do you not have questions?' Ben complained.

'Before you kidnapped me?' April shot back. 'Life wasn't so complicated then. Find the vampire, kill the vampire.'

'She's allowed to have questions,' Jack replied gruffly. April took the rolling of Ben's eyes as permission to fire at will.

'Let's say that we find the graves and do the spell ...'

'I know where they are. I buried them.'

'The area has probably changed quite a bit since then. A lot more concrete and tarmac ...'

'Your point?' April was going to point out that the graves might not be accessible anymore when she caught Jack's don't-you-dare glare in the rear-view mirror, although she wasn't convinced his we'll-deal-with-it-when-we-get-there approach was better. But he was trying to drive the car.

'How does it work? Summoning the dead, I mean. Oh God, Merlin's not going to climb out of the grave, is he? You know, one hand pops up first—' The boys' voices jumped over one another. April's poor little heart skipped a beat.

'It's not a zombie movie! Now that's in my head, it's a good job that I don't need to sleep,' Jack shrieked. 'And we're not resurrecting anybody ...'

'No, April. What's ... no!' Ben sounded practically traumatised. Which was distressing, given that he was already pretty distraught. April hovered on the edge of the seat, the seatbelt digging into her neck as she strained forward at the end of its reach.

'If he's ... dead,' Ben was still having trouble with that sentence, 'we'll see his ghost, and it won't crawl its way through soil.' After a beat, and so quietly April couldn't be sure she'd heard it, he added, 'I hope.'

'Reassuring. Ok, follow-up question.' April noticed both boys tense in anticipation.

'If Merlin's a no-show, who did you bury?' Ben dropped his gaze and turned back to the front of the car.

Apparently, they were done with the conversation.

Ambrosius's restless movement sent pins and needles flaring up and down Ben's arms. Ben had been trying his best to ignore Ambrosius since his earlier contribution. If there was any topic that the little orange irritant would have an opinion on, it would be ...

'*Merlin.*' Ben resisted the urge to groan.

'I never thought I'd say this but … I'm bored of thinking about Merlin.' The trouble with having magic was that Ben was never alone with his thoughts. And there was no fooling something that was a part of his own consciousness.

'*Want to talk about it?*' Ambrosius's concern was so present, Ben almost choked on it.

'Not particularly.'

'Come on, Ben. You and I both know that boredom is the thin tarpaulin you're using to hide what's going on.' Ambrosius was pushing his luck.

'I'm not ready to talk about it, and in another thousand years, the answer will still be the same.' It was getting harder to ignore what everybody else thought to be so obvious. Especially when they were using reason. *'What if Arthur is …'* Hot tears prickled at the corner of Ben's exhausted eyes.

'Don't think about that!'

'You're right.' Ben glanced at Jack, thankful that his vampire was unaware of this conversation.

'Things changed. There was no use in waiting for somebody who wasn't coming back.' Again, there was that reasoning that made sense to Ben's mind but not his heart. *'The past was never going to catch you up. Look, whatever happens next is what you need to focus on.'* Ambrosius's tone softened a little. *'Whilst it's hard to blow off the dust of the past, you must try. If, and I mean if, Merlin returns, he won't be the same. You're not the same, either. It's who he is now that we have to worry about.'*

'That's precisely my concern. I've got time aplenty to learn how to accept it, but as Guardian, I cannot overlook him working for Fate.' Ben forced himself to breathe, which only caught Jack's attention. His vampire reached over, and for

a second, Ben thought he was going to take his hand. That the fight was forgotten. But Jack simply pulled apart Ben's clasped hands with a cold efficiency. Ben hadn't realized that he'd been wringing them. *'Merlin taught me so much. I can't defeat somebody who knows my moves before I do.'*

'Then we had best pray for a ghost, Ben.'

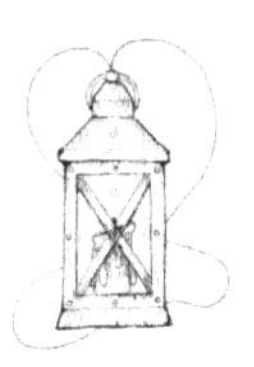

17

Ghost on the Dance Floor

Carmarthen, Wales

'Well, that's underwhelming,' Jack commented dryly. 'I was expecting a huge oak tree that dominated the town, not this potted plant by the side of the road.'

The trio stood in front of a six-foot-tall tree, which was lying on its side, in its circular planter at the side of the road.

'Trees take forever to grow,' April reasoned, wincing as the bright light of her phone pushed the night away from her.

'This one should be ginormous. It was planted two thousand years ago, right, Ben?' Jack looked sceptically at the row of terraced houses lined up beside them and running along the other side of the road. At least the majority of them were dark. It was hard to imagine the residential street with A-road ever being a part of history. 'It doesn't look like you could imprison a mouse in this thing, let alone a warlock.'

'That's a different tree. And Merlin wasn't trapped in it for long.'

'Why are we here then?' Jack screwed his face up. If it transpired that they had to travel to some other remote part of the country, Ben could walk.

'This is where Merlin was born, where he married and hid in the woods when said marriage broke down. This is where he'd have returned to.' Jack didn't bother to ask if "Merlin returned" meant in his physical or spirit form.

'Is now a bad time to tell you guys that they cut the original oak tree down in the seventies?' April piped up, the harsh blue light from the screen washing her out. Jack had to rub his eyes because, for a second there, she'd looked like somebody else. 'Well, what was left of it anyway. It was poisoned sometime in the eighteenth century.' April scrolled down a little further. 'HA! Apparently, a guy was annoyed by people meeting underneath it—'

'Let's hope his ghost isn't around,' Jack cut in, moving to right the planter.

'*And then* somebody set fire to it. The remains were removed in the seventies.'

'What? Let me see that!' Ben snatched the phone from April.

'That is both disappointing and insulting.' Ben chucked the phone back to April, having aggressively scrolled his way through the article, muttering about a lack of respect. It wasn't going well, but it could be worse.

'Don't we need the original tree for the spell?' April's joints cried out as she stretched, angry after the long car journey.

'Maybe they kept the original soil?' Jack poked doubtfully at the pot.

'It's not an ideal situation, but the energy should still be here …'

Ben grew quiet as he tuned into his surroundings. After a few deep breaths, he felt himself retreating backwards as Ambrosius rushed forward, for once unbridled and in charge. His magic rushed headfirst into a towering wall of matted energy that hung unseen around them. The singed air scratched at Ben's lungs. Something evil had come this way, and not too long ago.

'Why was the whole thing on its side?' Jack peered over April's shoulder at her phone. 'That has to be a bad omen. Search bad-tree omens.'

'The town had its worst floods after the tree was removed.' April frowned nervously.

'*When Merlin's Oak shall tumble down, then shall fall Carmarthen town.*' Ben's voice was still, calm and collected.

'That sounds like a prophecy, Ben. I don't like tangling with those.' Jack pulled on his ear. 'Don't tell me, it was one of Merlin's?' Ben quickly dropped his eyes to the floor, pretending to inspect the soil. 'Benjamin?'

'Merlin made many prophecies.'

'Benjamin?'

'You said don't tell you …'

'Of course!' Jack's sarcasm said everything he needed to.

'If it's not the original tree that falls, and nobody who cares is left, does the prophecy still count?' April squeezed herself in between the boys.

'I guess we'll find out. Are you getting anything from it?' Jack gestured at the tree.

'There's … something. It's not residual. It certainly doesn't feel like Merlin. It's …' Ben frowned, troubled by the heavy and oppressive atmosphere. 'It's dark.' He caught the flash of terror in April's eyes and rushed to change his mind. 'I could have misinterpreted the energies present, of course.'

'Not helping.' Ben was too unsettled to think of something reassuring. He looked over her head to Jack, silently asking for help.

'We've driven for over four hours to get here,' Jack sighed, rubbing his eyes. 'Caerleon is two hours in the other direction—'

'One hour and twenty-six minutes,' Ben corrected.

'With your navigation, we'll be lucky if we get there at all. Two hours is being generous.'

'There's nothing wrong with my sense of direction! You insist on using your phone, so I zone out. I don't know why you need me to reiterate the talking navigation's instructions.'

'Because I'm watching the road and sat-nav uses satellites rather than the stars!'

'Neither of you like asking for help, do you?' April crossed her arms.

'Ha!' Jack exclaimed, missing April's snide dig. 'Ben once got us so lost, we ended up in the wrong country. I love him, but he can be so stubborn!' April would have laughed harder, Ben thought, if she hadn't got hung up on something.

'That was different! We were travelling through portals and I misjudged it.'

'You could have asked that pixie for directions. Anyway,' Jack rushed on to stem the rising argument, 'the sooner you cast that spell, the sooner we can leave.'

'You've been in a foul mood since meeting Dirmynd. What's the matter?' There was something behind Jack's eyes, something that he needed to say but wasn't going to. At least not yet.

Jack shivered as the overwhelming feeling of being watched tapped him on the shoulder. 'I'm fine. You ready?'

This was his last chance to tell Ben what he knew.

Felling like the cowardly lion, unable to find his voice when it mattered most, Jack held his peace.

'As I'll ever be.'

'Ok. Don't spontaneously combust if Merlin appears, ok?' And maybe it would be easier for Ben if he found out on his own. And did it matter how Ben found out? No, so long as Merlin resumed his Guardianship, all would be well. 'I'm half-tempted to let Gaia collapse. There are other universes.'

'Hand me the spell.'

Jack's fingers had become quite fond of the weight of the parchment, and Ben had to pull it free. 'We're not resurrecting him, remember.'

'We'd need his bones.'

'Oookkkkayyy, I'm gonna ignore that. Where do you want the circle?' Jack produced twelve candles from a backpack, looking uncertainly at the houses across the street. 'This is how we get arrested and committed, isn't it?'

'In front of the tree. Evenly spaced.'

Ben carefully laid his talisman in the centre of the lit candles. With the point of Cerridwen's talisman, he slashed the palm of his hand, staining the sword crimson.

'What are you doing?' April tried not to yell, lest she disturb the calm of the night, her wide eyes darting between the flickering candles and the wound.

'I need something of Merlin's – his magic in the talisman; something of mine – blood; and something that connects us both.'

'I'm pretty sure there are other things that would have worked besides tearing your hand open!'

April looked to Jack for backup, but his intense stare was locked on Ben.

'Blood and magic. There are few things stronger,' Ben said, as if that was a perfectly good reason for inflicting harm on oneself. 'Besides, this is dark magic. We're not exactly summoning baby unicorns.'

Ben ignored thoughts of secrets, April and baby unicorns, and the throbbing creeping up and down the cut. Uncertainty and misgivings had no place beside him as he stepped into the circle. Ben raised both hands in front of him, palms facing the sky. The timing of his subconscious was inconvenient at best.

It was looping memories of Merlin's irritation at a young Ben's unorthodox spell-casting methods. Merlin's ancient disappointment hammered at his concentration. Ben scanned through his memories, trying to find one unmarked by anything other than happiness. There were but a few. The disappointment was crushing. Upon closer inspection, they didn't hold up to scrutiny either, but they were all he had. Ben took himself back to the first time he'd had dinner with Merlin and Arthur and smiled. Arthur lived at the centre of the good memories, whilst Merlin crept around the edge of them, watching and sniping.

Ben's hands dropped to his side, his breathing rapid.

'If something's wrong, we aren't doing this,' Jack said, car keys in his hand and worry in his voice.

'No, I'm alright.' Ben refocused. His arms were vibrating with Ambrosius's pins and needles. He clutched the happy moments close and slipped through the fabric of the realm to enter the night plane. It sat somewhere between Purgatory and the realms, and it was a pitch-black void of dark energy. The spell's energy shot past him as he catapulted it into the universe.

'I call forth from space and time, to a long-lost friend of mine.

Merlin Caledonensis, Myrrdin Aurelianus,

I call to you and Emrys, your magic,

Be thy living or dead,

Hear me and come to us who call you near, come to us and settle here,

I summon you to me, Merlin, to join us in the circle.

Blood to blood, I summon thee,

Blood to blood, return to me.'

Time slowed to a crawl. Ben didn't dare breathe, lest he miss the tell-tale beat of a heart still living. With each passing minute, hope died and trepidation grew, inviting in the oppressing energy that was so eager to dig its claws in. The night plane called to him, trying to break Ben's connection with Ambrosius. If Ben let the darkness in, it would be fatal.

His spell hurtled through the realms, until there were …

Three …

Two …

One …

None.

There was nowhere left to look. Ambrosius was sweeping back on himself, a burnt-orange tide returning to shore with not a waif or man adrift on it. The circle of light couldn't hold the emptiness in, and the black hole inside Ben greedily drank it.

Ben's chest constricted; his lungs had forgotten how to breathe. 'Merlin's always late. He's …' the giant hole inside of Ben swelled with his sorrow; the rickety supports that held it up crumbled.

'I'm—'

'He's late, Jack!'

The candles flickered and extinguished as Ambrosius collided with Ben. He staggered back, silently gasping for air.

'Ben—'

'Don't! Don't say it, don't say anything.' Ben scrubbed at his eyes and tried to keep his back to Jack. 'It was the spell. You tried to tell me to go to Caerleon but I didn't listen. I'll try it again!' Ben stared into the distance, his senses straining to detect anything – perhaps the spell was a slow burner.

'The candles are out, the circle's broken, love.'

'It can't be right – it's like Merlin never existed.' Ben's whole body was tingling, but not with magic. 'No, this isn't right.' He saw his thoughts mirrored on Jack's face and his stomach clenched – 'Merlin should be here.'

'So, what does that tell you?' The sympathy in April's voice said that she knew, but didn't want to be the one to say it. Ben's racing thoughts collided with one another in an explosion which left a coldness that spread from his core. Ben lifted his shaking hands, to do what, he didn't know. Neither

Jack nor April deserved his anger and Ben couldn't hold onto the evidence of Merlin's continued survival anymore. If Ben didn't think about it, he could breathe. If he could breathe, he could calm the stormy waters of his mind. If Ben didn't feel it, he could see the truth.

'Merlin's alive.'

'We can look for wandering warlocks in the morning.' Jack approached Ben slowly, the way he'd approach a wild animal. 'It's late, we could all do with some rest.' He gently tugged on Ben's elbow, trying to force eye contact, but Ben couldn't stop his eyes from roaming. 'Wherever Merlin is, he'll still be there tomorrow.'

Ben let Jack guide him back to the car. He couldn't seem to walk properly on his own. Jack held the door open with a weak smile, but Ben had to take one last look. Relief nearly folded him into the car seat – there was nothing there. The location had to be the weak link.

Horror gripped Ben by the throat. Leaning against the planter was Merlin, a little thinner than he remembered, but Merlin. He was wearing that infuriating grin.

'No, no.' Ben grabbed handfuls of his hair, tears streaming from his eyes. 'Merlin!' He was scared to look away to check if the others saw him too.

'There's nobody there.' April's certainty sounded like pity.

'He's right there!' Ben wrenched his eyes away from Merlin.

Jack gave him a doubtful smile and looked anyway. 'You're seeing things, love.'

'He's gone now. He was there.' Ben went to give chase but his sleeve caught on something. 'Damn it!' It was Jack, struggling to hold him back.

'There's nothing but leaves and a random raven.' The shock was enough to break the circuit. Ben blamed his distress for him missing the raven perched on the information board.

'Is it me or is the bird staring at Ben?' April asked, sword in her hands.

'What are you going to do with that? Throw it at the bird?' Jack snatched at the sword. Their bickering faded to a low hum as Ambrosius focused on the bird. The raven's head tilted sharply to one side, as if sensing Ambrosius's probing. Ben took one step towards it, and the bird responded with a shrill cry that halted him. It looked a little too ethereal for his liking.

'Feels like it belongs on the night plane. Did we bring something back with us, Ben?'

'I don't think so.' The bird gave one final cry and took flight on silent wings. 'Somebody's watching us.'

'Unless Merlin's turned into a raven, nobody's there, Ben.'

'Merlin used cats.' The raven banked steeply to the left and vanished over the rooftops, leaving behind an uneasy feeling in the pit of Ben's stomach. It took more energy than he cared to admit to lift his head and meet Jack's worried gaze. 'The spell searched heaven, hell, Purgatory and everything in between. Merlin's hiding well but nothing's lost forever.' Ben slumped down into the passenger seat, leaving a shocked April and Jack on the pavement as the wind picked up around them. 'We'll travel to Caerleon tomorrow.'

Jack wasn't sure why he felt so hollow. He could have avoided all of this by coming clean, but he couldn't be the one to shatter Ben's world like that. Looking at Ben now, all hunched over and defeated, Jack realized that not only had he been avoiding the inevitable, he'd compounded the injury.

'What the hell?' April mouthed at Jack over the open car door. He could only shrug and got into the car.

'This B&B place best not be a dive.'

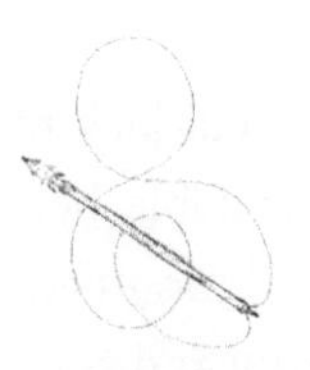

18

Devil's Dance Floor

Carmarthen, Wales

The sky was still empty of light when they finally pulled up outside the B&B.

Clinging ivy and shadows hid the face of the tired farmhouse, obscuring the mismatched brickwork looming over them. The long, lopsided building followed the slope of the eerily quiet farmland down towards the beach below. No light illuminated any of the thirteen dark brown, sash windows. Sat off-centre and framed by a pointed archway, was the uninviting doorway. Surrounded by fields, a deserted campsite and a sleeping town, nothing about the location suggested that Jack should be wary and yet nothing about it soothed his jumpy nerves. Maybe it was the way the angry waves relentlessly crashed against the beach, or perhaps it was the acute feeling of isolation that rolled across the campsite that had Jack on edge. 'I've been to livelier graveyards than this place.'

April edged a little closer to Ben. Nobody appeared to be in a rush to get to bed. Jack locked the car, shattering the silence.

'We can carry on driving if you prefer?' Ben reached out.

'This place creeps me out. But April needs sleep.' Jack pushed past his misgivings to pick up the bags.

'And we need to talk.' Ben agreed. *'After you.'*

'How chivalrous, letting your love die first.' Jack took his first tentative step towards the house. He had half a mind to suggest they camp but if given the choice, Ben would pick the eerie house over a tent.

April hung back, unable to shake her feeling of foreboding that wanted nothing more than to smother her. Images from the vision chased one another through her mind, reminding her to be vigilant. The boys had pulled ahead with their long strides. April took one step forward and a cold shiver ran down her spine, triggering another kaleidoscope vision. Ben and the stranger poked at the embers of her concern. The need to know why this was happening to her outweighed her fear of the answer. Visions weren't something that hunters had and Ben had asked her if there were any witches in her family. No, that was crazy – April couldn't be a witch. She'd know. Maybe she should curb her curses, in case she was a …

'April?' Ben called from the doorway. She shook herself free and hurried after them, pulling her kitbag further up her shoulder.

'Sorry,' she muttered as Jack opened the door for her.

April crossed the threshold and came face-to-face with a smiling old lady. April hoped that somebody else was about to appear to check them in, because the lady looked like the sort who'd trap you in conversation. She'd positioned herself at the foot of the dark mahogany staircase that ascended into darkness, framed by exposed beams and dark-red walls. April noticed that the carpet, presumably faded by years of sunlight, was the colour of dried blood. She should have checked the reviews.

'Um, Hi.' April's eyes protested at the thought of staying open a minute longer, maybe she could sneak off and leave the boys to it.

'Hello, dear.'

April didn't like how the lady's smile peeled back to reveal her teeth. She resigned herself to the fact that they were going to have to climb around the woman to get to their rooms.

'I'll find the booking confirmation.' The woman didn't even nod. 'Is she a G.H.O.S.T?' Jack and Ben recoiled from the old lady as one – whether in fear or disgust, April didn't know.

'Ghosts can spell. And no.'

Ben pulled her back by the shoulder, behind him and Jack. Curious to know if she'd been right, April peered through the gap. 'It is not with a spell that you've altered your appearance and you are not a shapeshifter. Only a God can alter their form at will.'

The old lady's smile stretched across her face. 'Your eyes see far more than they should.' She looked Ben up and down, her gaze never wandering to the other two. 'They always did.'

'You can change your hair but you can't fool me. I see you Mórrígan. Despite the glimmer. Age doesn't sit right on you, and beige isn't your colour, darling.' Ben tilted his head to one side, considering Mórrígan.

'This is War?' The only battle she looked ready for was for the last cheese and pickle sandwich. Jack swatted at April's shoulder.

'You were the raven in Merlin's tree?' Mórrígan answered Ben with a smile saved for co-conspirators, delighted that her memory had followed him through space and time.

'You saw what you wanted to, Benjamin. Can you not tell where the illusions start and end?' The old lady melted away, and her body elongated into a tall, muscular woman with long, wavy, feathered black hair. The whites of Mórrígan's eyes glowed, a contrast to her black dress which was made entirely of feathers, the straps delicate wings. She wasn't dressed for battle. April looked longingly at the door; it was so far away and she was too tired to run.

'You are a long way from home, Mórrígan.' And now here she was, with purpose and mischief shining in her captivating eyes. 'The last time I saw you, you were picking Merlin apart at the seams.' There was no telling somebody who thought they'd found love, that they'd found indifference.

'Even more reason for you to stay. I've travelled a great distance to see you. So come, sit, let us reminisce.'

'Ah, I'd love to, only, Jack left the oven on, and April has a cat.' Jack nodded enthusiastically. Ben moved towards the door, firmly pushing April backwards with his outstretched arm. 'Lovely to see you again. You look … like a raven.'

'We were hoping that you could stay a while.' The innocent tone was juxtaposed with the twisted smile that suggested they were certainly welcome to try and leave.

'We? Are you counting multiple personalities?' Ben looked around the otherwise empty hallway.

'There's somebody in the room behind her.' Ambrosius's warning was extraneous. The additional presence had been

making Ben uneasy since they'd entered. Mórrígan winked at Ben and clicked her fingers. Ben flinched in unison with Jack, but nothing happened.

'Unless you're planning on breaking out the jazz hands, I'm not sure what's supposed to have happened.' Ben shrugged at Mórrígan, underwhelmed by the anti-climax.

'Before you go,' Mórrígan left her threat unspoken, 'I thought that you might want to take a look at this.'

'Ooooh, your dress has pockets!' Jack cooed.

Mórrígan wound her fingers through a worn cord similar to Ben's. The shield. In Ben's mind, War bent over Merlin's dead body and snatched the talisman from his neck.

'Where did you find it?'

'The wee thing was tucked away in a tree. I'm not sure exactly. I had somebody find it for me. She's excellent at finding lost things.'

'That sounds careless. Even for Merlin,' Ben said dismissively, distracted by Jack's restlessness.

'Umm … What are those?' April asked, pointing at the walls behind Mórrígan.

War let out a delighted laugh at April's confused terror. Disembodied shadow hands were seeping through the walls, their long fingers with chewed nails scrabbling for purchase on the plaster. Ben repressed the urge to groan as the first batch dropped to the floor and crawled slowly towards them.

'Why is it always creepy hands?' Jack asked. 'I don't like the creepy hands.'

'No one likes the creepy hands.' Why anybody still used shadow magic, Ben didn't know. It was so clunky.

'They're behind us as well,' April cried. 'Shouldn't we be running away?'

'Where to? They will be everywhere. They won't stop until they have what Mórrígan wants.'

'And what is it that I want, Benjamin?'

'The sword.' Ben pulled it free, shocked to see that it was glowing again.

'It does nothing for a thousand years and then it comes alive twice in one day.' Ben trod on Jack's foot in a not-so-subtle warning. Cerridwen's bow and arrows pricked at his skin, threatening to burn him through his pocket if he didn't pay it some attention.

'How clever you were, outsmarting Barqan.' Mórrígan could be incredibly perceptive when it suited her.

'It wasn't so hard. In a shocking turn of events, I'm not giving you my talisman.'

'But what good is one half of a pair?' Mórrígan purred.

'I've managed alright so far.' Sooner or later, Mórrígan would grow tired of Ben's glib remarks, and she'd become careless.

'I need that little sword of yours. To complete the set. Besides,' Mórrígan added sweetly, 'a sword isn't much good on its own. It can't protect you, only attack.' Mórrígan spoke with mock sorrow. 'It's all that's left of our dear Merlin.'

The dig worked its way underneath Ben's composure, overriding his capability for rational thought. 'You of all people have no right to use his name, after everything you did,' he spat at her. 'And no one, immortal or otherwise, in this realm or the next, has any business handling the shield except me.' Ben stopped in his retreat. He'd waited forever to have it out with Mórrígan over this.

Mórrígan threw back her head and laughed. 'I should have known! That grudge must be eating you alive. Why drag the sorrow out for eternity?'

Something jerked violently at the bottom of Ben's jeans. Glancing down he realised that not only had the hands multiplied, but the forerunners had reached them. April was trying her best to kick them.

'Stand still. They'll get bored of you soon enough.' Ben watched one hand somersault through the air and collide with the opposite wall.

'How are you being calm about this?' April said, flailing about like one of those inflatable tube people.

'Because we've done this before. The more you fight, the more interested in you they'll become. Kinda like bees.' Jack didn't look away from Mórrígan. 'Got yourself a nice little collection of talismans, have you?'

'You could say that.' Barqan stepped out of the shadows. The blue flames of her eyes had reignited, but burned with less intensity than their former selves.

'What a surprise.' Ben glared but Barqan wouldn't meet his eye.

'What use to you is ours? It's supercharged and ready to go off if something threatens, Ben.' Ben turned his glare on Jack.

'Wouldn't you want to keep the things that hurt you locked away?' Mórrígan looked to Jack. Ben groaned.

'Huh, I thought you were gonna tell us about your plans to end the world. Obviously not.'

'If only you had the time, Jack. It's been lovely to catch up with you, Benjamin.' With a snap of her fingers, a fresh wave of creepy hands materialised and joined the rest.

Jack was up to his knees in hands. He looked wishfully at the door behind him, knowing that they'd never make it if they had to wade through a sea of extremities.

Behind him, the creepy hands pulled themselves on top of each other to form a column. A long arm, attached to the rest of the mass, grabbed hold of April's bokken. 'Let them have it, April!' Weighed down by hands, Jack waded slowly towards April. Another two strands grew from the ground up to pull her arms behind her back.

'Ah sh—' Jack ducked, narrowly avoiding being punched by a giant fist. The never-ending tide of hands pulled him off balance and away from April.

'Jack!'

He wrenched himself around to see Ben staggering under the weight of the hands, the vile things snatching at the talisman. Resolve pushed Jack towards Ben. Lifting one leg after the other, he managed two steps before a casual flick of Mórrígan's wrist sent him flying face-first into the wall beside Ben, denting it. Jack slid down the wall but didn't reach the ground; the hands scooped him up and set him on his feet. Mórrígan cleared herself a path. She smirked at Jack as she sauntered past him, coming to a halt in front of Ben.

'You've not fed.' Mórrígan watched Ben with the anticipation of a hawk who'd backed its prey into a corner. 'Such power, such strength and you let it go to ruin. A tragic waste.'

Jack struggled against the various forces holding him back, not liking the glint of malice in Mórrígan's eye and fearing the burning anger in Ben's.

'Talisman, Benjamin.' Mórrígan held out her hand, tsking at Ben's shaking head. 'Humans break so easily, you know,' Mórrígan paused, a cruel smile on her face, 'as do vampires.' Ben lunged forward, head-butting her with as much force as he could manage. Mórrígan, unhurt, hissed in irritation and pushed him back.

'So, the shield hurts you, big deal,' Jack said hastily, trying to draw her attention. 'You don't see me chopping down every tree in a five-mile radius.'

Mórrígan's stony-faced expression dissolved with her delighted laughter.

'He is simply adorable! Can I keep him?'

'You'll only get bored of him soon enough.' Jack found the time to look deeply offended. 'Let's skip to the part where your goons beat us up? Because I'm tired, it's past the kid's bedtime and it doesn't look like the shield is working.'

'I am not a kid!' Jack and April chorused, causing them to glare at each other.

'Lying is a sin, you know,' Mórrígan purred.

'I'm 891 years old …'

'I was talking to Benjamin.' Mórrígan's cold stare landed on Jack, freezing his reply. Satisfied, she turned back to Ben. 'Why else would you have come all this way if not for the shield?' The older Ben got, the more he turned into somebody who laughed at inappropriate times. Like funerals. Or being threatened by War.

'Is something amusing to you?'

'I was going to ask that.' Jack stared as Ben's disdainful laughter wound Mórrígan up.

'Merlin must have seen himself in you. You're both supercilious, opinionated fools who do not know when to stop talking.'

Jack would have facepalmed if he'd had a free hand.

'I see.' Mórrígan nodded and hit Ben in the solar plexus. Jack flinched in sympathy as Ben doubled over. Mórrígan pulled Ben up by his hair, punching him again. It was the sight of Ben's bloodied face and broken nose that compelled Jack to do the same to Mórrígan. Jack struggled against the hands restraining him, his eyes falling onto Barqan. Avalon's Guardian had stepped back, watching it all unfold with a blank expression. For his part, Ben remained silent, refusing to let them have the satisfaction of his pain.

'Are you going to stand by and watch this, Barqan?' Jack hoped she'd had enough of a conscience to be ashamed. Barqan didn't acknowledge Jack.

'Be easy, Jack.' Ben's voice found him through the white noise of his determination. *'I can almost reach the shield.'*

'Dammit, Ben. Mórrígan, if you want the sword, take it and let us go.' He wasn't willing to pay such a high cost for the talismans.

Still holding Ben up by his hair, Mórrígan paused to stare Jack down. His stomach tied itself in knots at Ben's lacerated and already swelling face. They weren't healing.

'Oh, I'll take the sword, little vampire.' Much to Jack's relief, Mórrígan dropped Ben and strutted over to him, the hands parting for her. 'But I won't be letting you go so easily.' Mórrígan trailed her fingers down the side of Jack's face.

He considered telling her that she was barking up the wrong tree, but his smart mouth went one better. 'It wouldn't work. See, I'm a Virgo and you're a bitch …'

'Jack!' Ben yelled, wincing at the pain in his jaw. 'Let them go, Mórrígan, and I'll give you the sword.'

'What?' April looked betrayed.

'*I can break free of the hand's grip,*' Ben said.

As if on cue, Mórrígan returned her attention to Ben, crouching down so they were eye-to-eye.

And Jack saw Ben's intention, clear as day. '*I do not approve of this plan. It's important to me that you know that.*'

'How noble you are, Benjamin.' Mórrígan held out her hand to receive the bokken that rode to her on a sea of hands. Without breaking eye contact, she deliberately wrapped the shield around the hilt of the wooden sword, a coy smile playing on her lips. The shield flickered into life. 'I have destroyed three realms already; do you believe you can stop me from ending Gaia?' Mórrígan drove the sword into Ben's chest.

Jack threw his weight to the side. The columns of hands wobbled but their grip never wavered. He threw himself violently to the right and knocked off a few pairs of hands. They were quickly swallowed by the mass of their counterparts. Jack frantically tried again and succeeded in falling onto his side. The hands swarmed over him, keeping him down. From Jack's side-on view, he saw Ben trying to stand on shaking legs that couldn't hold him. He crashed to his knees and toppled forward. All the while Barqan watched dispassionately. Mórrígan coldly sidestepped the growing pool of blood steadily making its way towards her.

'Ben?' Jack didn't recognise his voice, or the shocked acceptance in his partner's eyes. 'Ben?' Benjamin's face contorted with pain. His bloody hands clasped to his chest, he coughed up blood and fell out of consciousness.

This wasn't how it ended, not for them.

Jack violently threw himself from side to side. This time he managed to raise his leg and his sloppy kick connected with one of the columns. The hand gripping Jack's arms loosened enough to allow him to rip himself free of the second column. Jack gladly punched one of the columns restraining April. He grabbed her by her shoulders, but the hands pulled back. April stepped forward, straining against her captors. With a burst of strength, Jack ripped April free which caused the columns to explode. April pitched forward into Jack's arms, a creepy hand landing on her head.

'Sorry.' He quickly set her back on her feet. 'Yell at me later, ok?' April nodded. 'Great.' Jack darted a glance at Ben. The hands were regrouping and reforming into the shape of a person, the individual hands crawling about inside the form, sliding over one another.

'You can kill the girl,' Mórrígan said to the mass. It nodded stiffly and lumbered towards April. 'And you can kill the vampire, Barqan.'

Jack pulled his hunting knife from his belt. He pushed April behind him, forcing the mass to stop. It eyed him up, despite not seeming to actually have any eyes. Barqan remained still, back to the wall, watching.

The mass charged at him and by some sort of miracle, Jack managed to bury the blade into its chest. It caught on something that wasn't exactly flesh. It thrashed to the side, dragging Jack with it. Jack's feet struggled for purchase. He lost his grip on the handle. His knife disappeared into its body.

'Great.' A little too late, Jack realised that it had separated him from April. Its head looked past him to the hunter, the knife reappearing in its hand.

'No!' Jack lunged. It took a clumsy step out of his reach and he stumbled. Jack got back to his feet to see it backing April into a corner, knife poised to strike. Behind Jack, another human-like mass was forming and Barqan was moving slowly towards him, spear in hand.

And Ben hadn't got up.

He was lying on his back, forgotten in the chaos, on a patch of floor not covered by creepy crawlies. Wood might leave welts, maybe even a cut, but nothing more. But Ben was bleeding to death. Mórrígan swiftly closed the gap between her and Ben. She dropped to the floor, brushed a few stray hands from his chest and roughly patted him down. Ben groaned and stirred briefly, his hands pushing weakly at War's.

Jack glanced back to April. If he was quick, he could get Ben before Barqan got to April. A rope of hands tripped him over at the same time as April barrelled into him, having been thrown by Barqan. Jack yelled in outrage, aware that the pressure around him was changing. He wasn't sure whose magic it was charging up. Mórrígan's hand closed around the sword and was thrown back by a ball of aquamarine magic.

'That's handy.' Jack hauled Ben back to his feet.

'Jack,' Ben rasped, placing a hand on his chest, stopping him. 'Get April … ah. Outside.'

The look on Ben's face and the conviction in his voice forced Jack to reluctantly let go of his partner and grab April's arm instead. On his way to the door, bony fingers wrapped around Jack's ankles, tripping him. He hit the ground, rolled back to his feet and lunged for the door whilst April kicked away creepy hands at his back. Jack's fingertips brushed the handle. Barqan grabbed onto his legs and ripped them from under him. Jack clung onto the door, refusing to be pulled back into the room. April hit Barqan around the head with a stray chair. The djinn let go of Jack.

'It's a push, not a pull.' April gestured at the sign.

Jack tore the door off its hinges. 'It's neither now.' He used the door as a bat to fend off the mass of hands. Barqan charged at Jack, determined to end him. Like a matador, he held the door at his side, only moving it at the last second to let her pass. Barqan turned around and charged Jack again. He jabbed the door into Barqan's stomach and slammed it into her chin. She toppled over as she lost consciousness. Jack grinned, pleased with himself.

'Wow!'

'Out!' Jack shoved April outside into the cold early morning. Turning back to the scene inside, Ben had rolled onto his side. Clutched in his outstretched hand was the bokken, the shield still wrapped around the hilt. Jack couldn't work out if he'd simply lost consciousness. Or worse. Mórrígan picked herself up, ignoring the torn shoulder strap and cuts on her arm. She wobbled over to Ben, her eyes burning with fury, her face alight with rage. The very picture of war.

'You think you're so clever.' Mórrígan kicked Ben in the ribs. 'But you walked right into a trap, didn't you?' She was so focused on Ben that she failed to notice her hench-hands scattered around the room, nor did she notice the unconscious Barqan. Or the conscious vampire creeping over the threshold. Mórrígan's eyes darted down to the talisman.

And, the Gods help them all, both talismans were glowing with pulsating aquamarine magic.

The timing seemed all too convenient. Merlin was close, but Jack didn't know who Merlin was protecting.

Mórrígan let out a mad, triumphant laugh, her eyes wide with delight. 'Fate will be thrilled.' Jack crept closer. Talismans or Ben. He had two choices and not a lot of time to decide. Neither seemed like a winning option.

Mórrígan bent down, to end Ben's life or to snatch up the talisman, it didn't matter. Jack threw himself into her. As they crashed down, the shield and sword made contact with each other. And with Mórrígan. There was an almighty flash of aquamarine as the spell ripped through the room. The force of the explosion sent Jack into the opposite wall, ears ringing. Disorientated, he pushed himself onto all fours and crawled to Ben. Jack sunk to his knees beside his motionless partner. 'Ben? Mórrígan?'

Neither shtriga nor God answered before it all went dark.

19

Through Glass

Benjamin couldn't make out much through his blurred vision.

The little that he could see was at odds with his memory.

Ben had been indoors, not surrounded by copious amounts of large green smudges that he presumed to be trees, as he was now. Further proof of his change of location came in the form of birdsong. Day had broken, despite it having been hours away when he'd hit the ground. But there was the sun, high in the sky. Jack had got them clear, thank the Gods.

Ben closed his eyes, enjoying the warmth of the sun on his face whilst he struggled to reconcile time. Jack was going to give him hell for being out for an entire day. 'Gods, my … everything hurts.' A wave of nausea rocked Ben back and forth and he vowed not to fish for sympathy again. At least not straight away, not if it meant feeling like his rib cage was digging its way out. Physical pain *hurt*. It wasn't a hard concept to grasp, after all Ben was old friends with his hunger. But physical pain? He'd not known it in a long time.

The reason seemed clear. There was only so far he could run on empty. '*Ambrosius*?'

'*Ughhhh.*' Somewhere, deep inside, Ben's magic stirred and buried himself under the covers.

'*Same here. My mind hasn't felt this hazy since …*' Ben swam through the fog, trying to remember. '*Since the last time Merlin dragged me to the tavern. That man could drink anybody under the table!*'

'*Cheated. Used Emrys.*' With a huge amount of effort, Ambrosius managed to drag himself into view. '*We're concussed. Don't remember drinking.*' Content to let Ambrosius suss out their surroundings, Ben settled back into the strange feeling of serenity. Something cold collided with Ben's cheek and exploded, sending shards of glass across his face and rebooting his mind. He went to grab his talisman and found it was gone. A million possibilities chased his hands across his body as his pat-down turned to panic. Both his and Cerri's talismans were gone. Forgetting his aching-everything, Ben threw himself onto his side. Instead of feeling the solid security of carpeted floor, he fell a short distance to the snow-covered ground.

'Watch out, Benjamin!'

His befuddled mind recognised the voice, but like everything else in this world of anomalies, it was on the tip of his tongue. No attack followed. Relieved but confused, Ben lay on the frozen ground and despaired. He'd lost the talismans. Gaia must have fallen by now. Too drained to process it, he stared up uncomprehendingly at the treetops and patches of blue sky paled by a winter's sun. Heavy footsteps clattered towards him. Ben didn't bother turning to look. The symphony of aches, the bite of the cold and the burning shame would hopefully kill him before the footsteps arrived.

'Benjamin! What happened?'

'I'm only recently conscious, I don't know.'

'Are you hurt?'

Ben wanted to shut the voice out, if he couldn't name it. The footsteps repositioned so they were beside his head. 'I … Why am I in a forest?' Ben squinted up at the concerned face looming over him. 'Lancelot?! I'm dreaming. You're dead. Unless … are you immortal?' It was hard to make a conspiracy theory out of dying from old age, but Ben would, if it returned his friend to him. 'They said you died of a broken heart, but you ran out of time.' Benjamin forced out a shaky laugh, feeling a little smug at having worked it out. 'Jack must be worried. I've not woken up.'

'Jack?' Lancelot glanced back the way he came; uncertainty caused him to chew his bottom lip. 'I should fetch Merlin.'

'Merlin's here?' Benjamin clutched desperately at Lancelot's tunic, trying to pull himself up.

'Remain still!' Lancelot gently but firmly, pushed Ben back. 'Merlin is over there. See?'

Benjamin nervously followed Lancelot's pointing finger to where the other knights were setting up camp. All around him, horses were being relieved of saddles, blades were being sharpened and bedrolls laid out. In amongst the sea of activity and red cloaks stood Merlin, a scrawny spectre in black, the sleeves of his robes rolled up, sniping at an unfortunate squire. Ben took a deep breath of forest air and woodsmoke, and breathed out the knowledge that this was a dream. The heady cocktail of excitement and disappointment flooded his eyes with tears. Despite knowing it wasn't real, Benjamin couldn't get out of the way of his resentment and loathing. Wanting to rid himself of the bitter taste of betrayal, he summoned his courage, but found he couldn't stand on sheer determination alone.

His flailing arms took Lancelot down with him.

The commotion snapped Merlin's head round. Ben had to force himself not to look away first as Merlin's sceptical eyes darted up and down Benjamin.

'*None of this is real,*' Ambrosius tried to remind him.

'*Are we in Purgatory?*'

'*Nothing is looking at us like it wants to eat us.*'

'*It's too calm to be a dream state.*'

'*Merlin is looking at you like he knows you're here.*' They both saw how comprehension and intelligence weighed down Merlin's frown.

'Mer … Merlin?' The warlock huffed, dismissing the squire mid-sentence. The lad threw Ben a look of gratitude and scarpered off, pleased to have survived.

'Were you expecting somebody else?' Merlin grumbled but quickly made his way over, pushing a passing knight out of his way.

Benjamin couldn't answer; his conflicting emotions choked him.

'*Be careful, Ben.*'

'*I …*'

'Lancelot, do you have the map?' Shock froze Benjamin in place, his mouth slightly open. Ben had no trouble placing that voice.

Arthur.

Walking, talking, staring intently at Ben, Arthur. Concern danced in his piercing blue eyes, at odds with his blank expression. The king watched from a respectable distance, keeping a firm grip on the bridle of Benjamin's agitated horse.

'Ok, Ambrosius, either this place is a dream, or Jack and April were a dream.' But the pain of Arthur's death was too sharp and too present, to be imagined.

'We weren't out for that long. Jack and April are real. This place is crazy.'

'Well, let me see you.' Merlin snatched up one of Ben's arms, his movements sharp and rough. Benjamin paid him little attention; his gaze was locked with Arthur's. 'You are quiet,' Merlin observed, looking between his friends, 'and quite pale.'

Questions, thoughts and concerns bottlenecked, forcing an incoherent stream of noises out of Benjamin's mouth.

'What now? Have you misplaced your ability to speak?'

'Merlin.' Arthur, always overly-protective of Benjamin, cautioned his advisor. 'Benjamin is clearly hurt, be patient. I will never understand what drove you to become a physician when you despise people so deeply.' Arthur's rich laugh eased the way for Benjamin to blurt out,

'I fell off my horse!'

'Hmph.' Merlin prodded and poked at various limbs. 'Nothing appears to be broken. Can you sit?'

'Not sure.' Merlin shook his head in annoyance, motioning for Lancelot's assistance. Between them, they hauled Benjamin onto the log. Deciding that he was in safe hands, Lancelot patted him on the shoulder and left. Ben watched him go in awed disbelief, before returning his gaze to Merlin. He was surrounded by living ghosts.

'Stop staring. It's off-putting.' Ben laughed. Despite recent events, he had missed this disgruntled soul immensely. 'What is the matter? You are behaving as if you've not seen me in years.'

'I haven't. Lancelot's dead. You're dead. Arthur's dead. You're all dead,' Benjamin gestured with his free hand, 'apart from me.' He couldn't keep the bitterness out of his voice.

Merlin rocked back on his heels to stare right into the depths of his soul. 'Where have you been?'

Benjamin blinked, not understanding Merlin's question but before he could give it any real thought, Arthur knelt beside Merlin, ripping Benjamin's attention away.

'Are you alright?'

Ben could forget himself and he'd still know *that* voice.

'Arth—'

'Benjamin believes us all to be dead, if you can believe that?' Merlin complained. 'Dead! All of us. According to your physician.' Some things never changed, it seemed.

'Is that so?' The corner of Arthur's lips twitched, softening his stern face and stealing Ben's breath anew. Benjamin's mouth opened a little too wide – all of his words fled, leaving only inarticulate sounds. Merlin tutted his disapproval. Ben wished he could pass out again. He was a shambles. 'You lose consciousness for a few minutes and you forget us all.'

'Benjamin has lived another life.' Merlin's icy glare froze Ben's blood.

'What?!'

Merlin was the first to crack.

His shoulders shook with silent laughter whereas Arthur couldn't hold back his booming laugh. That wonderful, melodic laugh that shattered Ben's composure. 'What's so funny?' That made things worse – Merlin was turning blue. 'I do not understand what is happening.'

'We merely jest, Benjamin. Do not look so stricken.' Arthur's hand came to rest lightly on Benjamin's shoulder. Instinctively, he pushed his shoulder up and into the familiar warmth he'd never stop craving.

'Hell. We're in hell, Ambrosius,' Ben thought sadly. *'My mind has painted a pretty picture to distract me from whatever fate has befallen us.'*

'If this is hell, it's not so bad ...'

'What's this?' Arthur pulled up Benjamin's sleeve. The fabric peeled back to reveal a decent-sized cut on his arm and deep grazes on his hand. 'You are bleeding. Look!' Arthur exclaimed, prodding Merlin to inspect it.

Benjamin tore his eyes away from Arthur's face – there wasn't a line out of place – to look at the offending hand. He had to do a double take, his eyes growing wide. The pain and the cold, the ache in his head, they were real. 'Oh.' Ben swooned.

'It's a minuscule amount of blood, Benjamin,' Merlin huffed. There was actually quite a lot of blood. What Merlin mistook for a queasy stomach was actually bewildered confusion. 'I will bandage it, if you care to stay still.' He made another grab for Benjamin's hand as Ben snatched it free to inspect the wound that shouldn't be.

'You don't understand, I heal without delay.' Undernourished or not. Benjamin listened to the horses neighing and soldiers calling to one another. The hounds were barking and Arthur and Merlin were laughing, and for a second, all was right with the world. And that's what shoehorned clarity into Benjamin's mind:

He was home.

He was human.

He'd been poisoned.

This wasn't a dream, or hell. This was nefarious; it was torture. It *was* a dream state.

'The Gods be damned!' Ben closed his eyes to dam the flow of angry tears. He'd almost made it home. Almost ... It hit Benjamin with such force he swayed. Arthur's hand darted out to steady him, retreating as soon as the king was satisfied that his physician wasn't going to fall.

'How does your head feel?' Arthur asked, sitting down next to Benjamin, the sun flashing off the king's wedding ring. He followed Ben's gaze and his left hand disappeared from view. Benjamin would never stand in the way of Arthur's duty. He certainly wouldn't make the king choose. Doing the right thing had never felt so awfully wrong. 'Benjamin?' Arthur gave him a gentle shake, sending electricity shooting through him.

'Hmm? As if it's been bashed against a wall.' Benjamin flashed Arthur a sorry smile. 'I think I've been poisoned by Barqan ... Whatever this is, it's in my mind. Whether I die or wake, you'll fade away, all of this will fade to a vivid nightmare. Everything that could have been, laid out in front of me.' Benjamin chuckled at Arthur's sad concern. 'You think I've lost my mind.' Arthur watched him closely, his intelligent eyes searched Benjamin's, but said nothing – he was a perpetual thinker.

'If this is as you believe, would staying be so terrible?' Benjamin couldn't trust himself to speak. It didn't matter where Ben went, he'd always want to be right here. Arthur knew that. 'Would it?' Arthur gently nudged Benjamin with his shoulder, trying to provoke an answer. Benjamin shook his head as the dam broke. He had no use for tears, but this … this landed a million miles south of unfair. And how the tears fell, coming in great heaving sobs. 'What the …? I was teasing; it was cruel. I apologise.' Arthur hesitated for a second before wrapping his arm around Benjamin's shaking shoulders, drawing him in close, always conscious of those looking on. 'It's alright, Benjamin.' Arthur's armour was cold against Ben's cheek. His fingers traced the delicate engravings of dragons and roses. Benjamin had thought he'd never know Arthur's touch again, would never feel those strong arms encircle him. It was soul-crushingly sad.

'I couldn't stop it. It's my fault.'

Arthur looked to Merlin for help, utterly perplexed and a little disturbed by this strange outburst. Merlin, who loathed the display of any kind of emotion apart from exasperation, realised that this was one of those times where he had to do something solely for the benefit of somebody else. He finished preparing the bandage and knelt beside the couple. The man from his past looked into his soul once more. 'What happened?'

'The horse …'

'I know about your hand! What happened to *you*?' Merlin asked rather pointedly, cutting through Benjamin's spiralling thoughts, sharpening his focus. Ben knew where in time he was.

This scene had first been staged during the last Christmas. Ben had been riding to meet them. His horse had lost its footing on a patch of ice. The only subtle difference was Merlin. He was off-book and improvising.

'I don't follow,' Ben stalled, trying to find his way back on script. 'I am fine.'

'I can't tell if it's hunger or melancholy that consumes you. Or is it both?' Merlin spoke to him directly, as if he too existed outside of this loop.

'I don't understand …' Ben whined.

'You do have a haunted look about you.' Merlin's eyes shone a little too brightly for a memory that refused to fade.

'Is this poison or your magic?' Merlin gave him a knowing grin that silenced the sounds of the camp. Startled, Ben craned his neck around to see the clearing empty of people and animals. 'Where …?'

'They are away,' Merlin chuckled. 'The difference between them and Arthur and I, is you. You have kept us alive, Benjamin.' Considering Ben hadn't saved them, the dig was probably justified.

'You nearly fooled Ambrosius, but we can feel your magic running through this … illusion.'

'Took you long enough.' The warlock sighed in exasperation.

'Where are you, Merlin? You can't be far.' And had likely never been far.

'I am somewhere, it matters not where.' Merlin shrugged.

'Why is this the first time I've seen you?' Arthur flinched at the sound of Ben's anger. The sense of abandonment, the idea that Merlin had known and stood by, was throbbing in his mind.

'You do not dream anymore.' Merlin's tone suggested that this should have been obvious. 'You are dying.' Spots appeared in Ben's vision, one by one. 'Let the current take you.' Merlin reached around and pried his arm free of Benjamin's grip. 'Trust me.'

'Trust you?!' Ben lurched forward to grab Merlin, but Arthur pulled him back into a tight embrace. Arthur's chin came to rest on the top of Ben's head. It melted away Ben's anger.

'I can't be dying. Not now. It's so inconvenient.' In the distance, Jack was calling his name. 'Jack …' Ben wanted to stay but Jack... Ben dragged himself from Arthur's arms. 'Why?'

'Why, what?' Merlin's nostrils flared as his patience frayed.

'Why didn't you warn me?' Ben roared, blood thundering in his ears. 'Why did you give me Arthur's talisman? Why not give me yours?' The questions poured out of him like they'd never end. He felt lighter with each one. 'Why did you leave?'

'I had work to do. Arthur was lost, as you well know. You watched him die.' Ben didn't hear the rest of Merlin's excuses. Of course, Merlin had heard how the court physician had denied the king treatment. 'What are you seeking, shtriga? Absolution?'

'Answers, from you!'

Merlin threw his arms in the air, as if to say, *This is why I don't call!* and turned away. 'When you are not digging up the past, you are digging your own grave.'

Arthur took Ben's hand and gifted him with a genuine, fond smile. It tore his heart to pieces. 'I could have saved you; we could have …' He'd found all the things he should have said before, now he'd lost the time. 'I should have forgiven you for …'

'For the love of … We do not blame you for what happened, Benjamin.' Merlin spun back to face him, ever a comet racing through space. 'You had a purpose greater than ours.' Merlin shook his head, bored of teaching his former assistant. Ben wasn't sure, but he thought he heard some high notes of guilt.

'You're blaming Fate?' Merlin stilled, sending Ben back into Arthur's arms. Time, it seemed, hadn't erased his fear of Merlin's temper. And it was close to snapping.

'It's happened now, so dwell on it no more,' Merlin said quietly. Alarm bells clamoured in Ben's mind. Merlin had visited her. 'You had time enough to stop her, Benjamin, but you squandered it with that vampire!' Perhaps it was the light, but Arthur's ocean eyes turned a shade of green.

'I didn't know there was a deadline!' Merlin rolled his eyes, because the fault was never his. 'You could have told me instead of rambling about time dragging you around. It was wonderfully poetic but useless!'

'Never mind about that.' Merlin closed the short gap between them. 'Mórrígan can't be allowed to hold all of the talismans. She has the ability to wield such magic, but not the right intent. War will bring about an age of darkness far greater than any before. As soon as Mórrígan has the talismans, Fate will consume her and thus strengthen her magic significantly. Oh, don't look so disgusted! It's how the Gods settle most disputes. Fate must not be allowed to capture Chaos. The universe needs Chaos, Benjamin. Everything must remain in balance.'

Ben felt the coals of the old irritation ignite; here stood Merlin, inserting himself into Benjamin's life. 'As a matter of fact, that's what we were trying to—'

'Remember, Benjamin, when the dust settles, when it all comes clear, you will know. We will be here.'

'You haven't told me where "here" is!' Merlin smiled his crooked, all-knowing smile one last time and clicked his fingers, plunging Ben into darkness. 'Merlin!'

Merlin's breath came warm against Ben's ear. 'It was me.'

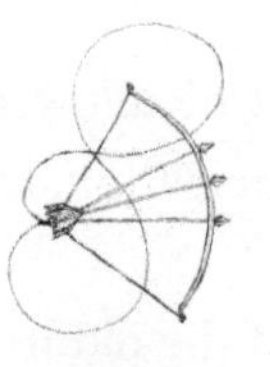

20

Wires

Wales

'Ben! Wake up. Please ...'

Past and present collided in a chaotic symphony built on clashing notes, Merlin as the high trill, Jack as the bass.

Ben was spinning, weightless in the darker-than-dark void that wrapped around him, squeezing him so tightly that he thought his skeleton would crumble to dust. The universe was folding in on itself and it didn't care that there was a shtriga trapped in the middle of it.

Jack's insistent call was the only object in the nothingness with any form and Ben reached for it, letting his favourite sound pull him out.

With great effort, Ben forced his eyes open to find Jack dominating his field of vision. Jack had that look of stubborn determination that he'd learnt from Ben. He wore it well but not so well that Benjamin couldn't see the worry poking out from the corners of Jack's mouth.

'What happened?' Pain screamed in every part of his body, nearly tipping him back into unconsciousness. Under

Ben's jacket, his shirt clung to his skin. He tentatively pulled it back, wincing at how it peeled away, sticky and red. 'Blood.' Ben numbly inspected his red hand. He'd been bleeding in his dream. A nice touch by his subconscious. As for the dream, it was fading fast, as dreams are wont to do. He latched onto the tail of the shadow before it slipped over memory's horizon, and rewound it.

'I know. We're going to get help.'

'Hand on you.'

'What? Ugh.' Jack danced a few steps, shaking the cursed thing off. Reaching the car, he ripped open the door and bundled Ben into the back seat where April waited.

'It was me? Wonder what he meant.' Ben closed his eyes, trying to listen carefully to everything Merlin hadn't said. Faking his own death, vanishing for over a thousand years and reappearing in a dream was so very Merlin. The ghost of Arthur's embrace wouldn't let him go and his voice still sung in Benjamin's mind, crystal clear. Everything seemed so huge, this close up. Ben could sort it out if he had the mind to focus on one thing at a time, but he didn't. He couldn't keep his eyes open, but shutting them was no good either. It allowed the nothingness to creep back in. Defeated, Ben let them close, content that they wouldn't open again.

Gravel crunched under wheels as Jack slammed his foot down, spinning the car around. There were but a few times in Jack's life where despair had stolen his confidence, and left him incapable of deciding what to do. This was one of them. His partner of over eight hundred years was treating consciousness like a revolving door and bleeding out in the back seat of his car, the talismans in his hand.

'We're not being followed.' He watched the B&B retreat in the rear-view mirror, his heart in his mouth.

'Great! Where are we going? To a hospital?' That sounded right, so Jack nodded. 'What are we going to tell them? "Excuse me, our friend, who is an ancient supernatural witch-creature, has been stabbed. And instead of healing like a good shtriga should, he's dying like the mortal he once was?"'

'I didn't say that it was a good plan!' Fear was jamming Jack from thinking properly. 'Feeding is an option but I don't know ...'

'I can't stop the bleeding. How much time do you need?' April pulled off her jumper, pushing it against the wound.

'More than he has.' The red stain grew rapidly, tainting the grey jumper. 'It'll wash out.' Jack's usually unfaltering humour stumbled and he couldn't hold the smile.

'Feel free to try but I'm going to burn this jumper first chance I get.'

'I'll buy you a new one ...'

'Need to stop Mórrígan.' Ben's weak voice managed to cut through their back and forth. 'Collecting the talisman ...'

'What?' Jack had to fight to keep his eyes on the road when they wanted so badly to look over his shoulder to find out why Ben wasn't answering him. 'Ben?'

'He's unconscious,' April said with more confidence than she felt. 'What happened inside, Jack?'

'Wish I knew.'

****

Jack pulled the car up in front of the emergency room doors, certain that they were too late. He rushed round to the passenger side and pulled a limp, unresponsive Ben free of April's tight grasp.

Medical staff, primed with questions, rushed out to meet them at the doors. Jack tried his best to answer but the shock and disbelief was settling deep into his bones. He looked down at Ben's blood-stained clothes, the paler-than-normal skin, the still and oddly peaceful face … This wasn't how Ben died, this wasn't how they parted. But that was exactly what was going to happen. Jack couldn't fix this and nor could the well-meaning nurses who ripped Ben from his arms with blunt efficiency. Free of Ben's weight, Jack staggered back, feeling detached from his body, unable to see Ben for all the people clustered around the bed. And the questions kept coming. Jack mumbled a yes or a no, acutely aware that he wasn't helping.

It felt like it took an eternity to begin the dash through the hospital corridors. Jack squeezed himself in between two nurses so he could at least see Ben. His breath caught in his throat as he took in the sight of his partner, unconscious and attached to an array of wires. Ben's eyes blinked open for a moment. He looked around him in confusion, unsure of everything. 'Jack?'

'I'm here.' Jack's voice cracked, so he took Ben's hand and squeezed it.

'I …' Specks of orange magic skittered over the backs of Ben's hands, unnoticed by the doctors. Ambrosius was dying. '… I saw them, Jack.'

'Who, Ben, who did you see?' Ben's eyes rolled into the back of his head. With more urgency, Jack again asked, 'Who did you see, Ben?'

'Merlin,' Ben sighed, his smile pushing back the pain. 'And Arthur.'

If Jack's heart still beat, it would have skipped. Something in Ben's voice convinced Jack that he wasn't talking about a dream. As they approached a set of double doors, somebody threw their hand out, stopping Jack in his tracks.

'We need to get him into the operating theatre, sir.' Jack watched them push Ben through the doors. It was the world's worst vanishing trick.

'Will he be alright?' Jack asked, desperate for an answer that he knew he didn't want to hear.

'At this stage it's difficult to tell. It's a case of waiting, here.'

Jack turned this way and that, not sure what to do with himself. He detested waiting. The prospect of an unknown number of hours of staring at white hospital walls in sterile conformity… Jack wanted to scream but couldn't, so he drove his fist into the nearest wall. Pent-up frustration extinguished, Jack turned his back to the wall and sunk to the floor, head in his hands.

****

April slowly lifted her head from where it rested against the steering wheel. She'd moored up in an awful multi-story car park that, according to the sign, charged five pounds an hour. She stared, unfocused, until the dirt-covered numbers and letters danced across her vision. Exhaustion was trying its best to pull her down. It was going to take all the comfort food to recover from this.

She made one last half-hearted effort to pull herself together, but the fact was she didn't want to. Nothing was ok, so April wasn't sure why she had to be. But she forced herself to look at her reflection in the rear-view mirror. 'Get a hold of yourself and get out of the …' in the bottom left-hand corner of the mirror, April spied a shadow nestled between two parked cars, '… car.' The hood of the cloak covered his features but for the tip of a long nose. April reached slowly for her bokken in the passenger seat, ignoring the dirty red stains on the blade. She should have asked the boys for something more substantial in the weapon department. 'Calm down. It could be anybody in a cloak loitering in a car park.' There was maybe twenty-five feet between April and the artificial glow of safety. Her many thanks went to the jerk who'd cut her off for a spot closer to the doors. She looked back into the mirror – no hooded figure. April whipped her head around, checking her blind spots, but he was nowhere to be seen. April wasn't quite a sitting duck – she could drive off. Or run him over. Panic wrapped her fingers around the door handle. Metal scraped against metal but there was no time to leave a note. She set off at a brisk walk, fighting to stay calm. Her hands automatically patted at her pockets. She had her phone but, 'Crap!' The key was still in the ignition. Oh well, she wasn't going back for it. Besides, if somebody nicked it, they'd be doing Jack a favour. Out the corner of her eye, a cloak swirled about a person in motion, effortlessly matching her hurried pace. April quickened her step. He matched it. She slowed her pace. He fell back in step with her. Six feet away and April's panic was tangible. Unable to hold her nerve any longer, she broke into a run. The sound of April's shoes hitting the concrete mixed with her rapid breathing, but he moved silently on his assassin's footsteps. The automatic doors sensed her coming and rattled into life. April jammed one shoulder into the parting and squeezed her way inside. Risking a quick look back, she stalled. Bathed in the rapid flickering of a harsh white fluorescent light, he watched her.

Two paces and he'd be able to touch April. His hands appeared from his sleeves.

April took off running. She skidded around a corner, into a busy waiting room and ducked behind a convenient pillar, pulling her phone out. 'Come on, come on!' Her lock screen pinged open. The dial tone screeched in her ear, her eyes coming to rest on the convex mirror across from her. Doctors and nurses moved around the hooded figure as if he wasn't there, standing in the middle of the room. 'Pick up, pick up.' The calm tone of the voicemail lady mocked her. April frantically hit redial, her eyes never leaving the mirror. He took a step forward. April broke cover and fled blindly down a corridor, colliding with people.

'April? April, are you there? April!'

'Jack!' she panted. 'Somebody's following me.'

'Where are you now?'

'Don't know.' April backtracked to consult a sign. 'Um, outpatients ...'

'Follow the signs for A&E.' April didn't need telling twice. The map was deceiving; it felt like she had to run forever before she found the emergency room. A startled nurse pointed her in the right direction. April turned another corner and collided with Jack.

'Where and what is he?' Jack's eyes darted back and forth from hers to the doors.

'I didn't think to ask!' April shouted. 'He was behind me. When. I. Phoned you.' She was breathing heavily, adrenaline pumping through her veins.

'Here.' Checking that nobody was looking their way, Jack produced a hunting knife with curious markings carved into the blade. He pushed it into her shaking hands, and she hid it up her sleeve.

Jack pulled her back so quickly that she dropped her questions. Over his shoulder, the hooded figure appeared at the end of the corridor. The sapphire cloak seemed to billow behind him, whilst revealing nothing of the figure beneath. Sensing Jack's challenge, he stopped, head to one side. The vampire's eyes narrowed in anger and April worried he'd charge.

'What kind of a coward chases a woman through a hospital? I have a sense, mind you.' With carefully measured steps, the man approached. 'That's close enough,' Jack barked, stopping the man just outside of arms reach. 'Declare yourself.'

'Hmph!' Weathered hands appeared, palms facing out as they inched up to remove the hood. He rested it atop his mop of chaotic brown hair which crowned a face dominated by pitch-black eyes and the previously glimpsed aquiline nose.

'I should kill you.' Something deep within April vehemently agreed with Jack.

'Perhaps you should hear what I have to say first.'

There was the strongest feeling of foreboding emanating from the cloaked man. Pins and needles prickled her arms. He had been or was going to be the root cause of Jack's unhappiness.

'Do you smoke?' The stranger nodded as if he'd thought that Jack would never ask. 'Alright.' Jack half-turned to April. 'Stay here?' She nodded. Curiosity sparked fires in her mind but she held her tongue. 'If anything happens, call me.' Jack didn't wait for the answer. He strode towards the sapphire cloak with a confidence that was worrisome. The cloaked man lingered, beholding April with an odd mix of intrigue and wonder that set her skin crawling. Jack turned back, his eyes dark as he grabbed the man by the shoulder and marched him away. Unsettled and with nothing else to do, April settled down to wait and see if she was right.

****

Faint voices and beeping called down to Ben. Jack was talking urgently with somebody, but it didn't matter anymore. Not here.

The trees stretched on their tiptoes, pulling back the clouds to reveal the moon and stars exactly as he'd left them when he'd shown April this memory. The only thing out of place in the spot-the-difference was the lack of a mob. Ben turned slowly on the spot, noting how the dew-soaked grass squeaked under his foot.

'This is Purgatory.' Ben's breath clouded the air in front of him.

'It sure is.' Ambrosius popped up on his shoulder. 'At least they've provided some entertainment.' A speck of white light flared brightly in the gaps between knotted tree trunks. It grew into a rectangle of static and white noise. A shower of sparks fluttered across the screens, bathing Ben in an orange glow. As Ben's eyes adjusted, the smudges took the shapes of his past in a silent, crystal-clear movie. Ben stared, entranced. Here, somewhere in between life and death, everybody he had ever known existed on the other side of the clearing. 'Look.'

Together, they watched a younger Ben stagger into the tavern where he'd meet Jack. Ben had saved the new vampire's life that night. Next to it, Ben stumbled through the battlefield to watch the king die. When the blade flashed out, Ben turned away, unable to watch himself do nothing to save the life he cared most about.

'Couldn't you have picked something else?'

'I'm not doing this! Try worrying about what is.'

Irritated by Ambrosius's lack of sympathy, Ben turned his attention back to watching an eighteen-year-old-Ben encountering Merlin for the first time. 'I treasure this memory,' Ben smiled a little, 'despite everything. It's so …'

'Disturbing. What? Watch, you'll see.'

Ben always felt the buzz of excitement at being in such a busy city. It had never called to him fully, preferring to live removed from the hustle and bustle, where it was quiet enough to think. Everything in the market was so full of colour and life. The constant clamour of traders calling out to passers-by was one of his favourite songs. The smells of freshly baked bread, spices and herbs were soothing to his soul as he wandered between stalls.

Free of his body, Ben could take in every little detail that he'd missed with his human eyes in the moment. Unnoticed, Merlin followed close behind. Purpose set Merlin's face into hard lines. His eyes narrowed as he moved with resolve, his calculating stare boring into Benjamin's back.

'If Merlin had wanted me dead …' Ben remembered the heat of the day scorching his skin, and yet Merlin was ensconced in his famous cloak of sapphire blue. 'That's the look that heralded the beginning of a Merlin-plan.' Ben shared a knowing look with Ambrosius.

'You're prey, Ben. Merlin's prey.' Ambrosius jumped down into Ben's hand, nudging at his thumb, wanting to get closer. 'There's no such thing as a coincidence, only Fate.'

'Merlin knew who I was and the road he was sending me down by stopping me from leaving.' Ben swallowed, numb with understanding. 'Merlin orchestrated all of it.' Ben watched on tenterhooks. 'Don't turn around. Keep walking,' he quietly urged his younger self.

'Is this your first time in Caerleon?' Merlin's smile was full of shark's teeth. Ben hadn't noticed that.

'It is, sir. I am passing through. I shall be gone by the week's end.' Ben smiled cheerfully. It had been all too easy to converse with Merlin. How ironic that, at the time, Ben had felt regret for the friendship that could have been, if only he had planned to remain in the city. That's the trouble with wishing – he never knew who had been listening.

'Hmph.' Merlin's signature sound preceded most sentences. And served to tell the world that Merlin was constantly exasperated with it. It also kept the majority of people from ever breaking past the grumpy exterior. Ben included. 'A pity. I see you looking at the tinctures and herbs. Tell me, are you a physician?'

Benjamin was on trial, and Merlin was the judge. Even now, Benjamin's anxiety twisted his insides. 'I am. Are you a physician also?'

'Amongst other things.' Perhaps the only honest words Merlin had ever spoken. Here, Merlin looked closer to being healthy. He wasn't so thin, his hair neatly combed without a fleck of grey.

'I have rooms booked at the Bear Inn.' Benjamin's painfully polite younger self stepped back, surprised he'd volunteered the information. Subtly extracting secrets from people was one of Merlin's many talents.

Ben's attention drifted to the brooch holding Merlin's cloak together; it bore the coat of arms of the king. Pinned above his heart, almost hidden by a blue fold, three swirls expanded from a central point, marking the man as a druid. Seeming to sense the next question, Merlin cut him off with his own.

'Do you like food?'

'Well, yes.' Benjamin laughed, surprised and relieved at the change of direction.

'Then it's settled! You will dine with me tonight. Ah, I will hear no protests.' And with that, Merlin slipped back into the crowd.

'Where shall I meet you? I don't even know your name!' Bewildered, Benjamin turned to the stall's owner, looking for confirmation that he hadn't dreamt the whole exchange.

'That was Lord Merlin, the king's advisor. Seems he likes you.' For a split second, it looked like he was going to say more, but thought better of it.

Ambrosius turned sharply, a worried frown on his little face, a tiny hand clinging to his ear. *'Benjamin, turn around.'*

'Oh.' The laughter of ghosts at a dinner party abruptly halted. The glow from the mob's torches crept closer. They advanced with synchronised steps, fanning out to surround Ben, forcing him into the centre of an ever-shrinking circle and bringing him within arm's reach.

Their silence was deathly and it sounded like doom.

21

Skylight

Hospital

'So, Mórrígan got the better of you, eh?' Jack was desperate, so he chose to ignore Merlin's provocation. 'Ah, well. It happens to the best of us, lad.'

Lad.

They'd only reached the doors and Merlin had already annoyed Jack into rummaging for a lighter. Jack wordlessly offered up the packet of cigarettes to Merlin.

'Ah!' Merlin snatched the lighter and made a beeline for the nearest bench. With a deep sigh, Jack joined him.

'Your tree is dead.' When in doubt, blurt something out.

'Oh no! Really? Whatever will I do?' Merlin rolled his eyes in exasperation.

'You took a huge risk chasing April. She's tougher than she looks.' Jack stared straight ahead, watching people who smelt like death or fear, or both, shuffle past in drab robes or street clothes. 'Funny to think that some of their lives could change forever today.'

'April's not a threat to me.' Merlin exhaled a cloud of smoke. 'Not yet anyway.'

Jack remembered how Merlin had looked at April and clenched his fists. 'She isn't a concern.'

'She is something.'

'Riddles? Really?' Merlin took another noncommittal drag, smoke curling from his lips. 'What are you doing, Merlin?'

'I was in the area.' Merlin chucked his cigarette and leant over Jack to help himself. Jack refused to pull away, despite the fact that his skin was crawling from the unwelcome breach of personal space.

'Wanna slow down? Warlocks can get cancer, right?' Jack stuffed the packet into a pocket. 'You picked a convenient time to rise from the dead.'

'Benjamin.' The name tripped out of Merlin's mouth. Left unspoken, names tended to fester, rearranging themselves into something difficult to pronounce. 'Feeding will only do so much. Do you know why?'

'Because Mórrígan used a wooden sword and your own talisman to stab Ben?' Jack took an angry drag on the cigarette to distract his hands.

'A crude theory, but yes. Benjamin is a creature born of magic; the wound was caused by magic. Ergo, magic is the cure.'

'Thank you, Merlin. I'd worked that out!' And magic was the only thing that Jack couldn't do for Ben. 'Had you the guts to show yourself earlier, this wouldn't have happened.'

'I came as soon as I could.' Jack's mouth twitched but Merlin didn't seem to notice – or care – that this matter was somewhat contentious. 'Why are we outside? Plenty of takeout strolling about, if you have a taste for blood.' Merlin asked deliberately loudly. A passing lady pulled her child away from the waving warlock in the cloak.

'Put your hand down!' Jack hissed, forcing Merlin's arm to his side. 'You can't smoke indoors. Especially at a hospital!'

'Take me to Benjamin and I shall begin. Nobody has to die today.'

Jack's head snapped up, hope and relief briefly lightening his mood, until he remembered who he was talking to and laughed darkly. He was still struggling with the welter of emotions kicked up by the day's events. 'As wonderful as that sounds, the problem, Merlin, is that you have a history of making terrible decisions. Especially where Ben is concerned. So, you'll forgive me if I don't fall to my knees in awe and gratitude.'

'By all means, continue searching for souls. Although it looks like slim pickings around here,' Merlin shouted gleefully.

'I'm glad you're enjoying yourself – stop it!' People had been giving them a wide berth before, but now there was a man talking to security. 'We don't need the attention that you bring.' Jack glared at the cloak, finished his cigarette, and immediately started another. The hypocrisy went unspoken.

'Does Benjamin know you smoke? I can't imagine he approves.'

'Does Fate know you're out? I can't imagine she'd approve. And I only smoke when I'm particularly stressed.'

'Hmph, it's our secret.'

'So kind.' Jack checked his phone – no calls. 'But Ben will forgive me. Assuming you're not here to kill him on Fate's behalf.'

'What Fate wants isn't for the best these days.' Merlin stubbed out his cigarette in the space between them. 'And what was Benjamin thinking? Letting himself get stabbed like that.'

'Letting … what? He was looking for you! Even though you're meant to be dead!' Jack's voice jumped in volume, drawing more stares. 'Why aren't you dead? How have you filled the time? If you can't explain yourself to me, how the hell are you going to face Ben?'

Merlin blinked slowly, letting Jack get his breath back. 'There is nothing I can say to clear me of my wrongs in your mind, so let's return to the subject of healing Benjamin. Perhaps I can help, for a change,' Merlin said earnestly.

'Nicely dodged. I don't want to steal a soul from a hospital patient. This doesn't mean that I trust you, Merlin.' Jack stood and crushed his cigarette with his heel. Merlin pushed himself up with both hands, earning Jack a reproachful tut from a posh lady with flowers clutched in both hands. 'He's fine. It's all an act.' She shook her head and moved off. 'Move it, Merlin!' Jack decided against shoving an apparently frail old man outside a hospital.

They found April dozing in the waiting room. Jack knelt beside her on the cold floor and gently shook her awake.

'Hello,' she mumbled. 'What are you doing here?'

'I could ask you the same thing. I told you to stay put.' Jack tried to keep his irritation buried; he could hardly tell her off for being exhausted.

'I couldn't find you,' April said around a yawn, 'so I waited here. They brought Ben out not long ago.' April frowned at her phone. 'I think.'

'Where is he now? Is he alright?' Jack's grip on her arm tightened.

'He's stable but critical.' April lowered her voice. 'They found a heartbeat. I thought Ben was joking about having a pulse!'

'He used that line on me too.' It had taken Ben six months to build up the courage to steal a kiss. Not that Jack had made much progress in that area either. He was still working out how to be a vampire, having been turned and then killing his entire town, all in one day. Ben had worried that it might be Stockholm syndrome, despite Jack insisting that he'd found where he was meant to be.

'Yeah, I suspected he'd already workshopped that line. They've stopped the bleeding. Ben's in a private room for now. Which is lucky because he keeps shouting in his sleep.' April's brows knitted together. 'If he carries on, they'll lock him up!'

'As a human, Benjamin often spoke in his sleep.'

April locked eyes with the man standing behind Jack, like some sort of half-arsed reaper. His hood was down this time, showing her his shark-like eyes. 'No.' April stood up hastily, knocking off Jack's hand. A mixture of dread and certainty filled her with a restless energy that was only satisfied by backing away from the stranger.

'He's going to help.' Jack sounded like he didn't believe it.

'He'll make everything worse.' April had never been so certain of anything in her life.

'Do you know each other?'

April shook her head, not looking away from the cloaked figure, not liking how he stared back at her, unconcerned by her accusation. And with such familiarity.

'A guy who dresses like a creep and hangs around in car parks is not going to help.' Jack dropped his gaze to the floor. 'Why is he even wearing a cloak? They haven't been fashionable this century.' Having sensed April's perturbation, Jack pushed himself between her and the creep, arms slightly raised.

'The cloak isn't that bad. Look, I don't much like this either, *but* it's the only way to help Ben, so … ok?' April considered Jack's position before reluctantly agreeing. She'd watch the stranger like a hawk, and the second he put a foot wrong, she'd pounce.

Jack straightened up but couldn't straighten out April's reaction.

He'd not seen her this spooked before. Whatever was going through her head right now, he was inclined to agree with it. But he let her take them to Ben all the same.

Merlin shoved his way past Jack to be the first into the cramped, sterile room. Best not let the lad think himself in charge. It wasn't the sight of Benjamin hooked up to machines and wires that were relentless with the orchestra of beeps and whirrs, that stopped Merlin in the doorway.

'You knew this day was coming, and still, you are woefully unprepared to meet Benjamin outside of a dream.'

'Thank you for your concern, Emrys, but I am completely fine with my lack of disguise. I can face Benjamin on the same plane, in the same realm, in the same room.'

'So why are you holding onto the doorframe?'

'There's never a convenient time to cop to the truth.'

'Fix him.' Jack, a tight bundle of apprehension and fear, shoved Merlin into the room. Merlin wanted a few more hours of calm before what promised to be a disastrous storm, but he'd run out of time years ago.

'This is how we start to cut ourselves free of my own spider webs, Emrys.' Merlin stepped forward, struggling to pin down the thoughts that kept flying away with his focus. And his focus had to be on healing and nothing else.

He raised shaking hands and cast the spell.

It was times like these that Jack cursed himself for not paying more attention to Ben's lectures. Jack was a lost cause when it came to magic. Merlin's eyes were half-closed, his lips were moving silently. Jack kept looking for the swirling ball of magic but it never appeared – not that that meant anything. He'd seen Ben cast spells without Ambrosius manifesting. 'Did it work?'

Merlin stepped back, looking perplexed. 'Well, I'll be—'

'Dead. If you fail. What's the problem?'

'He's got himself into a fine mess.' Merlin closed his eyes, listening to frequencies Jack couldn't imagine. 'Benjamin's stuck in between life and death.'

'He's a shtriga, that's how he rolls.' Jack's derisive tone earned him a long, menacing stare from Merlin that almost bowed the vampire's head.

'You misunderstand. Benjamin is passing through the veil as we speak.'

'He's in Purgatory.' April's voice cracked with lack of use. 'Purgatory isn't somewhere you come back from.' Jack glanced at her pale face, wondering how she knew that. Judging by her wide eyes and startled expression, April was asking herself the same question.

'That's what I said, was it not? I couldn't have been clearer. Hmph.'

'How do we get Ben back?' Jack demanded.

Merlin sent long, bony fingers reaching inside his cloak to retrieve a circular amulet. 'Sometimes, you have to swallow a spider to catch the fly.'

'Meaning?' Stories of Merlin's past deceits ran through Jack's mind, filling him with dread.

'Meaning, we need to send somebody, or rather, something, in after Benjamin.' Merlin carefully laid the amulet over Ben's heart. Jack didn't like the look of the two circles surrounding a pentagram and three heptagons. It was inscribed with the names of the new God's angels, but it looked downright demonic to him.

'What is it?' April edged a little closer, peering apprehensively at the thing.

'The Sigillum Dei.' Merlin's tone suggested that was obvious.

'How does it work exactly?' Jack hovered nervously at Merlin's side, fighting his instinctive urge to fling the man across the room.

'I cannot work with you standing on top of me!' Jack grunted and moved back half a step. 'You don't trust magic.'

'More like the caster.' The fact that Ben's fate lay solely in the hands of the person responsible for immeasurable amounts of physical and emotional trauma, wasn't helping. 'Magic wasn't an advantage for Ben. I hear he was one of the best in his day.'

'I taught him most of what he knows.' Merlin puffed out his chest. 'The curse turned his own brilliance against him. Tragic. Hold this.' A battered leather bag was thrust into Jack's unwilling arms.

'You seem to know an awful lot about an unconscious guy you've just met,' April said in a voice that spoke of past treachery, present danger and future deception. She'd no idea where the voice had come from – its scream had been building inside her ever since *he* had appeared. The Sigillum Dei was the last straw.

'I am aware of your many questions, my lady. I ask that you suspend your enquiry until later. I must focus on Benjamin.'

'Everybody keeps asking me to be patient. I'm done with patience.' April moved to the other side of the bed, forcing herself into *his* line of sight. *His* hands danced over Ben's body with care, despite the fact he wasn't one to care about anybody. April's concern had outgrown her vision. It might have been the way *he* moved like *he* was being pursued, or the way *he* didn't seem to care that *he* was wasting time, or the way the top of *his* nose scrunched up in concentration, but something spoke to April, insisting that she should remember. 'Who are you?'

'April,' Jack cautioned, a pained expression painted over his unhappy face.

She held a hand up to silence him. 'No.' There was that strange voice again, the one that belonged to a life April hadn't lived. 'I want to know.' April's mistrust gave her the confidence to challenge the stranger with the sapphire cloak. 'Your magic must be powerful if you're able to heal Ben.' *He* worked on in silence but she wasn't going to be ignored. Not by *him*. 'It's extremely difficult for another wizard—'

'Warlock.'

'Excuse me?' The arrogance was staggering.

'I am a warlock, not a wizard. Kindly remember the difference.'

April was going to call him a wizard at every available opportunity. 'Perhaps if you didn't wear a cape, people wouldn't confuse you with a wizard.' The corners of *his* lips pulled up into an approving smile. 'You can't undo another *wizard's* magic. Not without killing the spellcaster.'

Merlin dropped his head briefly and sighed. 'Jack possesses a rudimentary understanding of magic and yours, little hunter, is completely lacking.' *He* glanced at her, but lost interest when April gave him nothing for his insult. 'The talisman's power is strong enough to break through a creature's immunity and kill it.'

'Uh-huh. And you're powerful enough to undo it.'

'If *you* say so.'

'There can't be many people with such power.'

'Let the man work, April.' Jack's voice had emptied of emotion.

April knew that he was staring the reality of Ben's death in the face. But the voice didn't care that Jack couldn't comprehend living without the one person he'd always known. 'What did *he* say to convince you that his intentions were good?'

'It's not so much what he said, rather who he is.' Jack sighed, resignation written all over his face. He looked so beaten, so torn, so exhausted …

'Merlin!' That's what the voice had been trying to tell her. '*He's* …'

'Yes.' Jack said weakly, his hunched shoulders and drawn face said it all. April shook her head, backing away until she bumped into the wall. 'Alright,' Jack frowned, 'I'll bite. What's the matter with you?'

'I can't believe you let him in here,' April hissed, offended on Benjamin's behalf. 'I doubt death improved him. People don't change.' Not to mention that April was getting the worst vibes from Merlin.

'I never died. Therefore, I am who I was and I am who I am. Hmph. Now, if you don't mind, I am trying to work!'

April turned frightened eyes to Jack, sounding more like herself than she had a few moments ago. 'Make him leave. We'll find another way to help Ben. You don't understand …'

'No, you don't understand, April. I can't …' Jack closed his eyes, his voice catching. 'I can't lose Ben. This *is* our only option …'

'Nor does he trust me, if it's any consolation,' Merlin added. 'Only a fool would do that.'

'Has age made you honest, *wizard*, or death?' April had never felt such bitterness. Nor did she understand why Jack wasn't tearing Merlin apart.

'Ha! You sound like my wife!' Merlin snorted.

'Which one?' Jack asked.

With a disbelieving shake of her head, April left the dingy blue and white room.

'April …' Jack wasn't so committed to his grief that he couldn't feel guilt at having dismissed her.

'Let her go,' Merlin advised coldly. 'It's best she doesn't witness this. Make sure I'm not disturbed. It will not do for me to get stuck in there as well.' Merlin paused. 'It would be wise to put down salt lines.'

'To stop things getting in?' Jack's voice was rough with regret. Being at odds with April didn't feel right. He should have consulted her.

'To stop things getting out.'

Watching Ben being brought back from the brink of death by an assortment of demons and ghosts was Jack's new worst-experience-ever.

He heard the rasping voice of the night shade before he saw it. The tall, slender spirit in its black robe manifested beside Ben's head. It turned its featureless face to them, head tilted to one side, engaged in silent communication with Merlin. The night shade passed non-existent eyes over Jack, before resting its hand on Ben's chest. Jack rushed to chase the thing off, but came up against Merlin's unexpectedly strong arm.

'We need him,' the warlock said sternly, buying the spirit time to vanish. 'He is my guide. My magic has bound him to do no harm to Benjamin.' Merlin spoke in a near-whisper, glancing at the doorway behind him.

'April left, remember? She does not like you.'

'Hmph. The lady is human?' Merlin's lips pressed themselves together in a thin line. Jack nodded, curious as to why Merlin's eyes widened. Being human wasn't such a bad thing. 'Interesting.' Merlin's jaw worked, chewing over something that he didn't care to share. 'Regardless, do not let her re-enter.'

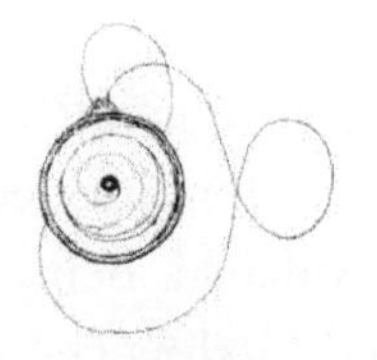

22

Breathless

Purgatory

Merlin sped his breathing up to match the rapid rise and fall of Benjamin's.

He waited, poised on the edge of Ben's consciousness, looking for a way into the

jumbled thoughts. With one hand raised over the Sigillum Dei, Merlin chanted the spell, calling on the spirits to help in retrieving the physician.

Merlin's skin prickled and burned, aflame with magic. Emrys was entirely wrapped up in the spell, flowing with the natural magic. Merlin took a deep breath, and on the exhale, Emrys drilled down, weaving with the realm's ancient energy from whence it came, before striking out of the realm altogether.

The hospital room melted away, submerging Merlin in the aquamarine hue of his magic. He was vaguely aware of Jack issuing a blunt warning about failure. It wasn't worth his attention because he was slipping through the planes like they didn't exist. Time and space sped past in a blur of every colour

Merlin knew and some he did not, until there was nothing but grey and black. Purgatory swallowed him whole, the cut he'd made beginning to seal as soon as he was through.

If Purgatory was a person, it would be an insatiable hoarder – taking whatever it was given, never throwing anything out. Merlin drew Emrys back to him slightly, to slow his approach. Glancing left and right, he spotted the burnt-orange glow of Benjamin's magic. Emrys cannonballed them into the gathered crowd, bowling into the creatures like skittles.

Merlin stood in the eerie silence with as much dignity as he could muster after rolling and tumbling his way in. *'Thank you, Emrys. I wanted to make an entrance.'* Merlin took a moment to stretch his neck and aching back, and another moment to straighten his clothing with a quick twitch. Out of the corner of his eye, Merlin saw the mob's true shape sticking out. Night shades like his guide but with mouths crammed full of razor-thin teeth. Merlin pushed his way through them, and his guide flashed into view, clearing a path to where Benjamin rocked back and forth, his back to Merlin. His former assistant was muttering something, his chin buried in his chest, his hair matted with sweat, his clothing torn and dishevelled, his tense shoulders pulled forward to hug his knees.

'You're not real. You're not, he's not, nothing's …'

'Everything here is real.'

Benjamin lifted his head slowly; a sad, defeated laugh crashed into the quiet. 'I suppose you're also real?'

'Of course I am!' Merlin bit down on the insult that instinctively tried to follow. It wouldn't do to quarrel now.

'I should have guessed you'd be back.'

Merlin's eyes narrowed at the bitterness, but let it pass. 'I did not startle you?' He shifted to the side, trying to see the wound.

'It's hard to sneak up on somebody in their own mind.' Ben sat up a little straighter, his hands planted on the ground, long legs bent. Ready to run. 'You gave yourself away in the woods. You didn't sound like a memory.'

'What a ridiculous thing to say!' Merlin glared at the puddle of red on Ben's right hand. 'How does one sound like a memory?'

'Distant, flat, rehearsed and always in the past. The you that exists in here,' Ben tapped his head, 'doesn't say anything that I don't remember you saying. And I remember, Merlin.' Ben dragged a hand through hair that was much longer than Merlin remembered.

'You need a haircut. And I thank you for not reducing me to nothing more than fiction.' Dark magic slammed into Emrys, trying to break their connection.

'Whenever I manifest you in my mind, the script is always in past tense.'

'Fair point.' The brush of a ghostly arm against Merlin's back stole his attention. The mob had come for dinner, not a show.

'You're losing your touch, Merlin.' Benjamin carried on, unaware of the growing tension and massing dark magic. 'Used to be that I couldn't tell the difference between you and one of your illusions.'

'Perhaps I was being intentionally careless?' Emrys engulfed Merlin's hands, curling around his arms in a not-so-subtle warning. The mob took a collective step backwards. 'As interesting as the back of your head is, I will tire of looking at it soon enough.' Merlin's light-hearted attempt at hurrying his assistant along, ricocheted off Benjamin.

'Oh, I'm sorry! What's five minutes looking at the back of my head compared to the fifteen hundred years spent looking for you?!' Benjamin hastily pushed himself to his feet, rounding on Merlin. 'Fifteen. Hundred. Years. Merlin! And now you appear, twice, as if a single day hasn't passed by.' Merlin saw for himself the pain and anger in those turbulent, storm-cloud eyes. He felt shame enough to step back.

'It has been a long time.' Merlin gave Ben a small smile in lieu of a peace offering. It was met with clenched fists. 'We must be ...'

'Were you too shy to say hello in front of the others?' Benjamin demanded, blood soaking through his shirt. 'I did see you, by the tree.' Night shades and shadow figures prowled around the fringes of the crowd, waiting for their chance to pounce on the two souls who weren't meant to be in Purgatory.

'I was close by.' Merlin had never mastered the trick of turning words into the truth. 'Look, hate me, if that's what's in your heart, but we must leave.' His assistant's eyes slid away from Merlin's for the hundredth time. 'Look at me. Benjamin?' Ordinarily, Merlin would have let the younger man pick his own path through the conversation, but he was all too aware of the opening through which he'd slipped, shrinking rapidly. 'You are dying.'

'I may have run into some trouble. In case you haven't noticed, we're reunited in Purgatory.' The truth of what he'd said dropped Ben's shoulders as centuries of waiting washed over him. 'All those years – it was for naught.'

'Yes, very good.' Blue flames winked at Merlin from a gap in the crowd. He threw up a shield in time to absorb the impact of an attack spell. 'Away with you, Barqan, you pest. Can neither of you sense the alarming amount of dark magic building around us.' Barqan shouldered her way past some night shades. 'You'll be trapped, djinn.' Barqan considered this and opened her own portal. 'As for you, Benjamin, now isn't the time for petty accusations.'

'We're having this conversation!' Judging by Ben's squared shoulders and determined fighting stance, he wasn't kidding.

'Tone deaf. You've always been utterly and helplessly tone deaf!'

'And your timing always suited yourself ...'

'That's not fair.' Merlin's face flushed with heat, the shrinking portal temporarily forgotten. 'I couldn't stop them!' Merlin yelled. 'Nor could I undo the twisted knots in your soul. It's like pulling shards of glass from drying cement. I'd have only hurt the both of us.' Merlin took a shuddering breath to compose himself. 'So, I gave you a chance to move on.' Merlin forced Benjamin's arm around his neck. 'Should've knocked you out. I thought it would be easier if you thought us dead.' A fresh wave of black magic slammed against Emrys, sending Merlin staggering forward.

'Easier?!' Benjamin spluttered, stepping forward a second before a pale hand caught his elbow. 'You've no right deciding what's *easier* for me, *Merlin*!' Benjamin spat the name as if it was a curse. 'You always do this! You twist a situation until you come out of it the wise martyr.'

'You survived, didn't you? You shook hands with the devil and walked away.' A second cold ghost-hand raked over Merlin's back, shocking him into action. 'That's it!' Merlin sprang forward, catching Benjamin around the waist before the mob pounced. Without having to be told, Emrys dropped the pair in a quieter, less crowded corner of Purgatory.

'Running away from your problems only works if you leave them behind,' Benjamin snapped, searching Merlin's face.

'I'm not running from … do you not see the hell hound?' Merlin forced Benjamin's head in the direction of the terrifying creature. With the spell still working, Merlin wasn't going to be able to take Benjamin with him. At this rate, Merlin was going to have to find another way out himself – his portal was halfway closed.

'You chose not to age.' Benjamin found no evidence of the one hundred and eighty-eight thousand days that had passed.

'Don't you prefer a familiar face?' The shtriga's teeth ground together. 'Obviously not.' Out of habit, Merlin placed a reassuring hand on his friend's shoulder.

Benjamin pulled back so quickly he tripped over his own retreat, his eyes searching Merlin's for a truth he didn't want to find. 'You followed me through the market. You convinced me to stay in Caerleon.'

'Would you stop forcing puzzle pieces together? Worry about your looming demise.' With tight lips, Merlin watched the inevitable and horrid thought land in Benjamin's mind.

'Were you ever my friend? Answer me truly or not at all. I'll hear no more lies from you.'

'We were at war, Benjamin. Friendship is inconsequential during war. And in the grand scheme of things, it doesn't matter at all.'

'Answer me!'

'Do you truly believe that I fabricated our friendship?'

Benjamin climbed clumsily to his feet, struggling as his life drained away. 'If it served a purpose.'

The accusing tone found a nerve.

'Look at you! Saving the world all on your own.' Merlin's mirthless laugh bounced off trees to fill the clearing. 'You've had a lifetime of freedom as a Guardian, thanks to my tireless, unseen work, and do you thank me? No. I shouldn't be surprised. You always fail to see the efforts of those supporting you.' Benjamin glared for a second longer before breaking away to pace in a fast, tight circle, like a trapped and dying animal who'd not accepted the end. 'Let me save you some internal struggling, Benjamin.' The shtriga's pacing quickened, his hand flying to clutch at the talisman. The portal sealed a little more. 'I have, and always will be, behind your every step. Yes, I introduced myself to you knowing full well we'd end up here. Yes, I introduced you to Arthur on purpose. Do I have regrets? None.' Merlin's voice cracked under the weight of one or two. 'You damage yourself by holding onto the past. But know this and never doubt it again, my friendship was true. It still is …' Merlin let his sentence trail off, leaving space for a reassurance that Benjamin didn't provide. 'Prophecy is a heavy burden to bear. There's much I can see and none of it I can change.' Benjamin's head snapped up, comprehension stilling his feet for a beat. 'I needed to ensure you were battle-ready – the realm in safe hands. Surely you understand that,

Benjamin, Guardian of Gaia.' Merlin held fast, watching his honesty cut deeper than the stab wound. 'You are as much an instrument of Fate as I.' Merlin didn't have to hear Benjamin's thoughts to know where they were heading. 'We used each other. Aye. Even you, in your own way, used me. You furthered your position; you had your affair with Arthur. You didn't like the outcome, so you blamed me. Stop making people your emotional crutch. It isn't fair.' With satisfaction, Merlin watched his accusation crumble some of Benjamin's resolve. A few more jabs like that and he'd have Benjamin completely uncertain of himself in no time.

'I shouldn't have stayed in Caerleon. That is unequivocally your fault.'

'The choice was not yours to make.'

'You knew how it was going to end and you still approached me. I … I don't know who you are, Merlin.'

'There is more than one way to interpret a prophecy. You can hardly expect me to achieve a one-hundred-percent success rate.'

The tiniest slit of the portal remained.

Ben closed his eyes, sinking further into the blackness. He should be feeling something – anything – but all sense of feeling had fled. His bones gave up and drew him to the floor. 'Can we fast-forward to the part where this turns out to be a dream and I wake up in the shower?' Ben looked to Merlin. Merlin, alive, breathing and solid. It was enough to drive all sense from his head.

'You'll awake soon enough. Why in a shower?'

Ben waved away the question, his entire body feeling heavy and tired, his rage extinguished. 'I'm not sure how much more I can stomach.' Everything he'd wanted to say had got itself confused. Was Ben happy to see Merlin? His mind changed whenever the warlock glanced at him. A warmth was spreading through Ben's body, chasing off the numbness. 'Whatever you're doing, it isn't working.' Merlin paled as Ben lifted shaking hands from his chest, revealing the wound. 'You're a little late, Merlin.'

'My timekeeping is exceptional. The only way to know for sure is to wake up.' Merlin huffed at the exasperated look thrown his way. The familiar knot of anxiety tightened in Ben's chest. But Merlin's flash of irritation wasn't enough to smother the little flicker of doubt.

'Why do I have a bad feeling about this? What have you done?'

'Perhaps I shouldn't say. Success is not a certainty.' Merlin's voice pitched up as the possibility occurred to the warlock for the first time.

'Would it kill you to give a straight answer for once?'

'Hmph, I've been trying to tell you … Oh, never mind.' Merlin cast his eyes skyward in a silent prayer for strength. 'The talisman is blocking all other spells from so much as tickling your big toe. Jack was reluctant to find you a soul …'

'You'd best not have laid that wretched thing over my heart!' If Ben's blood wasn't currently all over the hospital bed and floor, it would have run cold. When Merlin encountered the rare situation in which Emrys couldn't fix something, he had one ghastly fix-everything toy. 'You have! Merlin!' It explained why Ben felt as if something had crawled inside his body and was carelessly poking about. 'We talked about this.

I told you then, as I do now, I'd prefer death to—' A flash of intense pain cut Ben off.

'I've had to use force to save your ungrateful arse. Yes, there is currently a whole host of demons and ghosts in your body. Try not to consume any of them. Meanwhile, I have had to cross into Purgatory to drag you back, because you sure as hell can't find your own way out! Is that what you wanted to hear?'

'Not especially! I can't believe Jack agreed to this.'

'The lad knows nothing of magic. But you … he's devoted to you.' Merlin almost sounded jealous.

'Friends look after each other.' At least Jack wasn't around to hear the F-word.

'The sooner you stop yapping like a terrier, the sooner we can leave.' Merlin hauled Ben to his feet, letting him look about in greater detail.

Fear did its best to choke his words. 'The mob, they've found me.' Ben's weight dropped into Merlin's arms, dragging them both down. Bright flares of lit torches swam in his blurred vision. 'Don't let them get me.' Ben didn't recognise his own voice, so heavy with terror.

It dropped him to the floor of another memory. The mob closed in.

Benjamin could only hold Merlin's talisman for a few seconds – the tiny pendant knew that he wasn't the Guardian. 'The spells are unusual.' Ambrosius respectfully prodded at the silver shield with its miniature dragons.

'The binding spell is my own creation. I also worked in a protection spell, for good measure.' Intimidated by Merlin's spell casting and the weight of the warlock's responsibility, Benjamin handed the shield back. 'When they are all together in the hands of somebody with enough power to wield them, they are magnificent.'

'Let's hope that never happens! I'm glad to not be directly responsible for preventing that person from taking over the universe!' A strange, guilty look clouded Merlin's face, but the warlock shook it off.

'The spell has worked extremely well. Some of my finest work.' Only Merlin could compliment himself and make it sound as if the entire world agreed with him.

'Indeed.' Benjamin chuckled fondly. 'I must away. I will be late for my appointment with Arthur.'

'Oh?' Merlin drew the word out until it resembled a scandal. 'Will you be discussing business, or having lunch. As you usually do?'

'Lunch.' Ben confirmed with enough force to drive Merlin's eyebrows up his forehead.

'Move your legs, Benjamin! How can you be so slight but so heavy?' Merlin dragged Ben by the scruff of his neck. His feet caught on stones and roots, knocking something free from the memory.

'If they ... were ... bound ... with protection spells, why'd Arthur die?' Benjamin uttered between shallow breaths.

'Arthur was protected by a spell bound with Excalibur.'

'Arthur died with Excalibur in his hands ...'

'Are you really using your dying breaths to push for answers you've had all along?'

'I have to know. Did I do enough. For Arthur?'

'It's a little late now. Don't torment yourself.'

The crowd reached for Ben as one. After centuries of waiting, they were finally going to get their monster. 'Arthur!' he choked, the smoke from their torches reaching down his throat.

'You're no fun when you're dying,' Merlin groaned. Of all the cracks in his story, Benjamin had to slip into that one. His assistant's head lolled to one side. Merlin seized his chance. The mob took a synchronised step towards them, not letting Ben get too far away. A barrier between one world and the next, the mob had one job.

'All they've done is stare.' Benjamin complained around the pain, his feet scrabbling in a last attempt to stand. Merlin glanced away to hide his smile.

'You know the rules, Benjamin. You have to leave Purgatory on your own volition.'

'You're out of time, Merlin.' Emrys's voice rang in his mind. *'The rip is going to seal in the next minute. Open a portal for Benjamin and pray that nothing follows him back.'*

'Damn it.' Merlin dropped his assistant unceremoniously to the floor.

Ben craned his neck, trying to see what had caught Merlin's attention. 'I don't suppose,' Benjamin rolled onto his side with a groan, 'you're going to tell me where I can find you.'

'I'll come to you. Get yourself through the portal!'

'Riddles wrapped in riddles.'

'Now, Benjamin.'

It was the tone of voice that dared Ben to disobey. It wasn't far off Arthur's, the one that threatened all sorts of consequences if ignored.

'I'm no longer your assistant . . .' The air fizzled and popped as Merlin vanished into another portal. 'Damn it, Merlin!' The mob took another step behind him. Ben looked about in blind panic – he couldn't open a portal. 'Thank the Gods.' A mere three feet away, the air shimmered; Merlin hadn't shut his portal. With a great effort, Ben pushed himself onto his knees. The last grain of sand had fallen through the timer.

Shadows broke free of the mob, darting around Ben like a colony of bats. A few shot into the portal. 'Merlin!' Ben groaned and crawled for what felt like an hour. At least the portal was, mercifully, at ground level. Handy for someone whose legs had ceased to function. Exhausted, Ben peered into that familiar blackness and the vast expanse of the universe looked back. The deep blues, greens, purples and oranges of the universe that lay inside the tear, shimmered into view, along with the millions of pinpricks of light that stretched back forever, cradling the dramatic swirls of other universes. The whole thing would carry on with or without Gaia. The thud of hundreds of running feet reminded Ben to pitch himself into the portal. A pair of hands that clung to memories of calluses, wrapped around his calf. Ben hung, suspended over the abyss. With a teeth-rattling jolt, he was yanked back towards Purgatory. As he thrashed about, trying to roll out of the grip, Ben caught glimpses of a pale face with no features. Another kick and he loosened three fingers. The pale face grunted and leant into the portal, scrambling for a better grip.

'I'll drop myself into space.' The featureless face somehow managed to radiate scorn. 'I'm not afraid of falling forever in the nothingness.' Another pull and the trapped foot scrapped against solid ground. 'I'm certainly not giving you the satisfaction of ending my existence.' Ambrosius sparked into life, desperate to help but lacking the energy to do anything except flicker and fade like a dying nightlight. It was enough to startle the night shade into loosening its grip. 'Ha!' Ben's excitement died in his throat as something dark fell across the opening. The night shade's head snapped up before it was ripped backwards, dropping Ben's leg (and taking a chunk of skin with it).

Ben spun, nose over tail, through the portal. Behind him, the mob, Purgatory, the shadow, disappeared one by one.

23

Shadows

Jack could do nothing but fidget with a pen he'd found.

The nib of the pen shot back and forth like a cuckoo clock gone berserk.

There was nothing else to do whilst Ben's body convulsed, pulled this way and that by whatever unholy horrors flowed freely inside.

Click, click, clickity-click, click, click, clickity-click, click, click, clickity-click.

Beside him, Merlin remained perfectly still, his eyes fixed on Ben. Judging by the extremely irritated expression, Jack's fidgeting wasn't appreciated. He didn't want to throw Merlin off his game but lasted three seconds before his fingers felt compelled to move again.

Click, click, clickity-click, click, click, clickity-click, click, click, clickity-cli— The pen jammed. Merlin's eyes closed as he exhaled a heavily put-upon sigh. Jack hammered the top of the pen with the palm of his hand. The nib shot towards freedom with a satisfying pop. 'Yes!' The pen vanished into thin air. 'No! I was using that.' Jack twisted so violently he nearly fell out of his seat.

'Does your buffoonery ever rest?' Merlin huffed, his jaw tense.

'Only on high holidays.' Jack returned his gaze to Ben's sweat-drenched face.

'Hmph.'

Jack steeled himself, looking straight ahead. 'If I see a look of concern on your face, Merlin, I won't be responsible for my actions.'

'Be still, it's nearly done.' Merlin spoke to Jack as if he was ten years old. It wasn't far off how he felt. 'You made your choice, lad. See it through. Preferably with no more stationery casualties. Speaking of casualties, Benjamin will need to feed.'

'Call them what they are, Merlin. Victims.' Jack stared at a crack on the far wall, trying to detach himself from his growling hunger and the fact that he was surrounded by fast food.

'I call them so because they are necessary and, to my knowledge, neither of you take pleasure in the macabre business.' Merlin's tone was neutral, but his words were designed to cause feelings of inadequacy.

'I'm already bored of you.' Jack wondered if Arthur would be worse – he caught his train of thought and threw it out of sight.

'You could have arranged a meal ...'

'I'd like to know how you'd have got him to feed whilst he's unconscious?'

Merlin turned half-closed eyes to Jack, tilting his head from side to side, as if listening intently to a whispered conversation in a crowded room. Jack had seen Ben lost in the sweet song of his magic often enough to recognise the expression. 'There are other ways to extract a soul.' Jack shivered, not wanting to contemplate the meaning of *other ways*.

'Ben may forgive you, but he will never forget. I will make damn sure that you never again become a permanent fixture in his life. There's only so much healing spells and half-hearted apologies can resolve.' Merlin didn't so much as flinch at Jack's spiteful tone.

'Ben remembers.' Merlin's words came slow and steady. 'More than he thinks he does. So long as he lives.'

'What's that supposed to mean?'

'You don't care much for me, do you, Jack?' Merlin commented idly, his hands coming to rest lightly on Ben's arm.

Jack checked his instinctive reaction to floor Merlin.

It was because of his loss of control over his unhappy thoughts. It was because Jack was exhausted in the face of it all. It was because Merlin's presence set long-forgotten memories stirring in the fog concealing his human life. And it was because of so much else that Jack stooped to Merlin's level.

'I despise you, actually. For many reasons, one of which is your ability to make small talk right now.'

'There's nothing else to do. Be still, it's nearly done. So, you'd banish me from Ben's life forever if you could.'

'I would.' Jack pushed steel into his voice as if it was a blade running Merlin through. The thought of dealing with Ben, April *and* Merlin flying off the handle in different directions was almost enough to make Jack take a vacation.

'Benjamin and I, our paths criss-cross at many points.' Merlin turned back to Ben, leaning closer to the bed. 'Sometimes they run parallel; other times they are worlds apart. You've had him to yourself for the last eight hundred years, it's time to learn how to share.' Jack heard the subtext but could not decipher it. He should have got Ben to write a user manual. 'The three of you …' Ben groaned, his eyes fluttering open. Merlin threw out his hand to stop Jack flying from his chair. 'He's not quite home,' the warlock remarked, as if he were commenting on the arrival of a train. Jack, unable to restrain himself any longer, ducked under Merlin's arm and darted around to the other side of the bed. 'Have it your way.' Ben gave a violent shudder and his body relaxed, his head landing heavily on Jack's chest. 'Will you tell him of what happened here?' Merlin kept his eyes focused on his task of packing away the Sigillum Dei.

'I'll see how Ben is when he wakes up. With you returned …'

'Whatever calm he has created in his mind will be snuffed out.' Merlin almost sounded like he was sorry. His eyes flickered down to Ben.

Distracted, Jack followed Merlin's gaze. His heart sunk a little to see the restless shtriga continuing to toss and turn, eyes firmly shut.

'Now is a …' Jack turned back to the space recently occupied by Merlin. 'Son of a bitch!' A slight tremor from Ben pulled Jack away from his anger. With short, tight movements, Jack fished his phone from his back pocket and typed a hasty text to April.

Merlin has left. Ben is waking up. Where are you?

'Whenever you're ready, Ben. I'd love to get out of here.'

'Ben?' The shtriga's hands twitched and knotted themselves in the bed sheets, as if he was trying to claw his way awake. 'Ben!' The shoulders shuffled, rustling the sheets as his movement gathered momentum and knocked Jack off the bed. 'Breathe ... take it easy!' Jack scrambled back, throwing himself atop Ben, catching his partner's punches. 'It's me!'

'Merlin! You bastard!'

'You just missed him!' Jack looked down into wild eyes rapidly changing colour. 'Calm down or they'll sedate you.'

'Well, Ben has officially lost it.' Jack swung his head round to see April watching from the doorway, slightly out of breath. 'I suppose this is Merlin's doing?'

'You think? Help me, please?'

April added her weight to his, but still Ben managed to get a leg out of bed. 'Everybody can hear this.'

Bone shattered and blood flew.

Ben blinked once and sunk back heavily into the pillows, stunned. The world had come into painful focus.

'You punched him? Who does that?' April looked at Jack in total disbelief as she grabbed a handful of tissues and shouldered her way past him.

'I ... could hear the nurses walking over and ... I'm so sorry, love.'

Deflated, Jack sat beside his partner. Ben nodded weakly and muttered something about it being ok. Panic had been hovering at the back of Jack's mind since the B&B.

He'd lost his grip on it.

Ben managed a trembling smile that tore a little at Jack's heart. 'Not dying anymore?' Ben shook his head. As carefully as he could, Jack propped Ben up with pillows. Unable to support the weight, Ben's head dropped to his chest, eyes squinting at the floor as if the light bothered him.

'Jack?' His voice sounded lost and drowsy with magic. Jack drew a shuddering breath, his eyes misting over. 'Are you real?'

'What makes you ask that?' Jack laughed uncertainly.

With a great effort, Ben hauled his head up to look around the compact room, as if Merlin might be hiding in the sink. 'I thought I …'

'Saw Merlin?' Jack screwed his eyes shut. If he stayed still, his frustration might not show.

'How did you know?'

'Given that we don't sleep, I never thought I'd have experienced you waking up with another man's name on your lips.'

'Oh. Sorry.'

'It's alright.' After all, Jack was used to finding Ben far away, daydreaming about a dead king. Jack didn't like it, but dreams were harmless. 'You were ready to chase after Merlin.'

'He's alive.' Ben slouched in the bed, his disappointment digging its claws into Jack.

'So you yelled.'

'He was here, wasn't he?' Caught in the headlights, Jack nodded. 'And you let him leave?' Betrayed, Ben shook his head, pushing Jack away.

'I turned my back and he vanished into thin air!' Jack wasn't comfortable being the sole beneficiary of Ben's disapproval. 'What was I supposed to do? Find a portal and give chase?' No matter how many years they shared, Jack would always come second to Arthur and Merlin.

'More like you sent him away!'

'I gave you the spell – let's not do this.' Oh, how much simpler it would be if Ben had forgotten all he'd ever been. Without another word, Benjamin struggled to get up, his rounded shoulders and white knuckles screaming of his rage. 'You're hurt.' But the shtriga ignored Jack, along with the pain that pinched Ben's face into harsh lines. Stubborn feet planted themselves on the linoleum. He tipped forward and quickly sat back down, surprised at how his legs shook, unable to take his weight. Jack choked down a chuckle at Ben's mixture of shock and scandal. 'Have you finished being a stubborn goat now?' Keeping his gaze locked with Jack, Ben managed to guide his legs over the side of the bed again, promptly losing his balance. 'Obviously not.'

'Let go.' Ben pushed weakly against Jack's arm.

'See? You don't have the strength to argue with me.' Unable to disagree, Ben allowed himself to be lovingly shoved back into bed. 'I don't suppose he told you where to find him?'

'No!' Ben replied irritably, aggressively rearranging the covers, his breathing fast and heavy.

'Of course. How silly of me. We'll find him tomorrow.'

Ben lasted ten seconds before he attempted another advance on the door. This time Jack didn't comment as Ben yanked out the various wires and tubes. April took up position beside the door. Jack ignored her, shadowing Ben's movements. *Ten, nine, eight.*

'We need to go.' *Seven.* 'Find Mer ...' *Six.* exhaustion rapidly swept Ben away into unconsciousness, depositing him neatly into Jack's waiting arms. 'And, there he goes.' Jack felt a bit better with Ben pressed against him. 'It's like carrying a bag of bones.' He had the wild idea that if he was to let go, Ben would drift away. Jack wondered how the person who meant the most to him could feel so insubstantial.

'I wondered why you didn't stop him. It's like you've learnt the backroads and shortcut of Ben's soul!'

'I know where his thoughts are going before he does.' A sharp pang of sadness reminded Jack that, as a mortal, April would be gone in the blink of a vampire's eye. 'It's easier if Ben's unconscious a little longer.' Jack wanted to be anywhere but the hospital, where the smells of life and death were so entwined, he couldn't tell them apart. 'Go straight to the car. I'll be right behind.'

'Won't the staff have questions?'

'They're not going to see me.'

April nodded and turned to leave, her hand hovering above the door handle. 'You could have lied to him, you know?'

'I can't lie to him, April.'

24

Peace of Mind

Since leaving the hospital, Jack had driven the deserted back roads, unsure of where he was going, but certain he had to go somewhere.

So long as they were in motion, they couldn't be found – untraceable. It might slow Merlin down, but it wouldn't prevent him from trailing in their wake.

In the rear-view mirror, Jack watched April tap away on her laptop in between glances at Ben, slumped in the seat beside her. 'What are you up to?'

'Looking for somewhere to stay.' April added, 'Again.' She spoke so softly, Jack assumed he wasn't meant to hear.

The prospect of facing eternal life without Ben had been an all-encompassing devastation. It had robbed him of the ability to think clearly about, well, everything. Jack needed more friends. That was the thing about worlds, they tended to fall apart. And Jack's entire universe was centred on one person. 'See if there's a no-warlocks option.' Jack forced his fingers to relax on the steering wheel. Ben was alive. Jack had to stop clinging to what almost was.

'I've been thinking about Merlin.' April didn't look up.

'Don't waste your time. The pernicious twerp.'

'Couldn't he undo the shtriga spell? Or, I don't know, remove Ben's magic so he'd have been human again? No magic, no curse?'

Jack scowled at his unconscious partner. 'Please don't make me explain magic to a muggle.'

'I insist.'

'Ugh! Ben's magic is natural, right? He and Ambrosius are entwined. No magic, no curse, no Ben. That's the dark beauty of it.' Jack's wry smile reflected back at him.

'What does Merlin's magic feel like?'

'What makes you ask?' April shrugged, her eyes scanning the screen. 'It is … a weird hybrid of dark and light. Oppressive, wickedly powerful … You'll have to ask Ben. I can't smell it as well as he can.'

'Oh yeah, that's a good idea.'

'So much sarcasm!' The ghost of a memory tried to manifest itself, summoned by thoughts of Merlin, Jack was sure of it, just as he was sure that that was absurd. His eyes scrunched up in forced recollection. 'Damn it!' A black cat shot into his path, forcing Jack to swerve.

'Are you watching the road?!'

'Are you still staring at that screen?' Jack opened his eyes. 'Read a book or something.' An inkling of … No, it skittered away. Jack gently thumped the wheel. Whenever he got close enough to a memory, he ran into an invisible wall. And why, in a life Jack couldn't recall, the only discernible shape was Merlin, he didn't know. Perhaps he'd assigned so much blame to Merlin, on Ben's behalf, that the warlock had become Jack's cosmic scapegoat.

'I've been reading lore.' April cut into his thoughts.

'The spell can't be reversed. And not to be disparaging, but *lore* is often written by ill-informed, ignorant hunters ...'

'But ...'

'If it was possible, Ben would have figured it out by now.' Jack didn't want to know if it was a possibility or not. He changed gears and the subject. 'How's the digs hunt coming along?'

'Oh. There's a place in Caerleon. We need to get there by five though.' Jack swung the car into a sharp turn and accelerated back the way they'd come. The sharp tones of the sat-nav voice rose up from the back seat to boss him about. 'We're a weird-looking group; the owners will have questions.'

'Is it a holiday let or an estate agent?'

'Holiday let,' April confirmed with a few clicks.

'They'll know better than to ask.'

April's eyes narrowed as she caught onto Jack's meaning and, despite everything, he laughed.

****

'Who do you think you're fooling?' Impatience shortened Jack's words as he peered incredulously over April's shoulder at the not-so-thought-out disguise. 'Ben looks like somebody who's asleep. And Merlin will recognise Ben. Sunglasses or no sunglasses.' Although the chances of Merlin approaching them in a bustling council car park were slim.

'*And* I don't know what good you think locking him in the car will do. If he wakes up and wants out, he'll kick the doors off!' April stood back to admire her handiwork, hands on hips.

'Ben's not operating at full shtriga capacity. It will slow him down. Which is more than the hat will do.' Out of the corner of his eye, Jack spied a lady approaching with the furrowed brow of somebody trying to find an unfamiliar contact.

'Come on, let's get the keys. I don't want to leave Ben for longer than needed.'

'I can go alone, you know.'

'I'm well aware of that. But I've recently developed a distrust and, perhaps, a phobia, of B&B owners.'

'Her bright pink and yellow sun dress is the most offensive thing about her. There's no way she has fangs.' Despite her ability to spot vampires, April still looked to Jack for confirmation. Her trust in him had restored some of his self-belief.

'For the record, humans out-monster us easily. Finding a place on the internet and meeting the person in a car park is dodgy, that's all I'm saying.' Jack held his hands up in surrender.

'*And* staying at the local tavern where you'll wake to find your stuff's been nicked and/or your throat's been slit, is better, how?'

'What year do you think this is?'

****

Jack pulled up to the terrace house, wondering how long they'd be able to stay in the otherwise unassuming two-up, two-down abode on its average residential street. All they'd done for two days was run and it didn't matter how far they got, *responsibility* caught up with them. And Merlin. All the aggravation would be worth it, if Ben could escape being a Guardian. A small whimper punctured Jack's thought. Behind closed lids, Ben's eyes darted rapidly back and forth, up and down, like miniscule, out-of-control Scalextric. Jack couldn't help but wonder who his partner was seeing.

'Are you planning on teleporting yourself into the house?' April's teasing pushed Jack a little further inside his doubt as the hesitant patter of rain drummed on the windscreen. With a sigh that contained the weight of the world, Jack carefully retrieved Ben and carried him into the house.

Out of the corner of his eye, Jack saw April silently appear and mirror his stance, one shoulder resting against the bedroom door frame, arms crossed. 'You've an unusually light tread.' It was equal parts amusing and unnerving.

'I don't make a sound, thank you kindly!' April's voice rose, offended, of course.

'Perhaps humans can't hear you, but I'm part bat, remember?'

April snorted in amusement, her smile dying as quickly as it had arrived. 'So, are we going to talk about how you're delaying the inevitable?'

'He's sleeping, April.' Jack winced and straightened up. 'If there was another way … But it's what he needs. It's best you don't come with us.'

'Are you worried about my safety, or what I'll think of you?' Jack's head whipped around. His mouth opened and shut. Either answer would result in him being scolded. 'Both, then. I understand what you are, Jack.' Remarkably, there was no judgement in her eyes. 'Honestly, I'm surprised you're still upright. It's a needs-must situation.' Now it was April's turn to hesitate. Jack watched her eyes drop to the floor. Endorsing the loss of life, even for a good cause, didn't sit well with her. 'You can't go on like this. And Ben worries you're waiting too long between feeding as it is.' Surprise gently pushed Jack back into the doorframe. He hadn't realised how much Ben had confided in April. Had Ben spoken about Merlin? Arthur? Could he ask for a list of topics?

'How long has it been since Ben last fed? And you for that matter?'

Jack tilted his head to the ceiling as he tracked back through his memory. The longest Ben had waited was three years and he'd been a wreck for it. 'A year and a half.' As Jack said it, he realised he hadn't realised how long it had been. 'He should feed once a year, but he doesn't. Same for me.'

'And that's why he didn't heal on his own?' April kept looking to him for answers he didn't have.

'The two talismans haven't been in such close proximity for a long, long time.' April stared at him intently, with such belief and trust, it planted a new kind of worry in Jack's heart. He was going to let her down. Nobody looked at another person like that and had their expectations met.

'Merlin …'

'What? Knew that this would happen?' Merlin's voice filled the room, driving Jack and April into the bedroom. Side by side, they edged closer to Ben. 'I suppose you think me the mastermind of it all.'

'The hell?' April hissed quietly. 'Did you pocket dial him?'

'You should see somebody about that paranoia, Jack,' the disembodied voice mocked.

Jack growled. It was a warning as much as it was a signal of his lost patience. 'I swear to the Gods, if you flicker into existence behind me, I will rip your throat out, Merlin.' Messy hair bobbed on the stairs. The warlock was climbing the stairs in the most ordinary of unexpected entrances. 'Merlin! It's not funny, April!'

'When it's not happening to me, it is!' Her attention pivoted to Merlin and her laughter died. 'How did you get in here?' she screeched.

'The front door was unlocked.' Merlin flashed them a wicked smile that reminded them of who he was and how insufficient a barrier a door was, locked or otherwise.

'Fantastic. You need to leave, right now,' April ordered in the strange voice that wasn't quite hers.

'Easy, April.' Judging by the way her eyes sparked and her shoulders lowered, she was going to swing at Merlin. Jack didn't dare touch her, but he wasn't comfortable with how intensely Merlin was watching her. He took a big step back and bumped into the bed. April followed his lead.

'It's a shame salt lines won't keep you out.' If April put any more heat into her voice and face, she was going to ignite.

'Watch your tone with me, young lady,' Merlin snapped, sounding like a parent whose exasperation was bone deep. To Jack's surprise, Merlin didn't step over the threshold. April bristled at the condescending reproach. With considerable restraint, Jack held his hands up and stepped in between the two. 'She needs to learn some manners,' Merlin complained.

Common sense reminded Jack that he still needed Merlin. But common sense wasn't enough to keep the chill from his voice. 'Do you see how Ben sleeps, Merlin?' Jack looked at the warlock askance. His clipped words weren't quite enough to dispel the gathering storm clouds, but Merlin's gaze slid from April's.

'Aye, I see him well. He's tossing and turning more than is fitting.'

Jack opened his mouth to ask what the hell "more than fitting" meant but changed his mind. 'Rest is for mortals. We had to forgo that peace.'

'Some would call it a small price to pay for eternal life, lad.' Jack was shaking with anger. Merlin could win a battle with nothing more than words and wit, Ben had said.

'I was wondering what Ben was dreaming of, and then it dawned on me. He's being torn apart by memories that transcended time. Because of you.' Merlin made to step into the room. Jack surged forward, planted a firm hand on his chest and pushed. 'You go no further.'

'You flatter me. Truly.' Merlin let out a cruel laugh that sounded like ice splintering, sarcasm dripping from his words. 'Benjamin is long in the tooth. He has many faces of which to dream. I cannot claim the starring role. Perhaps it is you he sees. If you ask me,' the bastard's smile showcased his deteriorating teeth, 'he dreams of his love.'

'If it was me, he'd be calm.' Jack hated himself for rising to the bait. Ben loved him and Arthur was a very long time ago. And dead. That helped.

'Did I say love? I meant his true love.' Merlin smiled a grim smile, suspended over the threshold like a character frozen in a video game, one foot in the room, one outside.

'That's enough, Merlin,' Jack said in a low voice that promised trouble. Merlin's confidence faltered for a split second, before he defiantly brought his other foot into the room. 'Is it shame that slows your pace? I would have thought that you'd be extremely keen. After all, this reunion has been centuries in the making, what with this misunderstanding around you being dead.' Jack laughed sarcastically. 'It happens to the best of us.'

'I do not care much for your tone either, boy, though I shall allow you this moment. It seems to improve your mood when you ridicule me.' A bony finger poked Jack in the chest.

'It does. I assume you packed your agenda. Come on, out with it. I would hate to delay you further.'

April's anger gave way to nerves. Jack and Merlin stood chest to chest. 'Let's keep this clean. I cannot face the A&E staff again. We stole a patient earlier.' The air prickled around her; tension wasn't the only thing building in the room. Freaked out, April inched closer to Jack.

'Don't listen to him, girl. I'm not an evil warlock who has come to steal your soul.' The creep kept speaking to her and Jack like he was their dad, and it was doing her head in.

'Fantastic! But Ben does need a soul. Kindly vanish for a couple of hours.' Jack shoved Merlin back into the hallway. April breathed a sigh of relief. Merlin brought with him the same uncomfortable feeling as her visions.

25

Possibility Days

Daydreaming was a doddle.

Ben had mastered it in his spare time, back in the eleventh century.

He could pull himself out of a daydream when things got too vivid.

But dreaming, actual dreaming, was onerous.

It rifled through Ben's subconscious, unearthing things he couldn't remember forgetting. The years washed past, out of order, and forced their way into his mouth, scratching his lungs, drowning him. Ben couldn't turn away, couldn't skip a beat in the frantic rhythm of hide and seek. He could only slam into exposed nerves and wash up on the shores of places he'd left behind.

The sea narrowed into a river swelling with flood. It rushed him to the mouth of a waterfall and he was falling through heavy rain clouds and a torn blue sky choked by smoke. Ben braced for the impact that never came. He was lying on his back, unharmed but at risk of being trampled. The knights appeared like steel-clad giants and rushed past him to defend their king. 'Percival, behind you!' Ben scrambled to his feet, slipping in his rush to stop the broadsword from falling with deadly precision. The sickening sound of bone resisting steel drove Ben into a tight ball on the muddy ground. 'No more.' He squeezed his eyes shut, warm blood dripping down his face.

The ground shifted below him, tipping Ben onto his feet in the middle of a freezing winter night in a small Cornish town, whose inhabitants were sensibly tucked up in bed. 'The lake!' It shivered under its blanket of thin ice. Ben's panic clouded in the air. 'You never came back. You're not coming back.' The silent promise of the lake almost pulled Ben to sit on the grassy bank for another hundred years. 'I waited long enough, Arthur. I have to leave you here, love.' Ben's mind was sharper for the absence of fresh grief and loneliness that stretched to the bottom of his soul. With a heavy step, he turned away, wandering numbly through the deserted town with its wooden houses. The beat of a bird's wings pounded in Ben's ears, like battlefield drums, its heartbeat a whisper. Ben's hands flew to cover his ears. The hunger tore through him. He could eat until he threw up and it wouldn't be enough. So why bother? Ben could handle the pain. He had to, he couldn't – wouldn't. Wearing a shtriga's clothes would not influence his character. But Ben knew, in his heart of hearts, he wasn't strong enough to wait the hunger out.

The town slanted, and spat Ben out into the wilds of his subconscious. 'I hope I wake up soon.'

'No chance.' Ambrosius glowed dimly in the darkness. 'The door has been wedged open. The ghosts are coming in all at once and out of order.'

'It's making me dizzy.'

'What's that?' Ambrosius turned Ben around to inspect the moonlight streaming in, throwing silver streaks through the pitch black and setting Ben's pale skin aglow. Water dripped at the back of the dark, damp cave into which Ben had retreated. It had been five days since he had changed. The curse was twisting and turning through his subconscious, ripping him apart and reassembling him into something Ben didn't recognise. Was it not enough that it had taken his soul? Must it take his mind also? The madness felt worrying, so close to the surface. Mórrígan had tricked him. Ben should have known better; Merlin wasn't wounded or in trouble.

The sound of a battle exploded around him, dismantling the cave. Ben stumbled forward, not noticing the men who yelled at him. His attention fixed on the blade in his shaking hand. 'Not again.' But there was no use pleading with his own mind. Time skipped forward, pushing him in front of Arthur as the hooded figure emerged from the crowd. 'Arthur …' Nausea rocked Ben's body but he couldn't look away. As a ghost inside his own head, Ben couldn't do a damn thing but watch – again. Out of his control, time crawled to a near stop, freeing Ben to notice every little detail he'd missed the first-time round. The cloak was a sapphire blue so familiar it was comforting. Until the hood slipped as the killer glanced at Ben.

'Merlin?!'

Utter disbelief pushed Ben backwards, his eyes roaming over the pristine sapphire cloak. How, in the thousands of times he'd recalled this scene, had Ben not recognised it? Not noticed Merlin's magic humming in the air around him? Merlin's earlier reveal screamed at him. *'It was me.'*

Ben charged forward, forgetting it was a dream. 'Arthur!' He pulled on the king's gauntleted hand, the cold metal slipping in his clammy palms. 'Arthur!' Fate's blade appeared in Merlin's hand. 'Oh Gods.' There was no stopping it. And there was no coming back from the dead for the Once and Future King.

The blade tore its way across Arthur's soft skin as it always did. Only, Merlin didn't slit Arthur's throat, but tore a small cut in the middle. Aquamarine magic glowed faintly over the cut, stemming the bleeding. Bewildered, Ben listened intently as Merlin mixed up a death spell and a binding spell.

'Merlin never fumbles a spell ...'

Arthur sank to his knees, dying. Ben's mind sent him into a free-fall before the spell's completion. Merlin wouldn't kill Arthur. But Merlin did play games.

Back in the nothingness, Ben glided past Merlin, forcing the talisman on him, along with the pep talk that persuaded Ben to put one uncertain foot in front of the other.

Benjamin sneaked into the castle like a thief. Bypassing the guards via a servant's door, he slipped into the throne room and stopped dead in his tracks. He'd expected one corpse, not two. Trembling, Benjamin held his breath and gently removed the shroud obscuring the second body. A tortured howl ricocheted off the stone pillars, bouncing back to him with the truth. Hot, angry tears splashed onto Merlin's still chest. Ben was utterly alone. The only hope he'd had of acceptance, of a friend to see off eternity with, was as cold as the marble it laid on. Ben reached for the other shroud, but he couldn't bear to see Arthur's eyes closed forever, so he clutched his love's hands above the sheet. Gaia had won, but the Gods had left with everything he'd ever had. Ben collapsed onto the cold stone floor.

'I'm not brave enough to bury them again,' Ben argued with his mind. For once, the past was satisfied to remain behind him. It turned the light off on its way out.

****

The blissful nothingness didn't last.

Light crept over Ben's face, burning red behind his eyelids, and slid off into the darkness, like landing-strip lights guiding him to his next state. With a sickening sense of trepidation, Ben forced his bleary eyes to open, blinking in surprise at the carpeted ceiling above him. Light flashed in his eyes, all too real and all too painful.

So, having run out of content, his subconscious had released him back to the care of reality. The ethereal light was nothing more than the harsh glare of streetlights. Shifting his head to the left revealed Jack, cast in shadow, hands tightly gripping the steering wheel. Ben tried to find his voice, still feeling the reverberations of the past humming in his body. 'Where are we going?' he croaked out, failing to mask the tremor.

'You need to feed. We both do,' Jack replied wearily.

'Where's April?'

'At the house with …' Jack cut himself off, exhaustion tripping him up.

'Who is she with, Jack?'

'Hells,' Jack cursed softly. 'Promise me you'll feed before we turn back?'

'Who?' But Ben knew. Every fibre in his body knew. Ambrosius rumbled inside as he latched onto the traces of magic clinging to Jack.

'I should have recognised Emrys at your house! It's been so long.' Ambrosius felt like a thunderstorm in Ben's blood. Ben tried to sit up on weak, shaking arms and slumped back with a grunt, ignoring the concern in his vampire's eyes.

'Promise me, Ben.'

'I promise,' he said through gritted teeth, listening to Jack draw in a breath with which to release the truth.

'Merlin.'

The name hung in the air between them, stretching in the silence.

'Merlin and I don't like each other.' Jack rushed to fill the car with words. 'I don't envision a future where we will. But he saved your life, so I owe him for that.'

'Well, don't acquire any more debts with him.'

Jack returned Ben's questioning gaze in the rear-view mirror. 'You seem to be taking this rather well.' Jack's fingers tapped nervously against the steering wheel, the light rhythm singing of his disbelief and an unwillingness to ruin a good thing.

'It's best I feed with a clear and rational head. Anger will only serve to … escalate the situation.'

'Right you are. We're here.' The car squealed to a stop. 'I need to get the brakes looked at.' Jack disappeared from his seat and reappeared at Ben's door. The cool night air washed away some of the residual dream memories.

'You were meant to do that weeks ago.' Ben struggled to raise himself up again, unable to make anything out unless it was wrapped in the glow of a streetlamp's cold embrace. 'I can't see in the dark!' Panic flooded Ben's veins at the very human problem. He reached out for his vampire, feeling blind with his diminished sight.

'You're tired.' From where he knelt beside the car, Jack reached up to stroke Ben's hair. It would have been soothing but for the subtle tremor running through it. 'You've not fed and you're injured.' Jack shivered, but not from the cold, Ben thought. 'Merlin had to use the darkest of magic to bring you back.'

'I know.' Ben's eyes narrowed, remembering his conversation with Merlin in Purgatory. 'I'll see him dead for it.'

'If you need more than one soul, you will take it?' Jack held up his free hand to stem any protests. 'I need you back to your old self again.' Jack smiled adoringly at him. Ben couldn't resist that smile. He had to pull himself together, for Jack.

With what he hoped was a reassuring smile, he took Jack's raised hand into both of his. 'I will.'

Relief flushed through Jack's body. Wishing to be done with this business and unwilling to leave April alone with Merlin for longer than necessary, he stood and pulled Ben from the car. The shtriga swayed on his feet, unable to stand without assistance. 'Take it easy.' Jack caught Ben by the shoulders. 'It's a real shame that sugar does nothing for you.' Ben grunted, rubbing at his eyes with the palms of his hands. 'You can't hunt like this!' Without warning, Jack pushed Ben back into the car, ignoring the cries of protest that rose from the back seat.

'I'll do the chasing – I'll not hear another word from you. I'll ... bring them here. It's a remote enough spot.' Jack crossed his arms, his stubbornness clear for Ben to see.

'Be careful. You're always so careless when the bloodlust takes you.'

'Yeah, course. Be right back.' Jack smiled and planted a kiss on his forehead, and was slipping through the night like a shade from Hades before Ben could rethink it.

He let go, his breathing quickening with anticipation, his sharpened teeth gleamed in the moonlight. His hunger edged a little closer towards the surface as Jack loosened his tourniquet grasp on his cravings. All of those desires gleefully rushed to consume his entire being. It was euphoric.

It didn't take long to find prey. He didn't notice who they were. All he saw was the pulsing veins.

Displeased and without a leg to stand on, Ben had no choice but to let Jack vanish into the night. He dropped his head back against the headrest, eyes falling closed. How wonderful it would be if Ben could wrestle his irrational thoughts and fears into submission. He'd be content with an hour, or even a few minutes; a brief moment of reprieve from the constant bubbling volcano of uncertainty that formed the core of his being. His stomach turned at the thought of a hunter creeping up on a distracted Jack. Even if he'd accompanied his vampire, Ben would still have concerns racing through his mind. The difference now was that he couldn't do a damned thing to help. 'So, don't think about it,' Ben grumbled to himself.

What should he obsessively overthink about? The answer was obvious.

****

'How are you feeling?'

'Better.' Ben forced a smile, feeling neither one way nor the other, but hoping to stop Jack from trying to watch him intently and keep an eye on the road.

'You can't wait so long next time. That was way too close for comfort.'

'Ambrosius has kept me alive this long, hasn't he?' Ben could do without a lecture from his mother hen right now. Not when Mer—

'Merlin's magic saved you. We're a long way off the yellow brick road. You're being hunted down by a God.' Jack would've been wringing his hands if the steering wheel hadn't required them. 'Three realms have been destroyed – you nearly died. And there's a "dead" warlock …'

'Jack.' Ben kept his voice calm and even, trying to break through the wall of distress. 'You're going to crash the car at this rate.'

'Merlin's the original Guardian. You're going to give Merlin your talisman and we're going to walk away. Because this was too close. What if April gets hurt? Or you … again? What if—'

'Pull over,' Ben said firmly, his tone brokering no argument. Jack was hyperventilating, worrying about things he couldn't know.

Jack did so reluctantly, not looking up from the steering wheel until a gentle but firm hand under his chin forced his eyes to look into Ben's warm blue ones.

'Listen to me,' Ben said softly. 'You're fighting against a storm that is going to break regardless, so let it break.'

'Aren't you worried?'

'Of course. But Merlin's return does not give me permission to abandon my duties. Besides,' Ben paused, 'they're coming for me regardless. I'm not waiting for the inevitable. And fighting them is preferable to dealing with all of Merlin's mindfuckerery.' Ben always wanted to let the dots connect themselves. Jack wished he could be as pragmatic.

'Right. The Merlin thing.' That would do nicely as a change of subject. Finally remembering that April was trapped in a house with the world's most powerful and annoying warlock, Jack quickly retrieved his phone. 'April's sent twenty-six texts … She's complaining about being hungry in twenty-three of them.'

'What are the other three about?'

The other three said that the warlock had left the building. 'We should probably get back.'

'Yes. I can't believe that you left April with him!' Ben said as if he'd never had a lapse in judgement.

'I can't believe that you were friends with him! He's a jerk, Ben.'

'You—'

'Please don't tell me to get to know him. I've got to know him plenty.' Ben raised his eyebrows, taken aback by the venom in Jack's voice.

'What's happened whilst I was out?' Right, because Merlin couldn't possibly be anything but sweetness and light. 'How did April take to him?'

'Hard to say whether she hates him more than she's terrified of him – and she is. April legged it when they met. She's probably locked him out by now.' Jack chuckled at the mental image of Merlin perched on the doorstep, like the unwanted garden gnome he was. 'I'm telling you, Ben, when she gets over her fear, she's gonna run him through with her wooden sword.' Jack glanced over to Ben who wasn't laughing, and the smile died on his lips. Ben's eyes were glazed over and far away, staring unfocused out of the window. Jack got the impression that Ben's surroundings had disappeared and he was alone somewhere. 'Want to talk about it?'

'Hmm?' Startled, Ben half-turned towards the direction of Jack's voice, as if the vampire had appeared in the car, or he had.

'I have plenty to say, but I need to say it to him.'

'Sounds ominous.'

'The past is about to catch up with Merlin.'

If, on that fateful day, Ben had removed the hood himself, he would have denied it. How the world had changed.

****

The passenger door flew open and slammed shut before Jack had brought the car to a stop. With a lung-emptying sigh, he shoved the car into neutral whilst Ben hammered on the front door. 'Here we go.'

'Where is he?' Ben growled at the startled April. Her joyful smile at the sight of him recovered quickly evaporated as Ben shoved past her.

Jack exited the car with the deliberate slowness of someone wanting to delay an uncomfortable, impossible situation.

'You could have told him.' April's accusing eyes followed Jack up the pathway; Jack apologised with tired eyes. The pair stood together, listening to the cries of frustration bouncing from room to room. 'If Ben breaks anything, it'll come out of the deposit.' April winced at what sounded like a table being overturned.

'I didn't want him to freak out in the car.' Jack patted her shoulder. 'Best to stay out of the way. It shouldn't get any worse.'

After three hours, the sun was well and truly on its way up to the top of the world and Ben hadn't uttered a single word. Judging by the apocalyptic silence, Jack deduced that Ben had accepted Merlin's departure. There wasn't much to say, so Jack tried asking Ben how he was feeling for the hundredth time. To his surprise, Ben answered, his voice sandpaper rough.

'I don't know why you're both so concerned. I'm fine,' said Ben, convincing nobody. This new betrayal was a festering wound that nothing, or no one, was going to be able to close. 'Merlin left. It's what he does.' Ben's fake nonchalance cracked as he spoke the name.

'What aren't you telling me?' Jack's eyes narrowed, hearing something else scratching at the surface. Ben's body language couldn't have been more defensive if he'd built a castle around himself, complete with moat and drawbridge. 'Ben?'

His partner trembled, a volcano desperate to erupt.

'Merlin killed Arthur.'

Jack's instinctive response was to laugh, but the conviction in Ben's eyes killed his laughter. 'You're not joking?' Ben shook his head, a small, sharp, angry motion that conveyed more than his words could have. The anguish in his partner's face drove Jack's hand into a fist that promised to end Merlin.

'I saw the face beneath the hood.' Ben looked like his entire world had ended.

'Sometimes you need to look at things from a different angle,' April offered softly in that older, stranger voice. She ventured close enough to squeeze Ben's arm, a brave move given that Ben was at risk of ransacking the entire house in search of revenge.

'A drug-fuelled dream isn't absolute truth.' Jack frowned.

'Everything I saw before and after was exactly as it happened.'

'But you didn't see Merlin's face at the time. How—'

'He wanted to show me,' Ben said with a bitter laugh, shrugging out of his jacket to disguise him shaking April off.

'What are you planning on doing about it?' Jack didn't like the frosty tone, nor did he trust the black eyes. Ben was going to turn Merlin into a punch bag and Jack wasn't sure he'd intervene.

'I could trap him in a tree for a few thousand years, to make a point.' Ben's hands glowed orange with his magic, his mind cycling through the possibilities, giving Jack yet more cause for concern.

'Why don't you try summoning him?' April offered. Ben huffed and extinguished Ambrosius. 'Merlin came back to heal you. He followed you here. He still cares for you in his own messed up way.'

'Merlin's back because he needs something. From me. And I can't kill him until I know what that something is.'

'Coming in a bit strong there, Ben.' Jack had to get a better handle on this before Merlin reappeared. He'd put in a lot of hours to make this happen.

Ben had to know why.

They were friends – best friends. Merlin knew what Arthur meant to Ben. Merlin knew that without either of them, there wasn't a place in the world for Ben to call home. Merlin knew, Merlin knew … He turned away from Jack to hide the emotion turning his eyes a stormy shade of grey. 'Merlin killed Arthur,' Ben repeated softly, driving the truth home.

'In which universe does Merlin kill Arthur?' Jack protested. 'He was Arthur's advisor!'

'You're defending Merlin? For real? We don't like him, remember?' April rounded on Jack. Her bizarre aura flared, her anger strengthening its colour. If Ben could see it, so could Merlin. And Merlin could develop an interest in April over Ben's dead body. His money was still on her being a witch. 'He's a manipulative bastard who is no good for any of us. Least of all Ben.'

'That I will grant you, but I must insist, which universe?'

'In a universe where Merlin has been working for Fate all along. In a universe where he gets to play both sides of the field and come out the other end a hero. In a universe where he robbed me of choice. He showed me all I ever wanted and everything I couldn't have. I trusted him once and lived to count the cost—'

'Are you still whining about that?' Merlin cut him off. 'Let it go, Benjamin. It wasn't that bad.'

Ben closed his eyes, listening to three people breathing. He'd heard Merlin's voice multiple times in the last twenty-four hours, but this was different. Slowly, Ben opened his eyes to find Merlin standing across the room, framed by the doorway. 'For a one-thousand-year-old corpse, you're looking well, Merlin,' Ben said coldly, conflicting emotions crowding around him.

'I've missed you too.'

Ben ran his eyes up and down the length of the warlock, not trusting what he was seeing. Merlin took a tentative step forward. 'No.' Ben's hand flew up, preferring to maintain the distance. 'Where, in all the hells, have you been?'

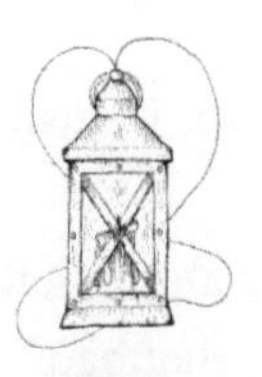

26

Secret of Life

Merlin could have been a statue.

There wasn't so much as a flinch as Benjamin let loose his verbal assault.

Benjamin, who had been ranting at him for some twenty minutes now, did not appear to be slowing down. Merlin had lost interest by the third minute. He'd resisted the urge to physically wander off and settled for dodging whatever Benjamin threw at him – verbally and literally. A plate smashed against the wall inches behind Merlin's head. They both knew full well that Benjamin was intentionally missing his target.

There were no words, in the hundreds of languages Merlin spoke, that could pacify Benjamin. So, he let the shtriga's anger wash over him, his unresponsiveness only aggravating the situation.

Benjamin's outburst could have been a little more honed, considering the amount of time he'd had to rehearse it. For all the words he yelled, screamed and spat at him, they could be distilled down to:

'Why, Merlin?'

Benjamin wasn't listening. He'd forgotten how to understand Merlin's silence. Everything that he wanted to hear, every answer, each overdue explanation, was right there, wrapped in all the things Merlin wasn't saying.

'At least he's speaking to you. Ambrosius is ignoring me,' Emrys grumbled.

'Silence is its own kind of magic, don't you think?'

'Please take this seriously, Merlin.' Emrys's disapproval almost burned a hole in Merlin's tangent.

'If I say the word out loud, I'd destroy it. If I remain quiet, nothing changes for Benjamin. But if he interprets the quiet to mean something, everything changes.' Merlin had spent hundreds of years mastering the art of silence. He knew when to hold his tongue. This wasn't one of those moments. But what to say?

'I have missed you,' would be a start. *'I'm sorry,'* a progression. The truth? Not yet. Merlin wasn't sure *he* was ready for that.

'All these years!' Benjamin roared. 'I thought you were dead. You can't even begin to comprehend … It damn near drove me mad.' Based on this performance, Merlin thought it had.

Merlin almost pulled a muscle trying not to roll his eyes as Benjamin blathered on about how Merlin should own his decisions, and how his actions had consequences.

'It's the least you deserve, Merlin.'

'Indeed. I'm not sure that I care particularly.'

'Give the poor man something! He's practically foaming at the mouth. And Ambrosius is building his energy.'

'You're scared of Benjamin? Ha! He won't do anything.' Merlin tilted his head to avoid another plate. *'I had to protect the realm, but that means nothing to these people.'* Merlin watched Jack trying to restrain Benjamin. *'That's not going to work.'*

'Read the room, Merlin. Nobody will believe you. Fate made you choose – her or them. You chose. And they are sad tales best kept for another day.'

'Look at the girl's aura! No wonder Fate can't see her future ...' A porcelain angel flew towards him.

'I looked for you for a century! Criss-crossed nine realms, hoping your death was a bloody parlour trick, for fu—'

'Language, Benjamin. There's a lady present.'

Ben must have misheard.

It sounded like Merlin had scolded him for swearing, as if nothing had happened? 'I can't even ... Fu—' He raised a vase high above his head.

'Ben!' Jack snatched the vase before it could be launched. 'You've broken enough pottery for one day. Where did you find this?'

'I've not even begun to swear, Merlin.' Benjamin looked around for something else to throw, not caring what damage he did. April snatched a chair away from him, thrusting a cushion into his hands instead. He gave her a withering look. Soft furnishings weren't going to cut it.

'Are you done?' Merlin asked, eyebrows raised.

'Far from it. You could have left clues, or a note.' Ben could hear how ridiculous he was being, but frankly ... 'Fifteen hundred years, Merlin!'

'I left all kinds of signs! You were too blind to see them.'

'Name one!' Ben folded his arms, confident he could catch Merlin out on this lie at least.

'Black cats,' Merlin said in all seriousness. 'If you think about it, you'll realise you see one wherever you go.'

'Cats? Of course, how obvious!' At some point, Ben was going to wake up from this dream.

'Has it ever occurred to you, that I didn't want to be found?' Merlin's glare softened a little. 'The mock burial was designed to cover our exit and give you sufficient closure. I should have known you'd cling onto the matter.' Merlin leant into April; both he and Jack tensed. 'When he gets an idea into his head, it takes the devil to shift it.' Merlin chuckled to himself as April stepped away from him. Smart girl, Ben thought. Smarter than he had been at that age.

'I swear, by the old Gods,' Ben could barely speak around the fury sitting tight in his chest, 'if the next words out of your mouth are along the lines of us having crossed paths, without me knowing, I will end you. Right here, right now. And it shan't be quick.'

'How shall I answer? Because you'll not like it.' Frustration carried Ben to the other side of the room to pace back and forth.

'Why him?' So, Ben had found a way to ask about his other ghost, without speaking the name. In place of anger, Merlin heard sorrow.

'It's—'

'Wait!' Merlin bit back his irritation at being shushed. 'You said *our* exit. In my dream … it wasn't a fatal wound. The spell wasn't intended to cause harm.' The veins in his neck were bulging, fists clenched so tightly, every fibre in Benjamin's body focused on the word *"our"*. Its three letters threatened to unravel everything. Jack inched closer to Benjamin, in an attempt to restrain him or extract him from the room.

'You should know better, lad.' Merlin tsked. Jack barely had time to scowl at him before he was dragged forward with each menacing step Ben took towards Merlin. Merlin straightened his back, head held high, and braced for the question he'd been avoiding since he created it.

'Is Arthur alive?'

27

It's Over when It's Over

Avalon

'What happened?' Mórrígan groaned, slowly coming around on a plush velvet sofa she didn't recall the B&B having. Sun blazed through the glass walls of the palace.

'Care to answer your own question? You had a simple task and you retreat here, empty-handed.' War froze at the barely concealed fury in Fate's voice.

'The talismans!' Mórrígan's hands frantically patted at her body. 'They're—'

'Gone. Both of them. Along with the trio of cretins,' Fate snapped. 'A malnourished shtriga, a mouthy vampire and a mortal, should have been no match for you. You are War, for crying out loud! I wanted Benjamin dead.'

'Benjamin is dead,' Mórrígan stated with all the haughty confidence of War, who never missed her target. Fate's face rearranged itself into offended surprise at having been questioned. 'I ran him through with Merlin's talisman and the girl's sword. Thought you'd appreciate the irony.'

Fate inclined her head in acknowledgement. 'But you failed. Benjamin's thread is still intact.' Fate stalked around the sofa. Barqan stifled a groan as she pushed herself into an upright position. Judging by her appearance, Fate's Guardian hadn't fared so well in battle. The djinn had never before struggled to make eye contact with Fate, and now her eyes remained tightly shut and directed at the ground.

'So, he's dying slowly. He'll linger in Purgatory for a few days, then he'll be gone. Same difference, no?'

'The difference, Mórrígan,' Fate wrestled with her patience, 'is that Benjamin is still breathing, buying Merlin time with which to repair their friendship. We cannot afford for Merlin to have another change of heart. Do I need to remind you that if Merlin goes to Chaos, we will all be returned home to live under Chaos's rule?'

'Do I need to point out that destroying realms is the quickest way to get Chaos's attention? I hope you're prepared for that eventuality, Fate.'

'I am preparing. Merlin is the only one who can trap Chaos. I knew he wouldn't return willingly, so I need to encourage him.'

'The shtriga's death would knock Merlin off course,' Mórrígan said knowingly.

'Precisely. If Benjamin dies, Merlin will come straight to me to demand I return his friend to life. I could string Merlin along for years.' Whether she realised it or not, Mórrígan's hand settled over a pocket. Fate would have to beat War to the double-cross draw. 'Merlin can get over his grief but he cannot abandon Benjamin if he is injured. I should never have trusted you with this.' Old suspicions and offences rushed to the surface as the conversation promised to escalate into a fight.

'Perhaps if you had given me your knife, you'd have had your desired outcome! Whatever magic Merlin wrapped around those pendants kicked in and took me down with it.' Mórrígan's eyes and temper flared; the sound of battle raged in her voice.

'I gave you my Guardian. That should have been adequate enough.'

'Your Guardian,' Mórrígan threw in Barqan's direction, 'doesn't have the stomach for the task.'

Fate's gaze briefly flickered over the djinn whose head remained bowed. Guilt must be a new sensation for one such as Barqan. 'I needed the knife.' Death was complicated and the blade was the only means to truly end an existence.

'My knife,' Fate chuckled softly, 'is missing.'

'How can that be?'

'I suspected you at first. Now I believe Merlin to be the thief in the night.'

'I wonder what he means to do with it.' Mórrígan stood carefully.

'No doubt it forms part of a plan designed to slight me. Return now. They will come looking for you. And Mórrígan?' The God of War turned back to Fate. 'Do not fail me a second time.'

28

Christ Jesus

Wales

'Arthur is neither alive nor dead,' Merlin chuckled, pleased with himself. 'He was never all that far away from you.'

The shock pulled the air from Ben's lungs. His mouth kept soundlessly forming itself around questions.

'Life and death still have such a pull on you, don't they? One's state of being is inconsequential. You're making a fuss over nothing.'

'Arthur … Where?' All these years, Ben had been dragging his guilt along and neither of them had been dead at all. Ben didn't know what to feel first but he was feeling everything all the same. If only he'd stayed on the battlefield, if only he'd looked closer. If he hadn't trusted Merlin. Arthur was alive – that was supposed to be tremendous news. So why was nervous fear raking its fingernails over his frayed nerves?

'Ah. You still love Arthur. Interesting.'

Ben made himself meet Jack's watery eyes. His vampire was trying to keep his face from crumpling. 'Jack, it's not … I don't …' Ben dropped the sentence, feeling his soul shake with the rumble of his life crashing down. Everything they'd built together was coming undone so easily because Ben hadn't let go of his past.

'What is this exactly?' Merlin gestured at the couple, the glint in his eye indicating that he knew full well what "this" was and just how much he was enjoying tearing it apart.

'What does it look like to you, oh great warlockie one?'

Ben reached for Jack's hand, but Jack snatched himself free.

'Oh, do I need to warn Arthur? Hmm, the news should come from you, Benjamin. Arthur will be devastated.' Merlin's cheeks bulged with stifled laughter. Judging by the way Jack braced himself, the vampire also predicted a spectacular fallout.

'Look at them, Emrys! Backs straight, jaws set and defiant in defence of their love. How fantastic! Even I couldn't have predicted this.' Out loud, he said, 'I'm not in the mood for answering your questions, Benjamin. You're being ridiculously dramatic. And War isn't going to kill herself.'

'Stop stalling, Merlin.' Benjamin sounded like he was being strangled. Merlin looked from one to the other with much amusement. His distinctive, high-pitched laugh finally broke free, filling the room. Jack tugged on Benjamin's arm, drawing him and April away from Merlin.

'Not that you asked, but laughing at them isn't helping. You could have neatened yourself up before you arrived. You look like a dishevelled lemur.'

'Watch Benjamin, Emrys. He's going to burst if he keeps allowing all of his useless emotions to rake him over the coals.'

'For the love of the Gods, stop tormenting me with it!' In a hushed, broken tone, Benjamin added, 'I would very much like to see Arthur.'

April snuck a glance at Jack, because that had to hurt. The vampire stood, adrift amongst the sea of history that, judging by the pain in his eyes, he wasn't built to weather.

'I'll tell you when I think you can handle yourself better.' Merlin's disgust was evident. 'Besides, there's something you must do first.'

'You're not in a position to make demands,' April heard herself say in the old voice that commanded respect and shocked the arguing men into silence. Merlin turned so quickly that April thought she was going to be lectured about speaking out of turn. Ben's arm flew out, catching the warlock and slamming him back into the nearest wall.

'Merlin.' It was a threat, a warning and a promise all rolled into one.

Sensing April's stare, Merlin turned his head towards her. His shark-eyes studied her, a terrifying co-conspirator's grin slowly growing. The bad feeling crawled onto April's shoulder again and something deep inside of her nodded in sage agreement.

'You're him!' How had April not seen it before?!

Merlin nodded once, the strange high-pitched giggle escaping the corners of his smile. He was the unknown man in her premonition.

'Over here, Merlin!' Ben slammed Merlin into the wall again and the moment disappeared. Ben might be in a tailspin, but he wasn't letting anybody get to her. April seriously hoped she could return the favour.

'I can't take you to him yet but if you have a little patience—'

'If he's hurt, Mer—'

'Slow, painful death, I know. He is perfectly fine. A little bored, but fine.'

'Does he know? That I'm still alive?'

'Well,' Merlin pursed his lips, 'he doesn't think you're dead.'

Ben's surroundings faded away, leaving only himself and Merlin's treasonous revelation. Ben couldn't straighten out his thoughts as comprehension pulled him under.

He'd abandoned Arthur.

Feeling sick, Ben reached for Jack but couldn't find him. With ears roaring, heart pounding, mind spinning and vision blurring, he pitched forward, hearing Arthur yelling for him.

'He's in trouble. He's … Arthur! I'm coming. I'm … I didn't know. I …' Ben had no control over his movements, just the all-consuming compulsion to find Arthur. Nobody was going to stand in his way this time. He wasn't—

'Ben, stop!'

Slowly, as if he was waking up, he recognised Jack's raised and pleading voice. Ben's entire body tingled with Ambrosius's rage and there was a persistent tugging on his left sleeve. Turning his sluggish head, he saw April, her face a mirror of Jack's urgent, desperate horror.

'What's the matter?'

Somewhere through the fog, Jack's voice found him and jolted him back into the present. 'You're hurting Merlin! You've just got him back – don't kill him now!'

Ben looked down the length of his arms to find his hands wrapped tight around Merlin's throat. He stared uncomprehendingly at Merlin's half-closed eyes and limp hands hanging by his side. Angry red patches marked the beginning of bruises, an unspoken accusation. Still, understanding lagged behind as Ben struggled to assimilate his actions with his intentions.

'Mer … Merlin?' Horror crept into Ben's mind as he shook the body still trapped in his grip. He hadn't meant to …

'Ben, for the love of … Let go of him!' Jack succeeded in squeezing his fingers between Merlin's throat and Ben's interlocked hands, forcing his fingers to break ranks. Merlin dropped to the floor like a puppet whose strings had been cut. Jack caught him before his head bounced off the floor.

Swaddled in shock, Ben watched Jack check Merlin over with more care than he deserved. 'He's breathing.' The vampire shook his head in disbelief, his tone flat and unamused.

'I was going to kill him.' Ben's voice was hollow with certainty. 'If you hadn't …' He stared at his trembling hands, not recognising them as a part of him. 'I would've.' His legs gave up, dropping him to the floor.

'You didn't mean to hurt him but it's done now. All we can do is hope he wakes up and is fine.'

'Or we could put him outside and hope that someone takes him,' April offered.

Merlin was still unconscious.

It had been long enough for Ben to worry, and he might have done if his entire being wasn't currently devoted to deconstructing his entire life. The realisation that Merlin was the architect of his downfall tore through Ben like cast iron. 'It's entirely his fault.'

Jack, who'd not moved from his side, wearily lifted his head from where it rested on Ben's shoulder. 'I've been telling you that for years.'

'I tried to leave Caerleon once, after a row with …' Ben caught Jack's wounded eyes and veered away from the name. 'Merlin made me feel so terrible for even considering it. I was so stupid.' But he couldn't articulate that particular loss. Ben hadn't learnt the words yet.

'No,' Jack sighed. 'You were settled and in love.' That was magnanimous, but it didn't soothe Ben's aching mind.

'If I retrace my steps, the path will always take me back to Merlin. He pushed me into the wrong place at the right time.' April had retreated to the corner, lost in her phone to avoid looking at them, her strange aura stronger than ever. 'Merlin's as much a tool of Fate as the rest of us.' Ben supposed the bitter taste in his mouth was what he got for unmasking his hero. 'Fate's always had such influence over him. I can't trust that he is his own agent.'

'He's a tool. Regardless of who picks him up,' Jack said with feeling. 'I'm sorry he was such a jerk.'

'If we can't trust him, he shouldn't be here.' Concerned by the way her voice quivered, Ben forced himself to focus on how the colour had drained from April's face.

'What's the matter?' April refused to look up from her phone.

'You look as freaked out as you did at the hospital.' Jack leant forward, probably wanting to snatch the phone away. 'Why are you being so weird? Come on, April, talk to us.' Ben squeezed Jack's shoulder, urging him to soften his approach.

April had her back to the wall, where she could watch the three of them and reach the door, if necessary. She felt trapped. Ben wondered if that's how Arthur felt, wherever he was. 'Merlin's out cold,' Jack reasoned, 'and even if he wasn't, we wouldn't let him hurt you.' April continued to ignore them. 'Don't make me come over there, kid. Seriously, I can't be sure that my boyfriend's spell of murderous intent has passed.'

Ben thumped Jack in the shoulder, but nodded in agreement. 'Has Merlin said something to you?' April shook her head. 'Has he done something?' Jack's fingers dug into Ben's arm at the thought. April's fingers ceased their dance across the screen, but she didn't look up.

'No. Not yet anyway. I keep getting the feeling that I've met Merlin before. I can't remember where.'

'You and me both, kid.' Well, Jack hadn't mentioned that. Were they both keeping secrets from him?

'And have you? Met Merlin before?' Ben shifted uncomfortably. Magic. That was the only plausible reason for Merlin's interest in her. 'It's alright, if you have. I won't be mad.'

'That's not what worries me. I can't put my finger on what it is exactly, but …' If there was a time to come clean about the vision plaguing her, it was now. 'It's just …' They leant forward, ready to defend her, to help her. April didn't deserve them. 'It's a bad feeling and it's worse around Merlin. That's all.'

'Like a premonition?' Ben's eyes narrowed a little at her shocked expression.

'Your guess is as good as mine.' Whenever April caught one of Ben's curious glances, she wanted to ask him if he'd finished the puzzle yet.

'Premonitions are a form of magic,' Ben said evenly, his eyes widening a little in understanding.

'I've been meaning to ask what's it like? Having another voice inside your head? Must be an inconvenience.' Ambrosius flared into life on Ben's shoulder, as if April had summoned him.

'Are you positive that there isn't a little witch in your family tree?' Seeming to respond to an unspoken request, Ben picked Ambrosius up and set the little guy on the floor. Much to Ben's surprise and April's unease, Ambrosius confidently strolled over to Merlin's prone body.

'I can't say it ever came up.' April wasn't sure why she felt so defensive about it. It seemed like a sensible question, given the circumstances. 'Does it matter?' Ambrosius inspected the purple-blue bruising on Merlin's neck. She had the horrible thought that he was going to rise up like a mummy. Ambrosius was a part of Ben and she didn't want any part of Ben so close to the sleeping lion. April busied herself with tying back the curtains, fighting the impulse to snatch Ambrosius away.

'It matters to me. If you have even a single drop of magic inside you, I don't want him to find out.' Ben indicated Merlin with his foot.

'Nope, no magic here. There's nothing up my sleeves either.' April laughed nervously.

Magic.

Well, that would explain the visions. The tiny bundle of embers stepped into view. His disarming smile interrupted her scowling at the threadbare carpet. 'Oh. Hello.' She peered down into the little round face. 'Um? What's the etiquette for interacting with somebody's magic/imaginary friend?' April wanted to touch Ambrosius, mostly out of curiosity.

'Flick him away if he's bothering you.' April shot Ben a disapproving glare. 'Or pick him up, it's up to you,' Ben amended with a surprised laugh, his head against Jack's shoulder. 'Either way, you do so with my permission.'

April cautiously bent down, hand extended. Ambrosius clambered up, his little extremities tickled. She stood, holding Ambrosius so he could see the room. The eyes were unmistakably Ben's, sad and distant. 'His tiny feet tickle! Feels a bit like localised pins and needles.'

'That's a good way to put it. Have you ever felt that within yourself?' Ben asked. April shook her head. Ambrosius tilted his head to one side, looking at her like he knew she was lying. People like April didn't have magic. She gently prodded Ambrosius with her little finger. 'Stop trying to use him as a voodoo doll!'

'Sorry! I think I'd have noticed if I had somebody like Ambrosius living in my head.' She went for smug, missed, and hit uncertain. Ambrosius climbed onto her shoulder and waved sarcastically at Ben. 'I'm kinda jealous. He seems fun.' Perhaps having a tiny bundle of magic attached to her wouldn't be terrible. Ambrosius must have been Ben's only companion for a long time.

'Not necessarily.' Ben's frown deepened.

In the hospital, April had spoken to Merlin in that strange voice. It had come from inside her – was that magic? No, April had been tired and worried, and those two things played havoc with a person.

'Magic runs deep. It could take you a lifetime to find it.' Ambrosius laughed as she jumped out of her skin.

'I forgot you can talk!'

'April,' Jack's concern mirrored Ben's, 'if you've seen or felt something, you've gotta tell us.' Like the classic deer in the headlights, April realised a fraction too late that they both knew. They just needed her to confirm their hypothesis. 'Even if to reassure yourself. No use sitting there worrying about it.'

April shifted, uncomfortable with the attention and speculation. She shouldn't have said anything and yet, Ben would have found his way to the heart of the matter all the same. In her hand, Ambrosius peered up at her with gentle, understanding eyes. It would be oh-so-typical if April had magic that was good for nothing besides disturbing her already pitiful sleep. 'Have you forgotten that Arthur is somewhere out there?'

'Did you have to?' Jack threw his hands up in the air. April shrugged unapologetically, relieved that, for now, the focus had shifted. Next time, the headlights were going to hit her.

'Merlin's the only one who knows what happened,' Ben decided.

'He probably said that so you wouldn't let him leave. We can find Arthur by ourselves,' Jack said with little feeling.

'Do you have a spell for that as well?' With that, Ambrosius vanished from her hand, reappearing in Ben's.

'Merlin only gave me the one spell. Which was a bit pointless.'

April dived back into her phone. This bit didn't seem applicable to the third wheel.

'Merlin appreciates drama. Scripted or improvised.' Ben gave a short bark of laughter. 'Yes, Ambrosius, I'm aware of your thoughts on the matter. Hey, April, you seemed keen on the idea of having a magical friend. Catch.' Ben bundled

Ambrosius up into a ball and pitched it. She panicked and dropped her phone, but Ambrosius disappeared mid-flight.

'Based on your reunion with Merlin, how do you see one with Arthur going?' Jealousy was not a good colour on Jack. It was the way that Ben spoke so highly of Arthur, the king who died to save Gaia. How was Jack supposed to follow that? He couldn't.

'Arthur will still be Arthur. He's resilient – and he'll be worried about the realm.'

'My bad. I forgot how brilliant Arthur was. I'm sure he's survived the under realms unchanged.' It was hard to decide who Ben would choose if he had to … and now he had the choice. Jack pulled himself away from the bottomless pit. This was bigger than his insecurities. This was about saving their home. So, against his better judgement, he reluctantly shelved his issues. 'The second this so much as interferes with us saving Gaia, or I think Merlin is screwing us, this rescue mission is over. Understood?' Ben nodded, but Jack knew he didn't agree.

'I should have seen what Merlin was doing at the time,' Ben sighed, prodding the warlock with his foot.

'Ugh!' the body complained, startling them all. 'You knew the company you kept and the dangers we brought.' The gruff voice didn't sound much like Merlin.

Ben's eyes clouded with guilt until he decided that damaging Merlin's vocal cords wouldn't be such a terrible thing. 'Aye, I knew it well. But I'm talking about one thing in particular.'

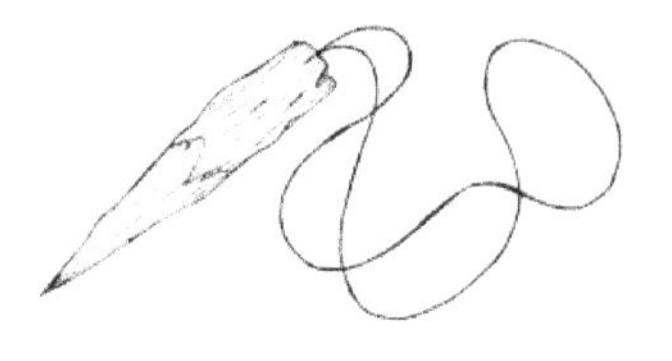

29

Let it Happen

'Did you betray Arthur for Fate?'

Ben had come up with all sorts of theories: Arthur was a casualty of war; wrong time wrong place; it was his time; part of a bigger picture. But the most likely of them all, was betrayal. He started to pace, but Jack's hand clamped on his arm. Ben glanced back, and Jack shook his head. Ben ran a hand through his hair, hoping he looked less like somebody desperate to hit Merlin.

'That's preposterous, Benjamin.' Merlin sounded so outraged and offended that Ben doubted himself out of reflex. The warlock was usually right about these things. 'Arthur was like a brother to me.' Merlin struggled to push himself into a sitting position. 'If anything, I saved him! And before you commence whining about yourself, you happened to get caught in the crossfire.' Ben sensed a lie, or at least a half-truth. He gathered his long legs under him, apparently undeterred from shaking the truth out of Merlin. 'Do you trust me, Benjamin?'

He almost choked on the humourless laughter that erupted from him. 'You can't be serious?' Merlin gave him that trademark solemn stare and slightly ruined the effect by rubbing at his neck. 'Trust you? I'm struggling to be in the same room as you! Fool me once – shame on you, Merlin. Fool me twice – not going to happen.'

'You, Benjamin, should know better than to let your emotions run rampant like that.'

Benjamin's conviction wasn't going to be anywhere near enough to deter him. Merlin sighed internally. 'You should have listened to me, Benjamin. You both should have listened to me. But no, you and Arthur had to become romantically tangled. Is the vampire broken?' Jack's fangs were out, puncturing his bottom lip and drawing blood.

'Oh, I don't know … maybe it's because you've just capsized our relationship?'

'Me? I've done nothing wrong! Honestly, Benjamin, you should have told Jack that you still harbour feelings for Arthur. It's unfair.'

'It was a little different when Arthur was dead.' Ambrosius burned like a bonfire on a grey October day, engulfing Benjamin's hands. And there was a third strand of magic. It was faint, but present. All anxious and uncertain, the nameless energy dogged Ambrosius's heels. It didn't like Merlin, not one little bit. And whilst there was a great deal of anxiety, animosity and confusion bouncing off the walls, the new magic had to belong to April. 'Who gave you the right to destroy so many lives? Was it Fate? I'd tell you that she's not good for you, Merlin, but you didn't listen the last two thousand times!'

'You're behaving like a spoiled child.' Emrys made his disapproval clear by way of an oncoming headache. 'Sometimes, Benjamin, being a good friend means being absent. I had work to do. It would have brought more trouble to your door. So, I've been little more than a stranger to you the past thousand years. Boo hoo.'

Benjamin's eyes bulged, his jaw working. 'You cannot fake your own death. Fake the death of the man I love.'

'Present tense, interesting.' Merlin smirked. Jack's lips pull downwards in dismay

'Being a *good friend* doesn't give you licence to destroy my soul.'

'Give me strength! I knew you'd overreact like this, Benjamin. It's why I didn't want to tell you.'

'I'm overreacting? If I was, you'd be dead.'

'You throttled me but ten minutes ago.' Merlin pinched the bridge of his nose. 'Perhaps I should have reached out earlier. Sent a letter.' Benjamin spluttered. 'You wouldn't have left it alone. Furthermore, the other Guardians would never have accepted you if they knew the appointed Guardians were alive. You're a shtriga!' Looking around the room it seemed only Merlin found it funny. 'I know how this all ends.' An unnatural stillness settled over Benjamin, his eyes pitch black. Merlin surprised himself by reaching for Emrys.

'I could have acted like you were dead?'

'The thought never occurred to me.' It seemed so simple with hindsight.

‘Unbelievable,’ Benjamin said softly. And, I’m scared to ask, Arthur’s “death?”’

‘It was best to let everybody think Arthur dead. But the death had to be convincing. And balance maintained – that’s important.’

Benjamin ripped the cushion in half. Merlin watched in silence as the shtriga drew in deep breath after deep breath, cushion stuffing falling to earth, plunging him into a snowstorm. ‘You could have told me! I would have dealt with it.’

‘Like you’re dealing with it now? I know you better than you know yourself. And the state you were in – you were a disaster-in-waiting.’ Merlin wanted to move on from this; he wanted to discover more about the delightful April. He’d been trying to reach her for some time. He wasn’t surprised that it took connecting with Ben to kick-start her premonitions.

‘I preferred you dead, Merlin.’

There it was again, that unfamiliar coldness in Benjamin’s voice. Merlin had thought their friendship to be stronger than that. ‘I’m not revealing Arthur’s location.’ Bejamin’s hands curled up into sledgehammer fists, a not-so-subtle warning.

‘You’ve come back armed with your revelations and your betrayals, and I can’t understand why you look so sad, Merlin.’ Merlin tilted his head to one side and considered the tortured expression on Benjamin’s long face. Merlin had expected to be consumed by guilt at this point, but he wasn’t even in the neighbourhood.

‘You can climb down from your high horse.’ Benjamin wasn’t the only one who’d spent the last thousand years gathering up baggage that weighed more than their long lifetimes put together.

'My high horse!' Merlin kept expecting steam to pop out of Benjamin's ears.

'What do you want from me, Benjamin? Aside from Arthur.'

'An apology. I assume that an acknowledgement of responsibility is too much to ask for. That would imply you've a moral code against which to transgress.'

'I didn't ruin your life, Benjamin. I gave you one! You'd have wandered off into obscurity, living your tedious physician's life if I hadn't intervened.' Benjamin took another step forward. Ambrosius flared, the angry flames looking ready to burn whatever they could touch.

Merlin calmly looked up at Benjamin. 'I am not to blame for your choices.'

'This is such bull—'

'Benjamin!'

'Everything I thought to be true has turned into an illusion, thanks to you.'

Merlin leant forward to interrupt, but he caught April's eyes glaring over the top of her phone. For a second, he saw her, sat atop a wall, framed by a sky so brilliantly blue, it looked fake. At her feet, roses and …

'There wasn't a moment when a plot wasn't brewing in that brilliant mind of yours. I've shouldered a responsibility that was never mine. I've made a new life with Jack, who makes mourning the past redundant. And without Jack, I had little reason to exist for quite some time. And in one day, you've swept the board clean!'

'Arthur never did like sharing your time. And he's a sore loser – part of the job description. Plus, I seem to recall that you can't bear to disappoint him. Really, Benjamin, you should have considered the facts before you created a new relationship.'

Ben looked around the room, not believing what he was hearing. 'I didn't have the facts!'

Merlin's derisive snort set off whispering voices in the back of April's mind. Wood smoke and incense filled her nostrils, transporting her back to a dark chamber with shelves groaning under the weight of books, jars filled with questionable objects, whilst the tables were hidden beneath bowls of herbs and beakers. It was a venerable wizard's bric-a-brac. Merlin turned from his work to stare her down for having said something so foolish. Only he looked without really seeing her. This wasn't a premonition; this was a memory.

'You aren't human!' Merlin scoffed.

The sounds of drunk, cheerful voices chased away the stale argument. A showreel of events and people filled the room, painting a picture of court life in that hazy vision that wasn't of the here and now. The unwelcome and unnatural feeling of déjà vu wrapped around April, constricting her breathing. She couldn't know Arthur, but her eyes picked him out in a crowded court, deep in animated conversation with Merlin, concern creasing his face. Her perspective shrunk, and from her new vantage point, close to the floor, April watched Fate glide into a room without walls, trailing her hand along Merlin's shoulders as she passed. And then Merlin, again. Only this time, he had a kind face as he manifested Emrys in his hand. The bundle of embers shifted from a person to a butterfly, to a miniature horse – whilst a child giggled with delight. The next moment, she saw Arthur, dishevelled and alone in a cold, grey castle perched above the sea. And how the wind howled around the solemn figure!

April's skin burned with pins and needles. What was the point in feeling out of place in her own body, if she couldn't make sense of it? April had to tell Ben. Whatever this was, it was a plague and April didn't like plagues. She reached out, blindly grabbing onto the rough wood of the windowsill so hard she felt the pinch of a splinter. The shock cleared her mind, slamming her back into the present with a touch of whiplash.

The argument had left Ben and Merlin standing in opposite corners of the destroyed room. Two beaten boxers unable to go another round, neither opponent willing to admit defeat, and in the middle stood Jack, a disgruntled referee.

'Ben ...' Merlin turned to answer her, that knowing grin on his stupid face. There wasn't anywhere to hide from him. Not that Ben was listening anyway. His rapid, shallow breathing nearly had April looking for a paper bag. 'Never mind.'

The stubbornness that Ben had once admired took a hold of Merlin, his attention switching to April. The book of the past had closed. 'If you are not inclined to answer my questions, there's no reason for you to remain here, Merlin.' Ben's formal tone had been intended to cut like a knife and, judging by the hurt that flashed in Merlin's eyes, he'd grazed the skin at least.

'If we pool our resources together, we can turn the tide, once and for all—'

'Can you hear yourself, warlock?' The last remaining picture – a framed print of an oak tree – lost its grip and clattered to the floor.

'Hmph! Fine. Finish what you have already failed to do. Once completed, you'll be free and I can leave – if that's what you want, Benjamin. You'll never hear from me again.'

Jack groaned. 'Hey, Ben, have you seen the one where a shtriga, a vampire, a hunter and a warlock have to work together to save the world? It's very original.' Ben shook his head.

'What do we have to do?' April asked cautiously, hauling the sofa back to its correct orientation. Bits of cushion stuffing and chunks of dust drifted about the living room. Some of it landed in Ben's hair, but he ignored it. Jack slipped over to her and collapsed onto the sofa. It groaned but maintained its structural integrity.

'Now that is an excellent question! If only there was a prophet in my life who I could have asked …'

'You've made your point, Benjamin!' Merlin stomped over to the sofa, plonking himself down beside Jack. He smirked as the vampire squashed himself against the armrest. Another grunt of protest came from the tortured piece of furniture. 'Thousands of prophecies were made, but they weren't all written down. So, yes, there are predictions known only to me.'

'Convenient. Isn't that convenient?' Ben looked from April to Jack. Neither wanted to encourage him.

'Go on, disregard me.' Merlin sighed. 'Remember what happened the last time you did so?' That put Ben on the back foot. Ambrosius squirmed, not liking the evil smirk.

Ben stalked over to Merlin, letting a little of his true form show in his face. 'You swore you'd never breathe a word of it to another soul.' Unintimidated, Merlin fell about himself laughing as Ben's skin flushed a deep, dark red.

'In-jokes are rude. Care to share?' Jack looked to Ben, his interest piqued.

'No. He doesn't,' Ben snapped in reply whilst Merlin tried to catch a breath.

'Benjamin muddled up the words casting a spell – ignored my warnings.' Merlin dissolved into another laughing fit. Jack raised his eyebrows at Ben who shook his head. 'He—'

'Hold your tongue, warlock!'

'Turned himself, into, a goat!' Jack was silent and still for a moment before his laughter exploded out of him and joined that of Merlin's and April's in a cacophony. The sofa shook under the weight of three people.

'And a fat lot of good you were! You opened the door so I could escape.' Ambrosius curled up into a ball. 'When I made my way back, Merlin convinced Arthur I was any old goat. Arthur gave me to a farmer! Three weeks, Merlin! Three whole weeks. I'd rather you'd left me as a goat than a shtriga. I'd be less conflicted about eating grass.' The sofa's frame snapped in the middle, dumping Jack, Merlin and April on the floor.

'For the record,' Jack ventured into the gap, 'I prefer you as a shtriga. I reckon that going out with a goat would get more looks.' Despite his embarrassment, Ben allowed himself a small smile. He hauled up Jack and April.

'I'm anxious to be done with all of this – goats included – so what's your plan?' Merlin's head tilted from side to side, as if Ben was a picture he couldn't quite see from his angle. There was no humour left in the cold, black eyes. 'Merlin?'

'Why didn't your magic heal you?'

'I'd not fed.' Ben glanced over to Jack; the vampire had crept forward.

'No, that's not it.' Merlin's voice was distant. 'It's all connected.' Merlin turned his faraway eyes to April. 'Even if you can't see how, you're all connected. Here, now, forever.'

'He's making it up.' April appeared beside Ben, her eyes were so wide that she resembled an anime character. Her elusive jade aura shimmered clearly for a moment. Out of the corner of his eye, Ben saw Merlin smile and he felt sick to his stomach.

'Why would I make it up? I am Gaia's second Guardian.'

'Is that so?' Ben laughed. 'Forgive me, Merlin, I must have missed you popping back to see how the realm and I were getting on.'

'I've had enough of this,' Jack cut in. 'You are both duty-bound to protect Gaia, yes?' Ben and Merlin nodded in chastised silence.

'Hallelujah! Something we all agree upon. Park your issues until Gaia is safe. Then, and only then, can you bicker like children. For now, we all have to play nice. Got it?'

'No!' April answered instead, falling into Ben. He let her lean against him, her face ashen, knowing eyes staring at the warlock. 'Merlin would destroy every realm if Fate asked him to.'

'How could you possibly know that, girl?' Merlin scrambled back to his feet.

'I'm not a girl.' With shaking arms, April cast off from Ben. 'I'm a hunter and I've got your card marked, Merlin.' Ben closed his eyes, trying to place her voice. April sounded like a haunted version of herself. She sounded … like somebody he knew … It was right there, on the tip of his tongue …

'That's adorable. Truly.' Merlin's laughter had a sharp edge to it. He stepped in front of April. 'Do not overestimate your abilities.'

'Good advice. You should heed it.' April shot around Ben to level the knife Jack had given her at Merlin's chest. Ben cursed himself for being distracted but didn't interfere.

'If you hurt either of them, I will send you back to Fate in pieces.'

'Ooo-kkk.' Jack leant forward and lowered the knife with one finger. 'The Gods give me strength to cope with the three of you.'

At least she'd lost some of her fear of Merlin. Unless it was fear that was driving April. Ben tapped her on the shoulder, letting her decide to move back a few steps, and she continued glaring from a safe distance.

'What is it you need us to do, exactly?' Jack spoke to Merlin but kept his gaze locked with April's, daring her to interrupt.

'Put an end to something that shouldn't have ever drawn breath.' Merlin took extra care to pluck a tissue from the box on the coffee table.

'Mórrígan,' Ben replied flatly.

'It always ends where it began.' Merlin nodded, folding the tissue into a pocket square with exaggerated movements. He had no pockets on his grubby tunic.

'What?' Jack asked, startled by Ben's cold, sharp bark of laughter.

'Oh, Jack,' Ben sighed. 'Merlin is guilty of many things, but I didn't think he was a coward. He can't face his ex-wife.'

'Need I remind you that my ex-wife is War? Mórrígan is a means to an end. Kill her and you'll have a clear shot at Fate.'

Ben didn't waste words discussing it with Jack, but he did look to April. She gave him a short nod of agreement. 'Where is she?' As Merlin made to launch into an explanation, Ben quickly added, 'Where, not how.'

'Where you left her. Oh, and Ben, does my return mean you'll finally stop writing to me?'

'How do you ...?' Ben's cheeks burned with embarrassment; he saw Jack make the connection. 'I never posted them. I didn't know where in the nine realms to send them.' Ben couldn't help but sound bitter.

'You are a nuisance. You couldn't leave me to my "death" – the Gods help you when I actually die. You projected your thoughts well and unknowingly.'

'You heard. And you never answered.' It didn't matter how low Merlin stooped, he always seemed to slip further.

'Stop talking. You're not helping.' If Merlin heard April's cold warning, he didn't let on.

'It was rather annoying. In particular, that day in 1802. You wrote two hundred and forty-eight, multiple-page letters. How does one think of enough content to produce that many letters within five hours?' Merlin shook his head in disbelief, like that was the greatest crime committed.

'I was having a mental breakdown. Because of you!' Ben shouted. 'It happens occasionally. Perhaps if you'd been here ...'

Merlin held his hands up in mock surrender. 'Too soon to tease?'

'Yes! I had a hunch you could hear me,' Ben muttered, hot, angry tears clouding his eyes, shuddering at the thought of Merlin mentally looking over his shoulder.

'No matter. Shall we prepare to leave?' The warlock meandered from the room, arms folded behind his back. Merlin had got what he wanted, and down the Merlin-rabbit hole they went.

'If you don't kill him, I will.' Ben did not doubt April's commitment to that vow.

30

We Don't go in There

In the bustle of activity that surrounded their departure, Jack found himself alone with Merlin. He'd been so concerned about making sure that neither April nor Ben had any solo interactions with Merlin, he'd forgotten about himself.

Jack took a deep breath and carried on, trying not to look like he was on the verge of running. As they passed in the cramped upstairs hallway, a slender hand reached out and wrapped itself around Jack's wrist, a smirk playing on Merlin's thin lips.

'You care deeply for Benjamin.' Frustration burned in Jack's cheeks. Whether Merlin understood it or not, the warlock continued to laugh at his relationship.

'Certainly, more than you do.' Jack tried to free his arm with a quick downwards pull but Merlin held fast, his strength out of place with his stature.

'If you know him inside out as you would have me believe, you must have realised that within him there is a violent storm brewing. He's rather overwhelmed.' Merlin's fingernails dug tiny graves in Jack's skin. His back bumped up against the rough wall.

'Speak plainly, Merlin. I am not of a mind to humour you.'

'If you prefer.'

'I would *prefer* it if you didn't spin lies and speculate.'

'Sometimes in war, things are asked of people, which under normal circumstances, would be unthinkable. I'm not suggesting anything ...' Merlin held up his spare hand as Jack's mind leapt to conclusions. 'People like Ben, who are so unhappy within themselves, tend to make rash decisions. He is smart, there's no question, but he charges headfirst into battle.'

'It's almost as if he's afraid he'll lose everything he cares about,' Jack said pointedly.

'Perhaps he's wise to fear such a repetition.' Jack couldn't be sure, but it sounded like a threat. 'You might need to keep him in line. We wouldn't want him rushing off to rescue Arthur, would we?'

'Gaia comes first. It always has.'

'Has it?' Merlin pulled Jack closer still. 'Around nine hundred years ago, Benjamin thought he could reach Arthur on the night plane.' Jack's insecurities rose up inside of him like a wave ready to break. 'Benjamin entered the plane without a second thought. It was a trap, of course. One of Fate's earlier attempts. Only it nearly worked.' Jack couldn't believe Ben would be so stupid, so desperate. So lonely.

'He'd never leave himself and Gaia open to attack like that.'

'I secured the realm and convinced Fate to free Benjamin. Mistakes can always occur a second time.' Jack ripped his wrist free, turned and grabbed Merlin's tunic. It would have been threatening if Merlin wasn't struggling not to laugh at him.

'You don't remember, do you?' Merlin asked softly. The dark hallway slanted on its axis.

'Remember what?'

'Me.'

'I don't follow.' Jack's entire being tried to recoil from Merlin. He glanced at the stairs, he was so close and yet so far from being free.

'We've met before, Jack. Prior to Dirmynd. It's curious that you don't remember.' Merlin held Jack's gaze for a moment before turning to leave.

'Wait!' Merlin turned on the first step and smiled a slow, deliberate smile. He'd got all he was going to get from Merlin today. Jack racked his brain for one meeting but … he couldn't remember anything. Unless … unless it was trapped in that thick fog of time.

'I am not trying to scare you,' Merlin's sincerity was questionable, 'but in my experience, it is ill-advised to go to war beside your love. If Benjamin loses you, he loses himself. You are both setting yourself up for heartbreak.'

'He's not going to lose me, Merlin. I promise.'

'I once heard Arthur swear the same to Benjamin. It's a promise you cannot keep, lad. Nobody can. Ask the millions who came before you.' Merlin's smile was almost kind.

Having heard enough, Jack shouldered his way past the warlock and headed for the car, haunted by Merlin's laugh.

Jack shook his head, unable to believe that they were going to (try to) kill a God. He'd not considered that Merlin's return would upset the balance of order between the Gods. And the three of them were caught in the swaying motion as the scales attempted to settle.

31

Victory Over the Sun

Jack drove carefully through the night, treating the oncoming potholes as landmines, fearful of triggering an explosion.

Beside him, Ben was wound so tightly that the sound of someone blinking could set him off. From the back seat, the sound of thick wool rustling against nylon threatened to disturb the calm.

Merlin was a planet around which Ben orbited, a sad, cold moon trapped in the gravitational pull of the charismatic warlock. Ben couldn't escape if he wanted to. Jack wasn't enough to break Ben free of that particular orbit. Perhaps he'd never be enough. Or maybe it felt like that because nothing had gone right recently. And apparently, they were going to lean into the trend by chasing after War. Jack tried to relax. One job. And then he could crawl into bed and stay there for as long as the pending apocalypse allowed him. With any luck it would be long enough to make a dent in his to-be-read pile. At least Jack assumed it was going to be a quick job with Merlin around. Had his human life been so stressful? Jack's glance darted from the road to Merlin and back, safe in the knowledge that if things went sideways, it would be Merlin's fault. At least Ben hadn't been inspired to dig out his cloak. That ancient atrocity was still safely stored in the loft.

Ben was feeling decidedly dizzy.

He couldn't keep his thoughts from butting up against the incomprehensible idea that Arthur was alive. Merlin's words tripped over themselves and fell into each other. Arthur – he was going to be devastated when he saw the state of Gaia. And Jack. But Arthur would understand. He'd have encouraged Ben to find happiness. Besides, the king had taken a queen. Ben hadn't done anything wrong … had he? And then there was the matter of Ben himself. The shtriga curse, time, solitude and Jack had shaped him into a new person. He'd be a fool to think otherwise. Aside from having to feed on souls, Ben was, more or less, content with who he had become. He'd thought he'd felt settled with Arthur, in the city he'd hated, but truth be told – and it wasn't hard to admit at all – the city wasn't at fault. Nobody else could shrink Ben's world to focus on them like Jack. He'd always love Arthur, but could Ben love the king now, after he'd been so many different people? He wasn't certain. He had to stop obsessing over it. He hadn't found Arthur yet but he was already trying to rehearse what he'd say.

A kick to the back of his seat sent a fresh wave of resentment to wash everything else away until all Ben could see was Arthur, trapped alone in an abandoned, isolated and cold castle. Although he was relieved that April had opened up, he wished she hadn't told him about *that*. Premonitions.

His thumb ran over a sharp crack. Ben looked at his tired watch and frowned. His only experience with that kind of magic came courtesy of Merlin. And Ben was determined April wasn't going to turn into Merlin. Scrolling aimlessly on his phone wasn't helping. Ben locked the screen with a sigh, his background photo of Jack reading in his bed appeared briefly. By getting what he most desired, Ben had found that it wasn't what he needed. Or wanted. The irony. Ben contemplated the fact that he'd survived Merlin, and to some extent, Arthur. There was nothing worthwhile that Ben could offer Arthur. There was never a future there. The truth had a way of making itself known, in its own time. And Merlin …

If only Ben had known that trusting Merlin would cost him more than he could afford to pay. This time, he would be more frugal.

Jack had barely said a word to him since they'd departed. Jack only had himself to blame. Ben hadn't wanted to listen to Merlin's nonsense but Jack had pushed him. His vampire couldn't distance himself from the issues that lay between Merlin and Ben. It ran deeper than that, of course. Or perhaps Jack was still upset about the strangling incident. Ben's hands twitched, remembering how easy it had been to squeeze Merlin's life from his body. A small part of Ben had not only acknowledged what he was doing, it had relished it too. That should have been turning Ben's stomach, yet he felt nothing until he recalled the look of terror in Jack's eyes. There had been something else there, some sort of reluctant acceptance. And he wasn't going to figure it out with Merlin banging on the metaphorical door of his mind.

'Benjamin?'

Merlin was met with a frosty silence. He wasn't worried. As wide as the distance between them had grown, as mad as his assistant was, Benjamin couldn't maintain a grudge. Sooner or later, he would need to vent the conflicting thoughts circling his head. Merlin had no patience for transgressing into the past. Doing so would only create more clutter, and he had run out of storage centuries ago. But Benjamin needed to talk. Especially if it only brought pain. Merlin truly wanted to repair their relationship but that would have to wait. He needed Benjamin angry, otherwise, he wouldn't have the stomach for the fight ahead.

'Benj—'

'I have nothing to say to you.'

Merlin fought to hide a smirk as the last straw snapped. *'I don't for a second believe that. The past is a trap that you keep tripping headfirst into.'*

'Unless you plan on telling me where Arthur is, you have nothing to say to me.' Benjamin crossed his arms defiantly. *'Return to your own road, Merlin. It was better that way.'*

'Ha!' Merlin carefully smoothed out the creases in his cloak, willing himself not to complain about the amateur dramatics. If Benjamin needed an apology so badly ... *'We've been over this ground several times. I wish I could undo what I've done, but I can't.'*

Ben sucked in a shuddery breath, turning to look out of the window. Merlin's best, begrudging, lacklustre attempt at pronouncing the word "sorry" hadn't fixed a damn thing. How unsurprising.

'That you got caught up in this was regrettable, but I had—'

'Don't!' The anger and disbelief cut Merlin short. *'It was all to further your position as Fate's errand boy.'*

Merlin was irritated enough to sigh aloud, drawing a quick, curious glance from Jack. Thank the Gods he didn't have to keep this up much longer. *'One day, I will explain—'*

Ben snorted. *'If you confess to even a quarter of your sins, old man, we will be here until the end of time itself.'* His temples throbbed in protest as headache one hundred of the day kicked in. Weary beyond expression, Ben pushed his cold knuckles against closed eyes and drifted in the kaleidoscope of colours. Merlin had been doing fine without him. So, wherever Arthur was, there was a strong possibility that the king's life had carried on untroubled by their separation. There was no such thing as miracles. Just poor timing and disappointment.

'Don't let War stab you this time. I don't think I can pull you back a second time, my friend.' Ben tensed at the F-word. *'Your talisman was created to protect you, not be used against you. Even I am unsure as to the full extent of the damage.'*

Ben twisted in his seat so violently that Jack swore loudly and with feeling. The car slowed and drifted into the slow lane.

'The talismans sensed a threat larger than they could handle, and they drew on the nearest energy source,' Merlin said casually, already having lost interest in Ben's latest disaster. *'Calm down.'*

Calm down? If the talismans had drained his magic, if Ambrosius ceased to exist … Ben ripped the cord from around his neck and shoved it into the glovebox. Jack cast a concerned glance over the scene but didn't ask.

'You fret too much. It's unbecoming.'

If Ben breathed through this, he might not kill Merlin.

Largely forgotten, April would have been concerned about the growing tension if her concentration wasn't funnelled into a single spot.

The pins and needles were back.

Her skin was on fire with thousands of tiny pinpricks – in both arms. And there was a humming in her chest that felt like she'd swallowed a beehive whole. And April had to be imagining the faint jade aura surrounding her hands. The product of her tired brain. Not magic. Sensing Merlin's stare, she chucked her jumper over her lap and hid her hands. Merlin's eyebrows crawled up his forehead. At least somebody was having a good time. Exhaustion or magic? Merlin knew. The delighted sparkle in his eyes confirmed it.

'Hey, quick question: what does having a heart attack feel like? Asking for a friend.' The next wave of pins and needles caused her to shudder. April screwed her eyes shut, and the darkness exploded. The premonition, which wasn't already etched behind her eyelids, flickered into view. Merlin had interrupted before April could tell Ben. April's veins froze over watching vision-Merlin take a step towards vision-Ben. Jade embers drifted from the top of the scene, dissolving it. A furious lady with long blonde hair, had her hands wrapped around Merlin's throat; Jack stood in a cave, afraid and up to his waist in freezing water that kept rising; a room full of creepy hands; something that looked like a trial in a place worse than hell; her, a resigned Merlin and a giant oak tree.

'Enough!'

April slammed the brakes on the spiral and forced her eyes to open, not wanting to feel the pressure of everybody else's experiences. They were suffocating her, taunting her even. If she didn't act on them soon, what would happen? April couldn't even say what the bad thing was but she was pretty certain a wooden sword wasn't going to be enough.

Breathing hard, April clocked Merlin's reflection watching her. She didn't know if his conspirator's smile was for her or Ben.

'What are the two of you whispering about?' Jack's voice boomed into the otherwise quiet car, promising a fight. Ben and Merlin jumped in unison, guilty looks on their faces.

Jack couldn't watch the silent movie any longer. He'd tried to ignore the odd muted hand gesture but he couldn't step around the pit that had opened up in his stomach. Jack hated how he didn't know what to do about Merlin.

'If it concerned you, we would have included you.'

'Don't speak to Jack like that!' Ben rounded on Merlin. 'I expect even you to treat my partner with respect.' Shock caused Jack's ordinarily steady hands to jerk the steering wheel, swerving violently before he could regain his composure.

Merlin snorted dismissively, causing Ben's eye to twitch. Jack placed a hand on his knee. *'Easy, Ben. You can't swing a cat in this car, let alone Merlin.'*

'You mistook my tone as harsh. I addressed Jack no differently to you.' Ben huffed, no doubt irritated by Merlin's condescending inflection.

'So,' Jack cut in, 'remind me why *we* have to find Mórrígan and *you* can't do it alone?'

'Benjamin has a destiny to fulfil,' Merlin said tartly.

'Isn't Arthur meant to be the act at the top of the "saving the world" bill? Where's he at?' It was out before Jack could demand to know what the hell he was thinking.

Merlin spluttered, choking on his laughter, tears streaming down his face. Jack barely had time to register Ben's right hand grab the steering wheel, forcing the car to the side of the road.

'Are you trying to kill us?'

Ben burst out of the car, all fury and no control. Jack could only watch in the rear-view mirror as he forcibly removed Merlin from the back seat, slamming the warlock against the car.

This time, Ben wasn't going to stop until he drew blood.

'Stay in the car, April.' She nodded, her nervous eyes following Jack as he rushed to intervene.

'Why. Are. You. Laughing?' Ben shook Merlin like a ragdoll, each shake punctuating his sentence. 'What. Have. You. Done. To. Arthur?' Merlin's laughter and blood bubbled from his mouth. 'He should be here for Gaia. Arthur should be here, with me. He should …' Ben's voice broke so he raised his fist to finish the sentence. Jack caught it on the downswing. 'Tell me!' Ben's left hand was free to cause damage, so it did. It caught Merlin in the ribs, snapping bones like brittle twigs. It was taking all of Jack's strength to restrain the one fist.

'Steady now, Benjamin,' Merlin snickered, despite his already swelling face. 'Wouldn't want you to overreact again.'

'What did I do to deserve such cruelty from you? To be thrown to the Gods? To watch you murder the man I love?'

Ben's inability to let go of the present tense slapped Jack across the face. It was his turn to yell.

'That's enough, both of you!'

'Ha!' Merlin gasped around hiccups and laughter. You'll find it ever so funny ...'

'I have had it up to here with the pair of you.' Jack hauled Ben off Merlin by his collar. 'Your bickering, your taunting, your lack of consistency.' Jack looked from Merlin's bloodied and mildly curious face to Ben's thunderous expression. 'Merlin, put Ben out of his misery. For all our sakes. Ben, Merlin's a bastard. But is your disappointment enough to drive you to murder?' The tension fell from Ben's shoulders. 'Play nice. Or you can walk to Caerleon.' They both stared at the ground as if it required their full attention. 'The ground isn't going to vanish if you look up, Merlin.' Jack staggered back, shocked by the light of galaxies burning in Merlin's eyes. Whatever the intention, it was for Ben's benefit.

Nausea and exhaustion drove Ben to his knees. He reached blindly for Jack – the only solid thing in his life – but a strange, weightless feeling possessed him all the same, and Emrys collided with Ambrosius. In the shower of blue and orange sparks, Ben caught sight of long-ago battles, hooded figures and hastily beat retreats. All the while, Merlin stared, his knowing smile insisting it was painfully obvious. Ben's stomach was aflutter, sensing irrevocable change approaching.

'Arthur's death was an illusion. A spell. The body was real enough.' Merlin ran a steady hand through his hair. If it got any worse, birds would nest in it. Merlin took a step towards Benjamin, testing his own mortality. 'The spell was harder than expected, but masking it from you was easier than it should have been.' Merlin's short, sharp laugh pierced Ben's confidence.

'The pain had you all to itself. You were so caught up in the melancholy of it all, you didn't notice how, as Arthur's soul fled into the ether, I caught it and stored it in the safest place I could think of.' Merlin leant forward and lightly tapped the sword where it sat hidden underneath Ben's top. 'I gave it to the one person who would never lose it.' Merlin straightened to his full height, his eyes wide and unfocused. 'Feels strange, telling you this after so long. I assumed you'd figure it out. The truth – it's sharped with age. Careful not to cut yourself, Benjamin.'

'You are winding me up.' Ben spun away, tearing himself free of Jack's grip.

'Not this time,' Merlin said with as much sincerity as somebody who'd lied for centuries could muster. 'I'm sick to my back teeth of wearing a skin that doesn't fit anymore.'

'You made me carry around the very thing in which you'd imprisoned Arthur … I've had Arthur with me the whole time …' No matter how Ben rearranged the words, it still sounded ludicrous.

'I said he was close but inaccessible.'

'Arthur wouldn't fit into this sword.' Ben yanked the cord from his neck and hesitated. He meant to throw it at Merlin but he couldn't let go of it.

'That is … Don't be ridiculous. A soul takes up no space at all! You could squash one onto the head of a pin, if you tried hard enough.'

Ben drew in a breath that didn't in any way slow down his spinning mind as pure joy bounced off doubt and uncertainty before colliding head-on with rage. 'What state is Arthur in?' Ben had been wearing the king and Guardian of Gaia around his neck for over a thousand years.

'He's a spirit in limbo, surely?' Jack asked, as horrified as Ben.

'Of course he's a spirit! I had to get his soul out somehow! It's easiest to trick the body into thinking it's dying. Don't worry, his body is safe. I think. The less said the better.'

'Well,' Jack tugged on his earlobe, 'that explains why you'd never take the damn thing off, even during—'

'It doesn't,' Ben said quickly and loudly. 'This might be the worst thing you've done, Merlin. Definitely the stupidest.' April watched from the backseat, flinching at passing cars. People were slowing down to stare at them.

'On the contrary. Only I can reverse the spell. Even Chaos and Fate can't find Arthur in there,' Merlin said smugly.

'How do we get him out?'

'With a spell.' Merlin looked a little uncertain.

'You can't remember the spell! Ergo, the stupidest thing you've ever done.'

'I can! Arthur's been in there for rather a long time, Benjamin. He may not remember who you are.' That hit like a freight train. Surely Arthur would remember him. 'So, before you go pulling him into a changed world, I suggest you devise a plan. And, as you keep mentioning, he'll need a body to inhabit. Preferably his own.'

'Take us to wherever you've stashed Arthur's body.' Ben shivered. 'There's a sentence I never thought I'd say.'

'Not until we've dealt with Mórrígan. Business first.'

Jack grabbed Ben's arm but Ben shook him off. 'This is business, Merlin. You've trapped the rightful Guardian and your king, in a pendant-purgatory. Forget your ex-wife, we're taking care of this right now.'

'Arthur has been safely hidden for a thousand years. He can wait a few more days. Skip the empty threats. On this, I will not budge.'

'Merlin has a point, Ben. As much as I hate to agree with him.' Ben shook his head, furiously thinking. 'We can't bring a confused Arthur back into the world on our way to kill War.'

'If we're lucky, Arthur will remember himself, thus requiring no explanation from you …'

'Not I, you, Merlin. You tore reality apart; you stitch it back together,' Ben snapped, earning him a stern and irritated sigh. 'Wait. If you spirited Arthur away before the Valkyries arrived … who died in his place?' A chill came over Ben and the nausea returned. 'Was I your sacrifice?'

'Life and death aren't so rigid for the three of us. Besides, it was a spell,' Merlin complained defensively.

'What's that supposed to mean?' Jack stepped in front of Ben. Anger squared his shoulders. 'If a prophecy comes next, *I'll* punch you, Merlin.'

'The realm cannot be without me. Benjamin is a Guardian and Arthur is the Once and Future King. The universe will always find a way to return us.'

'All stories have an element of truth to them.' Merlin shrugged. 'I left it too long to tell you, Benjamin.'

'Waiting for the right time, were you? I don't think they make *"Sorry for almost killing your boyfriend and trapping him in a necklace"* cards.'

'Yes, I was.' Merlin looked defiantly at Jack. 'Benjamin had settled. I'd sailed past the point of no return after introducing the two of you to one another.'

'What?' Jack and Ben chorused. Any more revelations, and Ben would never smile again.

'Oh, Jack. Still you don't remember?' Jack shook his head, glancing to Ben for a reassurance he couldn't provide.

'I sent you into that vampire's nest. I guided you into that tavern. You weren't supposed to fall in love. I thought Benjamin needed a friend.' Anger flushed Ben's cheeks, and he surged forward, incandescent. His right hook sent itself towards Merlin's jaw, but cold metal crumpled instead of bone. Jack made a small sound of protest.

'Merlin!' Ben screamed at skeletal trees. A car hurtled past quickly enough to shake their car.

'He's gone,' Jack said bitterly as he gently tugged Ben back towards the passenger seat. The door clicked open …

'What did Merlin say? And what did the car do to you? Where is Merlin? What happened?' April stalled for a second as she took in Ben's crushed and defeated demeanour, and the healing cuts on his knuckles.

'I'd forgotten I'd locked her in the car,' Jack said apologetically.

Ben nodded and reached for his seatbelt, his eyes filled with tears.

As Jack turned the engine over, April's seatbelt clicked at the edge of its range. 'What's Merlin waiting for, to be invited in?'

Ben threw himself out of the car. He had enough time to register the sad, wild look in Merlin's eyes, before the warlock vanished once more.

'How much longer can you run for, Merlin?' Ben vented to the uncaring SOS phone box that had witnessed the whole charade. 'Sooner or later, all of this is going to catch up with you.' Exhausted, he slipped back into the car.

'What happened?' April bravely ventured into the silence, letting the question float there. She expected Jack to answer, but it was Ben who surprised her.

'We've found Arthur.'

Ben's voice quivered under the strain. 'Ok, I'll bite. Where is he?'

'Here.' As stealthily as she could, April glanced about to make sure there wasn't a fourth person sharing the back seat with her. Ben held the sword up.

'The talisman?' April's disbelieving eyes found Ben's in the rear-view. She saw the truth in his sorrowful deep blue orbs. Her heart broke for him. 'How certain are you?'

'What makes you say that?' Ben turned to look at her properly, and April almost blurted out her original premonition. If Merlin had hidden a king inside a talisman, what else was he keeping up his sleeve?

'It's Merlin, so ...?'

'We're not sure.' Ben frowned.

'Oh, Ben.' She gave his shoulder a squeeze. April had no new clues to tell her why the feeling of doom and dread, that had dogged her since she'd first caught a glimpse of Merlin standing tall in an unknown place, tears slipping unnoticed down his cheeks but a determined smile on his face, refused to be silenced.

From the very back of April's mind came a discarded memory of Melvin. A cantankerous hunter in his forties, he'd taken her under his wing long enough to teach April about killing vampires. She hadn't thought of Melvin in a long, long time.

Not until he'd called her out of the blue that night.

He'd warned her that something was going down in the park, and could she handle it because he had his hands full with a nest? Why, April wondered, had she not realised before …? Merlin was a dead ringer for Melvin. 'Son of a bitch.'

Merlin was crafting his own script for the end of the world.

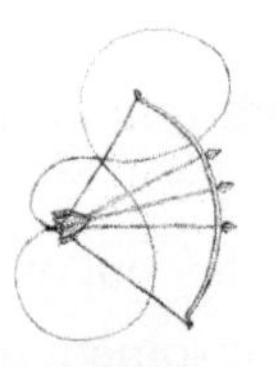

32

Joy

Jack let out a long low whistle as they pulled up to the B&B. The smouldering remains blended into the pale pink sky and rolling fields behind.

'Well, that's convenient,' Ben remarked, his voice jumping with irritation. Ambrosius appeared to inspect the situation. The place was humid with the static of spell-casting.

'Shame, I kinda liked it.' Ben turned to Jack, eyebrows raised. 'It was quaint.'

'I don't think there's anybody home.' April poked her head through the gap in the seats. 'What now?'

'Find Mórrígan, I suppose.' Jack looked around at the ruins, convinced he wasn't getting home to his books any time soon.

'She's set fire to everything in the area.' April unclicked her seatbelt, her breath warm on the back of his neck.

'I wondered what the burning smell was.' Sarcasm was a favourite coping mechanism.

'Well,' Ben leant forward for a better look, 'War has a tendency to destroy things ...' Ben's voice faded as he stared intently at something in the middle of the remains. 'Look.' Jack and April followed his pointing finger to the shimmering patch of air.

'She torched the place and portalled out. Classic,' Jack said flatly. 'We either just missed her or that's an invite.'

'It's an invite.'

'Where do you think it goes?'

'Hell,' Ben replied casually, 'Mórrígan's hall, probably.'

'So, Styx. Unpleasant doesn't exactly do that place justice.' Jack had visited once. Ben had been looking for Hades, who apparently sauntered around the under realms as he pleased. Jack had no desire to return.

'I vote we don't go through the portal.' April squinted into the smoke. 'Question: have either of you, with your supernatural eyesight, noticed the thing moving in the ruins?' Jack craned his neck, hoping it wasn't Merlin. 'It's a dog!' April tripped over her excitement as she flung herself from the car.

'Were we this stupid as humans?' Jack watched her sprint towards the alleged dog, stopping at what would have been the threshold of the building.

'At one point in both of our lives, we trusted Merlin. So, I'm going to have to say yes.' Ben slowly opened his door, not wanting to spook the dog.

'Good point.' Jack's door creaked open, protesting its age. 'Please don't pet it, April.'

April turned back, her hand reaching out for the dog, and laughed in surprise. Ben's nerves tangled with Jack's as they both wished April wouldn't turn her back on the dog.

'After the four days you've had, you're not suspicious? Not thinking it might not be as it seems?' Jack replied, shifting gears and looking for the best route to April.

'Looks like a dog to me.'

'Looks like a hellhound to me. And it's a bit too close to that there portal for my liking.'

'It's not a hellhound!' April glanced back again.

'Don't look at me! Eyes on the hellhound.' Jack was struggling to keep himself from yelling, but April's dismissive shrug made them both uneasy. 'Know what they look like, do you? Have the ability to see a being's true form, do you?' Ben lightly tapped Jack's shoulder, indicating they should approach April from either side.

'Look at its squashed nose! Hi, little fella. Who's a good boy?' The dog's stumpy tail wagged happily which only encouraged April's cooing.

'Its little squashed nose is going to be covered in your blood if you're not careful.'

'A tad harsh, Ben.'

'Better to cry over harsh words than April's wounds.' Ben shrugged.

'How are you guys seeing a hellhound?'

'Because we have messed-up supernatural eyesight, remember? Why are you doubting us?' Jack's hands went to his hips, in case she'd missed his disapproval. 'Seriously, April.' The pug gave a little bark as Jack and Ben closed the distance. They froze, staring the hellhound down. April hesitated, one foot inched slightly in front of the other, looking between the dog and common sense. *'April's too close to it, Ben.'* Fear caught fire in Jack and he surged forward, but Ben caught his arm and pulled him back. The hound's head swung to look at them – it had them over a barrel.

'If we so much as sprint, April becomes a chew toy, Jack.'

'Do you always have to be right. Damn it!'

'Demonic creature or not, it's still a strange dog in the middle of a burnt-out building. That should be setting off at least one warning bell.' Apparently forgetting his own advice, thin trails of orange magic emerged from the palms of Ben's hands. The hound pinned him with its hellish, button eyes. It's gaze slid to Jack and back to April. The cursed thing pulled back its lips into a smile full of razor-blade teeth and intent that had been sharpened on bones since it was a pup.

It was moving, tripling in size, its little squashed nose growing into the long, scarred snout of a creature that had never lost a fight. Razor-sharp claws extended from its paws, adding to the picture. The pulsating red light shining from its eyes suggested this was an animal that took no issue with dragging souls from their fleshy cage. The white and brown coat sunk beneath the black coat, and its transformation into the nightmare that Jack and Ben had seen all along, was complete.

Credit where credit was due, it was smart, tempting the slowest member of the group away by being all cute and fluffy. Neither vampire nor shtriga could stop it from sinking its teeth into April's side. They could only watch in horror as the hound dragged her backwards towards the portal, her screams ringing in their ears.

Jack's hand brushed against April's as she disappeared inside the portal. It sealed itself shut with a smug little pop.

'April! Ben, open another portal. Now.' Jack stared in horror at the trail of blood winding its way away from him, and his stomach flipped.

Ben opened his own portal and grabbed Jack's hand. 'Come on, let's go to hell.'

'I thought you'd never ask. I can't believe I'm about to say this, but we could do with Merlin right about now.'

'He's not answering.'

****

The world spun upside down, round and round, and time rushed past in a black tunnel. It bottomed out, exploding into colour. Sharp, tearing pain ripped through April's side, spreading to every inch of her being. A split second after that, the world disappeared altogether. April floated in the space between realms, her body weightless and formless. She didn't know what she'd expected the inside of a portal to look like, but April hadn't imagined it to be the most beautiful thing she'd ever seen. A galaxy of colours so bright, so vivid and so deep in their purples, blues, shivering silvers, golds and oranges enveloped her, stretching out as far as she could see. The dog's teeth sunk a little deeper and they flipped over, losing April in the perfectly crowded black sky that glowed with the intense white light of millions of stars. These stars were alive, April could feel it. Without knowing how she knew, April understood: she was staring down the length of time, right back to the centre of the universe. She managed to drag her eyes away from the majesty of time and space to look back over her shoulder. The sight of the worlds stretched out below, robbed April of the ability to breathe. Or it could've been the pain.

At the furthest point, the charred remains of the B&B shrank from view as the portal collapsed in on itself, cutting off any chance of Ben and Jack reaching her. April tried to ignore how alone she felt, bobbing along in the riptide of the cosmos.

The sinking feeling threatened to drown her. They were heading directly towards the dullest of the orbs. Hell. She should be concerned. But April was about to pass out from blood loss, so whatever happened next didn't seem to matter.

****

Merlin despised cold, damp, wood-panelled places. Particularly if they smelt of sulphur and were inhabited by his ex-wife.

It wasn't Merlin's surroundings that made him feel dirty, he reflected as he forced his feet to carry him in the direction of Mórrígan's great hall, it was the potent combination of shame and dread at the nefarious act he was about to commit.

April was one of those unfortunate consequences. Still, Merlin didn't like using her as bait. April didn't understand her own abilities. Merlin could have told her, but he preferred slow, dramatic reveals. He had to trample these feelings as he always did, for he was Merlin, the greatest warlock to ever live. Whilst April was nothing more than poor timing and bad luck. There was, however, one thing he could do. Fate's gilded gold knife felt heavy in his red right hand.

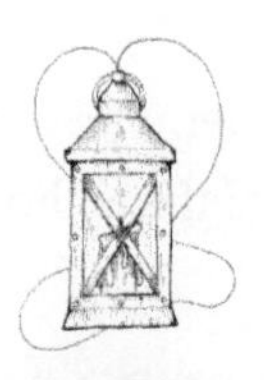

33

Precious

Styx

It wasn't the raven perched on the throne constructed of skulls that surprised April.

It wasn't the featureless dark shadows that darted across the walls of the long hall.

It wasn't the smoke that choked the room, stung her eyes and strangled what little light the wall sconces offered. It wasn't the ghosts, whose huge, empty eyes watched April from the rafters of a vaulted ceiling that mocked heaven. It wasn't the floor-to-ceiling stained-glass windows, their bloody battle scenes shrouded by the night.

It was the fact that April had woken up at all.

'I was starting to think you were dead.' Mórrígan's sultry voice slipped from the shadows, the sharp tap of heels on stone accompanying it.

'Starting to think I am.' April's head was throbbing. She gathered her clammy hands underneath herself and rolled onto her side. 'Nice black feather dress. Low cut at the back, right? I've seen it online.'

'This dress is made especially from crow feathers.'

'Right.' April tried to push through the fog rapidly taking over her mind, but the light-headedness threatened to pull her under for a second time. Her hands dragged over the flagstone, not finding her bokken.

'Are you looking for this?' The wooden sword sat perfectly balanced in the palm of Mórrígan's hand.

April eyed it up from her side of the two-foot gap and sighed with a mixture of exasperation and exhaustion. 'I guess we're doing this.' On motivation alone, April began the agonisingly painful forward crawl.

'I'm failing to see what all the fuss is about.'

April shivered as Mórrígan bestowed her haughty gaze upon her. It didn't help her nerves to see Mórrígan's circular shield and mahogany spear, laced with silver, leaning against the throne. A casual threat if April had ever seen one. 'It's a wooden sword.' April quickly bit down on the hoard of swear words that came to mind as the pain reached new heights.

'No! I'm referring to you.' Mórrígan's irritation sounded a lot like Merlin's. April's fingers brushed against her bokken. Mórrígan waited for her to inch a little closer and callously threw it over her shoulder. April expected no less. 'Something about you threatens Fate.' Mórrígan's cold fingers dug into April's chin, forcing her to look into eyes that had delighted in thousands of deaths. 'I can't see it.'

'Nothing remarkable about me,' April mumbled around the tight grip.

'Unless you haven't found it yet. No matter, if Fate wants you dead, then dead you shall be. It will upset Merlin, at least.'

'That's absurd! I wish people would stop hinting at destinies and talents I don't have.' There was no little voice, no spark. Just unhelpful premonitions – a cloak swirled around the side of the throne and then it was gone. Cloaks didn't necessarily equate to safety. 'Why doesn't Fate cut my thread, save War from such a lowly task?'

'There is a certain art to death. Life doesn't simply cease to be. For your exit, Fate has chosen death by my hand.'

'You're going to kill me on an order, despite seeing no reason to do so?' At this rate, April was going to annoy Mórrígan into killing her before she could be sure she'd actually seen something that looked like rescue.

'Is it right? Is it wrong? Is it fair? These are not questions for War. Morals are questions for lesser beings to ponder in smoking rooms after the dust has settled.'

'Morals require courage and faith. Things you'll never master, War. You fight without purpose.' April squeezed her eyes shut and rummaged inside for magic – it would explain the strange authoritative voice that kept leaping out of her throat. The disappointment was surprisingly sharp. She'd wanted Ben to be wrong, but right now April needed him to be right. Her hands shook but remained pale and devoid of magic. Mórrígan trotted back to her throne.

The softest thud by April's ear brought her face-to-face with the very sharp point of a gold gilded dagger. Stifling cries of pain, she reached for the handle, her heart in her throat. The knife slipped in her clammy palm. The blade scraped against the stone.

'What was that?' War's footsteps tapped their way towards her.

April quickly shoved the dagger underneath her torn stomach, her eyes locked with Merlin's over Mórrígan's shoulder. He made no move to help, just watched from inside a doorway. Remembering the knife, April gripped the gold handle tight. Merlin gave her a curt approving nod and slipped away.

'What's caught your eye?' Mórrígan turned, missing Merlin's exit.

'Thought I saw a ghost,' April said with feeling. Did Merlin intend the blade to be used for murder or mercy?

'I wouldn't look too closely. These souls are down here for a reason.' Mórrígan, confident in April's inabilities, stepped closer. Seeing her only chance, April channelled her remaining strength into plunging the dagger into War's thigh. 'You stupid girl!' Mórrígan's voice was far too quiet to be anything other than outrage. April collapsed back onto the floor. The furious God kicked the air right out of her lungs. Pain blazed around the original wound. In what could only be described as terrible timing, the creeping pins and needles returned. April's entire body hummed with the weird sensation.

Merlin's pride only extended so far. It was a deep cut but it wasn't going to slow Mórrígan down. April's magic spread across her body, a thin aura that she had no control over. Still, she wasn't a total disappointment, Merlin supposed.

Mórrígan tore the dagger free without flinching and tossed it aside. If she'd looked closely, she'd have recognised it as Fate's. The blade conveniently clattered its way over to Merlin's little pocket of shadows. There wasn't much else he could do without revealing himself. Merlin scooped up the dagger and turned to leave. April's cries of pain wrapped around his legs and he stumbled. *'Damn it.'* A swift kick from Mórrígan shunted April into the granite steps. The sound of bone breaking was all too loud in the empty hall. Merlin watched intently but April didn't stir. If April was anything like him, she'd be fine. Indecision clutched at his conscience, and he frowned at the blade in his hand. *'What's wrong with me, Emrys?'*

'Benjamin was right. It should be you who kills Mórrígan. Especially now.' Emrys was furious and ready to interfere.

'I'd hoped to spare myself the bother. I owe neither Fate nor War allegiance.' Merlin watched his ex-wife stalk towards April and unconsciously drew Emrys—

'Step away from her, Mórrígan!'

Benjamin sounded rather confident for somebody in his position.

'Look what the hands dragged in.' Mórrígan's dry remark lost a little of its impact as she spun on her heel and lost her balance, her pearlescent face twisted in pain. Merlin let Emrys die down. The flawless, pale spinning top came to rest, hands on hips, smiling her darkest smile at the pile of Benjamin and Jack in the middle of her floor. Merlin didn't look back to April.

'You have your pick of hell's worst creatures, yet you keep sending the hands. I've got to ask, why?' Ben brushed a few off his jacket, watching April out of the corner of his eye, willing her to move. The uncertainty felt a lot like his world was ending. As it had whenever he'd seen Arthur fall in battle. If Ben could get to her, he ...

'Sentimentality. That's twice I've sent them after the talisman.' Mórrígan bent to look pointedly at a pile of hands.

They had the good sense to scurry away. 'Although this time they brought me you.'

'Win some, lose some. You're bleeding.' Ben pointed to Mórrígan's thigh.

'And you're still with us.' She looked Ben up and down, an intrigued smile on her lips. 'I am surprised.'

'Can I say the same of April?'

'She's breathing. For now. I underestimated her.'

Ben craned his neck to look around Mórrígan – the faintest licks of jade magic were curling around April's hands. 'How so?' Ben quickly returned his attention to War.

'April has magic. She can't tap into it. Not for lack of trying.' Jack's fingers dug into Ben's arm, stopping him from tackling War to the floor as she twirled back to April. 'You should have taught her, Benjamin. Shame on you.'

Jack's grip tightened, watching Mórrígan brush hair from April's still face. They shared a tense, fearful look, and both simultaneously assumed the worse.

Mórrígan's eyes travelled down to the outline of the sword and shield beneath the material of his shirt. Her smile dipped slightly into a frown as she pointed. 'They are aglow.'

Ben's hand jumped up to cover the glow, trying not to shiver at the thought of Merlin's magic sitting so close to his heart.

'I'm looking for the special ones. The ones with kings and queens trapped inside them.' Ben's gaze locked with Mórrígan's as she stalked confidently towards them. Ben moved forward, putting himself in between her and Jack.

'How many people did Merlin trap inside jewellery?' Jack asked quietly, his disgust plain. 'And can he still do that?'

'Shush, Jack! That's ludicrous! This is you trying to start a war.'

'I've waited for a millennium – or longer - to have the king visit my court,' Mórrígan purred, her hollow smile not managing to disguise the mocking cruelty in her voice and eyes. 'That's an awfully long time to be patient.'

'I hate to disappoint you, but,' Ben looked around him with exaggerated movements, picking Jack up to check underneath the vampire's feet, 'Arthur's not here.'

'Ha!' Mórrígan scoffed, stepping close enough for Ben to get a whiff of poppies and death. 'Merlin thinks he outsmarted us all.' Her soft laugh almost sounded fond. 'It was a clever trick. Did it hurt? To discover that Merlin hid Arthur away, ready to bring him back when you screwed up.' Every muscle in Ben's face trembled as they clung tightly to his neutral expression. 'Merlin's a terror for keeping secrets. You weren't quite the last to know – Fate is unaware.' To Ben's surprise, Mórrígan stroked his hair, eliciting a possessive hiss from Jack. The flash of razor-sharp fangs caused Ben's stomach to drop. He hadn't noticed the copper smell. Ben's temptation would come later. Sweat beaded and glistened on Jack's forehead. The slight tremor shaking Jack's whole body said he was losing the fight. The pool of blood had grown considerably. Ben couldn't imagine the radius of twelve pints of blood spilled onto and smeared across a stone floor, but that didn't look quite enough – Jack lurched forward, dry heaving.

'You should have killed me when you had the chance, Benjamin.' Mórrígan threw her head back and laughed, returning to her throne. 'Think of the trouble you'd have saved yourselves. Your little human wouldn't be bleeding out at my feet.' The hunter grunted ever so faintly. Jack breathed a sigh of relief, his grip on Ben's arm loosening.

'Agreed. Erebus, Tuonela and Annwn and all who lived there would still be alive. That's on me.' Jack straightened up with a groan and glazed-over eyes. *'Hold on a little longer, love.'*

There was no escaping the smell of spilled blood assaulting Jack's nostrils.

Nor could he ignore the oh-so-familiar ache deep inside his jaws. Jack's strong will could only beat back the primitive instinct for so long. He had no intention of feeding on April but as his fangs shredded through his gums, and despite having fed recently, he felt sick with hunger.

April didn't stand a chance.

His body pushed against the firm blockade of Ben's outstretched arm – the irrational, blood-crazed voice in his head suggested Jack sink his teeth into Ben's shoulder. The girl was dying anyway – Jack darted forward but the shtriga pulled him back. The combined forces spun the vampire back on himself to face the obstacle standing between him and feeding, his arm trapped between them.

'Let go!' the vampire hissed and clawed at the shtriga's forearm, his nails tearing through Ben's shirt.

'Ah!'

Fresh, red blood bloomed over the gash he'd torn in Ben's chest. It was enough to break through the static.

'Did I hurt you?'

Ben shook his head but couldn't meet Jack's eyes.

'ENOUGH!' Mórrígan's thunderous voice shook the ground beneath their feet, reminding them that they were in the presence of a God. Ben's jaw worked harder than usual. His clenched fists were out in front as if they were bracing him, stopping him from advancing on War. 'You, Benjamin, are going to free Arthur from the talisman. And you will watch him die – for good this time. The pair of you is all that stands between Gaia and myself.' Ben rubbed Jack's back, encouraging him to breathe, to regain control.

This might be the one mistake Ben couldn't stop him from making.

Jack forced himself to focus on the frayed edge of Ben's collar instead of the somersaults his mind was doing.

'Why overthrow Fate and take Avalon? The two of you are friends.'

'Fate stole something from me. I was quite fond of it and still have a use for it.'

'Merlin.' Jack felt comprehension weigh Ben's heart down. He felt the reverberations of his realisation that Merlin had swum too far from shore. 'You would inherit Merlin, along with Avalon and the remaining universes. You'd be able to do as you pleased with both.'

'When all's said and done, Merlin lives to serve.'

'Ben, please ...' After everything, he should leave Merlin to wallow in the mess he had made. But Ben was Ben, and he wasn't going to abandon anybody.

'I have missed the wizard.'

'Merlin's a warlock. He was born with magic. But you should know that. You were married.'

'April is bleeding to death,' spots appeared on Jack's vision, *'and you're arguing semantics with War?! When she kills us, it will be your fault!'* If Jack could ignore the pain gnawing away

at his self-resolve, if he moved quickly enough and didn't breathe in, he might be able to do something useful.

Ben looked past Jack's incredulous gaze and found his own tipping point in April's fading aura. Like the northern lights on a cloudy night, it was translucent and scarcely there. Ben threw Jack back behind him and fired the first shot. Mórrígan's return attack crunched into Ben's chest with the force of a freight train at full speed. Pain exploded, rushing to fill every inch of him and extinguishing Ambrosius. Ben stumbled, arms flailing, until something caught him and held him steady. *'Ambrosius?!'* His magic groaned and retreated further. *'A few more spells. Then I won't use you for a whole week.'* Weak pins and needles crept down his arms, and one tiny ember of burnt orange sparked into life in his hands. Relief bubbled like laughter in Ben's throat.

'You're not bringing death and destruction to Gaia.'

'If you want the girl to survive, you will summon Arthur. She's practically a ghost. Wouldn't want such a pretty soul to become trapped down here.'

'I'm not going to do that, Mórrígan.'

'I wonder where Death will take you? Shall we find out?' The joy of inflicting death danced in Mórrígan's eyes. Her pitch-black magic formed a sphere in between her raised hands, illuminating her face.

'Dying. It's just another realm.' But Ben didn't want to learn who he would be without Jack. Mórrígan levelled her dark magic at Ben's heart and charged. He opened his arms and let her crash into him like a hurricane.

'Ben?' It was so faint, he hadn't been sure he'd heard April.

Jack heard her too.

Unguarded, he darted forward, stopping short of the pool of blood, his head to one side, his shoulders rising and falling with laboured breathing. Jack fought hard to keep his fangs retracted. A spell impacted and shattered Ben's ribs. He crashed to the ground whilst firing another attack just as Jack bent down but pulled back sharply, wringing his hands. Ben rolled away violently from Mórrígan and stood to see Jack double over again. His vampire looked back, indecision written across his face.

'Jack ...'

Mórrígan's hands found Ben's throat, crushing his windpipe. Jack pulled away from his instincts and scooped April up. Ben clawed at Mórrígan, his fingers digging for purchase. Ben jabbed a knee into her stomach. She found the leather cords and wrapped them around her fist, embedding them in his neck. The sword, unhappy with its new owner, turned from aquamarine to a pulsating dark and angry red. The shield answered with its own furious red light.

The talismans reached towards each other like separated lovers. The embrace was explosive.

Ben shot into the air, crashing through the roof and out into the cool night air, pulled by an unseen force. Mórrígan shot past him, arms tucked against her body, like an arrow, whilst Ben stumbled and tumbled from the emptiness into a blue abyss.

The talisman's magic had tried to take Ben away from danger, but danger had been holding the other half. Merlin should have thought about that. The blue found its place above and he slammed into the very solid green and rock-filled ground. To his right was the narrow entrance to a cave. He was back in Gaia. Ben looked around the woods in bewilderment. 'I'm never leaving the house again.'

He straightened up in time for War to barrel into him. His boots lost their fight for purchase on the mossy ground. Mórrígan landed atop him, driving the air from his lungs. Ben heaved her off and rolled away but she followed, screaming. Thunder rumbled in the distance, trying to beat the rain-heavy clouds that raced to cover the blue. Losing wasn't in Mórrígan's nature. Her eyes sparked as if little flints were being struck and she fired again. The scorching-hot magic brushed Ben's cheek. Ambrosius bristled, eager to reply with a death spell. Ben yelled the incantation, and the burnt-orange orb floating between his hands exploded into a fireball that filled his vision. Ben stepped back and slipped, one knee crashing to the ground. As he fell, he thrust the orb away from him with all his strength. Spots and patches of colour littered his vision. The one that looked like Ambrosius sailed away, climbing in a graceful orange arch that turned back on itself, painting a loop in the grey sky. Mórrígan couldn't avoid it. Ambrosius crashed into her, wrapping her around a tree trunk, crumpling her body with a sickening sound. She slid down to the ground, motionless, an arm across her face, hiding her eyes, her chest still. The charred air crackled from the energy that had torched it. Ben breathed in a lungful of air that smelt like burnt gunpowder and set off on unsteady legs, to assess the situation on the other side of no-man's land. His groan of pain sent birds flying from the trees. Seeing no outwards signs of life, he cautiously bent over her broken body and felt for a heartbeat that wasn't there.

'Alright.' With a deep, shuddering breath, Ben allowed Ambrosius to stand down, but his magic wouldn't go. They had to find April. Ben glanced back to the cave opening. *'The mortals entrance to hell. Probably the quickest route back ...'*

The whirling black cloud of magic punched him in the gut, driving him to his knees and swallowed him whole. Ben gulped for air but the cloud was suffocating him. His teeth clenched around the moan, his eyes streaming. Mórrígan had hit him with her own death spell. Her magic's tendrils were wrapping around his legs and arms, pulling him back. Unable to stand, Ben tried to crawl. Through the gaps in the cloud, Ben saw Mórrígan, propped up on one elbow, smiling triumphantly even as she swayed, feeling the effects of his spell working its way through her.

'Run!' Ambrosius yelled.

'No, I thought I'd wait here until I inevitably blackout!' A spell. He needed ... Ben shook his head, trying to form a coherent thought, but he couldn't hold onto words. So, Ben pictured Mórrígan dead on the ground and let Ambrosius fill in the gaps. The spell hit her straight in the heart. The dark light animating Mórrígan's eyes dimmed but still shone.

Mórrígan's grotesque magic twisted its way through his body, screaming in his mind like the banshees of old. The tendrils wrapped around his throat, strangling him with the weight of shadows and regrets. Mórrígan's body ricocheted backwards, struck with a new spell thrown by somebody whose magic was at full strength.

'Merlin?' The warlock's familiar silhouette appeared on the edges of the cloud, giving Ben the incentive to fight his closing eyelids. Merlin raised his right hand and approached the cloud with a confidence so full of conviction and purpose, it had to recede from the wall of aquamarine magic, driving it into the cave entrance.

'I didn't think I'd be glad to see you. What's the matter with your aura?' It was a tumultuous mix of black and blue, the colour of death. Merlin looked gaunt and downright ill. The bags under his eyes had morphed into craters; his eyes were haunted, and his nails bitten down to the quick. 'What have you done, Merlin?'

'Ben!'

'Jack!' Ben took in Jack's eyes, his thin mouth and every freckle and wrinkle on the face running towards him. It was the face he wanted to remember if things went south. 'It's alright ...' The glint of light thrown by a blade snagged Ben's attention. Merlin plunged a dagger into Mórrígan's heart. Her hate-filled gaze found Merlin's as the light fled and she slumped down.

'Have you ever noticed,' Merlin asked of nobody in particular, 'how a body always looks like it isn't dead? It accepts its fate easier than the soul.' Merlin looked about, moving like a sleepwalker for whom reality was an afterthought. 'The soul always thinks the heart should continue to beat whereas the heart knows it must stop.' Merlin teased the sword talisman free from hands that offered no resistance. He turned to face them, the sword swinging lazily in the air, threatening to send them into freefall.

34

Stolen Away

Merlin steadied his shaking hands, squinting into the watery afternoon sun.

'Mórrígan wore her measureless death count effortlessly. Mine hangs from me like an ill-fitting suit.' Merlin balanced the blade in the palm of his hand. 'Do you remember, Benjamin, my first fight with Mórrígan? Benjamin?'

'I'm busy, Merlin!' Orange magic weaved around April's wounds, trying to heal what it could not.

'You said, I didn't love *her*, rather the *idea* of her. You also thought she'd be the death of me.' Merlin laughed bitterly whilst Benjamin tore strips from his top for hastily made bandages. 'All anybody owns in life is their mistakes.' Merlin wiped the blade clean on his sleeve. 'I could have been a mediocre warlock, but no, I'm the only person preposterous enough to steal Fate's blade. And kill War. Curious,' Merlin muttered softly, 'such strong magic and April never noticed.' Her magic had formed a second skin over her wounds, keeping her alive.

‘A little help?’ Benjamin glanced over, his face all at sharp angles.

‘I’ve done enough, remember?’ In Merlin’s hand, the handle of the knife flipped over and over. ‘Fate didn’t like my rewrites.’ The knife spun hilt over point. ‘She’s not seen this new draft, though.’ Perhaps it was one or all of the above reasons that put Merlin in the mood to do something phenomenally stupid, something that would spark more wars. Or perhaps it was just destiny. The dagger soared into the air. The weight left as easily as a secret committed to the wind, whilst the talisman carried on its pendulum swing. The air crackled and popped with the three magics zipping about. Merlin’s mouth twitched, unable to restrain a shaky laugh that did little to hide the cracks. He had seen the end, he had. It was nobody’s fault. There had to be order, even in the chaos.

Merlin let go of the sword.

Ben heard the whistling of something small and metallic flying through the air. The shield strained at the end of its cord, trapped by his shirt. Jack snatched the shield talisman from Ben’s neck, but the tiny pendant ripped itself from his grasp before it could be thrown, desperate to be closer to the sword.

‘Duck!’ Ben pulled Jack to the ground, narrowly beating the shockwave of aquamarine magic that radiated out from the collision.

The sword had found its home, nestled atop the shield.

‘Sword and shield together as one, a kingdom protected,’ Merlin stated in a distant, prophetic voice that did not bode well for them.

'What's that supposed to mean, Merlin?' If Jack had started spitting fire, Ben wouldn't have been surprised. The talismans – Benjamin couldn't drag his eyes away from them. 'And where are you going?'

Ben gently brushed off Jack's attempts to restrain him, transfixed by the blue-green magic dancing around the little pendants that floated eerily between him and Merlin.

The world fell away as Ben plucked the talismans from their levitation, cocooning him in a bubble of Merlin's magic. April's wounds – Jack's concern – Merlin's betrayals – Arthur's imprisonment. He'd been tearing himself apart over things that, in this strange light, were out of his control.

'Feels light, doesn't it?' Merlin's voice drifted into the quiet. *'No responsibility, no obligations to bother you with.'* Ben's gaze drifted to Merlin, who mistook it for permission. *'Aren't you tired, Benjamin? I am. Eternally weary.'* Merlin gave an exhausted chuckle to emphasise his point. *'We've both borrowed time to finish a war created by Gods.'*

'You're not one for melancholy. Nor do you entertain doubt.'

'A thousand years of life is a thousand too many when you have to keep the worlds from colliding. This is the end.'

Somewhere in the twists, turns, ups and downs, Merlin had taken away everything good. And still the warlock held one of those things out of reach. *'Why, Merlin?'*

'Concealing you both would have been easy. Easy solutions are false guides.' Merlin shrugged. *'Rush towards it and you'll trip headfirst off the cliff.'*

'It wasn't you who fell, Merlin.' The blade spun in the air. *'I …'*

'You don't hate me, Benjamin.'

He wanted to turn away, but Merlin's eyes held Ben captive. Still the knife spun, hilt over blade. *'Summoning you was my second biggest mistake. Accepting your dinner invitation, the first.'* Merlin had been right. He did feel lighter.

'Fate, I can't deny her. But I deceived her for as long as I could.' The dagger landed with a soft thud. *'Help me see to it that she doesn't win this time.'*

'Merlin, if you're asking me to kill you, hand me the knife.' Ben held his hand out, all intent and no bluff.

'You're fed up with how I treat you. I'm fed up with how Fate treats me.' The knife rested innocently in Merlin's outstretched hand, blade pointed at his heart, the hilt at Ben's. He looked away briefly, not wanting Merlin to mistake the emotions spilling from his mourning-suit black eyes for compassion.

'Ben! Get away from him.' Fear was in April's voice and conviction in her eyes – she'd seen this before.

April's laboured breathing kept Jack tethered to her side and he looked to Ben with pleading eyes.

'She's dying, Ben.' It was head over heart or heart over head. April, determined to be listened to, shoved Jack away from her. 'You'd best still be here when I get back.' Jack pocketed his hesitation and sprinted to Ben, unable to look back.

'You've played your part, Benjamin.'

Jack inserted himself into the middle of them and swung at Merlin, but Merlin sent him flying with a casual flick of the wrist. He landed in a heap beside April.

'Let him up, Merlin.' The weight of a thousand soldiers pinned his vampire to the muddy forest floor, but he struggled against the invisible force all the same, his fear feeding his anger in a vicious circle of denial.

'You're free, now.' Fate's blade winked at him, keen to be put to use. *'Don't make me be the cause of any more pain for you.'*

'This is how you want to find peace?' Ben's fingertips brushed the hilt, their noses touching

'Benjamin!' He'd never heard so much torment in Jack's voice.

'I'd rather you found peace, actually.' Ben glanced back to Jack. He'd already found all the peace he needed.

Merlin darted forward, flipping the blade to catch the handle, and plunged it deep into Benjamin's chest. Benjamin gasped in shock and doubled over, blood rushing to form around the wound. Merlin wrapped his arm around Benjamin's shoulders, pulling his friend into an embrace. Benjamin's eyes widened as pain swept through him, his hands around the hilt.

'You'll only die quicker, if you pull it out.' Benjamin turned his dumbfounded stare to Merlin. 'It's Fate's dagger. In case you were wondering.' The accusation, the hurt and spite in those storm-cloud eyes … Merlin almost didn't recognise his own spluttering laugh as he lowered Benjamin to the ground. 'If I don't take you, Fate will.' Merlin's voice snagged on the last word, forcing him to take a breath and twist the knife. He had never detested himself more than he did then. 'You need to trust me, one last time.' Benjamin reached up, gripping Merlin's arm tightly. Ben coughed sending teardrops of blood flying.

'Nothing grows in my company; I'm so ensnared in my own destructive destiny – I know. Save your breath, Benjamin.' Merlin patted his shoulder, speaking louder to drown out Jack's gut-wrenching screams. 'How foolish we were. To think we could change the world!' A tsunami of emotion rose from Jack to crash down around where they knelt, flooding the woods with sorrow.

'Arthur—'

'It's not fair but that's the beauty of it – there's a lot of living mixed up with dying.'

Jack. April. Ben was going to have to say goodbye despite having neither the time nor the words to do so. Merlin wasn't searching for a way out for himself. The warlock had never been anything other than Ben's demise in disguise.

A spasm of intense pain quickened Ben's breathing, turning it into short, sharp pants.

'Jack!' Ben had to … tell … his vampire … something, but the tightness in his chest kept that thing from him. His mind galloped through epiphanies, lingered on regrets, snaring on the sharp barbs of things he would never get to say, and stung him with the things he'd wished he'd hadn't. And wherever eternity took Jack, Ben would never know. There was no time for anger because there was no time left. The regrets crowded forward, fighting for the best room in a soon-to-be abandoned house, evacuated in a hurry.

'Look up, Benjamin. Before you die, look up.' Ben dragged his head back but before he could ask, what in the Gods' name Merlin was talking about, the warlock leant forward and whispered in his ear.

The oppressive force lifted without warning. Jack pitched forward and came up snarling. His vampiric self tore through. He grabbed Ben's knife from his belt on his way past. He grabbed handfuls of the warlock's robe, body-slamming the old man to the ground.

'Oaf!'

Jack hauled the warlock to his feet and jammed the tip into Merlin's neck – blood bloomed, crimson and red. The smell barely registered. Some people's blood wasn't worth losing himself over. 'Undo it, Merlin.' The knife trembled.

'I cannot. It is done.'

Jack couldn't stop the inevitable from happening, not for all of his strength and speed. They'd missed their chance to retreat, but what good was eternity now? The heaviness would always weigh Jack down, anchoring him to this single event.

Jack's right hook sent Merlin crashing to the floor. He loomed over the warlock, about to rip his throat out—

'Jack?'

Ignoring the ache in his wrist, Jack pulled his partner into his arms as gently as he could, willing Ben to open his eyes. If Jack held onto him tightly enough, he couldn't leave. A spasm rocked Ben's body, and with his nose pressed into Jack's shoulder, those multi-coloured eyes opened to reveal irises that were spheres of burnt-orange magic. 'Find Arthur,' he took a great, shuddering breath, 'tell him … I …' The longing in Ben's voice shattered Jack's heart so he nodded reluctantly. 'Look after April.'

'Obviously.'

Ben's smile ripped a new hole in Jack's soul. With great effort, Ben uncurled his fingers to reveal the cursed talismans sitting in a pool of blood. Jack let Ben weakly force the damned things into his own hand where they hummed and happily burned his palm. The calming presence Jack had always felt within himself was diminishing rapidly.

'This doesn't mean you can leave.' Benjamin sighed, unable to comply with Jack's wishes. He smiled softly at Jack, squeezing his hand.

Jack understood what Ben was trying to ask.

Jack couldn't say no but he couldn't say yes, either.

Ambrosius's familiar burnt-orange orb spluttered into life in Ben's hand. It shone as best it could and slowly faded out.

The last thread of their connection snapped.

'Ben?' But Death had pulled Ben away in their unrelenting undercurrent. 'Oh Gods, please.' Tears wouldn't fall, despite Jack feeling like he was drowning.

'Let him go, lad. It's for the good of the realm.'

Jack buried his face in Ben's hair, breathing in his scent. Pain, like nothing he'd ever known, ripped his heart out, put it back and ripped it out again. Merlin was muttering under his breath, but it all seemed so inconsequential now. The world was ending? Good. Let it implode. There was no future for Jack. The wind cried out in sympathy, rattling brown leaves loose that couldn't hold on to branches any longer. Leaves that looked pretty as they fell, as they decayed on the forest floor.

Jack fumbled for some strength to lift his head above his sorrow. And there was Merlin, kneeling on the other side of Ben, clutching the shtriga's shoulder. 'Take your hands off him!' Jack reached to knock him off, but Merlin caught Jack's wrist with his spare hand.

'I must maintain balance. I've considered all the possible scenarios.' Merlin shrugged, as if he'd not murdered his best friend five minutes ago. He finally looked up and his black eyes bored into Jack's. 'The other options were worse. Trust me.'

'What am I supposed to do with that? Take it home and sit it in Ben's spot?!'

'There's no right ending to this story.' Merlin dug at his eyebrow with a knuckle.

'I'm not ready ...' Jack clung tighter to Ben. His sadness swelled up inside, like a balloon fast running out of space.

'If I gave you another century, you'd still ask for more time. You'll never be ready. Nobody is,' Merlin said, not unkindly.

'I promise you, this isn't over.'

The warlock forced his creaking joints to stand. 'If only you knew how right you are, Guardian of Gaia. At least until we retrieve Arthur.' Jack couldn't feel enough to argue. 'I'll be seeing you, Jack. Perhaps by then, you'll have gained some perspective. Take care, there are villains here.'

'You'll leave when I let you.' Jack lunged forward to grab his tunic.

With a snap of his fingers, Merlin sent Jack into a deep sleep, sighing as the vampire collapsed beside Benjamin, and turned his back on all that had happened.

'Ah! I'd almost forgotten about you.'

April was stirring. She wouldn't want to hear him, Merlin knew. But April couldn't escape and a captive audience was his favourite kind. Merlin transported himself to her side, delighted to have company. 'You know,' he sat cross-legged on the ground, 'I can't shake the image of star-crossed lovers – I hope it's not a premonition.' April was staring at Benjamin and missed Merlin's pointed stare. 'Nasty things, premonitions, wouldn't you agree?' April looked up at him, eyes overflowing. 'Couldn't put the pieces together in time, eh? I thought as much. No matter, we will work on that. Hmph.'

April's response was to crawl away from him. 'Charming.' Her progress was slow and painful to watch but he wasn't inclined to intervene. Yet. Tough love was a wonderful teacher. 'Come now, I am not a threat.' That wasn't exactly true – Jack had called it right. Merlin was a villain, the proof of which lay ten feet away, with a knife in his chest. 'There is a certain wildness in Jack. Should I be concerned?'

Merlin didn't need April to like him, although it would be nice. Nobody ever wanted to see him again. 'Jack's mad with grief, I suppose. To have his partner die in his arms … I saw it in his eyes, April. The eyes always have the truth of it. At least he didn't flee, as Benjamin did with Arthur.' Merlin tsked.

April's struggling caused her uncontrolled and unnamed magic to flare and she yelped in surprise. 'Oh shush, it's your magic trying to heal you. Let it.'

Merlin watched her like an over-eager parent, keen to see progress. Her fear was tangible. 'You're not going to die. You're tough, like your father.' April ceased her pointless crawling. 'I had hoped Benjamin would teach you a little. I suppose that falls to me now.'

April resumed her crawling, her hands desperately grabbing at rocks, roots, anything to propel herself forward. 'For the love of the Gods.' Merlin halted her escape with a click of his fingers, and set Emrys to work sewing up ripped skin and organs. 'I'm pleased you've remembered who you are. We have a lot to do, so you'd best be a quick study. Unlike Benjamin.'

April rallied against the exhaustion tucking her in. She didn't win. Merlin stood slowly, each of his years weighing him down. 'Smells like rain.' His eyes settled on Fate's dagger still buried in Benjamin's chest. The forecast was a category five hurricane, at best.

'Everybody is asleep or dead, all the better for taking my leave.' With both hands, Merlin pulled the dagger free of its gruesome cage, careful not to look at the pale face, and threw up. With hands on his knees, he tried to take a deep breath, tasting the enormity of what he'd done, along with the sharp tang of sick. He'd seen the end. He'd set it in motion.

'You did the right thing.' Emrys stepped into the gap in his thoughts, equally exhausted.

'Hmph. I am less certain.' Merlin's aquamarine friend popped into life in his hand.

'Time will tell. Besides, you're being summoned.' Thunder rolled across the clearing as the rain started lashing down. 'Ready or not, Fate's coming for you, Merlin.'

'Who does she think she is exactly? The God of weather? She's upset – message received. There's no need for a literal storm to demonstrate the metaphorical one she's about to unleash,' Merlin grumbled to cover up his growing dread. He'd disobeyed Fate for the last time. 'Her theatrics grow more irritating with age.'

'Best not keep her waiting.' Emrys vanished and reappeared on Merlin's shoulder, a little hand hanging onto the warlock's ear for balance.

'She's not out of time yet.'

'The universe is still at risk. We'll have to deal with Chaos too.' The urge to vanish filled Merlin's entire being, but Emrys refused his wish. 'You need to pick a side. You cannot fight a war on three fronts.'

'Sometimes, Emrys, I do not want to see what I don't want to see. We need to keep Fate distracted whilst April—'

'April won't give you the time of day. Nor will Jack. You're out of options.'

'At least I made this right. Benjamin was a walking, letter-writing advertisement of my faults.' It was natural to want to bury that in the woods. The rain clouds looked set to follow him. 'Perhaps it's time to buy a raincoat.' Merlin squinted up into the falling rain and wondered how on earth he'd painted himself into a corner.

'Everything you fear – everything you've seen – will still come to pass. All of that outmanoeuvring was for naught.' Emrys sighed. 'At least April found Benjamin and Jack.'

'Erm.' In the not-so-distant future, Merlin was going to be returned to the shadows of the past where they could all rest together.

'Who will mourn me, when I go, Emrys?' But Emrys had extinguished in the rain. 'That's what I thought.' With one final glance at the laden sky, Merlin ran his hand through the air, cutting the fabric of the realm. Fate, Death, Chaos, Arthur, Jack, and April. They all had reasons to break his bones. Some would get the chance, but not just yet. He still had a few moves left before he followed Benjamin.

Jack and April will return in
Make Damn Sure

It's been a month since April's premonition.

She is struggling with her magic, the ramifications of her premonition, and the expectations of everybody around her. Plus, the only person who seems inclined to help cannot be trusted.

Jack is reeling from the cost of saving Gaia and ignoring his new role as Guardian.

Merlin is in the wind, trying to retrieve Arthur, but is he prepared for the consequences of playing God (or Fate)?

More secrets come to light as the balance of the universe shifts, and Death does not tolerate an unbalanced universe.

About the Author

Caroline is an Italian-English production coordinator based in the UK. Inspired by anything supernatural, historical, and the myths and legends of Europe, she writes for stage and screen. When she's not writing, Caroline bakes (a lot).

Milton Keynes UK
Ingram Content Group UK Ltd.
UKHW011814061023
430090UK00001B/1